2011 不求人文化

2009 懶鬼子英日語

www.17buy.com.tw

2005 意識文化

2005 易富文化

2003 我識地球村

2001 我識出版社

2011 不求人文化

2009 懶鬼子英日語

www.17buy.com.tw

2005 意識文化

2005 易富文化

2003 我識地球村

2001 我識出版社

全新制 TOEIC Listening

50次多益滿分的怪物講師

多益聽力

攻略＋模擬**試題**＋解析

只學考試會出的內容就夠！

現在的社會，報考多益已經成為一件不得不做的事情。想要就業或升遷，高分的多益成績單就跟履歷、作品集一樣，是不可或缺的條件，分數愈高，受到公司青睞的機會也會愈高。

你正在為了一張「好像只有我沒有」的高分多益成績單，翻著堆疊如山的相關書籍、在各家補習班間奔波嗎？

很累吧？讓我們來幫你終結這痛苦的生活。這本《全新制50次多益滿分的怪物講師TOEIC多益聽力攻略＋模擬試題＋解析》可以讓各位的實力有明顯的變化，同時也改變你的人生！

無可取代的特色！

1. 內容包括多益改制前後的考試總整理，以及怪物講師們對於多益出題模式的研究、在補習班教授的考試專用祕訣……等。簡單來說，就是滿分50次的怪物講師們，將分析考題與挑選答案的全部過程公諸於世。為了避免造成學習者的混淆，我們秉持最基本的原則——就是把考試裡不會出現的冷門內容排除掉！

2. 淺顯易懂的說明方式，就算學習者的英文程度是只認得英文字母，也能逐步學習、一讀就理解。從Part 1到Part 4，為什麼這是答案、為什麼那個不是答案，每個選項都一一解釋。這是因為我們相信——基礎實力必須要穩固，才不會遇到難題就逃避。

3. 當學習者差不多看完這本書的時候，會發現我們藏在書中的一個禮物——看完這本書，不只能掌握多益聽力考試的技巧，連多益口說（Speaking）也都學會了。

在多益改制之後，為了做出符合最新趨勢、最好的多益教材，我們不斷進出考場，蒐集與研究多益改制前後的資料，以求提供學習者最完整的學習內容。為此，透過序言我們要向朋友們表達謝意：謝謝一起經過漫長辛苦作業的同仁們，還有出版以來一如往常支持我們的忠實讀者們。

怪物講師教學團隊（韓國）代表作者 **鄭相虎、金映權** 敬上

真的可以公開這些祕訣嗎？！

看了「怪物講師的祕訣」之後，真的忍不住說「哇！真的很棒」。「進入下一個考題前先填寫答案」這樣細膩的建議非常受用。

申寶美（26歲，準備考研究所當中）

讓人不斷翻頁閱讀的多益攻略！

跟市面上其他的書不同，這本書不是讓你用頭腦過度思考的理論書，能讓人順利地讀下去！不僅看完，還能充分理解書中內容，如果有人問我書上的問題，我可以馬上說明與講解！

金水宣（26歲，上班族）

怪物講師的解題祕訣，直接搬到書裡了！

這本書根本是直接收錄「怪物講師們的解答順序和技巧」嘛！將「看考卷之後預測 → 選擇性地聽錄音」的解題順序，完全不藏私地告訴讀者。

李美真（22歲，全北大學，英語系）

實戰型書籍，讓我變成順利戰勝多益！

第一次看到這種「實戰型」的書籍，只要照書中內容練習後再去考試，就可以順利考到好成績吧！現在每寫一道練習題，都好像看到實際考題一樣！

周惠理（28歲，上班族）

超神奇，看完就把所有祕訣記住了！

所有的章節都安排了Review Test和Preview，只要依照書本的順序一直學下去，就不需要另外安排預習與複習的學習進度，十分方便。

黃志敏（26歲，檀國大學，不動產學系）

細膩解說，看一次就懂了！

怪物講師仔細地講解每道題目的每個選項，看完講師細膩的解說後，感覺好像已經考過多益十多次一樣。怪物講師更挑選出多益考試的核心內容，並把考題相關的所有東西都完整說明了。

許昌勇（28歲，韓國綜合技術專門學校）

怪物講師的技巧，就是考場上最實用的技巧！

這是在考試裡能直接用上的技巧！只要把這些內容都看完的話，在考場上可能就會看到滿分成績單了。

秋明熙（20歲，漢陽大學，分子生命科學部）

策略性地了解多益，順利考到滿意的分數！

這本書籍的內容經過策略性的安排，攻略說明、各種專欄、單字、例句、解題技巧……等，只要有所疑惑，馬上就會看到補充說明，這樣的安排，讓人能夠不間斷地順利學習下去。

李吉洙（32歲，上班族）

目錄

Part 1　對照片的描述

Part 2　疑問與回答

多益是什麼？

TOEIC是Test of English for International Communication的縮寫，針對非英語母語者以工作或日常生活裡需要的「溝通」為主測驗實用英語能力的考試。因此裡面大部分出現商務以及日常生活裡所使用的實用主題。

多益考試的出題領域以及特色

公司內研發	研究、產品開發
財務相關	投資、稅務、會計、結帳
餐飲	業務上的聚會、聚餐、晚宴、預約
娛樂、文化	電影、音樂、藝術、博物館、大眾媒體
一般業務	合約、協商、併購與合併、行銷、業務
健康相關	健康保險、診療、牙科診療、醫院
住宅／公司不動產	建設、採購與出租、電氣／瓦斯費用
人事相關	僱用、退休、升遷、申請工作、錄取公告、薪水、年薪
製作	組裝工程、工廠管理、品質管理
辦公室相關	理事會、委員會、參觀、電話、傳真、電子郵件、辦公用品
購買相關	購物、訂單、配送、費用請款單
旅行相關	大眾運輸、船舶、入場券、廣播、飯店、延遲、取消

多益考試會盡量避免只屬於特定文化的內容，各個國家的人名與地名都平均地分布在考試題目裡面。另外，美國、英國、加拿大、澳洲等的發音與語調也平均分配出現。

考試的結構

結構	Part	內容	考題數目	時間	分數
聽力測驗	1	照片描述	6	約45分鐘	495分
	2	應答問題	25		
	3	簡短對話	39		
	4	簡短獨白	30		
閱讀測驗	5	句子填空	30	75分鐘	495分
	6	段落填空	16		
	7	單篇閱讀	29		
		多篇閱讀	25		
Total	7個Parts		200	120分鐘	990分

考試時間介紹

時間	內容
9：30～9：45	分發答案表格，以及說明填寫表格方法
9：45～9：50	休息時間
9：50～10：05	第一次身份證檢查
10：05～10：10	分發考卷，以及檢查考卷上的瑕疵與否
10：10～10：55	進行聽力考試
10：55～12：10	進行閱讀考試（第二次身份證檢查）

＊ 無論如何，在九點五十分以前得入考場。以上時間視考場狀況可變。

多益報名方法

報名期間與報名處：**請參考多益委員會網站／考試費用：1,600元**

❶ **網路報名**：費用1,600元，加網路處理費40元。

  報名網址：http://www.toeic.com.tw/register/index.jsp

❷ **通訊報名**：費用1,600元，須以郵政匯票方式繳費。

  報名表可臨櫃或致電索取
  （台北市復興南路二段45號2樓，02-2701-8008分機109）。

❸ **臨櫃報名**：費用1,600元，平日早上9:00至下午5:30。

  地址：台北市復興南路二段45號2樓。

❹ **APP報名**：可使用APP報名，在便利商店繳費。

Android下載　　iOS下載

考試準備事項

❶ **身份證**：限中華民國國民身分證或有效期限內之護照正本。沒有身份證的話，絕對不能參加
  考試。一定要記得喔！

❷ **文具**：電腦用鉛筆（先弄成粗一點比較方便；一般鉛筆或自動鉛筆也可以，但不可使用有墨
  水的筆），橡皮擦。

確認成績以及成績單寄發

在指定的發表日期，在多益官方的網站或透過電話可以確認成績。成績單是以應考生指定
的方式領取，且僅有第一次成績單是免費的。

Part 1

出題趨勢

此部分已不再能說是最容易得分的題型了，因為近幾年常常出現以東西描述為主的陌生說法。這些說法是以前完全沒有出現過的，所以應考生的錯誤機率也劇增。有人可能會想，在Part 1裡錯兩題左右也不會有礙於考到高分，畢竟數目不大嘛。但千萬別這麼想，如果把失去的分數類推到聽力考試其他部分，就等於在各個部分裡錯六題那麼嚴重。只要錯一個考題，也有可能會造成很大的影響，而不容易得到高分數。

出題比例分析

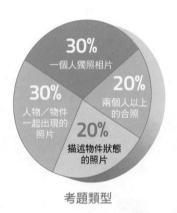

考題類型

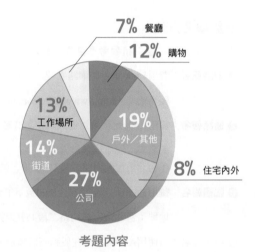

考題內容

學習策略 & 應考策略

1　人物照片的出現比例為60～70%，所以得熟知人物的動作以及狀態相關的說法。

2　要達到一看照片就能判斷是什麼狀況的程度。即使聯想不到動作或狀態相關的英語說法，還是要能先正確分析照片，在聽錄音的時候才能容易選出答案。

3　若出現描述在照片裡沒出現的東西或動作的選項，立刻排除在答案之外，然後繼續看別的選項。

4　聽錄音的時候應該同時填寫答案。在Part 2之前的單元立刻填寫答案會節省時間。

5　有時也會發現找不出完美答案的情形。此時得選擇最接近的答案。

Part 2

出題趨勢

即使是同樣類型的考題，前面第7～19題大部分很簡單，但愈到後面題目通常會愈難。尤其在第25題以後，混雜出現了能評鑑出高分數應考生的高難度考題的情形。因此，第25題以後回答考題時得特別注意。最近陳述句的比例正在增加當中，且疑問詞疑問句裡常出現why與how。

出題比例分析

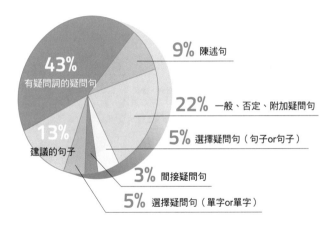

43% 有疑問詞的疑問句

9% 陳述句

22% 一般、否定、附加疑問句

5% 選擇疑問句（句子or句子）

13% 建議的句子

3% 間接疑問句

5% 選擇疑問句（單字or單字）

學習策略 & 應考策略

1 需要依照疑問句前面部分出現的疑問詞來決定答案。即使聽到了考題後面的部分，但如果一開頭沒有聽到疑問詞，還是無法找出正確答案。

2 最近常出現看起來很容易，但聽起來很難的說法。Part 2的答題線索沒有在考卷上，必須專心聽這些說法。

3 若將類似的發音、時態、同義詞等先整理下來學習，會有幫助。尤其是如果先將自己很容易弄錯或選錯的選項整理好，可以提高以後選出正確答案的機率。

4 聽選項的時候，偶爾會記不住剛聽過的疑問詞或句子開頭的地方。即使多麼專心，進行25個考題時還是會失去集中力。

出題趨勢

Part 3前面的部分（第32～40題），對話長度很短且考題也是有關地點、說話者、下一個行程等，比較容易回答的問題為主。但在後面部分（第53～70題），對話長度比較長且選項為句子形式的「詢問具體內容的考題」最常出現。「詢問概括性內容的考題」是與主題、地點、說話者、要求與建議事項、以及下一個行程相關的為多。Part 4裡，電話留言以及活動開始公告的類型在增加當中。

出題比例分析

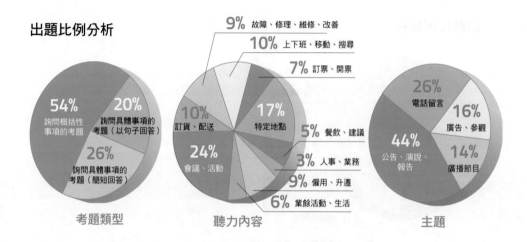

| 考題類型 | 聽力內容 | 主題 |

學習策略 & 應考策略

1 無論如何，在聽錄音之前，需要了解考題裡的核心詞彙。先知道是哪種考題，才能有選擇性地聽錄音，聽到考題重點時也不要猶豫，要立刻選擇答案。

2 需要多做邊聽錄音邊看考題與選項的訓練。雖然先看了考題再聽錄音是好的，但還是需要將所看過的考題做確認的過程，這種練習剛開始的時候很難適應，但經過多次就會熟練的。

3 大部分的情形之下，考題的順序與錄音內容進行的順序一樣，所以需要做依序回答考題的練習。

4 在錄音前段部分出現答案的情形尤其多，得專心聽該部分！

5 有些主題、情況的內容大部分相似：影印機總是故障、想找的人都是出差當中，因此若習慣了這些刻板的內容模式，會更容易回答考題。萬一真的沒有時間或不想讀書，起碼看看錄音內容的翻譯吧。

Part 5, 6

出題趨勢

雖然每個月都有所不同,但文法與詞彙考題佔各一半。大部分的考題與以前的類型和難易度沒有太大的差別,高難度的考題仍然會出現。另外,大部分的考題長度以及詞彙難度正在慢慢調高當中。Part 6裡所使用的詞彙量更大,而且也會出現了解脈絡才能回答的考題。

出題比例分析

Part 5 考題類別

55% 詞彙相關考題
45% 語法相關考題

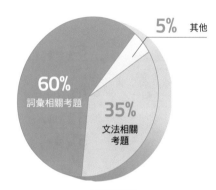

Part 6 考題類別

60% 詞彙相關考題
35% 文法相關考題
5% 其他

學習策略 & 應考策略

1 Part 5 & 6是可以最有效率找到答案的部分。回答考題的時候,要先很快看過選項,判斷此題是否為需要經過翻譯才能回答的。

2 若有不知道怎麼回答的考題,先標記之後直接進入別的考題更省時。最多要在二十五分鐘之內結束Part 5 & 6,才有充分的時間完成Part 7。

3 無論如何,文法考題的部分全部都要答對。多益總分數高的人,大多是在詞彙考題方面獲得高分。

4 學詞彙的時候,得將常用的組合一起背下來。有些句子是我們看來沒問題,但在以英語為母語者的眼裡是很奇怪的說法。將詞彙常用的組合熟記,才能在考試時縮短答題時間且提高分數。

Part 7

出題趨勢

Part7是最近難度變得最高的部分。除了考題的難度提高，文章的長度也變長，所以讓應考生感到吃力。除了最容易的詢問主題類的題目，現在考生也需了解文章裡隱藏的含意。詢問具體事項的考題也是如此，在選項裡找出線索變得更不容易。推論相關考題也提高了難度，且持續出現同義詞相關的考題。信函與電子郵件類型仍然最常出現，此外，說明文與報導類型文章的出現機率最近也增加當中。愈後面部分的文章長度會愈來愈長，有時可能會出現考生無法看完文章的情形。

出題比例分析

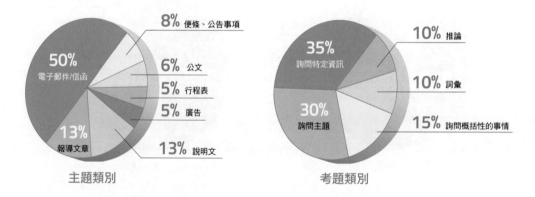

主題類別

8% 便條、公告事項
6% 公文
5% 行程表
5% 廣告
13% 說明文
50% 電子郵件/信函
13% 報導文章

考題類別

35% 詢問特定資訊
10% 推論
10% 詞彙
15% 詢問概括性的事情
30% 詢問主題

學習策略 & 應考策略

1　若沒有自信管理好時間，先完成Part 7再進入Part 5 & 6也是個好辦法。

2　要練習先看考題，之後在文章當中閱讀需要的地方。選擇答案時沒有必要將長篇文章都看完，只要了解考題的核心，然後有選擇性地閱讀。

3　為了得到高分數，選出答案之前還是得再次思考。多益裡不常出現一眼就能看出答案的考題，若再多想一次，常有會找出別的答案的情形。

4　文章最後部分也有答案。有時在文章最後出現的幾個說法會決定考題的答案。

「多益只不過是一種考試。
為了這種考試，學該學的東西就好！」

若是英語很好的人，可以用自己的實力將考試考好，這樣該多好呢？但想在多益考到高分不是一件容易的事情，何況我們又不能整天只學英語就好。然而英語夠厲害就會自動得到多益滿分嗎？不是！因為所有的考試都有為了預防得滿分而設計的陷阱，這就是為什麼不太可能用英語實力而得到分數。

那麼，眼前面臨考試的我們要怎麼辦？最重要的就是，即使只學一道題目，都得學有助於解決實際考題的方式。透過徹底符合實戰考試的學習法，並依照最適當的答題法來準備多益才行。前面說過，所有的考試裡都有陷阱吧？如果有陷阱也就會有漏洞。出題者挖陷阱不是什麼卑鄙的事情，所以應考者鑽漏洞同樣不是卑鄙。即使只學一題，我們也要使用在考場上行得通的方式來學！

面對新制題型，不可不知的要點！

Part 3、4是三題一組的題型，多益改制之後，這兩個Part各有新增搭配圖表的題組，通常題組中會有一題需要搭配圖表作答，面對這樣的題型，考生需要眼耳並用。且Part 3的題目也新增了三人對話的錄音內容，愈多人講話就會有愈多的資訊，不熟悉攻略法的考生就愈容易被過多的資訊混淆。

覺得很難嗎？其實一點也不！對話內容變長、變多人，但對話的邏輯沒有改變。新增的圖表內容，反而有助於考生判斷對話或是獨白的發生地點，一般來說，會搭配的圖表多半為：報價單、地圖、優惠券、產品資訊、報表……等。

其中Part 3會搭配的圖表，80%是報價單、優惠券、產品資訊，Part 4搭配的圖表，則80%會是地圖、產品資訊、報表等。

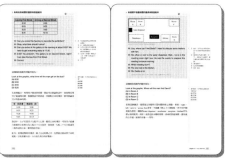

教你真實考場上可以立刻使用的方法！

這本書是基於「多益只不過是一種考試而已」的想法誕生的。大部分的多益教材是教你把「英語」與「考試」兩隻兔子都要抓住。

但「多益」是在有限時間之內，答對愈多考題的人，就可望得到愈高分數的一種遊戲。即使是英語相當不錯的人，如果不太懂遊戲規則，十之八九會失敗。

這本書是徹底為了實際考試撰寫的。因此將考場上用得到的內容放在裡面，並用實戰演練的方式，把找出答案的方法一起教給你。

不僅是單純的理論書，更是實戰手冊！

這本書不同於別的多益參考書，不是單純的修改幾個句子或增加幾張頁數，而是脫胎換骨的「全新版」。雖然多益的考試模式沒有變得很多，但我們想要脫離多數多益書有的盲點。

學了文法理論之後，實際考聽力部分時，不知道到底要將什麼理論應用於考題，而為此懊惱過吧？因此我們加入了「依照考題直接聯想適當理論」，做為找出答案的過程與練習活動。

以前準備多益聽力考試時，會將理論、考題、與錄音分開學習，而且也沒有一本書將其做乾淨俐落的整理，所以大家都曾感到困擾混亂過吧？因此這本書提供「看考題→預測→聽」的學習流程，這樣就能有便於考生學習了。

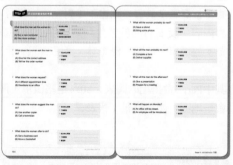

訓練你最適當的解題方式！

這本書的每個單元以「理論→Quiz→沒有答對會後悔的考題（低難易度）→考題實戰練習（實際難易度）」的四個學習階段而構成。

「沒有答對會後悔的考題」裡，學習者可以將前面透過理論學到的解題方法逐一應用。按照例子練習的過程中會發現，即使沒有看過很多考題，但自己正使用怪物講師的解題法。國內沒有任何教材是這種「實戰型」的學習書。

一目瞭然地整理所學過的內容！

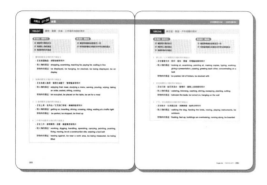

無論是上補習班還是自己學習，最重要的就是複習。但這一點可不容易，為了讓讀者有效的整理所學過的內容，每個單元後面的部分都安排了「一目瞭然整理」的專欄。透過易懂的圖示化方式，學習者可以很快在頭腦裡整理內容。考試前總複習所學過的內容時，沒有什麼是比這個專欄更有效的。如果學習者沒有太多時間從頭學習，看這個部分也能提高分數。

比任何參考書還要詳細的解說！

這本書不同於其他書的解說，除了理論說明以外，解題的部分比起任何書還要詳細。怪物講師根據自身長久以來的經驗，不只有解說錯誤的理由，同時也很仔細說明為什麼是正確答案。如果你想找一本仔細解說的書來學習，就算學一個題目也想要明確了解，那你就找對書了。

自我診斷考試

Part 1 Listen and choose the statement that best describes what you see in the picture.

1

(A)　　(B)　　(C)　　(D)

2

(A)　　(B)　　(C)　　(D)

3

(A)　　(B)　　(C)　　(D)

4

(A)　　(B)　　(C)　　(D)

Part 2 Select the best response to the questions.

5 Mark your answer.   (A)   (B)   (C)

6 Mark your answer.   (A)   (B)   (C)

7 Mark your answer.   (A)   (B)   (C)

8 Mark your answer.   (A)   (B)   (C)

9 Mark your answer.   (A)   (B)   (C)

10 Mark your answer.   (A)   (B)   (C)

11 Mark your answer.   (A)   (B)   (C)

12 Mark your answer.   (A)   (B)   (C)

▶ ▶ ▶ GO ON TO THE NEXT PAGE

Part 3 Listen to the conversation and select the best response to the questions.

13 Where are the speakers?

(A) In a bank
(B) In a shopping center
(C) In a hotel
(D) In a restaurant

14 What does the woman want to do?

(A) Place an order
(B) Make a deposit
(C) Change her room
(D) Clean some clothes

15 When is the interview?

(A) This morning
(B) This afternoon
(C) Tomorrow morning
(D) Tomorrow afternoon

16 Who most likely is the woman?

(A) A salesperson
(B) An athlete
(C) A security manager
(D) A museum curator

17 What does the man want to do?

(A) Purchase a musical instrument
(B) Visit a museum
(C) Attend a performance
(D) Make a travel itinerary

18 What will the man probably do next?

(A) Complete a form
(B) Talk to the manager
(C) Listen to the music
(D) Purchase tickets

19   Which department needs a new manager?

(A) Personnel
(B) Customer service
(C) Accounting
(D) Marketing

20   What qualification does the man mention?

(A) Willingness to travel
(B) Strong references
(C) Relevant experience
(D) A university degree

21   What does the woman recommend?

(A) Contacting a possible candidate
(B) Transferring to another branch
(C) Placing an advertisement on the Internet
(D) Rescheduling some interviews

22   What is the woman asked to help?

Leaving Curvent Ave.	Arriving in Johnson St.
7:05	7:25
7:40	8:00
8:10	8:30
8:40	9:00

(A) Reviewing a record
(B) Filing a report
(C) Decorating a stall
(D) Finding a bus schedule

23   Look at the graphic, what time will the woman get on the bus?

(A) 7:05
(B) 7:25
(C) 8:10
(D) 9:00

24   What advantage does the man mention?

(A) Free meal
(B) Promotion
(C) Double pay
(D) Short work hours

▶▶▶GO ON TO THE NEXT PAGE

Part 4 Listen to the following talk and select the best response to the questions.

25 Who is the caller?

(A) An accountant
(B) A clothing maker
(C) A sales manager
(D) A fashion designer

26 What might be the problem?

(A) An item is not available.
(B) Some documents are missing.
(C) Some products were damaged.
(D) The delivery is late.

27 What does the caller need to know from Erica?

(A) The type of model she wants
(B) The time she will return to the office
(C) The cost of a specially ordered item
(D) The expected arrival time of delivery

----

28 Who is the speaker?

(A) A sales manager
(B) A maintenance worker
(C) A software designer
(D) A repair technician

29 What will happen in July?

(A) A company will stop its operation.
(B) Renovations on a new building will begin.
(C) The speaker will transfer to a new city.
(D) A presentation will be made at a meeting.

30 What does the speaker ask the listeners to consider?

(A) Meeting a project deadline
(B) Moving to a different office
(C) Recruiting more employees
(D) Modifying a building design

31 Who is Mr. Park?

    (A) An author
    (B) A conference organizer
    (C) A bookstore owner
    (D) A hotel receptionist

32 What will Mr. Park talk about?

    (A) His experience
    (B) His book
    (C) His health
    (D) His role as an analyst

33 What can the listeners do at the back of the auditorium?

    (A) Buy a book
    (B) Read some signs
    (C) Take a coffee break
    (D) Register for future lectures

---

34 Who is David, most likely?

    (A) A hotel manager
    (B) The speaker's boss
    (C) A ticket agent
    (D) The speaker's assistant

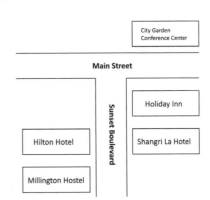

新
35 Look at the graphic.
    Which hotel would the speaker prefer?

    (A) Holiday Inn
    (B) Shangri La Hotel
    (C) Hilton Hotel
    (D) Millington Hostel

36 Why does the speaker need to return early?

    (A) To participate in a project
    (B) To attend an academic exchange
    (C) To see an old friend
    (D) To avoid traffic jam

做過自我診斷考試了嗎？請你根據結果判斷自己屬於A、B、C哪一型，客觀地了解你的應考實力，然後選擇適合自己的學習方法吧。

自我診斷表

A型
答對的數目為十二個以下初級學習者

在這個階段，剛開始學習多益或學習不到幾個月的應考者居多。基本的聽力能力相當不足，而且對多益的模式也還沒完全熟悉。因為基礎很弱，所以即使是看錄音內容仍然無法完全了解。

此階段學習者的特色

- 聽錄音時不太能抓住大概的脈絡。只能聽到零散的單字，也不太能聽到完整的句子。即使聽到單字，很多時候都不知道意思。
- 在播放考試指南時會浪費時間的人。在每分每秒都不得浪費時間的時候，甚至有人看別的地方發呆。
- 由於對考試本身不熟悉的關係，對四十五分鐘的考試時間覺得太長的學習者都屬於這類型的。即使英語實力多好，為了發揮本身的能力還是需要考個幾次才行。
- 這類應考生對於很多單字不知道怎麼發音，只是背了單字而已，沒有確認過這些單字的發音為何。

B型
答對的數目為十三～二十五個中級學習者

這個階段的學習者當中，以準備多益考試好幾個月的人居多，在某種程度上對多益的出題模式有所了解。雖然具有基本的聽力能力，但只要出現陌生一點的說法，在理解意思方面，會感到很大的困難。這類的學習者尤其在Part 3、4裡，會覺得先看考題與選項很難。

此階段學習者的特色

- 對錄音裡出現的商務相關詞彙感到困難。
- 翻譯句子時習慣看後而順序錯亂，所以無法順著聽來了解句子。
- Part 3、4的每一個題組裡都會錯一題以上，也不太能掌握錄音內容的脈絡。
- 在英國式以及澳洲式發音的聽力上很弱，總是覺得很陌生。

C型
答對的數目為二十六～三十六個高級學習者

這個階段的學習者對多益的考題模式已經很熟悉，是在全方位的英語聽力上沒問題的人。另外，他們都知道多益考試裡出現的詞彙，以及這些詞彙怎麼發音。因此，屬於這個階段的學習者必須以減少錯誤為目標。這類學習者覺得比起Part 3、4，Part 2反而更難。尤其在看起來很簡單、但聽到的時候無法立刻了解其意思的陌生說法方面很弱。

此階段學習者的特色

- 能聽懂大部分的內容，但有時候會恍神而無法選出答案。
- 選擇答案時，總是在兩個選項之間猶豫不決。
- 常常執著於已經過去的考題，這樣當然不能好好聽下一個考題。
- 在考試時，填寫答案之後一直猶豫不決，最後改選錯誤答案的情形很多。
- 花了相當長的時間準備多益考試的學生居多。

A型

答對的數目為
十二個以下

若你是這個類型的學習者，透過六十天計畫來學習吧！

剛開始學多益考試的人，大多屬於這個基礎不足的類型吧。但請別失望，因為這裡有解決方法了。對該類的學習者而言，首要就是將這本書重複學習並累積基礎做為最優先的事項。尤其是透過「Warming-up」和「若沒答對會後悔的考題」部分，熟悉找答案的過程。如果想養成更明確的實力，將題目的錄音台詞背下來吧。

六十天學習計畫

第一週	Day 1	Day 2	Day 3	Day 4	Day 5
教材	自我診斷考試	Warming-up		Chapter 1理論	Chapter 1考題
解析本				Chapter 1	
第二週	Day 6	Day 7	Day 8	Day 9	Day 10
教材	Chapter 2理論	Chapter 2考題	Chapter 3理論	Chapter 3考題	Chapter 4理論
解析本	Chapter 2		Chapter 3		Chapter 4
第三週	Day 11	Day 12	Day 13	Day 14	Day 15
教材	Chapter 4考題	Part 1複習		Chapter 5理論	Chapter 5考題
解析本	Chapter 4	/		Chapter 5	
第四週	Day 16	Day 17	Day 18	Day 19	Day 20
教材	Chapter 6理論	Chapter 6考題	Chapter 7理論	Chapter 7考題	Chapter 8理論
解析本	Chapter 6		Chapter 7		Chapter 8
第五週	Day 21	Day 22	Day 23	Day 24	Day 25
教材	Chapter 8考題	Chapter 9理論	Chapter 9考題	Chapter 10理論	Chapter 10考題
解析本	Chapter 8	Chapter 9		Chapter 10	
第六週	Day 26	Day 27	Day 28	Day 29	Day 30
教材	Part 2複習		Chapter 11理論	Chapter 11考題	Chapter 12理論
解析本	/		Chapter 11		Chapter 12

第七周	Day 31	Day 32	Day 33	Day 34	Day 35
教材	Chapter 12考題	Chapter 13理論	Chapter 13考題	Chapter 14 理論考題	Chapter 15 理論考題
解析本	Chapter 12	Chapter 13		Chapter 14	Chapter 15
第八週	Day 36	Day 37	Day 38	Day 39	Day 40
教材	Chapter 16 理論考題	Chapter 17 理論考題	Part 3複習		Chapter 18 理論考題
解析本	Chapter 16	Chapter 17	/		Chapter 18
第九週	Day 41	Day 42	Day 43	Day 44	Day 45
教材	Chapter 18考題	Chapter 19理論	Chapter 19考題	Chapter 20理論	Chapter 20考題
解析本	Chapter 18	Chapter 19		Chapter 20	
第十週	Day 46	Day 47	Day 48	Day 49	Day 50
教材	Chapter 21理論	Chapter 21考題	Chapter 22理論	Chapter 22考題	Chapter 23 理論考題
解析本	Chapter 21		Chapter 22		Chapter 23
第十一週	Day 51	Day 52	Day 53	Day 54	Day 55
教材	Part 4複習	Part 1錯題複習	Part 2錯題複習		Part 3錯題複習
解析本	/	/	/		/
第十二週	Day 56	Day 57	Day 58	Day 59	Day 60
教材	Part 3錯題複習	Part 4錯題複習		模擬試題	模擬試題 錯題複習
解析本	/	/		/	/

B型

答對的數目為
十三～二十五個

為了該類型的學習者，我們推薦三十天學習計畫！

這類型的學習者對多益考試模式很熟悉，但還沒達到高分數的水準。他們都能了解句子或錄音內容的基本脈絡，但具體內容還不太行。而且一旦出現陌生的詞彙，集中力容易被破壞，覺得考題變得很難。屬於該階段的學習者最好將整本教材很仔細地看，然後透過「聽寫練習本」熟悉各種說法。另外需要重複練習「若沒答對會後悔的考題」的解題方法，要懂得考試時如何有效安排時間。

三十天學習計畫

第一周	Day 1	Day 2	Day 3	Day 4	Day 5
教材 解析本	自我診斷考試	Warming-up		Chapter 1	Chapter 2
第二週	Day 6	Day 7	Day 8	Day 9	Day 10
教材 解析本	Chapter 3	Chapter 4	Part 1複習 /	Chapter 5	Chapter 6
第三週	Day 11	Day 12	Day 13	Day 14	Day 15
教材 解析本	Chapter 7	Chapter 8	Chapter 9	Chapter 10	Part 2複習 /
第四週	Day 16	Day 17	Day 18	Day 19	Day 20
教材 解析本	Chapter 11	Chapter 12	Chapter 13	Chapter 14-15	Chapter 16-17
第五週	Day 21	Day 22	Day 23	Day 24	Day 25
教材 解析本	Part 3複習 /	Chapter 18	Chapter 19	Chapter 20	Chapter 21-22
第六週	Day 26	Day 27	Day 28	Day 29	Day 30
教材 解析本	Chapter 23	Part 4複習 /	錯題複習 /	模擬試題 /	模擬試題 錯題複習 /

C型

答對的數目為
二十六～三十六個

對該類型的學習者，適合二十天學習計畫！

為了得到滿分而學習的人。與其學習大量的內容，不如進行減少錯誤的訓練。因為已經知道大部分的考題類型與出現詞彙，需要做更仔細觀察考題的練習。另外，透過教材裡「怪物講師的祕密」來提高實戰考試能力，同時經由題目來熟悉很多說法。除了學習多益考試，為了讓耳朵更靈敏，也需要聽或看英語新聞與電影。

二十天學習計畫

第一周	Day 1	Day 2	Day 3	Day 4	Day 5
教材 解析本	自我診斷考試	Warming-up	Chapter 1, 2	Chapter 3, 4	Chapter 5, 6
第二週	Day 6	Day 7	Day 8	Day 9	Day 10
教材 解析本	Chapter 7	Chapter 8	Chapter 9	Chapter 10	Chapter 11
第三週	Day 11	Day 12	Day 13	Day 14	Day 15
教材 解析本	Chapter 12	Chapter 13	Chapter 14-15	Chapter 16-17	Chapter 18
第四週	Day 16	Day 17	Day 18	Day 19	Day 20
教材 解析本	Chapter 19	Chapter 20	Chapter 21-22	Chapter 23	模擬試題 /

Warming-up

英語發音，只要懂這些就夠了！
美國式發音 vs 英國式發音
連音、重音、發音省略現象
Check up Quiz

1. 英語發音，只要懂這些就夠了！

1) 聽起來相近的發音

[p] vs [f] 的發音

[p] 的發音是先將嘴唇閉合起來充氣，再如破裂地發出的聲音。[f] 是將下唇輕輕地含在門牙下面，然後將氣息由此之間吐出去的聲音。

fill [fɪl] 填滿	pill [pɪl] 藥片	suffer [ˋsʌfɚ] 遭受	supper [ˋsʌpɚ] 晚餐
file [faɪl] 檔案夾	pile [paɪl] 堆積	full [fʊl] 充滿的	pool [pul] 水池
fair [fɛr] 公平的	pair [pɛr] 雙	face [fes] 臉	pace [pes] 步速
often [ˋɔfən] 常常	open [ˋopən] 打開	staff [stæf] 員工團隊	step [stɛp] 腳步、台階

✏️ check up 01　請聽錄音而選出正確答案。

1. (1) copy
    (2) coffee

2. (1) chief
    (2) cheap

3. (1) cuff
    (2) cup

[l] vs [r] 的發音

[l] 是舌尖先碰觸上牙齦之後唸出的發音。[r] 是將舌頭往後退了之後再發出的聲音。

light [laɪt] 光線	right [raɪt] 正確的、右邊的	late [let] 晚	rate [ret] 比率
load [lod] 貨物、裝載量	road [rod] 道路	low [lo] 低	row [ro] 排
glass [glæs] 玻璃	grass [græs] 草	flame [flem] 火焰	frame [frem] 架構、框
law [lɔ] 法律	raw [rɔ] 生的	fly [flaɪ] 飛	fry [fraɪ] 炸
lead [lid] 領導	read [rid] 閱讀		

✏️ check up 02　請聽錄音選出正確答案。

1. (1) lane
    (2) rain

2. (1) file
    (2) fire

3. (1) flea
    (2) free

|答案|　**Check up 01**　1. (1) copy　2. (1) chief　3. (2) cup　**Check up 02**　1. (2) rain　2. (2) fire　3. (1) flea

[b] vs [v] 的發音

[b] 的發音如 [p] 的發音一樣,在口腔裡充氣了之後發出的聲音。[v] 是與 [f] 一樣,將下唇輕輕地含在門牙再唸出的發音。[b] 和 [p] 的嘴唇形狀一樣,但 [b] 有震動聲帶,[p] 沒有該現象。同樣的,[v] 和 [f] 的嘴唇形狀是一樣的,但 [v] 也是震動聲帶,而 [f] 沒有這種現象。

boys [bɔɪz] 男孩子們	voice [vɔɪs] 聲音	curb [kɝb] 鑲邊石	curve [kɝv] 曲線
base [bes] 基礎	vase [ves] 花瓶	boat [bot] 小船	vote [vot] 投票
ban [bæn] 禁止	van [væn] 箱型車	bend [bɛnd] 彎曲	vend [vɛnd] 販賣
best [bɛst] 最好的	vest [vɛst] 背心		

Check up 03　請聽錄音選出正確答案。

1. (1) bow
(2) vow

2. (1) vet
(2) bet

3. (1) vine
(2) bind

[d] vs [t] 的發音

[d] 與 [t] 都是將舌尖貼在上牙齦的部分唸出的發音,但 [t] 是將舌尖突然脫離牙齦而吐出來的發音。

bid [bɪd] 投標	bit [bɪt] 一點點	dance [dæns] 跳舞	tense [tɛns] 緊張的
desk [dɛsk] 書桌	task [tæsk] 任務	do [du] 做	to [tu] 向…
bud [bʌd] 萌芽	but [bʌt] 但是	sad [sæd] 難過的	sat [sæt] sit的過去式

Check up 04　請聽錄音選出正確答案。

1. (1) feed
(2) feet

2. (1) dry
(2) try

3. (1) letter
(2) ladder

|答案|　Check up 03　1. (1) bow　2. (2) bet　3. (1) vine　Check up 04　1. (2) feet　2. (2) try　3. (1) letter

[ð] vs [θ]

兩個發音都是先將舌頭輕輕地含在上下排門牙之間，然後用力吐氣來唸出的發音。但是 [ð] 是震動聲帶，而 [θ] 沒有該現象。

worthy [ˋwɝðɪ] 配得上的　　worth [wɝθ] 有價值的　　bathe [beð] 浸洗　　bath [bæθ] 沐浴

✎ **Check up 05**　請聽錄音寫出正確答案。

1. world population _____

2. winning a _____ competition

[ε] vs [æ]

[ε] 與 [æ] 的發音相似，但 [æ] 是將嘴巴用力左右張開來唸的。

bed [bεd] 床　　　　bad [bæd] 壞的、不好的　　letter [ˋlεtɚ] 信函　　ladder [ˋlædɚ] 梯子
mess [mεs] 一團亂　　mass [mæs] 大量、多數　　bet [bεt] 賭　　　　bat [bæt] 蝙蝠

✎ **Check up 06**　請聽錄音選出正確答案。

1. (1) set　　　**2.** (1) men　　　**3.** (1) bend
　　(2) sat　　　　　(2) man　　　　　(2) band

|答案|　Check up 05　1. growth　2. math　　Check up 06　1. (1) set　2. (1) men　3. (2) band

[ɪ] vs [i]

[ɪ] 是不張開嘴巴短短地唸。 [i] 是將嘴巴左右張開來唸。

live [lɪv] 居住	leave [liv] 離開	rich [rɪtʃ] 富裕的	reach [ritʃ] 到達
hit [hɪt] 打	heat [hit] 熱氣	bit [bɪt] 一點點的	beat [bit] 拍打
sit [sɪt] 坐	seat [sit] 座位	fill [fɪl] 填滿	feel [fil] 感覺
list [lɪst] 目錄	least [list] 最少的		

🖊 **Check up 07** 　請聽錄音選出正確答案。

1. (1) pill
(2) peel

2. (1) knit
(2) neat

3. (1) meet
(2) meat

[ɔ] vs [o]

若不專心聽，聽起來都很相似的發音。尤其需要注意 [o] 的發音。

want [wɔnt] 想要	won't [wont] will not的縮寫
saw [sɔ] see的過去式	sew [so] 縫
caught [kɔt] catch的過去式	coat [kot] 外套
law [lɔ] 法律	low [lo] 低的
cost [kɔst] 費用	coast [kost] 海岸
flaw [flɔ] 缺點、瑕疵	flow [flo] 流動
bought [bɔt] buy的過去式	boat [bot] 小船

🖊 **Check up 08** 　請聽錄音選出正確答案。

1. (1) hall
(2) hole

2. (1) called
(2) cold

3. (1) raw
(2) row

|答案| **Check up 07** 1. (2) peel 2. (1) knit 3. (2) meat 　**Check up 08** 1. (1) hall 2. (2) cold 3. (2) row

2）發音相同或相似，但寫法不同的單字

working [ˋwɝkɪŋ] 工作的	walking [ˋwɔkɪŋ] 走路的
weak [wik] 弱	week [wik] 週
contact [ˋkɑntækt] 聯絡	contract [ˋkɑntrækt] 合約
wait [wet] 等候	weight [wet] 重量
department [dɪˋpɑrtmənt] 部門	apartment [əˋpɑrtmənt] 一戶公寓
whether [ˋhwɛðɚ] 是否	weather [ˋwɛðɚ] 天氣
new [nju] 新的	knew [nju] know的過去式
attend [əˋtɛnd] 出席	tend [tɛnd] 傾向
address [əˋdrɛs] 演說、地址	dress [drɛs] 衣服、穿
ride [raɪd] 搭乘、騎	write [raɪt] 寫
train [tren] 火車	rain [ren] 雨
right [raɪt] 右邊的	write [raɪt] 寫
sale [sel] 銷售	sail [sel] 帆
flu [flu] 流感	flew [flu] fly的過去式
steak [stek] 牛排	stake [stek] 賭金、木樁
break [brek] 打破	brake [brek] 剎車
fare [fɛr] 車錢、乘客	fair [fɛr] 公平的、博覽會
ate [et] eat的過去式	eight [et] 八
our [ˋaʊr] 我們的	hour [ˋaʊr] 小時

2. 美國式發音 VS 英國式發音

多益考試裡常出現的發音，主要可分成美國、加拿大、英國與澳洲的發音。但是，這些發音也可以概括的分類成美國式發音與英國式發音。我們比較熟悉美國式的發音，但世界上有很多國家是用英國式發音的。以下來仔細學習兩種發音的差異與發音方法吧。

1）子音 [r]

美國式發音與英國式發音當中，考生最容易感到有差異的地方就是 [r] 的發音。美國式發音裡將 [r] 都唸出來，但英國式發音裡面，如果母音後面出現 [r] 就會不唸，其前面的母音的發音會變得很長。換言之，[r] 的發音就被省略。反之美國式英語很明顯的特色就是 [r] 的發音。

car 車子	美 [kɑr]	英 [kɑ:]	carpet 地毯	美 [ˋkɑrpɪt]	英 [ˋkɑ:pɪt]
dark 暗的	美 [dɑrk]	英 [dɑ:k]	store 商店	美 [stor]	英 [stɔ:]
parking 停車	美 [ˋpɑrkɪŋ]	英 [ˋpɑ:kɪŋ]	part 部分	美 [pɑrt]	英 [pɑ:t]
art 藝術	美 [ɑrt]	英 [ɑ:t]	stair 階梯	美 [stɛr]	英 [stɛə]
repair 修理	美 [rɪˋpɛr]	英 [rɪˋpɛə]	turn 轉	美 [tɝn]	英 [tə:n]

2）子音 [t]

以下的單字裡，美國式與英國式發音的共同差異，就是最後的 [t]。美國式英語裡，若母音之間出現 [t] 傾向於變成 [d] 或 [r]。但在英國式英語裡，將 [t] 唸得很明顯。

sitting 坐著的	美 [sɪtɪŋ]	英 [ˋsitɪŋ]	later 較晚的	美 [ˋletə]	英 [ˋleitə]
better 更好的	美 [ˋbɛtə]	英 [ˋbetə]	bottom 底部	美 [ˋbatəm]	英 [ˋbɔtəm]
nurse 護士	美 [nɝs]	英 [nəs]	matter 事情	美 [ˋmætə]	英 [ˋmætə]
waiter 男服務生	美 [ˋwetə]	英 [ˋweitə]	letter 信函	美 [ˋlɛtə]	英 [ˋletə]
meeting 會議	美 [ˋmitɪŋ]	英 [ˋmi:tɪŋ]	setting 環境、背景	美 [ˋsɛtɪŋ]	英 [ˋsetɪŋ]
total 總共	美 [ˋtotl̩]	英 [ˋtəutl̩]			

3）子音 [tn]

[tn] 在美國式發音裡聽不到 [t]，同時有很深的鼻音，但在英國式發音裡都照著唸。

mountain 山	美[ˋmauntn̩]	英[ˋmauntin]	button 鈕子	美[ˋbʌtn̩]	英[ˋbʌtn]
curtain 窗簾	美[ˋkɝtn̩]	英[ˋkɜtn]	carton 紙盒	美[ˋkartn̩]	英[ˋkɑːtən]
certainly 確實	美[ˋsɝtn̩lɪ]	英[ˋsɜːtənli]	shorten 縮短	美[ˋʃɔrtn̩]	英[ˋʃɔːtn]
important 重要的	美[imˋpɔrtn̩]	英[imˋpɔːtənt]	fountain 泉水	美[ˋfauntɪn]	英[ˋfauntin]

4）母音 a

在美國式發音裡都唸成 [æ]，但英國式發音裡常常唸成 [ɑ]。

ask 詢問	美[æsk]	英[ɑːsk]	after …之後	美[ˋæftə]	英[ˋɑːftə]
bath 沐浴	美[bæθ]	英[bɑːθ]	chance 機會	美[tʃæns]	英[tʃɑːns]
half 一半	美[hæf]	英[hɑːf]	fast 快的	美[fæst]	英[fɑst]
manager 經理	美[ˋmænɪdʒə]	英[ˋmænidʒə]	answer 回答	美[ˋænsə]	英[ˋɑːnsə]
pass 通過	美[pæs]	英[pɑs]	can't 無法	美[kænt]	英[kɑnt]

5）母音 o

母音 o 在美國常唸成 [ɑ]，但在英國唸成 [ɔ]。

stop 停止	美[stɑp]	英[stɔp]	copy 複印	美[ˋkɑpɪ]	英[ˋkɔpi]
doctor 醫生	美[ˋdɑktə]	英[ˋdɔktə]	not 不	美[nɑt]	英[nɔt]
got 收到了	美[gɑt]	英[gɔt]	lot 多數	美[lɑt]	英[lɔt]
job 工作	美[dʒɑb]	英[dʒɔb]	rock 石頭、振動	美[rɑk]	英[rɔk]
body 身體	美[ˋbɑdɪ]	英[ˋbɔdi]	contact 聯絡、接觸	美[ˋkɑntækt]	英[ˋkɔntækt]

6）其他需要注意的單字

還有一些美國式發音和英國式發音完全不同的情形，這些與之前列出的子音母音的規則無關。最具有代表性的單字為schedule。

advertisement 廣告	美 [ˌædvəˈtaɪzmənt]	
	英 [ədˈvətismənt]	
often 經常	美 [ˈɔfən]	英 [ˈɔːfən]
vase 花瓶	美 [ves]	英 [veis]
garage 車庫	美 [gəˈrɑʒ]	英 [ˈgærɑːʒ]

data 資料	美 [ˈdetə]	英 [ˈdeitə]
schedule 行程	美 [ˈskɛdʒul]	英 [ˈskedʒul]
laboratory 實驗室	美 [ˈlæbrəˌtorɪ]	英 [ləˈbɔrətəri]
water 水	美 [ˈwɔtə]	英 [ˈwɑːtə]

3. 連音、重音、發音省略現象

1）子音與母音合起來的時候

子音和母音相逢的時候，其發音會合起來。意即前面單字的最後子音與後面單字的開頭的母音合起來的現象。此時大致上保留原有的發音，但有時候也會產生全新的發音。

Did you leave it on the desk?	你把它留在桌上了嗎？
The bicycles are **parked in** rows.	這些腳踏車排列停車。
This store **closes at** twelve.	這家店在十二點打烊。
Where **would you** like to go?	你想去哪裡？
Are there any single **rooms available**?	有可用的單人房嗎？
A lot of companies **participated in** the job fair.	很多公司參加這場就業博覽會。

2）發音的省略

舉例而言，將next train唸快的時候next的t與train的t當中一個會被省略。另外，若單字最後出現 [d] 或 [t]，有時候會被省略。

I don't want to go **with them**.	我不想跟他們一起去。
See you **next time**.	下次見吧。
We couldn't find any laundry shop **around the** place.	我們在這附近無法找到洗衣店。
I **don't know** the exact size of the item.	我不知道那個物品的正確大小。
He **can't speak** Japanese.	他不會說日語。
The shipping company decided to **send back** the items.	貨運公司決定把那些物品送回去。

3）重音

在英語裡，除了很短的單字以外，都有重音。在多益考試裡出現的某些單字，依照重音的變化，其詞性與意思會不同。名詞的重音是在前面，而動詞是將重音放在後面。

address	名 [ˋædrɛs] 地址	動 [əˋdrɛs] 演說
conduct	名 [ˋkɑndʌkt] 行為	動 [kənˋdʌkt] 實施
export	名 [ˋɛksport] 出口	動 [ɪksˋport] 輸出
decrease	名 [ˋdikris] 減少量	動 [dɪˋkris] 減少
increase	名 [ˋɪnkris] 增加量	動 [ɪnˋkris] 增加
object	名 [ˋɑbdʒɪkt] 東西	動 [əbˋdʒɛkt] 反對
refund	名 [ˋriˏfʌnd] 償還金額	動 [rɪˋfʌnd] 退費

Check up Quiz 請聽錄音填寫空欄。

01 The truck is _____ next to containers.

02 The _____ has been signed.

03 According to the _____, how can someone purchase the product?

04 The cars are _____ at a traffic light.

05 The lamp has been _____ on.

06 _____ all our experts have spoken, we will collect the cards.

07 A ship is _____ under the bridge.

08 Have you _____ the manager about it?

09 What kind of shoes did you _____?

10 They are _____ the plants.

11 What is being _____?

12 I'd like to _____ a reservation of the room I booked yesterday.

13 To _____ an appointment, please press '1' now.

14 The _____ staff will participate in the conference.

15 We _____ exciting tour packages during your stay.

16 I hope you take the _____ to relax.

17 You will need a heavy _____.

18 Some trees are being _____.

19 Our _____ stop on the city tour is Eco World.

20 Why has the man _____ the woman?

21 _____ please _____ this form?

22 I forgot to _____ bus at the last stop.

23 We are willing to _____ some samples.

24 The president of our company is set to _____ the employees.

25 He _____ get here on time.

| 答案 | 1. parked 2. contract 3. advertisement 4. stopped 5. turned 6. After 7. passing 8. asked 9. purchase 10. watering 11. rescheduled 12. confirm 13. schedule 14. entire 15. offer 16. opportunity 17. coat 18. planted 19. last 20. contacted 21. Would you, fill out 22. change 23. send you 24. address 25. couldn't

Part 1
對照片的描述

一人獨照相片
需了解該人物的動作與狀態！

▶ 在Part 1得滿分的策略

Part 1總共有六個考題，每一個考題中出現一張描述人物或背景的照片。應考生需邊看照片邊聽四個選項，從中選出一個正確的描述。該部分為聽力測驗中最基本的，亦為聽力測驗4個Part中難易度最低、題目數量最少的。一般而言，大多都是容易作答的考題。

1 動詞80%為進行式！

大部分句子的主詞為人，同時在主詞後面接著的動詞也幾乎都是進行式。約80%左右的正確答案為be -ing的進行式。

2 選項中出現的說法都是固定的！

選項無論是正確與否，每次都以固定的說法描述。大約80%左右是重複出現的，所以請將這些說法統整出來。

3 大部分為概括性的句意！

舉例來說，若照片裡有個男生在彈吉他的話，相較於A man is playing a guitar.（有個男生正在彈吉他。）的準確描述，A man is playing a musical instrument.（有個男生正在演奏樂器。）此類型的句子出現較多。

Preview

1 一人獨照相片考題的特色

該類考題有一半左右的題目為詢問人的動作或狀態。以獨照方式呈現的照片，只要能看得出來人的動作和狀態，就很容易選出答案。

2 看獨照相片考題需考慮的重點

❶ 顯示人的動作的照片，從大動作猜測出小動作。
❷ 人的動作以現在進行式來描述。
❸ 沒有敘述到人的動作，就很可能不是正確答案。
❹ 描述人的狀態的時候，使用standing（站著）、sitting（坐著）、holding（握著）等不含動作，但描述狀態的動詞。

攻略法 **01**

對人物動作的描述

描述動作為最基本的的考題，因此動詞相當重要。一個小提醒：在聽錄音之前，只看照片也能夠得到很多線索。

第1階段：觀察照片 看著照片，從大動作開始描述

❶ 先確認照片裡面人物的性別，再預測主詞！
❷ 將人物的動作依從大動作到小動作的順序做預測！

1 主詞	He, The(A) man, A worker	1 他，那（一個）男生，一位工作人員
2 大動作	working, handling	2 在工作，操作
3 小動作	pushing, moving	3 在推，在搬動
4 背景／場所／其他	boxes, a cart, a warehouse	4 箱子，手推車，倉庫

主詞是使用**代名詞**或**表示職業的名詞**來表達。人的動作以**大動作**（用全身的動作）、**概括性動作**：如「在購物（shopping）」、與**小動作**：如「在寫（writing）」、「在吃（eating）」、「在看（looking at）」等，用手、嘴巴或眼睛的動作）來描述。描述動作時一般都使用現在進行式（be + -ing）。

《講師的補充說明》

以下的動詞若使用全身或腳，分類為大動作，若使用以上半身為主的手、嘴巴、眼睛等，分類為小動作。using或washing等概括性的詞彙的話，依照狀況可當大動作也可以是小動作，所以先分類為大動作。

1 表示大動作的動詞

描述一般使用全身動作（如「走」、「工作」）的動詞！

walking, working, running, boarding, shopping, loading, cleaning, posing, bending over, sweeping, driving, washing, using

在走，在工作，在跑，在搭乘，在購物，在裝載，在清洗，在擺姿勢，在彎曲，在清掃，在開車，在洗，在使用

2 表示小動作的動詞

描述一般使用上半身、嘴巴、眼睛的動作（如「放」、「指」、「吃」）的動詞！

putting, pointing at, reaching for, raising, packing, repairing, looking at, examining, reviewing, drinking, eating, speaking

在放，在指示，在伸手，在舉起，在包裝，在修理，在看，在檢查，在審查，在喝，在吃，在說

第2階段：聽錄音 邊想著預測的答案，邊聽錄音

❶ 依照與預測的動作一致與否，確認圖片內容。

❷ 在選項當中若聽不見正確地描述動作的動詞，只有聽到背景、場所、或其他名詞的話，該選項很可能不是答案。

(A) A man is walking on the street. (X)
圖片不是街景，所以不是答案！

(B) A man is washing a car. (X)
圖中沒有車輛，所以不是答案！

(C) A man is pushing a cart. (O)
因為是推著手推車的場面，正是答案！

(D) A man is loading boxes. (X)
不是正在裝載箱子，而是已經裝載好的，所以不是答案！

(A) 有一個男生在街上行走。
(B) 有一個男生在洗車。
(C) 有一個男生在推著手推車。
(D) 有一個男生在裝載箱子。

一般菜鳥考生只要聽到與照片有關的一個單字就開始猜測答案。選項沒有street或car等詞彙，所以不正確。聽到了boxes，但沒有正確描述動作，所以還不是答案！「在推手推車」是預測到的動作，所以（C）就是答案。

1 與大動作有關的說法 🎧 01-02.mp3

「工作」、「上車」、「跑」、「搬運」等是屬於使用全身的大動作。「購物」和「使用」的話屬於概括性的動作。

He's working outdoors.
She's boarding a bus.
The man is running along the path.
A worker's carrying a bucket.
The man's shopping for groceries.
He's using a shovel to dig a hole.

他正在戶外工作。
她正在上公車。
那個男生正在沿著路跑。
有個工人正在搬桶子。
這個男生正在購買食品。
他正在使用鏟子挖洞。

2 與小動作有關的說法 🎧 01-03.mp3

「在寫」、「在放」是用上半身的，「喝水」、「打電話」是用嘴巴的，「看」、「查看」是用眼睛的，所以這些都是與小動作有關的句子。

She's writing with a pen.
She's placing a file folder in the rack.
He's drinking some water.
She's talking on the telephone.
He's looking at some paper.

她正用筆在寫。
她正把檔案夾放在架子裡。
他正在喝點水。
她正在講電話。
他正看著一些紙張。

A woman is examining some jewelry.

有位女性正在檢查一些珠寶。

怪物講師的祕密

1. 聽錄音之前必須觀察照片。
2. 若聽到照片裡沒有顯示的單字，一定不是答案。
3. 若沒有正確描述動作，很有可能不是答案。
4. 進入下一題之前將答案填好。

Quiz

01-04.mp3

請聽錄音之後填寫以下空欄，然後選出正確答案。

Q1

(A) She is _____ .

(B) She is _____ .

Q2

(A) He is _____ .

(B) He is _____ .

▶ 答案在解析本第012頁

攻略法 02

對人的狀態的描述

對狀態的描述是指表達「服裝」、「站著」、「握著」等靜態的狀況，與「在戶外」等場所或位置的說法。應考生需先看照片人物的動作，之後預測可能出現的詞彙。

第1階段：觀察照片 看著照片，從服裝開始描述

1 看了照片裡面的人物之後預測主詞

2 描述人物的服裝和狀態

1 主詞	She, The(A) woman	1 她，那（一個）女生
2 服裝	wearing a hat	2 戴著帽子
3 靜態的狀況	standing, holding	3 站著，拿著
4 背景／場所／其他	plants, a garden	4 植物，花園

在英語裡「wearing（穿著）」是描述服裝的說法。

描述人物的時候也會用standing（站著）、sitting（坐著）、holding（握著／拿著）等「描述靜態動作的動詞」。

1 主要服裝相關說法

若照片裡看到以下的名詞，常與wearing結合成為答案，所以請特別注意。但是若與putting on、taking off、trying on一起用，則不是答案。

hat, glasses, wristwatch, watch, uniform, backpack, gloves, helmet, protective glasses, toolbelt, work vest, coat, long sleeved shirt, short sleeved shirt

帽子，眼鏡，手錶，錶，制服，背包，手套，安全帽，護目鏡，工具腰帶，工作背心，外套，長袖襯衫，短袖襯衫

2 表達人物的靜態狀況的動詞

只專心觀察照片動作時，很可能會錯過對靜態狀況的描述。在喝水的狀況裡，不止drinking water能成為答案，holding a cup也能成為答案。

standing, sitting (seated), holding, resting, kneeling, (waiting) in line, has + 名詞

站著，坐著，拿著，在休息，跪著，在排隊等著，擁有

be outdoors, be alone, be gathered, has gathered, be + 介系詞 （near/by/at/in/on）+ 場所和位置的名詞

在戶外，獨自，聚集著，集合了，在（…附近／旁邊／在／裡面／上面）

🎧 01-05.mp3

第2階段：聽錄音 邊想著預測的答案，邊聽錄音

❶ 依照與預測的動作一致與否，確認圖片內容。

❷ 除了動作之外，也注意聽狀態的描述。

(A) A woman is putting on her glasses. (X)
圖中沒有眼鏡，也不是戴的動作，所以不是答案！

(B) A woman is watering some plants. (X)
只聽見plants嗎？沒有正確描述動作，所以不是答案！

(C) A woman is wearing a hat. (O)
圖中女士戴著帽子，就是答案！

(D) A woman is planting trees in the garden. (X)
只聽見花園嗎？沒有樹，也不是在栽種，所以不是答案！

(A) 有位女士正在戴上眼鏡。
(B) 有位女士正在為一些植物澆水。
(C) 有位女士戴著帽子。
(D) 有個女士正在花園種樹。

若只專心於動作的描述，會錯過（C）「戴著帽子的狀態」。若錯過（B）或（D）裡動作的敘述，很容易產生疑惑。選項（A）因為出現了putting on，所以不是答案。

1 對服裝的描述　　　　　　　　　　🎧 01-06.mp3

對服裝的描述是一律在wearing之後加上服裝名詞。除了wearing，若使用taking off、putting on、trying on就不是答案。

The man is wearing a wristwatch.

The woman's wearing a hat.

He's wearing a watch.

She's wearing protective glasses.

She's wearing gloves.

The man has a bag over his shoulder.

那位男士戴著手錶。
那位女士戴著帽子。
他戴著手錶。
她戴著護目鏡。
她戴著手套。
那位男士肩上背著包包。

2 表達靜態狀況的說法　　　　　🅐 01-07.mp3

「站著」、「坐著」、「拿著」等為表達靜態狀況的說法。也有以「場所介系詞＋場所名詞」表達位置的說法。

He's standing on the ladder.
He's holding a fuel pump handle.
A woman has a microphone in her hand.
She's resting on a bench.
She's waiting by the train tracks.
A woman is near a display board.

他站在梯子上。
他握著燃料泵的把手。
一位女士手上拿著麥克風。
她正在長椅上休息。
她在鐵路旁等著。
一位女士在顯示板附近。

怪物講師的祕密

1 出現獨照人物的通常是相當簡單的問題。

2 描述服裝的部分裡，若聽見putting on（正在穿）、taking off（正在脫）、trying on（正在試穿）、adjusting（正在調整）等的動作動詞，大部分不是答案。

🅐 01-08.mp3

✍Quiz

請聽錄音之後填寫以下空欄，然後選出正確答案。

Q3

(A) He is _____ .

(B) He is _____ .

Q4

(A) A man is _____ .

(B) A man is _____ .

▶ 答案在解析本第012頁

攻略法01　對人物動作的描述

第1階段：觀察照片

1. 預測主詞（確認性別）
2. 預測大動作
3. 預測小動作
4. 確認背景／場所／其他名詞

第2階段：聽錄音

1. 確認與預測的動作是否一致
2. 沒有正確描述動作，但只聽見背景／場所／其他東西的名詞，很可能不是答案
3. 聽見照片裡沒有的名詞，就不是答案

大動作的動詞

walk, work, run, board, shop, load, clean, lose, bend over, sweep, drive, wash, use

小動作的動詞

put, point at, reach for, raise, pack, repair, look at, examine, review, drink, eat, speak

攻略法02　對人的狀態的描述

第1階段：觀察照片

1. 預測主詞（確認性別）
2. 確認服裝
3. 確認有沒有「站著」、「坐著」、「拿著」
4. 確認背景／場所／其他名詞

第2階段：聽錄音

1. 確認與預測的動作是否一致
2. 除了動作的描述以外，也注意聽狀態的描述
3. 服裝的名詞是對的，但若聽見taking off、putting on、trying on，就不是答案

表示服裝的名詞

hat, glasses, wristwatch, watch, uniform, backpack

靜態動詞

standing, sitting (seated), holding, be outdoors, be alone, be gathered, has gathered

STEP 01　若沒答對會後悔的考題

請按照mp3錄音的指示進行以下的考題

例子

① 觀察照片

1 主詞	He, The man, A worker
2 大動作	working, using
3 服裝	wearing a helmet
4 背景／場所／其他	brick wall, bricks, a construction site

② 聽錄音

(A)　(B)　(C)

1

1 主詞

2 大動作

3 小動作

(A)　(B)　(C)

4 背景／場所／其他

2

1 主詞

2 服裝

3 靜態的情況

(A)　(B)　(C)

4 背景／場所／其他

▶ 答案在解析本第012頁

3

1 主詞 ....

....

2 小動作 ....

....

3 服裝 ....   (A)   (B)   (C)

....

4 背景／場所／其他 ....

....

4

1 主詞 ....

....

2 小動作 ....

....

3 靜態的狀況 ....   (A)   (B)   (C)

....

4 背景／場所／其他 ....

....

▶ 答案在解析本第013頁

1

(A)　　(B)　　(C)　　(D)

2

(A)　　(B)　　(C)　　(D)

3

(A)　　(B)　　(C)　　(D)

重要
4

(A)　　(B)　　(C)　　(D)

▶ 答案在解析本第013頁

重要

(A)　　(B)　　(C)　　(D)

6

(A)　　(B)　　(C)　　(D)

高難度
7

(A)　　(B)　　(C)　　(D)

8

(A)　　(B)　　(C)　　(D)

▶ 答案在解析本第014頁

包含兩個以上人物的照片
掌握概括性動作與個別動作！

Review Test

請回答以下的問題，同時整理前面所學的內容。

1 進行Part 1考試時，最優先要確認的是？ ▶ ....

2 預測人物動作的順序為何？ ▶ ....

3 若聽到照片中沒有出現的名詞？ ▶ ....

4 在Part 1考題中，最重要的部分為何？ ▶ ....

5 描述人物服裝的主要名詞為何？ ▶ ....

6 描述人物狀態的主要動詞為何？ ▶ ....

Preview

1 包含兩個人物的照片考題特色

與人物有關的照片當中，在一張照片裡出現兩個以上人物的考題，其中一、兩個考題的主詞為they、some people、或the men等形式，大部分是在測試能否對兩個以上人物進行概括性或群體性的描述。另外兩、三個考題，其四個選項是以不同的主詞來對某特定人物的動作或狀態進行描述，選項中若出現對人物以外的東西做描述的內容，就可能不是正確答案。

2 顯示兩個人物的照片考題需考慮的重點

❶ 將人物的動作概括性地、群體性地描述。

A woman is playing the piano.
A man is playing a guitar. ▶ They are playing musical instruments.

❷ 沒有完整顯示的、位於太遠的人物、或畫面模糊的東西與人不會成為答案。

❸ 在顯示兩個以上人物的照片裡，若有描述個別人物時，依照中心人物到其他人物的順序預測其動作與狀態。

❹ 若聽到從照片的狀況聯想的說法（looking for、going upstairs to sleep）或無法以一張照片來描述的抽象說法（folding、adjusting），大部分不是答案。

[答案] 1.照片 2.從大動作開始確認到小動作 3.不正確答案 4.動詞 5. hat, glasses, wristwatch, watch, uniform, backpack 6. standing, sitting (seated), holding, be out doors, be alone, be gathered, has gathered

攻略法
03 對兩個以上人物做概括性的描述

有顯示兩個以上人物的照片時，必須先確認的事項為人物的概括性與群體性的動作。例如：一個人在敲釘子，而另一個人在梯子上面，則可說他們正「工作中」。

第1階段：觀察照片 看著照片，從群體性的動作開始描述

❶ 先確認照片裡面人物的性別，再預測主詞！

❷ 將人物的動作依概括性／群體性的動作與狀態的順序預測！

1 主詞	They, The women, Two women	1 他們，那些女生，兩個女生
2 概括性的/群體性的動作	examining	2 仔細看著
3 概括性的/群體性的狀態	sitting, seated	3 坐著，坐著
4 背景／場所／其他	documents, stairs, building	4 文件，階梯，大樓

對兩個以上人物做描述的時候，其選項的主詞為群體性的（如they、(some) people、two men、the men、two women、the women）。概括性的動作是指「正在上班（working）」、「正在處理（handling）」等，群體性的動作是指一群人「正在跨過（crossing）」、「正在吃（eating）」等。

1 表示概括性／群體性動作的動詞

「正在上班」、「正在處理」等對幾個人的動作概括性地描述時用的說法！

working (together), handling, shopping, attending, walking, strolling, playing instruments, crossing, using, having a meal, eating, having a conversation, shaking hands, watching, talking together, greeting each other, facing each other, looking at each other

（一起）上班當中，處理當中，購物當中，參加當中，走路當中，散步當中，演奏樂器當中，跨過當中，使用當中，用餐當中，正在吃，對話當中，正在握手，看著，一起說話當中，正在打招呼，面對著，互相看著

2 表示概括性／群體性狀態的動詞

若一群人「在坐著」、「在站著」或「在戶外」，就是對群體性狀態的描述！

standing, sitting, seated, (waiting) in a line, wearing, being helped, be outdoors, be in boats, be on opposite sides of

站著，坐著，坐著，在排隊（等著），穿著，正得到幫助，在戶外，在小艇上，在…的對面

第2階段：聽錄音 邊想著預測的答案，邊聽錄音

❶ 依照與預測的動作一致與否，確認圖片內容。

❷ 在選項當中若聽不見正確描述動作的動詞，只聽到背景、場所、或其他名詞的話，該選項很可能不是答案。

(A) The women are going up the stairs. (X)
　　這是故意讓你聽到stairs（階梯）的誤導選項！

(B) The women are adjusting their hats. (X)
　　照片裡沒有帽子，所以不是答案！

(C) The women are examining some papers. (O)
　　兩個女生都在看著文件，是群體性的動作！

(D) The women are looking at each other. (X)
　　不是互相看著，所以不是答案！

(A) 這些女生正在上樓梯。
(B) 這些女生正在調整她們的帽子。
(C) 這些女生正在查看一些文件。
(D) 這些女生正互相看著。

這是很容易看到兩個女生的群體性動作（看著文件）的照片。（A）是用照片裡面的名詞（stairs）來誤導考生的選項，（B）描述了與照片無關的狀態，所以不是答案，（D）則為故意採用有兩個人物就很容易聯想到的說法來誤導的選項。

1　與概括性／群體性動作相關的說法　🎧 02-02.mp3

「一起做事」、「演奏樂器」或「開會當中」等，是屬於概括性／群體性的動作。

They're working together at a desk.
Some people are playing instruments.
They're having a meeting.
Some people are strolling along the water's edge.
Some people are attending a concert.
The women are greeting each other.

他們正在桌上一起做事。
有些人正在演奏樂器。
他們在開會當中。
有些人正在沿著水邊散步。
有些人正參加演唱會。
這些女生正在互相打招呼。

2　與概括性／群體性狀態相關的說法　🎧 02-03.mp3

「穿著制服」、「一群人站著」或「在戶外」等的說法，常出現在概括性／群體性描述的選項當中。

The men are wearing uniforms.
Some people are standing on the road.
Some people are outdoors.

這些男生正穿著制服。
有些人正站在路邊。
有些人在戶外。

Some people are being helped at a counter.

They're on a stairway.

The women are seated on the lawn.

怪物講師的祕密

1 和具體的描述相較之下，概括性的描述通常會成為答案。

2 被刪掉的畫面或位於太遠的人物不會成為答案。

3 畫面模糊的東西或人物不會成為答案。

🎧 02-04.mp3

Quiz

請聽錄音之後填寫以下空欄，然後選出正確答案。

Q1

(A) They are _____ .

(B) They are _____ .

Q2

(A) The men are _____ .

(B) The men are _____ .

▶ 答案在解析本第015頁

攻略法

04 對兩個以上人物個別描述

顯示兩個以上人物的照片中，也有對個別人物做描述的選項。若是對人物以外的東西做描述，則不是正確答案。對人物沒有概括性描述的話，也可能會出現對個別動作的描述。

第1階段：觀察照片 看著照片，對個別人物做描述

❶ 確認照片裡面的中心人物之後預測主詞！

❷ 先預測中心人物的動作／狀態，再預測其他人物的動作／狀態！

1 主詞	One man, A man
	One of the people
2 中心人物	pointing, explaining, standing
3 其他人物	looking at, sitting
4 背景／場所／其他	chart, meeting room

1 一個男生，一個男生，一群人當中的一個
2 指著，正在說明，站著
3 看著，坐著
4 圖表，會議室

在照片上出現兩個以上人物時，若沒有概括性／群體性的動作／狀態描述，會出現對個別人物的動作／狀態的描述。而不正確的選項則是對別人或週遭的東西做描述。在此先預測中心人物的動作／狀態，或者從最左邊人物的個別動作／狀態開始預測。

1 兩個男女當中，個人的主詞

The man, The woman

這個男生，這個女生

2 兩個同性人物當中，個人的主詞

One man, A man, One of the men, One woman, A woman, One of the women

一個男生，有個男生，這些男生其中之一，一個女生，有個女生，這些女生其中之一

3 三個人物當中，個人的主詞

One man, A man, One woman, A woman, One of them

一個男生，有個男生，一個女生，有個女生，這些人其中之一

第2階段：聽錄音 邊想著預測的答案，邊聽錄音

① 依照與預測的動作一致與否，確認圖片內容。

② 注意聽出現人物的動作。

(A) A man is taping a presentation. (X)
的確有presentation，但無法知道錄音與否，所以不是答案！

(B) The men are speaking to a microphone. (X)
聽到了照片裡沒有的麥克風，所以不是答案！

(C) Some people are entering a conference room. (X)
不是有人進入會議室的狀況，所以不是答案！

(D) One man is pointing at a chart. (O)
描述了中心人物的個別動作，正是答案！

(A) 有個男生在錄報告。
(B) 這些男生正對著麥克風說話。
(C) 有些人正進入會議室當中。
(D) 有個男生正指著圖表。

描述了中心人物的個別動作的（D）就是正確答案！（A）與（C）選項，若只想著「開會當中」或「發表當中」等概括性／群體性動作會很容易選錯的項目。（B）用了照片裡沒有的名詞（microphone），所以不是答案。

1 個別動作相關的說法 🎧 02-06.mp3

如一群工人之中的一個人在挖土，或一個女生將筆記本拿給一個男生的狀況等，都是將焦點放在中心人物的描述。

One of the workers is digging.
The woman is passing a notebook to the man.
A bicyclist is crossing the street.
A man is trimming some bushes.
The man is cutting hair.
A man is making a purchase.

其中一個工人正在挖土。
這個女生正把筆記本拿給這個男生。
有個騎腳踏車的人正在過馬路。
有個男生正修剪灌木。
這個男生正在剪頭髮。
有個男生正在採購中。

2 個別狀態相關的說法 🎧 02-07.mp3

一群人當中有一個人在站著、坐著、或自己在某個角落的狀況，對個別狀態的描述。

One person is standing apart from the crowd.
The woman is standing behind the counter.
Some people are seated on the lawn.
A woman is holding up some merchandise.

有個人遠離人群站著。
這個女生站在服務台的後面。
有些人坐在草坪上。
有個女生用手拿著一些商品。

One man is holding the back of his chair.
One man is near a corner of the room.

有個男生正用手抓著他的椅背。
有個男生在房間角落附近。

怪物講師的祕密

1. 概括性的描述比個別描述出現得更多。
2. 對個別動作的描述模糊時，對東西的描述會成為答案。
3. 若聽到從照片的狀況聯想的說法（looking for、going upstairs to sleep）或無法用一張照片來描述的說法（folding、adjusting），這大部分不是答案。

🎧 02-08.mp3

Quiz

請聽錄音之後填寫以下空欄，然後選出正確答案。

Q3

(A) Some shoppers are _____.

(B) A man is _____.

Q4

(A) A woman is _____.

(B) A man is _____.

Chapter 02_ 包含兩個以上人物的照片 **061**

攻略法03　對兩個以上人物做概括性的描述

第1階段：觀察照片

1 預測主詞（確認性別）
2 確認概括性／群體性動作
3 確認概括性／群體性狀態
4 確認背景／場所／其他名詞

第2階段：聽錄音

1 確認與預測的動作是否一致
2 沒有正確描述動作，但只聽見背景／場所／其他東西的名詞，很可能不是答案
3 聽見照片裡沒有的名詞，就不是答案

表示概括性／群體性動作的動詞

working (together), handling, shopping, attending, playing instruments, crossing, having a conversation, shaking hands, talking together, greeting each other

表示概括性／群體性狀態的動詞

standing, sitting, seated, (waiting) in a line, wearing, being helped, be outdoors

攻略法04　對兩個以上人物個別描述

第1階段：觀察照片

1 預測主詞（確認性別）
2 預測中心人物的動作
3 預測週遭人物的動作
4 確認背景／場所／其他名詞

第2階段：聽錄音

1 確認與預測的動作是否一致
2 除了動作的描述以外，也注意聽狀態的描述
3 對照片裡不完整的東西或對心理狀態描述的，就不是答案

1 兩個男女當中，個人的主詞

The man, The woman

2 兩個同性人物當中，個人的主詞

One man, A man, One of the men, One woman, A woman, One of the women

3 三個人物當中，個人的主詞

One man, A man, One woman, A woman, One of them

STEP 01 若沒答對會後悔的考題　　　　請按照mp3錄音的指示進行以下的考題

例子

① 觀察照片

1 主詞	They
2 概括性／群體性描述1	having a meal
3 概括性／群體性描述2	looking at each other
4 背景／場所／其他	food, dishes, table

② 聽錄音

(A)　(B)　(C)

1

1 主詞

2 概括性／群體性描述

3 個別描述　　　　　　　　(A)　(B)　(C)

4 背景／場所／其他

2

1 主詞

2 概括性／群體性描述1

3 概括性／群體性描述2　　(A)　(B)　(C)

4 背景／場所／其他

▶ 答案在解析本第016頁

3

1 主詞 ....

....

2 概括性／群體性描述 ....

....

3 個別描述 ....   (A)　(B)　(C)

....

4 背景／場所／其他 ....

....

4

1 主詞 ....

....

2 概括性／群體性描述 ....

....

3 個別描述 ....   (A)　(B)　(C)

....

4 背景／場所／其他 ....

....

▶ 答案在解析本第016頁

STEP 02 **考題實戰練習** 請留意前面兩個階段的內容進行以下的考題 答對的題目數：_____

高難度

(A) (B) (C) (D)

2

(A) (B) (C) (D)

高難度

(A) (B) (C) (D)

4

(A) (B) (C) (D)

重要
5

(A)   (B)   (C)   (D)

6

(A)   (B)   (C)   (D)

7

(A)   (B)   (C)   (D)

重要
8

(A)   (B)   (C)   (D)

▶ 答案在解析本第017頁

對照片裡的物件與背景的描述
由物件的立場來想像吧！

Review Test

請回答以下的問題，也同時整理前面所學的內容。

1 有兩個以上人物的照片其特色為何？　　　　　　　　▶ ....

2 照片裡的畫面若焦點模糊或不完整的話？　　　　　　▶ ....

3 概括性／群體性動作的動詞有哪些？　　　　　　　　▶ ....

....

....

4 若個別人物的動作模糊，則描述物件的說法大部分為答案。▶ ....

5 若聽到從照片的狀況來聯想的說法，或無法只用一張照片來
　描述的內容的話？　　　　　　　　　　　　　　　　▶ ....

Preview

1 物件與背景描述照片考題的特色

即使在照片裡有人出現，不止對該人物的動作描述可能會是答案，對周遭東西的描述有時也會成為答案。考題大約會出現兩張左右沒有人物出現的照片，此時需要的就是對物件的描述。對物件做的描述像是：A car is parked.（有一輛車子被停放著。）這類不具動態的，指的就是對靜態的描述，或是物件有動作，如A car is being parked.（有一輛車子正在被停放當中。）這類的，就是對動態的描述。

2 看東西與背景描述照片考題需考慮的重點

❶ 若照片裡的物件沒有動作，大部分以被動式或被動現在完成式來描述。看這種照片時，需要能預測被動式或被動現在完成式的說法。

❷ 若照片裡沒有人物出現，卻有與人物相關的說法或進行被動式說法being出現的話，則不是答案。
The chairs are being arranged.（這些椅子正在被擺放當中。）

❸ 描述物件的動作時，最常用的說法為被動進行式（be being p.p.）。
He is driving a car.　▶ The car is being driven by him.

|答案| 1.概括性／群體性動作或狀態的描述　2.不正確答案　3. standing, sitting, seated, (waiting) in a line, be outdoors, be in boats, be on opposite sides of　4. O　5.不正確答案

攻略法

05 對物件靜態狀況的描述

若照片裡沒有人物，或即使有但周遭的物件、背景較為突顯，通常對物件描述的選項即為答案。物件包含有動作或沒有動作的，對沒有動作的物件做的描述稱為靜態狀況描述。

第1階段：觀察照片 看著照片，對靜態狀況做描述

① 先確認照片裡面的主要物件，再預測主詞！

② 對靜態狀況用被動式或被動現在完成式預測說法！

1 主要東西	Products, Merchandise	1 產品，商品
2 靜態1	(be/have been) displayed	2 被陳列
3 靜態2	(be/have been) stacked/stocked	3 被堆放／被貯存
4 背景／場所／其他	store, shelves, rack	4 商店，架子，掛物架

描述東西的靜態狀況時最常用被動式（be p.p.）或被動現在完成式（have been p.p.）。假如有一輛車子停放著，可用A car is parked.（有一輛車子被停放著。），或A car has been parked.（有一輛車子被停放的狀況。）來描述。

1 用被動式描述東西的狀態

最常以「be + p.p.」的形式用於描述東西。

（產品）displayed、（產品）arranged、（散步的路）boared by a wall、（車子）being parked、（箱子）stacked、（座位）occupied、（籃子）filled with、（地板）covered with、（辦公室）stocked with supplies

（產品）被陳列、（產品）被擺著、（散步的路）被牆圍著、（車子）被停放著、（箱子）被堆放著、（座位）被佔滿、（籃子）裝著、（地板）覆蓋著、（辦公室）被存貨塞滿

2 用被動現在完成式描述東西的狀態

若從現在的立場看，其意思與被動式一樣。請注意have been的發音。

（餐桌）has been set、（椅子）have been arranged、（書）have been organized、（梯子）has been propped against、（東西）has been placed、（石頭）have been piled

（餐桌）被準備好、（椅子）被擺好、（書）被整理好、（梯子）靠著、（東西）被擺放、（石頭）被堆積

3 用There is/are或「be＋場所介系詞片語」描述物件的位置

若用場所介系詞（in, on, at, near, next to, behind, around），可以描述位置！

There is/are＋東西＋場所介系詞＋場所名詞

There are cars in the parking area.

物件＋is/are＋場所介系詞＋場所名詞

Cars are in the parking area.

> 有些車子在停車場。
>
> 車子在停車場。

4 用「be＋形容詞」描述物件的狀態

也可以用形容詞描述物件的狀態！

（畫）hanging、（產品）on display、（空位）available、（抽屜）full of、（登機口）empty、（鐘面）round

> （畫）掛著、（產品）陳列著、（空位）可用、（抽屜）裝滿著、（登機口）空的、（鐘面）圓形的

5 將物件擬人化來描述狀態

「沙發面對著」是將沙發擬人化的表達方法！

（梯子）casting a shadow、（大樓）overlooking、（沙發）facing each other、（小路）lead to、（圍牆）run along、（水果）growing on a vine

> （梯子）投影著、（大樓）俯瞰著、（沙發）面對著、（小路）通到、（圍牆）圍繞著、（水果）長在藤蔓上

🎧 03-01.mp3

第2階段：聽錄音 邊想著預測的答案，邊聽錄音

❶ 依照與預測的狀態描述一致與否，確認圖片內容。

❷ 若照片裡沒有人物出現，卻聽到與人相關的說法或being，則不是答案。

❸ 注意分辨has been與is being的發音。

(A) Some shoppers are trying on shoes. (X)

因圖片裡沒有人物，所以聽到shoppers就不是答案！

(B) There are clothes hanging in the closet. (X)

圖中畫面不是衣櫥，所以不是答案！用clothes故意誤導的選項！

(C) Merchandise is displayed in a store. (O)

商品陳列在商店裡面，正是答案！

(D) Shelves are being stocked. (X)

在沒有人物的照片聽到being就不是答案！

> (A) 有些客人正在試穿鞋子。
> (B) 有些衣服掛在衣櫥裡。
> (C) 商品陳列在商店裡。
> (D) 架子正被裝著東西。

這是在沒有人的商店裡陳列著商品的照片。（A）出現了人物相關的說法，所以不是答案。（B）出現了照片裡沒有的closet，所以不是答案。（D）若要成為答案，必須先要有人針對物件做動作才行。

1 以被動式／被動現在完成式描述狀態　🔊 03-02.mp3

Cars are parked. 或Cars have been parked. 都能成為答案！

Cars are parked along the street.
Some sofas are arranged around the table.
The office is stocked with supplies.
A picture has been placed above the bed.
A table has been set for a meal.
Some lights have been turned on.

> 車子被沿路停放著。
> 有些沙發繞著桌子擺著。
> 這間辦公室裝滿著貨物。
> 有一張畫被擺在床的上方。
> 為了用餐，有張桌子被擺設了。
> 有些燈被打開了。

2 用場所介系詞片語描述位置　🔊 03-03.mp3

There are chairs around the table. 或Chairs are around the table. 都能成為答案！

There are chairs around the table.
There are cabinets under the counter.
There are vehicles on the highway.
Some plants are behind the sofa.
A vehicle's at an intersection.
The train is near the platform.

> 有些椅子繞著這張桌子。
> 服務台下面有些櫥櫃。
> 在高速公路上有些車輛。
> 沙發後面有些植物。
> 有一輛車子在交叉路上。
> 這輛火車在月台附近。

3 用形容詞或擬人化的方式描述狀態　🔊 03-04.mp3

「椅子靠著」或「火車站俯瞰著」都是將東西擬人化來表達的方法，round/empty/hanging等，是用形容詞來描述東西狀態的說法。

Chairs are leaning against the table.
The train station overlooks a parking area.
The ladder is casting a shadow.
The clock faces are round.
The platform is empty.
Some guitars are hanging from a wall.

> 椅子靠著這張桌子。
> 這座火車站俯瞰著停車場。
> 這個梯子投射出影子。
> 這個鐘面是圓的。
> 這個月台是空的。
> 有些吉他在牆上掛著。

🎧 03-05.mp3

Quiz

請聽錄音之後填寫以下空欄，然後選出正確答案。

Q1

(A) Trees are ⸺⸺⸺⸺⸺⸺⸺ .

(B) Trees are ⸺⸺⸺⸺⸺⸺⸺ .

Q2

(A) ⸺⸺⸺⸺⸺ has been set for a meal.

(B) ⸺⸺⸺⸺⸺ are having their meals.

▶ 答案在解析本第019頁

攻略法
06

對物件動態狀況的描述

物件有動作時，其動作大部分是由人發生的。若由人使物件有動作，也可以從物件的立場表達說法。這種描述方法叫做動態狀況描述。

第1階段：觀察照片 看著照片，描述動態的狀況

❶ 若預測到了人物的動作，再從物件的立場想像吧！

❷ 從物件的立場用被動進行式預測吧！

1 人物的動作	They are carrying a basket.
2 物件的立場	A basket is being carried.
3 背景／場所／其他	grass, grassy area

> 1 他們在搬一個籃子。
> 2 一個籃子正在被搬動。
> 3 草，草地

描述物件的動作最常用的說法為被動進行式（be being p.p.）。例如有人在停車當中，可以表達為He is parking a car.，若由車子的立場描述，也可以說A car is being parked.

人物 is making a purchase.
→ A purchase is being made.

人物 is examining some documents.
→ Some documents are being examined.

人物 is applying paint to a wall.
→ Paint is being applied to a wall.

人物 is giving a presentation in a lecture hall.
→ A presentation's being given in a lecture hall.

> 有人在購買當中。
> →被購買當中。
>
> 有人正在查看一些文件。
> →一些文件正在被查看。
>
> 有人正在牆上塗油漆。
> →油漆正在被塗在牆上。
>
> 有人正在演講廳報告當中。
> →有一份報告正在演講廳被發表當中。

第2階段：聽錄音 邊想著預測的答案，邊聽錄音

❶ 依照與預測的動作一致與否，確認圖片內容。

❷ 沒有動作的物件後面若聽到being，就不是答案。

(A) The man is carrying a bag. (X)

這個男生搬的東西不是包包，所以不是答案！

(B) Trees are being planted in the garden. (X)

圖片裡看不到樹，所以不是答案！

(C) A basket is being carried. (O)

從籃子的立場來看就是被搬運的，所以是答案！

(D) A blanket is being loaded in the car. (X)

圖片裡看不到車子，所以不是答案！

(A) 這個男生在搬包包。
(B) 有些樹正在花園裡被種植。
(C) 有個籃子正在被搬運。
(D) 有一張毯子正在被裝上車子。

將有些人正在搬運籃子，以籃子的立場來描述的（C）就是答案！（A）、（B）、（D）都用了照片裡沒有出現的名詞，所以不是答案。

1 用被動進行式描述東西的動態狀況　🎧 03-07.mp3

車子被洗、容器被搬運等，都是從物件的立場描述有人洗車、有人搬運容器等動作的說法。

A car is being washed.
A container is being carried by a man.
Plants are being watered in a garden.
A map is being examined.
A piece of wood is being measured.
A purchase is being made.

有一輛車子正被清洗。
有一個容器正被一個男生搬運當中。
花園的植物正在被澆水。
有一張地圖正在被查看。
有一塊木頭正在被測量。
有一筆交易正在被進行。

2 將東西擬人化來描述物件的動態性狀況　🎧 03-08.mp3

煙飄上去、噴泉噴水的狀況等，可以視為將物件擬人化來表達的說法。

Smoke is rising into the air.
Some trucks are crossing a bridge.
The fountain is spraying water into the air.
A train is traveling on the tracks.
The fog is coming in from the sea.

煙正在飄到天空。
有些卡車正在過橋當中。
這個噴泉正在噴水到空中。
有一輛火車正走在鐵軌上。
霧氣正在從海上過來。

Some ducks are swimming near a boat.

有些鴨子正在一艘小船附近游著。

怪物講師的祕密

1 被動進行式是不正確答案的機率較高。

2 請注意：is being的發音比has been長。聽到is being，必須有人物才能成為答案，但has been的話，沒有人物也能當作答案。

3 常用的擬人化說法最好背下來（overlook、face、run、surround等）。

🎧 03-09.mp3

Quiz

請聽錄音之後填寫以下空欄，然後選出正確答案。

Q3

(A) A map is _____.

(B) A telescope is _____.

Q4

(A) The _____ is _____ into the air.

(B) Some _____ are _____ in the garden.

▶ 答案在解析本第019頁

攻略法05　對物件靜態狀況的描述

第1階段：觀察照片

1 確認照片裡的主要物件

2 預測主詞

3 以被動式或被動現在完成式預測物件的靜態狀況

第2階段：聽錄音

1 確認與預測的狀態是否一致

2 若照片裡沒有人物卻聽到being或人物相關說法，就不是答案

3 聽錄音時注意分辨has been與is being

對物件靜態狀況的描述

1. 被動式：A car is parked next to a building.
2. 被動現在完成式：A car has been parked next to a building.
3. 使用場所介系詞片語的：A car is next to a building.
4. 使用There is的：There is a car next to a building.

*若要表達A car is being parked.，照片裡必須有人物。

攻略法06　對物件動態狀況的描述

第1階段：觀察照片

1 確認照片裡的主要動作

2 從物件的立場用被動進行式，預測物件的動態狀況

第2階段：聽錄音

1 確認與預測的動作是否一致

2 若沒有動態的東西後面聽到being，就不是答案

對物件動態狀況的描述方法

1. 被動進行式 : A car is being parked.
2. 擬人化：交通工具、噴泉、煙、霧氣、動物、建築物、家具等會被擬人化。

A train is traveling on the tracks.

Smoke is rising into the air.

The fountain is spraying water into the air.

Some ducks are swimming near a boat.

STEP 01 若沒答對會後悔的考題　　　　　請按照mp3錄音的指示進行以下的考題

例子

① 觀察照片

1 主要物件	lights
2 靜態性狀況1	(be/have been) turned on
3 靜態性狀況2	(be/have been) lined up
4 背景／場所／其他	wall, corridor, pedestrians

② 聽錄音

(A)　(B)　(C)

1

1 人物的動作	
2 物件的立場	
3 背景／場所／其他	

(A)　(B)　(C)

2

1 主要物件	
2 靜態性狀況1	
3 靜態性狀況2	
4 背景／場所／其他	

(A)　(B)　(C)

3

1 人物的動作	
2 物件的立場	
3 背景／場所／其他	

(A)　(B)　(C)

4

1 主要物件	
2 靜態性狀況1	
3 靜態性狀況2	
4 背景／場所／其他	

(A)　(B)　(C)

▶ 答案在解析本第019頁

重要

(A)　　(B)　　(C)　　(D)

重要

(A)　　(B)　　(C)　　(D)

3
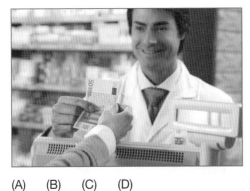

(A)　　(B)　　(C)　　(D)

4

(A)　　(B)　　(C)　　(D)

5

(A)　　(B)　　(C)　　(D)

6

(A)　　(B)　　(C)　　(D)

高難度
7

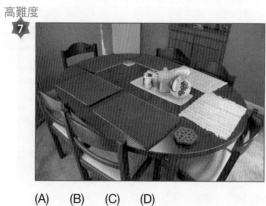

(A)　　(B)　　(C)　　(D)

8

(A)　　(B)　　(C)　　(D)

▶ 答案在解析本第021頁

出現特殊狀況的照片

預想各種狀況裡常出現的說法！

Review Test

請回答以下的問題，也同時整理前面所學的內容。

1 照片裡描述的物件與背景的狀態一般為何？　　　　　▶ ....

2 靜態狀況的物件是以何種動詞形式描述？　　　　　　▶ ....

3 若照片裡沒有人物卻聽到being就不是答案。　　　　▶ ....

4 若沒有動態的物件但在之後聽到being，這就是答案。　▶ ....

5 將物件擬人化的動詞主要有哪些？　　　　　　　　　▶ ....

Preview

1 出現特殊狀況的照片之特色

Part 1的照片中有大約70%是以前考試出現過的。每張照片大多是使用特定主題反覆出現。例如：購物的照片中，常常出現商品陳列的畫面、正在購物的畫面、在服務台互相面對著的畫面等等。這些即為常出現的特殊狀況照片，大致上可分為購物、餐廳、街道、工作場所、公司、家庭、戶外等類別。

2 看特殊狀況照片考題需考慮的重點

❶ 特殊狀況照片都各自有該狀況裡常出現的固定說法。

購物：A man is holding up some merchandise. (hold up, merchandise)

餐廳：A table is being set for a meal. (table, set for a meal)

公司：A woman is using a photocopier. (use, photocopier)

家庭：Some people are resting on a porch. (rest on, porch)

❷ 最常出現的辦公室相關照片考題，大部分的答案為「仔細看著文件」、「正在工作」、「座位是空的」等的說法。

A man is sitting at his desk.

A woman is seated on a chair.

Some of seats are empty.

❸ 有時也會出現沒有特殊狀況或複合狀況的照片。

|答案| 1.靜態狀況　2.被動式或被動現在完成式　3.O　4.X　5. overlook, face, run, surround

攻略法 07 購物、餐廳、街道、工作場所相關的照片

每次考試都會出現，有購物、餐廳、街道、工作場所等畫面的考題。因此如果將各種狀況之下可能出現的說法特別學起來，不但可以減少預測描述的時間，也能降低選錯答案的機率。

第1階段：觀察照片 看著照片，判斷是哪種特定狀況

❶ 先確認是否為常見的特定狀況照片！
❷ 根據特定狀況中常用的說法來預測答案！

1 判斷狀況	購物		2 購買一些食品
2 對人物的描述	shopping for some groceries		3 陳列著
3 對物件的描述	be displayed		4 商店、食物、手推車
4 背景／場所／其他	shop, food, cart		

若照片裡有人物購買商品，則可能出現的說法大概只有3～4個。先了解是與購物相關的照片，就要想到shopping、pushing、examining、paying for等常出現的人物描述與displayed、arranged、stacked等的物件描述。

1 購物

挑選商品與排隊結帳的畫面為常出現的！

對人物的描述： shopping, examining, reaching for, paying for, waiting in line, holding up some merchandise, standing behind the counter

購物當中、檢查著、正在伸手、付錢當中、正在排隊、用手拿著一些商品、正站在服務台後面

對東西的描述： be displayed, be hanged, be arranged, be stacked, be being displayed, be on display
A purchase is being made.

陳列著、掛著、擺著、堆放著、陳列著、陳列著
交易正在進行當中。

2 餐廳

為客人點餐、服務員端盤子、或整理餐桌的畫面為常出現的！

對人物的描述：enjoying their meal, studying a menu, serving, pouring, wiping, taking an order, seated, sitting, cooking	享用餐點中、仔細看著菜單、服務當中、正在倒、正在擦、正在點菜、坐著、坐著、正在做菜
對物件的描述：be occupied, be placed on the table, be set for a meal	正被佔用中、被放在桌上、為了用餐而備妥的

3 街道

上車、在月台／十字路口等待、或車輛移動的畫面為常出現的！

對人物的描述：getting on, boarding, driving, crossing, riding, waiting at a traffic light	上車當中、搭乘當中、開車當中、穿越當中、乘坐當中、於紅綠燈等著
對物件的描述：be parked, be stopped, be lined up	被停放著、被停止、被排列著

4 工作場所

工作、修理、測量、或搬運材料的畫面為常出現的！

對人物的描述：working, digging, handling, operating, carrying, painting, pushing, hammering, fixing, moving, be at a construction site, holding a ladder, wearing a tool belt	正在工作、正在挖、正在處理、正在操作、正在搬運、正在塗、正在推、正在捶打、正在修理、正在移動、在工地、握著梯子、穿戴著工具腰帶
對物件的描述：leaning against, be near a work area, be being measured, be being lifted	倚靠著、在工地附近、正被測量、正被抬高

🎧 04-01.mp3

第2階段：聽錄音 邊想著預測的答案，邊聽錄音

❶ 依照與預測的說法是否一致，確認圖片內容。

❷ 特別注意聽在各種狀況之下常當作答案的說法。

(A) A man is paying a clerk. (X)
因照片裡看不到錢，所以付錢的說法就不是答案！

(B) Some food is being placed in the cart. (X)
沒有人針對食物做動作，所以不是答案！

(C) A man is shopping for some groceries. (O)
商品陳列在商店裡面，正是答案！

(D) A man is eating in a restaurant. (X)
看起來不是餐廳，也不是正在吃，就不是答案！

(A) 有個男人正付費給服務員。
(B) 有些食物被放在手推車裡。
(C) 有個男人正在買一些食品。
(D) 有個男人正在餐廳裡吃著。

由於是與購物相關的照片，因此可以想到「購物」、「伸手」、「推手推車」與「商品陳列著」等說法。

符合這些條件的（C）就是答案。其他選項都使用了照片裡沒有出現過的名詞，或paying、food等說法來故意誤導。

1 商場

🎧 04-02.mp3

大部分以「購物」、「看商品」、「商品陳列著」等說法作為答案。

She's examining some produce.
The man is shopping for groceries.
A man is making a purchase.
Baked goods are displayed in a shop window.
Some clothes have been hung from hooks.
Products have been organized in two rows.

> 她正在檢查著一些農產品。
> 這個男人正在購買食品。
> 有個男人正在交易當中。
> 烘焙類的商品被陳列在商店的窗邊。
> 有些衣服被掛在鉤子上。
> 產品被整理為兩排。

2 餐廳

🎧 04-03.mp3

大部分以「用餐中」、「看著菜單或點菜」、「菜上桌了」等說法作為答案。

A group has gathered at a table for a meal.
They're having a meal.
Diners are seated near the curb.
Dishes have been placed on the table.
The cup is being filled.
Menus have been provided for the diners.

> 一群人為了用餐聚集在餐桌旁。
> 他們正在用餐。
> 用餐的人坐在路邊附近。
> 盤子（菜餚）被擺放在桌上。
> 這個杯子正被填滿。
> 菜單被提供給用餐的人。

3 街道

🎧 04-04.mp3

「上車」、「穿越馬路」、「等紅綠燈」、「車子停放著」等說法常常出現。

She's boarding a bus.
A passenger is getting out of a car.
Pedestrians are crossing the street.
A stairway is located near some railroad tracks.
There are cars parked along the street.
The intersection is deserted.

> 她正在上公車。
> 有個乘客正從車子裡出來。
> 行人正穿越馬路。
> 樓梯位於一些鐵軌附近。
> 有些車輛被沿路停放著。
> 這個交叉路口無人蹤影。

4 工作場所

🎧 04-05.mp3

「工人在上工」、「將什麼東西修理」、「測量」、「搬運」等說法常常出現。

He's working outdoors.

A worker is concentrating on cutting a piece of wood.

A worker is holding a sign.

The man is wheeling a cart across the floor.

The building is under construction.

A piece of wood is being measured.

他正在戶外工作。
有個工人正專心切著一塊木頭。
有個工人正拿著標誌。
這個男人正推著手推車橫越樓層。
這棟大樓正在施工。
有一塊木頭正被測量。

怪物講師的祕密

1 be being displayed也描述物件的靜態狀況，與be displayed是一樣的意思。

2 若照片裡沒有出現錢，卻聽到paying for或purchasing等，就不是答案。

3 照片裡出現車輛時，不是答案的選項中很常會聽到driving等說法。

🎧 04-06.mp3

Quiz

請聽錄音之後填寫以下空欄，然後選出正確答案。

Q1

(A) People are _____ .

(B) The food is _____ .

Q2

(A) Workers are _____ .

(B) The men are _____ .

攻略法
08

辦公室、家庭、戶外相關的照片

在Part 1當中，辦公室／公司相關狀況的照片佔將近一半。因此若特別學習各種狀況之下可能出現的說法，不但可以減少預測描述的時間，也能降低選錯答案的機率。

第1階段：觀察照片 看著照片，判斷是哪種特定狀況

❶ 先確認是否為常見的特定狀況照片！

❷ 根據特定狀況中常用的說法預測答案！

1 判斷狀況	辦公室／公司	
2 對人物的描述	using a photocopier	2 正在使用影印機
3 對物件的描述	be being used	3 正在被使用
4 背景／場所／其他	office, paper, copier	4 辦公室，紙，影印機

Part 1中，與辦公室／公司有關的照片，其出現比率幾乎有50%那麼多。若想到辦公室／公司相關照片的話，就要想到examining、making copies、typing、working、passing等對人物的描述，與posted、stocked等對物件的描述。

1 公司

在看文件、影印、報告、開會、用電腦做事中等狀況，會經常出現的！

對人物的描述：looking at, examining, pointing at, making copies, typing, working, giving a presentation, passing, greeting each other, concentrating on a task

看著、檢查著、指著、正在影印、正在打字、正在工作、正在報告、正在經過、正在互相打招呼、正在專心做事情

對物件的描述：be posted, full of folders, be stocked with

貼著、裝滿著文件夾、⋯裝著

2 家庭

正在打掃、給花草澆水、整理床、在牆壁上掛著畫等狀況，為經常出現的！

對人物的描述：watering, trimming, washing, stirring, sweeping, resting on a porch, sprinkling, planting, cutting

正在澆水、正在修剪、正在洗、正在攪拌、正在掃、正在陽台休息、正在噴水、正在栽種、正在剪

對物件的描述：between the beds, be turned on, hanging on the wall

在床和床之間、被開著、掛在牆壁上

3 戶外／其他

在散步、在湖邊走路、演奏樂器、船停泊當中等，為常出現的照片！

對人物的描述：walking the dog, feeding the birds, rowing, playing instruments, hiking up the mountain, be outdoors

正在遛狗、正在餵鳥、正在划船、正在演奏樂器、正在步行上山、在戶外

對物件的描述：floating, tied up, buildings are overlooking, running along, be boarded

浮著、被綁著、大樓俯瞰著、沿著跑、被覆蓋著

🎧 04-07.mp3

第2階段：聽錄音 邊想著預測的答案，邊聽錄音

❶ 依照與預測的說法一致與否，確認圖片的內容。

❷ 特別注意聽在各種狀況之下常作為答案的說法。

(A) A woman is typing a document. (X)
　用與影印機相關聯想的說法document當做誤導的選項！

(B) A woman is using a photocopier. (O)
　正在使用影印機當中，所以正是答案！

(C) A woman is making a cup of coffee. (X)
　故意製造coffee與copy可能聽錯發音的選項！

(D) A woman is speaking on the phone. (X)
　沒有電話，也不是說話的狀況，所以不是答案！

(A) 有個女士正在打文件。
(B) 有個女士正使用影印機。
(C) 有個女士正在煮一杯咖啡。
(D) 有個女士正在講電話。

對使用影印機的狀況來做描述的（B）為答案。（A）與（D）是使用和公司可能相關的狀況來誤導的選項。（C）用近似發音coffee來故意誤導的選項。

1 辦公室／公司　　🎧 04-08.mp3

「看著文件」、「正在工作」、「座位空著」等說法常作為答案。

She's placing a file folder in the rack.

They're working at a table.

They're examining some papers.

The chairs are unoccupied.

Some equipment has been arranged in front of the man.

The drawer is full of folders.

> 她正把文件夾擺在架子裡。
> 他們正在桌上做事。
> 他們正在仔細看著一些文件。
> 這些椅子空著。
> 有些設備被放在這個男人前面。
> 這個抽屜裝滿著文件夾。

2 家庭　　🎧 04-09.mp3

「正在澆水」、「正在廚房水槽做事」、「牆壁上掛著畫」等說法常作為答案。

She's using the sink.

He is watering some plants.

She's packing a suitcase.

A picture has been placed above the bed.

Some lights have been turned on.

A balcony is attached to every apartment.

> 她正在用水槽。
> 他正在為一些植物澆水。
> 她正在打包行李。
> 有一張畫被掛在床的上方。
> 有些燈被打開了。
> 每一間公寓都附有一間陽台。

3 戶外／其他　　🎧 04-10.mp3

「正在散步」、「看著表演」、「正在演奏樂器」、「有圍牆」等說法常作為答案。

Some people are attending a concert.

They're strolling along the water's edge.

Some people are playing instruments.

The parkway is boarded by a wall.

A fence runs along the edge of the road.

There are clouds in the sky.

> 有些人正在聽演唱會。
> 他們正在水邊散步。
> 有些人正在演奏樂器。
> 這條林園道路被圍牆圍繞著。
> 有座柵欄沿著這條路的邊緣。
> 有雲彩在天空上。

1 若考題有戶外／其他狀況的照片，對物件的描述常作為答案。

2 piano、guitar以外的樂器，都以musical instruments描述。

3 考題當中也會出現沒有顯示特定狀況或包含多種狀況的照片。

🎧 04-11.mp3

✏️Quiz

請聽錄音之後填寫以下空欄，然後選出正確答案。

Q3

Q4

(A) Some musicians are _____ .

(B) People are _____ .

(A) She's _____ .

(B) She's _____ .

攻略法07　購物、餐廳、街道、工作場所相關的照片

第1階段：觀察照片
1. 確認照片裡的狀況
2. 預測對人物的描述
3. 預測對物件的描述

第2階段：聽錄音
1. 確認與預測的狀態是否一致
2. 特別留意聽在各種狀況中常出現的說法

1　購物相關常出現的照片與說法
- 正在挑選商品、排隊結帳等照片
- 對人物的描述：shopping, examining, reaching for, paying for, waiting in line

對物件的描述：be displayed, be hanging, be stacked, be being displayed, be on display

2　餐廳相關常出現的照片與說法
- 正在為客人點菜、服務生端盤子、整理餐桌等照片
- 對人物的描述：enjoying their meal, studying a menu, serving, pouring, wiping, taking an order, seated, sitting, cooking

對物件的描述：be occupied, be placed on the table, be set for a meal

3　交通相關常出現的照片與說法
- 正在上車、在月台／交叉路口等候、車輛移動等照片
- 對人物的描述：getting on, boarding, driving, crossing, riding, waiting at a traffic light

對物件的描述： be parked, be stopped, be lined up

4. 工作場所相關常出現的照片與說法
- 正在工作、修理東西、測量、搬運東西等照片
- 對人物的描述：working, digging, handling, operating, carrying, painting, pushing, fixing, moving, be at a construction site, wearing a tool belt

對物件的描述：leaning against, be near a work area, be being measured, be being lifted

攻略法08 辦公室、家庭、戶外相關的照片

第1階段：觀察照片

1. 確認照片裡的狀況
2. 預測對人物的描述
3. 預測對物件的描述

第2階段：聽錄音

1. 確認與預測的狀態是否一致
2. 特別留意聽在各種狀況中常出現的說法

1 辦公室／公司相關常出現的照片與說法

- 正在看著文件、影印、報告、開會、用電腦做事等照片

- 對人物的描述：looking at, examining, pointing at, making copies, typing, working, giving a presentation, passing, greeting each other, concentrating on a task

  對物件的描述：be posted, full of folders, be stocked with

2 家庭相關常出現的照片與說法

- 正在打掃、給花草澆水、整理床、牆壁上掛著畫等照片

- 對人物的描述：watering, trimming, washing, stirring, sweeping, planting, cutting

  對物件的描述：between the beds, be turned on, hanging on the wall

3 戶外／其他相關常出現的照片與說法

- 正在散步、在湖邊走路、演奏樂器、船停泊等照片

- 對人物的描述：walking the dog, feeding the birds, rowing, playing instruments, be outdoors

  對物件的描述：floating, tied up, buildings are overlooking, running along, be boarded

STEP 01 若沒答對會後悔的考題　　　　　請按照mp3錄音的指示進行以下的考題

例子

① 觀察照片

1 確認狀況	餐廳
2 對人物的描述	×
3 對物件的描述	be unoccupied
4 背景／場所／其他	table, outdoors, shadows

② 聽錄音

(A)　(B)　(C)

1

1 狀況 _____

2 對人物的描述 _____

3 對物件的描述 _____

4 背景／場所／其他 _____

(A)　(B)　(C)

2

1 狀況 _____

2 對人物的描述 _____

3 對物件的描述 _____

4 背景／場所／其他 _____

(A)　(B)　(C)

3

1 狀況 _____

2 對人物的描述 _____

3 對物件的描述 _____

4 背景／場所／其他 _____

(A)　(B)　(C)

4

1 狀況 _____

2 對人物的描述 _____

3 對物件的描述 _____

4 背景／場所／其他 _____

(A)　(B)　(C)

▶ 答案在解析本第023頁

STEP 02 考題實戰練習　　請留意前面兩個階段的內容進行以下的考題　答對的題目數：_____

高難度
1

(A)　　(B)　　(C)　　(D)

2

(A)　　(B)　　(C)　　(D)

高難度
3

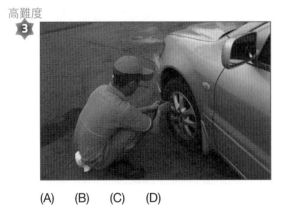

(A)　　(B)　　(C)　　(D)

重要
4

(A)　　(B)　　(C)　　(D)

重要

5

(A)　　(B)　　(C)　　(D)

6

(A)　　(B)　　(C)　　(D)

高難度
7

(A)　　(B)　　(C)　　(D)

8

(A)　　(B)　　(C)　　(D)

Part 2
疑問與回答

Chapter 05

Who、Where 疑問句

只要聽到疑問詞就知道答案！

▶ 在Part 2得滿分的策略

Part 2的考題總共有25題，而每個考題裡將一個疑問句或陳述句與三個選項連續聽完後，需選出正確答案。大部分的考題即使沒聽完選項還是能回答，所以若先學習各種考題類別與各類別之下的答案，就不難作答。

1 注意聽第一個單字吧！

先要知道第一個單字為疑問詞、助動詞、還是名詞主詞，才能確定是哪種形式的疑問句。因此第一個聽到的單字為最重要的線索。

2 若以疑問詞詢問，Yes/No不可以作為答案。

若聽到的疑問句裡有疑問詞，而選項當中有Yes/No的話，大膽地將這個選項排除吧。依照常理想也知道，詢問「什麼」、「誰」、「如何」、「什麼時候」、「什麼地方」、「為什麼」的時候，用「對」、「不對」來回答也很不搭吧。

3 對一般疑問句而言，大部分以Yes/No開頭的選項作為答案。

若疑問句以助動詞或be動詞開頭，其答案60%以上為以Yes/No開頭的。

Preview

1 Who、Where類疑問句考題的特色

Part 2的考題可以分類為「以疑問詞開頭的疑問句」、「不以疑問詞開頭的疑問句」、與「陳述句」，其中「以疑問詞開頭的疑問句」是出現率達一半以上的重要考題。「以疑問詞開頭的疑問句」只要注意聽疑問詞就可以回答，但若沒聽到疑問詞，即使都聽完剩下的部分也不容易答對。

2 出現Who、Where疑問句的考題需考慮的重點

❶ 聽到疑問詞是最重要的。
❷ 疑問詞Who的後面常接著出現「負責」類的說法。
❸ 對Who疑問句而言，人名常作為答案。
❹ 對Where疑問句而言，場所介系詞片語常作為答案。
❺ Where與When疑問句，因為文法結構很像而很容易混淆。

攻略法

09

回答Who疑問句的方法

有疑問詞的疑問句當中,最常出現且最容易掌握的就是Who疑問句。只要聽到Who,90%的考題就可以回答。那麼我們一起學習Who疑問句吧!

🎧 05-01.mp3

第1階段:聽考題 注意聽疑問詞

❶ 聽到第一個出現的疑問詞是最重要的。

❷ 若沒聽到疑問詞時卻聽到「負責」類的說法,其疑問詞很有可能為Who。

❸ Who的後面出現過去時態的機率比未來時態多。

Who疑問句的主要例子

Who is in charge of safety inspections for your plant?
Who is going to organize the reception?

Who called me earlier this meeting?
Who left the party first?

Who's going to pick the director up at the airport?
Who will notify the employees of these changes?

Who is that sitting in the first row?
Who has the key to the supply closet?

Who do you think will be the new head officer?
Who should I ask if I need more paper for the printer?
Whose duty is it to send the newsletter to the customers?

Part 2的考題當中最簡單的為以Who開頭的疑問句。沒聽到疑問詞Who的話,想想是否聽到「負責」類的說法。如果是,該句子很有可能為Who疑問句。Who的後面傾向於出現過去時態。表達「誰的」Whose也與Who疑問句沒兩樣吧?

常出現的「負責」類的說法

be in charge of, deal with, handle, be responsible for, take the responsibility for, organize

---

《講師的補充說明》

你們覺得多益聽力考題中,最難的部分是哪裡?就是Part 2。其原因在於「一次性」:僅僅只讓你聽一次,也不提供任何線索可參考。而且最近的趨勢是高難度的句子出現率愈來愈高。為了因應這一點,考生除了針對疑問詞以外,對整個句子也需要完全了解、熟悉。

誰負責你們工廠的安全檢查?
誰要籌辦這場歡迎會?

稍早的會議是誰打電話給我?
誰是第一個離開那場派對的?

誰要在機場接那位主任?
誰要將這些變更事項通知員工?

坐在第一排的人是誰?
誰有倉庫的鑰匙?

你覺得誰是新的總幹部?
如果我需要影印紙要問誰?
誰負責將通訊報寄給客戶?

對…負責,處理,處理,對…有責任,對…承擔責任,組織

第2階段：聽選項 選擇性地聽吧！

❶ 對Who疑問句而言，最常出現的答案選項為以「人名」來回答的。有時候也加入職務或單位的名稱來提高難度。

❷ 有時候不容易聽辨人名。（例如不尋常的名字Mrs. Lawyer、Ms. Duffy、Ms. Soto等）

❸ 最近選項當中也常出現迴避性或反問的說法。

Who疑問句題型主要出現的回答說法

Q：Who's going to speak at the meeting after work?
A：Mr. Gomez, I think.
　　以Who來詢問，因而出現了人名。這個就是答案！

Q：Who is responsible for the project?
A：I think the vice president is.
　　雖然不是人名而是職稱，還是應該會答對吧？

Q：Who is going to the demonstration?
A：The public relations team will go for it.
　　單位也能當作人物的角色！

Q：Who is in charge of taking notes of this meeting?
A：I think I am.
　　又快又短地回答說「我是」的情形。

Q：Who has the copy of the financial report?
A：It's on my desk.
　　只認為這是針對Who的答案就錯了！此回答也可以作為答案！

Q：Who do you think will be the new General Manager?
A：It depends on the situation.
　　迴避性或反問的說法對任何疑問句都可以當作回答。

> Q：誰要在下班之後的會議中發言？
> A：我想是戈麥斯先生。
>
> Q：誰負責那項企劃案？
> A：我想是副總。
>
> Q：誰要去參加那場展示會？
> A：公關部門會去。
>
> Q：誰負責這場會議的記錄？
> A：應該是我。
>
> Q：誰有那份財務報告的複印本？
> A：它在我的桌上。
>
> Q：你覺得誰會當新的總經理？
> A：依狀況而定吧。

對Who疑問句最常出現的答案為「人名」，所以很容易選出答案，但有時候也會出現不尋常的人名，最好還是得小心一點。另外，雖然不是常出現，但也有一些又快又短的回答方式。

1 常出現的職務與單位名稱

manager, secretary, director, vice president, supervisor, personnel department, maintenance department, accounting department, advertising department, sales department

> 經理，祕書，主任，副總，主管，人事部門，維修部門，會計部門，廣告部門，業務部門

2 常出現的迴避性或反問的說法

I'm not sure.

Let me check.

Karen probably knows.

It hasn't been decided yet.

Have you asked the manager about it?

我不確定。
讓我確認一下。
凱倫有可能知道。
還沒決定下來。
有關那個，你問過經理了嗎？

怪物講師的祕密

1 只要將第一個出現的疑問詞聽好也能選出答案。

2 確定答案了，就大膽地進入下一題吧。

3 若在選項裡聽到與問句相似的發音或單字，大部分不是答案。

4 對疑問詞問句絕對不可以用Yes/No回答。

🎵 05-03.mp3

✐ Quiz

Q1 請邊聽邊填寫以下空欄。

(1) _____ speak at the meeting after work?

(2) _____ complaints regarding our products?

(3) _____ contact for the meeting?

(4) _____ of safety inspections for your plant?

Q2 請聽問題之後選出適當的回答。

(1) ⓐ John, our vice president.　　ⓑ I meet him quite often.

(2) ⓐ They are Mr. Parks.　　ⓑ I think Jackson will.

(3) ⓐ I have some time right now.　　ⓑ It's our custom.

▶ 答案在解析本第025頁

攻略法

10

回答Where疑問句的方法

Where疑問句是詢問場所的考題。因此只要事先學習表達場所的說法，大家都能答對。Where疑問句與Who疑問句一樣，是在Part 2當中最容易答對的考題。

🎧 05-04.mp3

第1階段：聽考題 注意聽疑問詞

❶ 聽到第一個出現的疑問詞是最重要的。

❷ Where與When類的句子結構相似，所以很容易會混淆。

❸ 需要注意Where的英國／澳洲發音。

Where疑問句的主要例子

Where is the nearest train station?
Where's the nearest place I can buy some toothpaste?

Where can I find room 28?
Where can I get directions to the convention center?

Where should I put these file folders?
Where should I sign my name on these forms?

Where did you leave the fabric samples?
Where did you buy this digital camera?

Where does Jason live?
Where are you going for your holiday?

最近的火車站在哪裡？
我能買到牙膏最近的地方在那兒？

28號房間在哪裡？
在哪裡可以詢問往會議中心的方向？

該把這些檔案夾放在哪裡？
該在這些表格上的哪裡簽名？

你把那些布料樣本放在哪裡？
這台數位相機你在哪裡買的？

賈森住在哪裡？
休假的時候你要去哪裡？

Where疑問句與Who疑問句一樣，只要聽到一個疑問詞就行。但若不小心，有時候會與When混淆。另外，因英國／澳洲發音裡r會消失而可能聽成 [uea]，所以得特別留意。一半以上的Where疑問句都呈現「Where is the closest/nearest 名詞？」的結構。若沒聽到疑問詞卻聽到can I get/find等說法，其前面的疑問詞很有可能是Where。

1 考題中常尋找的場所

department, bus stop, bookstore, platform, post office, train station, pharmacy, headquarters, library, bank

部門，公車站，書店，月台，郵局，火車站，藥局，總部，圖書館，銀行

2 考題中常尋找的對象

doctor, cashier, file folder, key, copy machine, sales record, identification card, digital camera, office supply, printer paper

醫生，收銀員，檔案夾，鑰匙，影印機，行銷記錄，身份證，數位相機，辦公用品，印表機用紙

🎧 05-05.mp3

第2階段：聽選項 **選擇性地聽吧！**

❶ 對Where疑問句而言，最常出現的答案包含場所介系詞片語（介系詞 + 場所名詞）。

❷ 有時候不容易聽辨街道、國家／都市、餐廳名稱等。（例如Main Street、Hanoi、Singapore、Alabama等）

❸ 尋找的對象有時候為「人物」。

Where疑問句題型主要出現的回答說法

Q：Where is the nearest public library?

A：Near the hospital.

　　以「場所介系詞（near）＋場所名詞（hospital）」回答，所以是最優先的答案！

Q：Where can I find room 27?

A：It's on the second floor.

　　在場所介系詞片語（on the second floor）上，增加別的說法來回答也是答案！

Q：Where did you leave the office calender?

A：Ms. Jackson borrowed it.

　　尋找的對象不只是場所，有時候是人物。

Q：Where is the post office?

A：Two hundred meters from here.

　　這是以距離回答的情形。

Q：Where does the company have its headquarters?

A：It's about twenty minutes from here.

　　這也是以距離回答的情形，但是以時間來呈現。

Q：Where do you plan to go for the holidays?

A：We haven't decided yet.

　　迴避性、反問的說法對任何疑問句都能作為答案！

Q：最近的公共圖書館在哪裡？
A：在醫院附近。

Q：27號房間在哪裡？
A：在二樓。

Q：你把辦公室的月曆放在哪裡？
A：傑克遜小姐借去了。

Q：郵局在哪裡？
A：距離這邊兩百公尺。

Q：那家公司的總部在哪裡？
A：距離這邊大概二十分鐘。

Q：休假的時候你們要去哪裡？
A：我們還沒決定。

對Where疑問句而言，最常出現回答為「場所介系詞片語」。雖然有時候不容易聽辨場所名詞，但若只要聽清楚介系詞還是很容易選對答案。不過還是得注意，除了場所以外也會出現「人物」或「距離為多少」等的說法。

尋找的場所或對象的位置

across the street, near the park, at the front counter, on the third floor, from our supplier, beside the window, on the bottom line, down the hall, to the dentist, right over there, in front of the lobby, on my desk

在馬路的對面，在公園的附近，在前面的服務台，在三樓，來自我們的供應商，在窗戶旁邊，在最底下一行，在走廊的末端，到牙醫診所，就在那邊，在大廳前面，在我桌上

怪物講師的祕密

1 Where疑問句與When疑問句的文法結構相似情形很多，所以在Where疑問句的回答選項中，常出現When疑問句的回答方式。
2 Who與Where疑問句常出現於Part 2的前半部分。
3 Who與Where疑問句是在Part 2裡面最容易的，所以一定得答對。

🎧 05-06.mp3

Quiz

Q3 請邊聽邊填寫以下空欄。

(1) _____ sign my name on these forms?

(2) _____ plan to visit this weekend?

(3) _____ the nearest pharmacy?

(4) _____ the company have its main office?

Q4 請聽問題之後選出適當的回答。

(1) ⓐ On page 12 in the newspaper.　ⓑ Yes, last Thursday.

(2) ⓐ I like coffee.　ⓑ We don't have one.

(3) ⓐ I can give them to you.　ⓑ He's a new director.

▶ 答案在解析本第026頁

攻略法09　回答Who疑問句的方法

Who疑問句

聽到Who就是關鍵。即使沒聽到Who，但只要聽到「負責」類的說法，其前面的疑問詞很有可能是Who。

Who疑問句的主要例子

Who is in charge of safety inspections for your plant?

Who left the party first?

Who's going to pick the director up at the airport?

Who will notify employees of these changes?

Who has the key to the supply closet?

Who should I ask if I need more paper for the printer?

Who疑問句題型的主要答案

以人名、職務或部門名稱回答。想得高分的應考生也需要知道「我是」、「在我桌上」等應用類說法。另外「不太清楚」等間接迴避性的回答，無論何時都能作為答案。

Who疑問句題型的主要回答方式

Mr. Gomez, I think.

I think the **vice president** is.

The **public relations team** will go for it.

I think **I am**.

It's **on my desk**.

It **depends on the situation**.

攻略法10　回答Where疑問句的方法

Where疑問句

只要聽到Where也能選出答案。因為其文法結構與When一樣很容易混淆，所以除了疑問詞以外，也需要將疑問句的前段全部一起記下來。

Where疑問句的主要例子

Where's the nearest place I can buy some toothpaste?

Where can I find room 28?

Where can I get directions to the convention center?

Where should I put these file folders?

Where did you leave the fabric samples?

Where are you going for your holiday?

Where疑問句題型的主要答案

大部分以「場所介系詞片語」或將此包含在內的句子為答案。「距離」或「走該距離時需要的時間」也能作為答案。「不知道」、「還沒決定」類的「間接迴避性答案」，無論何時都能作為答案。

Where疑問句題型的主要回答方式

Near the hospital.

It's **on** the second floor.

Two hundred meters from here.

It's about **twenty minutes from here**.

Ms. Jackson borrowed it.

We haven't decided yet.

STEP 01 **若沒答對會後悔的考題** 請按照mp3錄音的指示進行以下的考題

例子

Who's going to pick me up at the airport?

❶ 聽考題

1 疑問詞	Who
2 動詞（動作）	is going to, pick up
3 對象／場所／其他	at the airport

❷ 聽選項

Mark your answer.

(A)　(B)

1

1 疑問詞

2 動詞（動作）

3 對象／場所／其他

Mark your answer.

(A)　(B)

2

1 疑問詞

2 動詞（動作）

3 對象／場所／其他

Mark your answer.

(A)　(B)

3

1 疑問詞

2 動詞（動作）

3 對象／場所／其他

Mark your answer.

(A)　(B)

4

1 疑問詞

2 動詞（動作）

3 對象／場所／其他

Mark your answer.

(A)　(B)

5

1 疑問詞

2 主詞／動詞（動作）

3 對象／場所／其他

Mark your answer.

(A)　(B)

▶ 答案在解析本第026頁

STEP 02 考題實戰練習　　　　　請將以下部分當作真實考試，邊計時邊回答吧。

1　Mark your answer on your answer sheet.　　　　(A)　(B)　(C)

2　Mark your answer on your answer sheet.　　　　(A)　(B)　(C)

3　Mark your answer on your answer sheet.　　　　(A)　(B)　(C)

高難度
❹　Mark your answer on your answer sheet.　　　　(A)　(B)　(C)

5　Mark your answer on your answer sheet.　　　　(A)　(B)　(C)

6　Mark your answer on your answer sheet.　　　　(A)　(B)　(C)

7　Mark your answer on your answer sheet.　　　　(A)　(B)　(C)

8　Mark your answer on your answer sheet.　　　　(A)　(B)　(C)

9　Mark your answer on your answer sheet.　　　　(A)　(B)　(C)

10　Mark your answer on your answer sheet.　　　　(A)　(B)　(C)

重要
⓫　Mark your answer on your answer sheet.　　　　(A)　(B)　(C)

重要
⓬　Mark your answer on your answer sheet.　　　　(A)　(B)　(C)

▶ 答案在解析本第027頁

Chapter 06

When、Why 疑問句

聽到疑問詞與後面的另一個單字就能選出答案！

Review Test

請回答以下的問題，也同時整理前面所學的內容。

1 有關Who、Where疑問句，最重要的是？　　　　▶ ....

2 Who疑問句之後最常出現的答案為何？　　　　▶ ....

3 Where疑問句之後最常出現的答案為何？　　　▶ ....

4 若聽到「負責」類的說法，其前面的疑問詞為何？ ▶ ....

5 若選項裡聽到與問句相似的發音或單字？　　　▶ ....

6 無論何時都能作為答案的選項為何？　　　　　▶ ....

Preview

1 When、Why類疑問句考題的特色

出現When、Why疑問句的話，將疑問詞與接著出現的另一個單字聽清楚才能選出正確答案。When疑問句是單純詢問時間的，所以時間、星期幾、日子等作為答案。Why疑問句除了詢問某事的原因或理由以外，也常當作提出建議的句子。

2 出現When、Why疑問句的考題需考慮的重點

❶ When的後面常出現未來相關的內容。When疑問句裡面的動詞即使是現在式，仍然表達未來的事情。

　　When does the train leave for Seoul?　　　　When does this ticket expire?

❷ 對When疑問句最常有的答案為「未來時間點的介系詞片語」。

❸ 疑問詞When是單純詢問時間的，所以時間、星期幾、日子等作為答案。

　　Q: When are you going to visit the factory?　　A: Sometime next week.

❹ 若Why後面沒有don't，是屬於詢問理由的，所以表達理由的句子為答案。

　　Q: Why isn't that printer ever used?　　A: It's not connected.

❺ 若Why後面聽到don't，是提出建議的說法。

　　Q: Why don't you take a day off tomorrow?

　　A: I'd love to. But I have an important meeting tomorrow.

[答案] 1.聽疑問詞 2.人名 3.場所介系詞片語 4. who 5.是錯誤答案 6.間接／迴避性回答

攻略法
11
回答When疑問句的方法

When疑問句是詢問特定時間點的考題，因此聽完疑問詞後面出現的單字，再判斷是詢問過去時間點還是未來時間點，然後對此選出答案。

🎧 06-01.mp3

《講師的補充說明》

第1階段：聽考題 注意聽疑問詞

❶ 除了疑問詞以外，也得聽接著的單字。
❷ 在When後面聽到動詞，大部分會產生有關未來的回答。

When疑問句的主要例子

When will construction start on the Cooper Building?
When are you leaving?

When did you buy your car?
When did you sign up for the conference?

When does the train leave for Seoul?
When does this ticket expire?

When is the deadline for submitting news articles?
When is the inspection?

When was the copier repaired?
When were those reports written?

Part 1的「be+ing」是現在進行式，表達「正在發生的狀況」，但在Part 2，用來表達近期未來的狀況。例如「When are you leaving?」是表達「你預定什麼時候離開？」的句子。

什麼時候將開始庫伯大樓的建設？
你什麼時候離開？

你什麼時候買了車子？
你什麼時候報名那場會議的？

這班火車什麼時候開往首爾？
這張票什麼時候過期？

新聞交稿的期限是什麼時候？
視察是什麼時候？

這台影印機是什麼時候修理的？
那些報告是什麼時候寫的？

考題為When疑問句的話，也要將後面動詞的時態一次聽到才能選出答案。實際考試裡，詢問未來時間點的考題（When後面出現will或現在時態的情形）出現得更多。

When疑問句裡常出現的說法

開始相關：start, begin, take place, be held, leave, move into, join, go out, release

結束相關：end, expire, complete, finish

意見相關：be supposed (scheduled) to+V, expect to+V, plan to+V, be planning (going) to+V

開始，開始，發生，舉辦，離開，搬進，加入，出去，上市

終止，過期，完成，結束

預訂做…，預計做…，計劃做…，將要做…

活動相關名詞：inspection, seminar, presentation, appointment, deadline, product demonstration, workshop

其他： approve, submit, hand in, send, arrive

檢查，研討會，報告，約定，期限，產品示範，工作坊

贊成，呈送，提交，寄送，抵達

🎧 06-02.mp3

第2階段：聽選項 選擇性地聽吧！

❶ 對When疑問句而言，最常出現的答案是以「未來時間點介系詞片語」來回答的。有時候也會用包含未來時間點的句子來回答。

❷ 即使在When的後面聽到is、are、do、does等現在時態，還是以「未來時間點的說法」作為答案。

❸ about、approximately、maybe等的副詞常出現在時間點說法之前。

When疑問句題型主要出現的回答說法

Q：When will you move to Chicago?

A：At the end of the year.

因為「在年底」是表達未來時間點的副詞片語，這就是答案！

Q：When did John complete the inventory project?

A：He finished it last week.

這是把過去時間點的副詞片語last week包含在句子裡回答！

Q：When does the software demonstration begin?

A：In an hour.

雖然是以現在時態（does）詢問的，但其回答是指未來時間點！

Q：When did you buy your mobile phone?

A：About two weeks ago.

這是故意用「大略」一詞，讓你不容易聽到答案！

Q：When is John going to mail the proposal?

A：As soon as he finishes it.

也可以用未來時間點的副詞片語來回答！

Q：When was the copier repaired?

A：Was it last Wednesday?

迴避性或反問的說法對任何疑問句都能作為答案！

Q：你什麼時候會搬到芝加哥去？
A：在年底。

Q：約翰什麼時候完成了存貨清單？
A：他在上個禮拜完成的。

Q：那場軟體示範會什麼時候開始？
A：一個小時之內。

Q：你什麼時候買的行動電話？
A：大概兩個禮拜前。

Q：約翰什麼時候要把提案書寄送？
A：他一完成就會立刻寄的。

Q：這台影印機是什麼時候修理的？
A：是上個星期三嗎？

對When疑問句而言，最常出現的答案是用「表達未來時間點的介系詞片語」。即使用現在時態（does）來詢問，對此回答仍然是指未來時間點。回答當中的「in +期間」、「not for + 期間」等都是表達未來時間點的說法，意思為「…之後」。表達過去時間點的說法不多，只有yesterday、last...、...ago等而已。

1 作為答案的未來時間點說法

this afternoon, on December 10th, at the end of the year, on Tuesday, the day after tomorrow, in twenty minutes, within a week, not for another 2 weeks, not until next year, sometime next week, a year from the date of issue, later today, in less than 6 months

在今天下午，在12月10日，在年底，在星期二，在後天，在二十分鐘之內，在一週之內，下兩個星期之後才，明年才，在下週的某一天，發行日期之後一年，今天稍晚時，不到六個月以內

2 作為答案的過去時間點說法

yesterday, last week, last month, earlier today, about three years ago

昨天，上個星期，上個月，今天稍早時，大概三年以前

3 未來或過去時間點常搭配使用的副詞

about, approximately, almost, sometime, maybe, probably, perhaps, at the latest, exactly, I think, we are hoping

大概，大略，幾乎，有時候，也許，很有可能，或許，最晚，確切地，我想，我們希望

怪物講師的祕密

1 When疑問句與Where疑問句的結構相似，所以選項當中常常出現對Where疑問句的回答。

2 對過去時間點的回答方式為數不多，所以一定得答對。When were與When will的發音很容易混淆，此判別方法為：在最後加上形容詞的，是were；加上動詞原形的，就是will。

3 提出建議的why疑問句，可以用Yes、No來回答。

🎧 06-03.mp3

✏ Quiz

Q1 請邊聽邊填寫以下空欄。

(1) ＿＿＿＿＿＿＿＿＿＿ your flight leave?

(2) ＿＿＿＿＿＿＿＿＿＿ you sign up for the conference?

(3) ＿＿＿＿＿＿＿＿＿＿ the new manager start?

(4) ＿＿＿＿＿＿＿＿＿＿ those articles written?

Q2 請聽問題之後選出適當的回答。

(1) ⓐ At least twice a week.　　　ⓑ In October, I believe.

(2) ⓐ In less than two months.　　ⓑ At the new plant.

(3) ⓐ At her office.　　　　　　ⓑ About three hours ago.

▶ 答案在解析本第030頁

攻略法 12

回答Why疑問句的方法

Why疑問句有兩種：詢問理由的「為什麼…？」類與提出建議的「…如何？」類。

🎧 06-04.mp3

第1階段：聽考題 **注意聽疑問詞**

❶ 若Why後面沒聽到don't，是詢問理由的Why疑問句，若聽到don't的話，是提出建議的Why疑問句。

❷ 錯過疑問詞，但聽到「so 形容詞」或「too 形容詞」的話，大部分是詢問理由的why疑問句。

Why疑問句的主要例子

Why is the radio so loud?
Why isn't that printer ever used?

Why did you work so late last night?
Why didn't the directors approve our proposal?

Why was the meeting rescheduled?
Why was that company so profitable last year?

Why are you walking so fast?
Why are the applications on the desk?

Why don't we finish this tomorrow?
Why don't you buy this camera?
Why don't I help you organize the welcome reception?

Why的後面多聽一個單字來確認有沒有don't，這點很重要。若接著聽到「so 形容詞」或「too 形容詞」，大部分是「理由」的Why。

常出現的so形容詞

so much, so many, so early, so fast, so profitable, so empty, so late, so hot, so bright, so busy, so loud

《講師的補充說明》

英國與澳洲的發音裡，母音後面r的發音會消失。如Part 1所學的，park的話唸成[pa-k]。依此道理，另一個不易聽到的發音就是Why are you：因為沒有r的發音，實際聽到的發音好像是[why you]，因此得特別小心。

廣播聲音為什麼這麼大？
那台印表機為什麼都沒用過？

你昨晚為什麼工作到那麼晚？
那些主管們為什麼不准許我們的提案？

那場會議為什麼重新安排時間？
那家公司去年為何獲利那麼多？

你為什麼走路走得那麼快？
那些申請書為什麼在桌上？

我們明天把這個做完如何？
你們買這台相機如何？
我幫你一起準備那場歡迎會如何？

很多，很多，很早，很快，盈利，很空，很晚，很熱，很亮，很忙，很吵

第2階段：聽選項 選擇性地聽吧！

❶ 對Why疑問句而言，最常出現的答案選項為表達理由的。此時，將 Because省略直接以「主詞 + 動詞」回答的情形較多。

❷ 也會出現以「to + 動詞原形」、「due to / because of + 名詞」、「for 名詞」的回答方式。

❸ 若有don't，不可以選擇針對理由why的回答。

Why疑問句題型主要出現的回答說法

Q：Why isn't that printer ever used?

A：It's not connected.

這是用沒有because的句子來回答的，就是候選答案的第一名！

Q：Why did Ms. Lawyer leave a message at the front desk?

A：Because she couldn't find your number.

有時會以「Because + 句子」回答，所以還是得注意喔！

Q：Why did you call the doctor?

A：To make an appointment.

正確答案的10%是以這種方式回答。為什麼撥電話？為了約時間！

Q：Why was that flight delayed?

A：Because of a storm.

正確答案的5%是以「理由的介系詞（because of / due to / for）+ 名詞」回答的！

Q：Why hasn't Eric signed the invoice yet?

A：I'll find out.

迴避性說法、反問句等是對任何疑問句都能作為答案！

Q：Why don't we go for a walk during the lunch break?

A：Sure, that's a good idea.

請留意don't！這不是詢問理由！是提出建議的，因此以肯定／許可來回答！

Q：那台印表機為什麼都沒有用過？
A：它還沒被連接。

Q：羅樂小姐為什麼在服務台留言？
A：因為她找不到你的電話號碼。

Q：你為什麼打電話給醫生？
A：為了約時間。

Q：那班飛機為什麼延後？
A：因為暴風雨的關係。

Q：艾瑞克為什麼還沒簽收那張發票？
A：我會再問問。

Q：我們在午休的時候去散步如何？
A：好的，是個好主意。

一般只要聽到Why就想到because，也選出有because的選項。為了避免這一點，大部分的正確答案是沒有because的句子。另外，也會以「to 動詞原形」或表達理由的介系詞加名詞來回答。若是提出建議的why，以肯定、許可、否定、拒絕來回答。

對提出建議的why常出現的回答

肯定、許可：That's a good idea.

Okay. I'll see you then.

Thanks. That would be great.

這是個好主意。
好的。到時候見吧。
謝謝。這樣很好。

否定、拒絕：It doesn't sound very interesting.
Thanks, but I have other plans.
No, now is not a good time.
I can't. I've got too much to do.
Sorry, I'm going out of town.

迴避性：　　I'll see if I am available.

聽起來不太好玩。
謝謝，不過我有別的打算。
不行。現在不是時候。
我不行。我有太多事情要做。
抱歉，我要出城。

我看看有沒有空。

怪物講師的祕密

1 請注意：Why are you在英國與澳洲的發音裡聽起來像Why you。
2 若沒聽出針對理由why的答案，大部分以長的句子為答案。
3 提出建議的why的話，可以用Yes、No來回答。

🔊 06-06.mp3

🖊 Quiz

Q3 請邊聽邊填寫以下空欄。

(1) _____ you walking so fast?

(2) _____ that company so profitable last year?

(3) _____ the meeting started yet?

(4) _____ we meet after lunch to discuss the budget?

Q4 請聽問題之後選出適當的回答。

(1) ⓐ By train. ⓑ It's closed for road repairs.

(2) ⓐ Have a seat. ⓑ That's a bus stop.

(3) ⓐ I can't. I've got too much to do. ⓑ Sorry, I didn't mean to break it.

攻略法11　回答When疑問句的方法

When疑問句

需要聽When後面的另一個單字，來判別是否did/was/were。若不是過去時間點，未來時間點會成為答案。

When疑問句題型的主要答案

過去時間點若有yesterday、last...、...ago等就是答案。未來時間點大部分以未來時間點介系詞片語，或包含這種片語的句子為答案。

When疑問句的主要例子

When will construction start on the Cooper Building?

When are you leaving?

When did you buy your car?

When does the train leave for Seoul?

When is the deadline for submitting news articles?

When was the copier repaired?

When were those reports written?

When疑問句題型的主要回答方式

At the end of the year.

He finished it last week.

In an hour.

About two weeks ago.

As soon as he finishes it.

Was it last Wednesday?

攻略法12　回答Why疑問句的方法

Why疑問句

不可以只聽到Why就判定為詢問理由的疑問句。若以Why don't開始，是提出建議的why。萬一錯過了疑問詞，但聽到「so 形容詞」的話，就是詢問理由的why。

Why疑問句題型的主要答案

理由的why大部分以沒有because的句子來回答，因此比較長的句子為答案。對提出建議的why，Sure類的肯定／許可的回答或No、Sorry等的否定／拒絕類的回答之後，會出現附加說明。

Why疑問句的主要例子

Why is the radio so loud?

Why did you work so late last night?

Why was the meeting rescheduled?

Why are you walking so fast?

Why don't we finish this tomorrow?

Why don't you buy this camera?

Why don't I help you organize the welcome reception?

Why疑問句題型的主要回答方式

理由的Why

It's not connected.

To make an appointment.

Because of a storm.

I'll find out.

提出建議的Why

Sure, that's a good idea.

No thanks, I've already got plans.

STEP 01 　若沒答對會後悔的考題　　　請按照mp3錄音的指示進行以下的考題

例子

	① 聽考題	② 聽選項
When will you move to Chicago?	**1** 疑問詞 + 時間點　　When will **2** 主詞／動詞（動作）　you move **3** 對象／場所／其他　to Chicago	Mark your answer. (A)　(B)

1

1 疑問詞 + 時間點

2 主詞／動詞（動作）

3 對象／場所／其他

Mark your answer.

(A)　(B)

2

1 疑問詞 + 助動詞

2 主詞

3 動詞（動作）

Mark your answer.

(A)　(B)

3

1 疑問詞 + 時間點

2 主詞

3 動詞（動作）

Mark your answer.

(A)　(B)

4

1 疑問詞 + 助動詞

2 主詞

3 動詞（動作）

Mark your answer.

(A)　(B)

5

1 疑問詞 + 時間點

2 主詞

3 對象／場所／其他

Mark your answer.

(A)　(B)

▶ 答案在解析本第030頁

STEP 02　考題實戰練習

1　Mark your answer on your answer sheet.　　(A)　(B)　(C)

2　Mark your answer on your answer sheet.　　(A)　(B)　(C)

重要
⭐3　Mark your answer on your answer sheet.　　(A)　(B)　(C)

高難度
⭐4　Mark your answer on your answer sheet.　　(A)　(B)　(C)

5　Mark your answer on your answer sheet.　　(A)　(B)　(C)

6　Mark your answer on your answer sheet.　　(A)　(B)　(C)

高難度
⭐7　Mark your answer on your answer sheet.　　(A)　(B)　(C)

8　Mark your answer on your answer sheet.　　(A)　(B)　(C)

9　Mark your answer on your answer sheet.　　(A)　(B)　(C)

重要
⭐10　Mark your answer on your answer sheet.　　(A)　(B)　(C)

11　Mark your answer on your answer sheet.　　(A)　(B)　(C)

12　Mark your answer on your answer sheet.　　(A)　(B)　(C)

▶ 答案在解析本第031頁

Review Test

請回答以下的問題，也同時整理前面所學的內容。

1 When後面出現的單字若為was、were或did，此為詢問何種時間點的疑問句？ ▶ ....

2 Why後面出現的單字若為don't，該疑問句是哪種句子？ ▶ ....

3 有關未來時間點，對When疑問句而言最常出現的答案為何？ ▶ ....

4 理由的Why詢問時，最常出現的答案是？ ▶ ....

5 聽到「so 形容詞」或「too 形容詞」，是理由的Why還是提出建議的Why？ ▶ ....

6 in less than one month是未來時間點還是過去時間點？ ▶ ....

Preview

1 What、How類，疑問句考題的特色

將What are you going to do this weekend?（你這個週末要做什麼？）與What time do you want to meet me this weekend?（你這個週末何時想與我見面？）一起看就會發現，What 不會提供回答這些問題的線索，在前句是詢問行為，而後一句是詢問時間點的。在此為 了認出類型，對前者而言最重要的是do，對後者而言最重要的是time。因此，出現What 與How疑問句時需要依照類型來了解。

2 出現What、How疑問句考題需考慮的重點

❶ 出現What/How疑問句時，除了疑問詞，還需聽到另一個單字來確認其類型。

What's the problem with the sales report?

How many computers will you need for the training session?

❷ What疑問句當中，詢問對象的What是出現機率最高的。

Q: What was the main agenda of the conference?

A: It was about the frequent power failure of our factory.

❸ How疑問句當中，「How + 形容詞」的形式是考試裡最常出現的。

How many chairs do we need for the meeting?

How often should we clean the water dispenser?

|答案| 1.過去時間點 2.提出建議的句子 3.未來時間點介系詞片語或將此包含在內的句子 4.（沒有because的）表達理由的句子 5.理由的Why
6.未來時間點

攻略法

13

回答What疑問句的方法

What疑問句中，只聽到疑問詞「什麼」是無法回答的。要再聽到決定類型的另一個單字才能作答。

🎧 07-01.mp3

第1階段：聽考題 **注意聽疑問詞**

❶ 除了疑問詞以外，再聽另一個單字來確認類型。

❷ 在考試裡最常出現詢問對象的What。

What疑問句的主要例子

1）詢問對象的What（及物動詞／介系詞的受詞）

What did you study in school?

What kind of carpet should we get for the waiting room?

> 你在學校學什麼的？
> 我們要幫等候室買哪種地毯？

2）詢問對象的What（be動詞的補語）

What's the problem with the sales report?

What's the room rate?

What's the weather like in Hong Kong?

> 銷售報告有什麼問題嗎？
> 訂房價格為何？
> 香港的天氣怎麼樣？

3）詢問時間的What

What time does Stan's plane arrive?

What's the due date for this report?

> 斯坦坐的飛機幾點到達？
> 這份報告的繳交日期為何？

4）詢問行為或意見的What

What are you doing after work?

What do you think of the new office?

> 下班之後你要做什麼？
> 你覺得新辦公室怎麼樣？

5）詢問理由或提出建議的What

What's causing all the noise upstairs?

What if I call you from the airport?

> 是什麼造成樓上的那些噪音？
> 我在機場打電話給你如何？

出現What疑問句時，只聽到疑問詞還是無法回答，需再聽到核心詞彙來確認該疑問句的類型後，才能預測其答案。舉例而言，What did you study in school?中的study就是讓你知道該句中的疑問詞為詢問對象的What的核心詞彙。

What疑問句當中常出現的說法

詢問對象的What：flavor, color, kind, currency, problem, new position, best way, topic, extension, weather, price, round-trip fare, monthly service fee, projected budget, shipping charge, hourly pay rate

詢問行為的What：this afternoon, after work, after he retires, if I have a question, with these sales receipts

詢問意見的What：our proposal, the new office, design proposal, advertising strategy, this month's budget

味道，顏色，種類，貨幣，問題，新的職位，最好的方法，話題，分機號碼，天氣，價格，來回車費，月付費，預計的經費，運費，鐘點費

今天下午，下班之後，他退休之後，若我有疑問，帶著這些銷售發票

我們的企劃案，那間新的辦公室，設計企劃案，行銷策略，這個月的預算

🎧 07-02.mp3

第2階段：聽選項　選擇性地聽吧！

❶ 詢問對象的What：以及物動詞的受詞「對象名詞」作為答案。
❷ 詢問時間的What：以未來、過去的時間點作為答案（與When相同）。
❸ 詢問行為的What：以包含行為的說法作為答案。
❹ 詢問意見的What：以表達意見的句子（常包含形容詞）作為答案。
❺ 詢問理由的What：以表達理由的句子作為答案（與Why相同）。

What疑問句題型主要出現的回答說法

Q：What did Anne discuss at the meeting?
A：The new budget.
　　「詢問及物動詞的對象的What」，用該動詞的「對象名詞」來回答！

Q：What is Mr. Wolbio's new position?
A：I think he's the assistant director.
　　「詢問be動詞的補語的What」，也是用「對象名詞」來回答。

Q：What time did Mr. Rose leave the office?
A：At five thirty.
　　「詢問時間的What」與When一樣以「時間點」回答！

Q：What should I do if I have a question?
A：You can call me.
　　「詢問行為的What」以包含「行為（call）」的說法來回答！

Q：What did you think of our proposal?
A：I was impressed.
　　「詢問意見的What」以「表達意見的句子（常包含形容詞）」回答！

Q：What's causing all the noise upstairs?
A：They're installing shelves.
　　「詢問理由的What」與Why疑問句一樣以「表達理由的句子」來回答！

Q：在那場會議安妮討論了什麼？
A：新的預算。

Q：伍拜爾先生的新職位是什麼？
A：我想他是副經理。

Q：羅斯先生幾點離開辦公室的？
A：在五點半。

Q：若我有疑問的話該怎麼辦？
A：你可以打電話給我。

Q：你對我們的企劃案有什麼想法？
A：我很欣賞。

Q：什麼造成樓上的那些噪音？
A：他們正在裝架子。

請注意：What疑問句不像who、where、when、why疑問句有常出現的答案，而是在各類別之下才有固定的答案。

1 對詢問對象的What常作為答案的對象名詞或代名詞

something that's easy to 動詞原形, the one close to the stage, the ones in the folder I gave you, a glass of water, the chicken sandwich, orange juice

容易做…的東西，離舞台較近的那個，在我給你的檔案夾中的那一份，一杯水，那份雞肉三明治，柳橙汁

2 作為答案的行為相關說法

finish a report, have a celebration, take courses at the university, go shopping, call me, travel to Asia

完成報告，舉辦慶祝活動，在那所大學上課，去購物，打電話給我，到亞洲旅遊

3 表達意見時常使用的說法

It looks like, I think, I believe, I assume, I guess, bigger, nice, good, impressed

它好像，我想，我相信，我認為，我猜測，更大，很好，很好，印象深刻

怪物講師的祕密

1 雖然詢問對象的What為最常出現的考題，但因為其及物動詞的部分經常出現於句子末段，快聽完句子時才能判斷出類別。因此平時需要熟知許多What疑問句。
2 在What疑問句的選項中，常出現針對When或Where疑問句的答案。
3 對提出建議的What疑問句而言，可以用Yes、No來回答。

Quiz

Q1 請邊聽邊寫以下空欄。

(1) _____ of ticket did you _____?

(2) _____ did Mr. Rose leave the office?

(3) _____ are you _____ after work?

(4) _____ do you _____ of our advertising strategy?

Q2 請聽問題之後選出適當的回答。

(1) ⓐ No, thanks. I have one.　　ⓑ The chicken sandwich.

(2) ⓐ Next Friday.　　ⓑ Only three.

(3) ⓐ I'm going fishing.　　ⓑ She's not at home.

▶ 答案在解析本第034頁

攻略法 14 回答How疑問句的方法

How疑問句與What疑問句一樣，判斷類別很重要。但和What疑問句相較之下，How疑問句的種類更多，所以在確認類別時很容易混淆。

🎧 07-04.mp3

第1階段：聽考題 注意聽疑問詞

❶ 除了疑問詞以外，再聽另一個單字來確認類型。

❷ 在考試裡最常出現「How + 形容詞」。

How疑問句的主要例子

1）How 形容詞

How many computers will you need for the training session?

How long do you think it will take to fix the car?

How often do you go on business trips?

How much did the dinner cost?

How late is the restaurant open?

2）詢問方法／方式的How

How do you get home in the evenings?（交通方式）

How do you usually buy airline tickets?（其他方式）

How can I contact Carl in the office upstairs?（通訊方式）

How do I pay for the merchandise?（支付方式）

3）詢問狀況或意見的How

How's the newspaper article going?

How do you like the new software?

4）提出建議的How

How would you like to see a movie tonight?

How about a game of tennis this weekend?

《講師的補充說明》

「你的咖啡想怎麼調製？」的英語怎麼說？就是How would[do] you like your coffee?或How would you like your coffee done?。這是一種詢問意見的How。對此答案有With sugar, please.（請加糖。）、I like it black.（我喜歡喝黑咖啡。）等。

為了那個訓練課程，你需要幾台電腦？
你覺得修理那台車子需要多久？
你多久去出差一次？
那份晚餐花了多少錢？
那家餐廳開到多晚？

晚上你怎麼回家？
你通常怎麼買飛機票？
我要如何和樓上辦公室的卡爾聯絡？
那些商品我要如何付費？

那篇報紙文章進行得如何？
你覺得那個新的軟體如何？

今晚看電影如何？
這個週末來一場網球比賽如何？

How疑問句與What疑問句一樣，得聽另一個核心詞彙判斷出類別才能預測答案，所以是有疑問詞的句子中最難的。但是，只要聽到後面的單字就能判斷出類別的「How+形容詞」形式佔一半以上，所以比起What疑問句，找出其答案實際上更容易。

How疑問句當中常出現的說法

方式的How：get, go, commute, contact, get in touch with, pay

狀態的How：trip to Tokyo, coffee, newspaper article, new job, inspection

詢問意見的How：the work, the new vice president, the new office furniture, your coffee

提出建議的How：see a movie, meet at three, join us for some dessert

到達，去，通勤，聯絡，聯繫，支付

到東京旅行，咖啡，報紙文章，新的工作，視察

那個工作，那位新副總，那間新辦公室的家具，你的咖啡

看電影，在三點見面，和我們一起吃些點心

🎧 07-05.mp3

第2階段：聽選項 **選擇性地聽吧！**

❶ How + 形容詞：答案傾向於包含數字。數量、期間、頻率、價格、時間點等為答案。

❷ 方式的How：交通、通訊、支付方式或方法的句子為答案。

❸ 狀態／意見的How：表達狀態或意見的句子（通常包含形容詞）為答案。

❹ 提出建議的How：表達肯定、允許或否定、拒絕的句子為答案。

How疑問句題型主要出現的回答說法

Q：How many rooms do you need to reserve?

A：Just one for me.

包含數量（one），所以就是答案！

Q：How long will it take to get to the office supply store?

A：About 30 minutes.

以期間（30 minutes）為答案。

Q：How do you get home in the evenings?

A：I take the city bus.

詢問交通方式的How，所以包含交通方式（city bus）的說法為答案！

Q：How did you learn about our store?

A：I was just walking by.

詢問其他方法的時候，包含「方法（只是走路經過）」的說法為答案！

Q：How was the trip to Osaka? / How do you like the new bag?

A：It was great. / It looks really nice.

詢問狀態或意見時，包含形容詞的句子常作為答案。

Q：How would you like to see a movie tonight?

A：That would be nice.

具有建議色彩的How的話，以肯定／允許或否定／拒絕來回答。

Q：你需要訂幾間房間？
A：只要給我自己的一間房間就好。

Q：到那家辦公用品店要多久？
A：大概三十分鐘。

Q：晚上你怎麼回家？
A：我搭市內公車。

Q：你怎麼知道我們店的？
A：我只是剛好路過。

Q：去大阪的旅行怎麼樣？／你覺得那個新的包包怎麼樣？
A：很好。／看起來非常好。

Q：今晚看電影怎麼樣？
A：很好啊。

若先判斷How疑問句的類別，就能找出各類別之下固定出現的答案。對「How+形容詞」而言，包含數字的說法常作為答案；對方式的How來說，表達各種方法的說法為答案；若是詢問狀態或意見的How，大部分以包含形容詞的句子為答案；對建議的How，答案與其他建議說法的答案一樣。

1 對方式的How常出現的答案

通訊方式：by taxi, I walk there, She took a taxi, by bus
聯絡方式：by fax, by phone, in person
支付方式：in cash, by credit card
其他方式：through my travel agent, with a dry cloth, by filling out a form

搭計程車，我走路到那邊去，她搭計程車，搭公車
用傳真，用電話，當面
用現金，用信用卡
透過我的旅行社，用乾布，填表格

2 對狀態或意見的How常出現的形容詞（或副詞）回答說法

great, quite good, pretty well, wonderful, very challenging, harder, friendly, nice

極好，相當好，相當好，非常棒，很有挑戰性的，更難，友善，不錯

怪物講師的祕密

1 請注意：在How many的回答說法中，也有以almost all或almost every等非數字的方式。
2 How long疑問句的答案與When疑問句的答案很容易混淆。例如問句How long have you been working for the company?，若用Two days ago.來回答就錯了。
3 對提出建議的How，可以用Yes、No來回答。

🎧 07-06.mp3

✏️ Quiz

Q3 請邊聽邊填寫以下空欄。

(1) _____ did your interview last?

(2) _____ did the lunch cost?

(3) _____ your coffee?

(4) _____ shipping the orders this afternoon?

Q4 請聽問題之後選出適當的回答。

(1) ⓐ Just one.　　　　　　ⓑ Around 3 o'clock.

(2) ⓐ No, not every day.　　ⓑ By train.

(3) ⓐ Unfortunately, I didn't.　ⓑ Yes, that's a good idea.

攻略法13　回答What疑問句的方法

What疑問句

為了知道是哪類別的What疑問句，需要接著聽決定類別的核心詞彙。

What疑問句的主要例子

What did you study in school?

What's the room rate?

What's the weather like there in Hong Kong?

What time does Stan's plane arrive?

What are you doing after work?

What do you think of the new office?

What's causing all the noise upstairs?

What疑問句題型的主要答案

詢問對象的What是以對象名詞；詢問時間的What是以時間點介系詞片語；詢問行為的What是以包含行為的句子；詢問意見的What是以表達意見的句子；詢問理由的What是用與理由的Why一樣的句子來回答。

What疑問句題型的主要回答方式

The new budget.

I think he's **the assistant director.**

At five thirty.

You can **call me.**

I was **impressed.**

They're installing shelves.

攻略法14　回答How疑問句的方法

How疑問句

How疑問句也不能只聽How就找答案。為了判斷屬於哪類別的How疑問句，得接著聽決定其類別的核心詞彙。

How疑問句的主要例子

How many computers will you need for the training session?

How long do you think it will take to fix the car?

How often do you go on business trips?

How do you get home in the evening?

How's the newspaper article going?

How would you like to see a movie tonight?

How疑問句題型的主要答案

「How 形容詞」是以數字；方式的How是以包含方式（名詞）的句子；狀態／意見的How是以包含形容詞的句子；建議的How是先說Sure、OK等肯定允許說法，或No、Sorry等否定拒絕說法後，再加附加說明回答。

How疑問句題型的主要回答方式

Just **one** for me.

About **30 minutes.**

I take the city **bus.**

I was just **walking by.**

It was **great.**

It looks really **nice.**

That would be nice.

STEP 01　若沒答對會後悔的考題

例子

①聽考題

②聽選項

What did you
study in school?

1 疑問詞　　　　　What

2 決定類別的單字　study

Mark your answer.

(A)　(B)

1

1 疑問詞

2 決定類別的單字

Mark your answer.

(A)　(B)

2

1 疑問詞

2 決定類別的單字

Mark your answer.

(A)　(B)

3

1 疑問詞

2 決定類別的單字

Mark your answer.

(A)　(B)

4

1 疑問詞

2 決定類別的單字

Mark your answer.

(A)　(B)

5

1 疑問詞

2 決定類別的單字

Mark your answer.

(A)　(B)

▶ 答案在解析本第035頁

STEP 02 考題實戰練習　　　　　請將以下部分當作真實考試，邊計時邊回答吧。

1　Mark your answer on your answer sheet.　　　　(A)　(B)　(C)

2　Mark your answer on your answer sheet.　　　　(A)　(B)　(C)

重要
3　Mark your answer on your answer sheet.　　　　(A)　(B)　(C)

高難度
4　Mark your answer on your answer sheet.　　　　(A)　(B)　(C)

5　Mark your answer on your answer sheet.　　　　(A)　(B)　(C)

6　Mark your answer on your answer sheet.　　　　(A)　(B)　(C)

7　Mark your answer on your answer sheet.　　　　(A)　(B)　(C)

8　Mark your answer on your answer sheet.　　　　(A)　(B)　(C)

高難度
9　Mark your answer on your answer sheet.　　　　(A)　(B)　(C)

10　Mark your answer on your answer sheet.　　　　(A)　(B)　(C)

高難度
11　Mark your answer on your answer sheet.　　　　(A)　(B)　(C)

12　Mark your answer on your answer sheet.　　　　(A)　(B)　(C)

▶ 答案在解析本第036頁

Chapter 08

提出建議的句子與選擇疑問句

隨著聽過的句子的量，分數也會不一樣！

Review Test

請回答以下的問題，也同時整理前面所學的內容。

1 聽What疑問句時，最重要的是？　　　　　　　▶ ⋯⋯⋯⋯⋯⋯⋯

2 對時間的What的答案是？　　　　　　　　　　▶ ⋯⋯⋯⋯⋯⋯⋯

3 對意見的What回答時，常用的詞彙為哪類？　　▶ ⋯⋯⋯⋯⋯⋯⋯

4 與疑問詞How常一起出現的詞彙為哪類？　　　▶ ⋯⋯⋯⋯⋯⋯⋯

5 方式的How是詢問哪些？　　　　　　　　　　▶ ⋯⋯⋯⋯⋯⋯⋯

6 對詢問狀態或意見的How回答時，常用的形容詞為何？ ▶ ⋯⋯⋯⋯⋯⋯⋯

7 建議的How可以用Yes或No來回答。　　　　　▶ ⋯⋯⋯⋯⋯⋯⋯

Preview

1 提出建議的句子與選擇疑問句考題的特色

Are you going to see a movie after work?（下班之後你要看電影嗎？）與 Would you like to see a movie after work?（下班之後你想看電影嗎？）都是沒有疑問詞的問句，看起來也相似，但其實類別完全不同。第二個句子裡面包含詢問者的期待，也就是希望對方以Yes來回答的。這種就是「建議」疑問句，與必須聽see a movie才能找出答案的一般疑問句不同，其特色為只聽到Would you的部分就能選出答案。另外，提出「想看電影嗎？」後面再加「還是要不要先吃飯？」這種讓對方做選擇的句子叫做選擇疑問句。

2 出現該類考題需考慮的重點

❶ 建議的句子是以would、could、can、may開頭，翻譯成「可以⋯嗎？」。

❷ 有疑問詞的疑問句或陳述句也可以作為建議的說法。

❸ 若中間出現or，就是選擇疑問句。

❹ 選擇疑問句出現「兩個都好」、「兩個都不是」之類的選項，這就是答案。

攻略法

15

回答建議的句子的方法

期待著肯定的回答而用「可以…嗎？」來詢問的形式，叫做建議的句子。與聽到動詞才能選出答案的一般疑問句的不同之處是，若只聽到建議的句子的開頭就可以選出答案。

🎧 08-01.mp3

第1階段：聽考題 注意聽是否為建議的句子

① 若以Would、Could、Can、May開頭，就是建議的句子。

② 若包含Let's、Please、mind，也是建議的句子。

③ 以疑問詞開頭，有時也會是建議的句子。

建議的句子的主要例子

1）用助動詞的建議

Would you like me to send this invoice now?
Would you like another piece of fruit?
Could you hold this suitcase for a minute?
Can you help me find my seat?
May I buy you lunch?

> 你要我把這張發票現在寄出去嗎？
> 你要再吃一片水果嗎？
> 你可以暫時拿著這個行李箱嗎？
> 你可以幫忙我找我的位子嗎？
> 我可以請你吃午餐嗎？

2）間接的建議

Don't you want to go out for lunch?
Shouldn't we have our passports ready?
Wouldn't it be nice to take the clients out for lunch?
Couldn't we reschedule our meeting for tomorrow?
Don't you think we should take a short break?

> 要不要出去吃午餐？
> 我們不需要準備我們的護照嗎？
> 帶客人出去吃午餐不是很好嗎？
> 我們能否把我們的會議重新安排到明天？
> 你不覺得我們需要休息一下嗎？

3）用陳述句的建議

Let's have lunch at the restaurant across the street.
Please call me when you have your itinerary.
We should review our presentation for this afternoon's meeting.

> 我們在馬路對面的餐廳吃午餐吧。
> 等你定了你的旅程後，請給我電話。
> 為了今天下午的會議，我們得再看一次我們的報告內容。

4）用疑問詞的建議

Why don't we finish this tomorrow?
How would you like to see a movie tonight?

> 我們明天把這個完成如何？
> 今晚看電影如何？

5）包含mind的建議

Would you mind turning off your mobile phone?

> 你介意關掉你的手機嗎？

若以Would、Could、Can、May開頭，就知道「可以…嗎？」類的建議的句子。另外，「是否…？」來詢問的句子也是建議類的。有時也有以疑問詞開頭的建議的句子。還有以「我們…吧」的陳述句形式的建議。

考試裡常出現的建議的內容

建議用餐，食物，飲料，訂房，寄送文件，表演，電影，安裝商品，搭乘交通工具，休息，幫忙，檢查文件

🎧 08-02.mp3

第2階段：聽選項 **選擇性地聽吧！**

❶ 若Sure、Certainly、Yes等肯定、允許的說法或Sorry、No等否定、拒絕的說法後面再加附加說明，就是答案！

❷ 有時也有將Sure、Sorry等省略，直接進行附加說明的回答方式。

❸ 對建議的說法而言，That's a good idea. 這類句子絕對是答案。

建議的句子主要出現的回答說法

Q : Would you help me wash these dinner plates?

A : Sure. I'll be right there.

　　肯定／允許的Sure後面出現附加說明，所以就是答案！

Q : Would you like to take a short break?

A : No, I want to finish this report.

　　否定／拒絕的No之後出現附加說明，所以就是答案！

Q : Would you send me a copy of the report?

A : I'll send it this afternoon.

　　這就是沒有Sure或Sorry等的說法，直接說附加說明的情形！

Q : Could I have a few minutes of your time?

A : Sure, how can I help?

　　請記得反問句也能成為附加說明！

Q : Would you like to go hunting this weekend?

A : That would be great!

　　對建議的句子來說，這是絕對正確的答案！

Q : Do you mind if I open a window?

A : Not at all.

　　對包含mind的建議的句子，以否定的說法回答才是允許的意思！

對建議的句子而言，肯定、允許的回答很常出現。肯定、允許的話，Sure、Yes、Thanks的說法後面用簡單的附加說明來回答。否定、拒絕的話，No、Sorry等的說法後面再加簡單的附加說明。

《講師的補充說明》

對建議的說法而言，肯定／允許的回答（Sure、Yes、Okay等）比否定／拒絕的回答出現的更多。其原因在於，提出建議或請求時，大部分是期待肯定／允許的回答才詢問的。若期待否定／拒絕的回答，根本不會提出詢問吧。但是Would [Do] you mind ~這類的疑問句是「你介意～嗎？」的意思，所以若對此要肯定／允許的話，反而要用否定的說法。例如詢問Would you mind opening the window?時，不可以為了肯定／允許而用Yes來回答。

Q：要不要幫忙我一起洗這些碗盤？
A：好。我馬上來。

Q：你想暫時休息嗎？
A：不要。我想把這份報告完成。

Q：你要不要給我一份那個報告的影本？
A：我今天下午會寄給你。

Q：我可以佔用你的幾分鐘時間嗎？
A：當然可以。我能如何幫你？

Q：你這個週末想去打獵嗎？
A：好啊！

Q：你介意我開窗戶嗎？
A：完全不會。

有時候也會用反問句來作為附加說明。另外，有時只有附加說明也會成為答案。對包含mind的建議的句子而言，若回答裡有No、Not、Nope等，就是以肯定或允許的回答方式成為答案。

1 只要聽到就知道是答案的肯定、允許的說法

Sure, Certainly, Of course, Okay, Right, Thanks, Sure, No problem, Sure, why not?, I'd be happy to, That would be great, That's a good idea, That sounds good, That's a great idea, I'd appreciate that, We'd be delighted, That's an excellent idea, I'd be glad to, You're right, That sounds fine with me, Sounds like a good idea

當然，一定可以，當然了，OK，正確，謝謝，當然，沒問題，當然了，有何不可？，我很願意，這樣很好，這是好主意，這聽起來很好，這是很好的想法，感謝你，我們很願意的，這是非常好的想法，我很樂意，你是對的，這對我來說聽起來很好，聽起來是個很好的想法

2 只要聽到就知道是答案的否定、拒絕的說法

That's OK, No thanks, No, Sorry, I'm afraid...

沒關係，不用了，謝謝，不要，抱歉，恐怕…

怪物講師的祕密

1 對建議的句子而言，出現肯定、允許的回答頻率高的不計其數。若選項裡有Sure、Yes、Thanks、Okay等，大部分都是答案

2 對建議的句子以肯定、允許來回答時，不會有以過去時態來回答的情形。若句子不是否定或拒絕卻聽到過去時態，大部分不是答案。

3 否定、拒絕的理由為「忙」、「要去出差」、「取消了」、「已經做了」、「我要自己做」等等。

Quiz

08-03.mp3

Q1 請邊聽邊填寫以下空欄。

(1) _____ like to join us for the party?

(2) _____ lend me your newspaper?

(3) _____ to see the baseball game tonight?

(4) _____ try the new cafeteria.

Q2 請聽問題之後選出適當的回答。

(1) ⓐ I've already put it on your desk.　ⓑ Sure, I'll call you around five.

(2) ⓐ He's moving to the city.　ⓑ I'd appreciate that.

(3) ⓐ That sounds good.　ⓑ The food wasn't ready.

▶ 答案在解析本第038頁

攻略法
16
回答選擇疑問句的方法

出現選擇疑問句時都得聽完其選擇的範圍，因此屬於相當難找出答案的考題類別。但是選擇疑問句有一半以上是即使沒有聽完選擇範圍，只要知道該句子為選擇疑問句，就能找出答案。

🎧 08-04.mp3

第1階段：聽考題 **注意聽A or B**

❶ 若中間出現or，就是選擇疑問句。

❷ 長度很長的話，就是選擇疑問句。

❸ 將常出現的A與B記憶下來！

選擇疑問句的主要例子

1）單字 or 單字

Would you rather eat before or after the meeting?

Is Yoko's office upstairs or on this floor?

Did we send the document to Mr. Jenkins by e-mail or fax?

你要在會議之前還是之後吃？
洋子的辦公室在樓上還是在這層樓？
我們是透過電子郵件還是傳真把那份文件寄給詹金斯先生？

2）句子 or 句子

Will you deposit the money yourself, or is Eiko going to do it?

Are you busy with work right now, or could you help me move my desk?

你要自己存那筆錢還是埃可要做？
你正忙著工作嗎？不然可否幫忙我一起搬我的桌子嗎？

3）動詞片語 or 動詞片語

Would you rather have dinner first or go to the cinema?

Should I set this package on Mr. Parker's desk or put it somewhere else?

你想先吃晚餐還是去電影院？
我需要把這件包裹放在帕克先生的桌上還是放別的地方？

4）Which 疑問句

Which website design do you prefer?

Which jacket do you think I should buy?

你比較喜歡哪個網頁的設計？
你覺得我應該買哪件外套？

判斷是否為選擇疑問句不太難。首先，大部分的選擇疑問句長度比較長，而且若中間聽到or就能知道該句子為選擇疑問句。不過為了更正確選出答案，還是得聽完選擇事項（A或B）。另外若以Which開頭，這也是選擇疑問句。

常作為A與B的事項

第一名：時間 or 時間	Can I expect your reply <u>today</u> or <u>tomorrow</u>?
第二名：場所 or 場所	Would you like to meet in the <u>cafeteria</u> or <u>my office</u>?
第三名：你…? or 我…?	Did you <u>write</u> the report, or <u>would you like me to</u> do it?
第四名：食物種類 or 食物種類	Do you prefer <u>green tea</u> or <u>black tea</u>?
第五名：東西 or 東西	Do you want to send a <u>gift</u> or just a <u>card</u>?
第六名：通訊方式 or 通訊方式	Will you send the document to Mr. Kim <u>by e-mail</u> or <u>fax</u>?
第七名：交通方式 or 交通方式	Is that better to travel to Beijing <u>by car</u> or <u>by bus</u>?
其他：要列印 or 看螢幕?	Would you like me to <u>print out the document</u>, or can you <u>read it on the screen</u>?

我在今天還是明天能得到您的回應？
你想在自助餐廳還是在我辦公室見面？
你寫那份報告了嗎？還是你要我做？
你比較喜歡綠茶還是紅茶？
你想寄禮物還是卡片就好？
你要把那份文件透過電子郵件還是傳真寄給金先生？
開車還是坐公車去北京比較好？
你要把那份文件列印出來，還是你能在螢幕上看？

🎧 08-05.mp3

第2階段：聽選項 選擇性地聽吧

❶ 「兩個都好」、「兩個都不是」類的選項絕對是答案。

❷ 包含one的句子或短語常作為答案。（尤其是有Which疑問句時）

❸ 有時會將A or B變化後作為答案。

選擇疑問句題型主要出現的回答說法

Q：Would you rather see a movie or go to a concert?

A：Either one is fine.

　　「兩個都好」類的說法絕對是答案！

Q：Is today's meeting about communication or planning?

A：Neither. It's about strategy.

　　「兩個都不是」類的說法絕對也是答案！

Q：Which website design do you prefer?

A：This one's more professional.

　　Which疑問句來詢問時，以代名詞（one）來回答的情形為90%！

Q：Will Mr. Park retire this year or next?

A：He plans to leave this May.

　　「今年五月」是將「A or B」當中的A部分（this year）變化的說法，所以就是答案！

Q：Do you want to talk about it now or should we meet later?

A：I'm available this afternoon.

　　「今天下午有空」是將B部分（晚一點見面）變化的，所以就是答案！

Q：Are we buying ballpoint or felt tip pens?

A：Which is better?

　　對選擇事項反問的說法有時也作為答案！

Q：你想看電影還是去看演唱會？
A：都可以。

Q：今天的會議是有關通訊還是企劃的？
A：都不是。是有關策略的。

Q：你比較喜歡哪個網頁的設計？
A：這個比較專業。

Q：伯克先生是今年退休還是明年？
A：他打算今年五月離開。

Q：你想現在談那件事，還是我們晚一點見面談？
A：我今天下午有空。

Q：你要買圓珠筆還是簽字筆？
A：哪個比較好？

若知道考題為選擇疑問句，就能知道答案可能為「兩個都好」、「兩個都不是」這類的回答方式。另外若代名詞one在選項裡面，有時會是答案，尤其對以which來詢問的疑問句來說，90%以上的答案包含one。但若想得到更高的分數，還得要知道選擇疑問句答案中，大約有三分之二是將A或B的部分變化的。

只要聽到就知道是答案的「兩個都好」、「兩個都不是」類的回答方式

Either (one) is fine (with me).
I have both of them.
Anywhere is fine.
It doesn't matter to me.
It's for all of us.

Neither do I.
Whichever costs less.
Some of each, please.
Whatever you like.

哪個都好。
我也不是。
我兩個都有。
只要比較便宜的都可以。
哪裡都好。
每個都要一些，謝謝。
對我而言無所謂。
你要什麼都可以。
這是為了我們全部的人。

怪物講師的祕密

1 若對選擇疑問句以Yes、No來回答，就不是答案。但若是「句子 or 句子」的選擇疑問句的話，則可以用Yes或No來回答。不過這種情形之下Yes或No的意義不大。

2 若選擇疑問句以Would或Could開始，因為其開頭的部分和建議的說法相似，在選項當中常常出現對建議說法的回答方式，關於這點得特別注意。

3 「兩者都好」這類的答案當中，最常出現的是either。但是該單字的英式發音和美式發音不同，所以考生有時候很容易錯過。

《講師的補充說明》

若句子以Which開頭，就是選擇疑問句，但以What開頭的話不是。What與Which的文法結構一樣，例如What color do you like? 與Which color do you like? What與Which之間只有意思差別。What是「不特定的什麼」，Which是「固定項目當中的哪個」。因此，Which color do you like?，就知道可選的顏色有限制，所以是「（在這些紅色、藍色、黃色當中）你喜歡哪種顏色？」的意思。

🔊 08-06.mp3

✎ Quiz

Q3 請邊聽邊填寫以下空欄。

(1) Should we order _____ dishes or _____ ?

(2) Can we _____ or are _____ ?

(3) Should I just _____ or _____ ?

(4) _____ parking area is for employees?

Q4 請聽問題之後選出適當的回答。

(1) ⓐ Either one is fine with me.　　ⓑ Sure, you can sit here.

(2) ⓐ I'd prefer to take an airplane.　　ⓑ The training should be very useful.

(3) ⓐ We can meet today.　　ⓑ Either one is fine.

▶ 答案在解析本第039頁

攻略法15　回答建議的句子的方法

建議的句子

以Would、Could、Can、May開頭的話就是建議的句子。另外，像How about以疑問詞開頭，有時也是建議的句子。Let's（「我們…吧」）這類陳述句也可以作為建議的句子。

該類題型的主要答案

若Sure、Certainly、Yes等肯定／允許的說法之後再加附加說明，或Sorry、No等否定／拒絕說法後面再加附加說明，則就是答案。另外，有時也會有將Sure、Sorry省略，直接用附加說明來回答的情形。

建議的句子的主要例子

Would you like me to send this invoice now?

May I buy you lunch?

Let's have lunch at the restaurant across the street.

Please call me when you have your itinerary.

How would you like to see a movie tonight?

Would you mind turning off your mobile phone?

該類題型的主要回答方式

Sure, I'll be right there.

No, I want to finish this report.

I'll send it this afternoon.

Sure, how can I help?

一定作為答案的說法！

That would be great! / Sounds great!

對包含mind的建議的句子而言，絕對是答案的說法！

Not at all. / No. / Sure. / Certainly (not).

攻略法16　回答選擇疑問句的方法

選擇疑問句

若出現A or B的形式，就是選擇疑問句。疑問句的長度很長的話，也很有可能是選擇疑問句。

選擇疑問句題型的主要答案

若有「兩個都是」、「兩個都不是」說法在其中的，一定是答案。以Which詢問的時候，答案的90%以上包含代名詞one。想得高分的應考生，在聽到將A或B變化的部分後，應該能判別出是否為答案。

選擇疑問句的主要例子

Is Yoko's office upstairs or on this floor?

Did we send the document to Mr. Jenkins by e-mail or fax?

Are you busy with work right now, or could you help me move my desk?

Would you rather have dinner first or go to the cinema?

Which website design do you prefer?

選擇疑問句題型的主要回答方式

Either one is fine.

Neither. It's about strategy.

This one's more professional.

He plans to leave **this May**.

I'm available **this afternoon**.

Which is better?

STEP 01 若沒答對會後悔的考題　　　請按照mp3錄音的指示進行以下的考題

例子

Would you help me wash these dinner plates?

①聽考題

1 決定類別的線索　　Would you

2 動詞與其他　　help me wash these dinner plates。

②聽選項

Mark your answer.

(A)　(B)

1

1 決定類別的線索　_____

2 動詞與其他　_____

Mark your answer.

(A)　(B)

2

1 決定類別的線索　_____

2 動詞與其他　_____

Mark your answer.

(A)　(B)

3

1 決定類別的線索　_____

2 動詞與其他　_____

Mark your answer.

(A)　(B)

4

1 決定類別的線索　_____

2 動詞與其他　_____

Mark your answer.

(A)　(B)

5

1 決定類別的線索　_____

2 動詞與其他　_____

Mark your answer.

(A)　(B)

▶ 答案在解析本第039頁

STEP 02 考題實戰練習　　　　請將以下部分當作真實考試，邊計時邊回答吧。

重要
1 Mark your answer on your answer sheet.　　　　(A)　(B)　(C)

重要
2 Mark your answer on your answer sheet.　　　　(A)　(B)　(C)

3 Mark your answer on your answer sheet.　　　　(A)　(B)　(C)

4 Mark your answer on your answer sheet.　　　　(A)　(B)　(C)

5 Mark your answer on your answer sheet.　　　　(A)　(B)　(C)

6 Mark your answer on your answer sheet.　　　　(A)　(B)　(C)

7 Mark your answer on your answer sheet.　　　　(A)　(B)　(C)

8 Mark your answer on your answer sheet.　　　　(A)　(B)　(C)

9 Mark your answer on your answer sheet.　　　　(A)　(B)　(C)

高難度
10 Mark your answer on your answer sheet.　　　　(A)　(B)　(C)

11 Mark your answer on your answer sheet.　　　　(A)　(B)　(C)

高難度
12 Mark your answer on your answer sheet.　　　　(A)　(B)　(C)

▶ 答案在解析本第040頁

Review Test

請回答以下的問題，也同時整理前面所學的內容。

1 建議的句子大部分翻譯成什麼？ ▶ ....

2 建議的句子大部分以什麼開頭？ ▶ ....

3 陳述句形式的建議的句子大部分以什麼開頭？ ▶ ....

4 句子當中出現什麼單字就叫做選擇疑問句？ ▶ ....

5 若出現「兩個都是」、「兩個都不是」類的選項，絕對是答案。 ▶ ....

6 Which疑問句題型若出現含有one的選項，不是答案。 ▶ ....

Preview

1 一般、否定、附加疑問句考題的特色

When are you leaving the office?

Are you leaving the office?

將以上兩個句子比較會發現，雖然只有一個單字的差異，但其實是完全不同特點的疑問句。第一個句子的焦點在於When，而且也必須聽到When才能知道答案。第二個句子是詢問「要不要離開」，其焦點在於「離開（leave）」這個動詞上。若要離開就用Yes，不是的話就用No來回答。像這樣沒有疑問詞而以助動詞（have、will、do、did）或be動詞開頭的疑問句，稱為一般疑問句。另外，像Aren't you leaving the offce?以否定詞開頭的，稱做否定疑問句；Are you leaving the office, aren't you? 等有附加尾巴的，稱做附加疑問句。

2 出現一般、否定、附加疑問句考題需考慮的重點

❶ 與別的疑問句不同，一般疑問句的核心在於動詞。若沒聽到這個部分，什麼都沒有用。

❷ Are you、Do you、Did you、Have you、Will you等，常出現於一般疑問句考題裡。

❸ 一般疑問句的答案裡，有時會出現反問句。

　　Q: Have you seen Mr. Jones today? 　　A: No, has he returned from England already?

❹ 否定、附加疑問句需要將否定詞與尾巴先去掉不看，再判斷其答案。

　　Q: Isn't she at her desk right now? 　　A: No, she went to payroll department.

攻略法 17

回答一般疑問句的方法

沒有疑問詞而以助動詞或be動詞開頭的疑問句，稱做一般疑問句。與用句子開頭決定類別的疑問詞疑問句或建議的句子不同，一般疑問句的核心部分為動詞，所以得注意聽到其動詞。

🎧 09-01.mp3

第1階段：聽考題　注意聽動詞與時態

❶ 動詞的部分以0.1秒的速度講過去！

❷ 除了動詞以外，也得注意時態！

❸ 考試裡常出現Are you、Do you、Have you等。

一般疑問句的主要例子

Are you going to Ms. Chang's party on Saturday?
Are there more pens in the cabinet?

Do you think this article is well written?
Did you go to the seminar last night?

Have you heard about the rent increase in our building?
Has the mail been delivered yet?

Is the fax machine working yet?
Will you speak at the sales meeting?
Should I give him your business card when he returns?

> 星期六你要去張小姐的派對嗎？
> 櫃子裡還有筆嗎？
>
> 你覺得這篇文章寫得好嗎？
> 你昨晚去那場研討會了嗎？
>
> 你聽說我們大樓的租金上漲的事嗎？
> 那個郵件已經寄出了嗎？
>
> 那台傳真機現在正常運作嗎？
> 你願意在那場銷售會議上發言嗎？
> 等他回來時，我應該給他你的名片嗎？

一般疑問句的核心部分為動詞。為了聽到動詞，先記下來Are you、Do you、Did you、Have you、Will you等常出現的助動詞與主詞的部分，然後再去掌握後面的內容。

一般疑問句裡常出現的「助動詞＋動詞」

Are you going, Are you planing, Are there any, Do you think, Do you know, Do you have, Do you like, Did you go, Did you find, Did you see, Did you contact, Have you seen, Have you heard, Have you been, Have you finished

> 你將要…，你打算…，有什麼…，你覺得…，你知道…，你有…，你喜歡…，你去…，你發現…，你看…，你聯絡到…，你看過…，你聽過…，你去過…，你完成…

⏺ 09-02.mp3

第2階段：聽選項 選擇性地聽吧！

❶ 除動詞以外，也得注意時態！
❷ 肯定回答是Yes加附加說明，否定回答是No加附加說明的形式。
❸ 30%的答案裡沒有Yes/No，而直接出現附加說明。

一般疑問句題型主要出現的回答說法

Q：Did you see the briefcase I left in here?
A：Yes, I put it on the table.
　　說「放在桌子上」，所以對於「看」的正確附加說明！

Q：Does this vending machine give change?
A：No, you'll need the exact amount.
　　「需要確切的金額」，所以這是對於「不找錢」的附加說明。

Q：Are you going to the laboratory this afternoon?
A：I'll be a bit late, but I'll be there.
　　「雖然晚一點，但還是會去」是對於「會去」的肯定附加說明！這裡省略了Yes！

Q：Have you checked your e-mail yet?
A：I've been too busy.
　　「很忙」是對於「看e-mail」的否定附加說明！把No省略了！

Q：Have you heard about Betty's promotion?
A：No, what's her new title?
　　反問句有時會當作附加說明！

Q：Do you know if all employees need to submit a time sheet?
A：I'll ask Dana.
　　「向…詢問」這類間接迴避性的回答一定是答案！

Q：你看到我留在這邊的公事包嗎？
A：是，我把它放在桌子上。

Q：這台自動販賣機會找零嗎？
A：不，你需要用確切的金額。

Q：你今天下午要去研究室嗎？
A：我會晚一點，不過我會去的。

Q：你已經看過電子郵件了嗎？
A：我一直很忙呢。

Q：你有聽說貝蒂升遷的事情嗎？
A：沒有，她新的職稱是什麼？

Q：你知道是否所有的員工都得交工作時間記錄卡？
A：我問問黛娜。

答案的形式為：動詞加時態的句意若是肯定就用Yes，若是否定就用No，然後再加上附加說明。但是答案的30%是省略Yes或No之後直接加附加說明的，所以得注意！另外，反問句有時也當作附加說明。

考試裡常出現的附加說明

Yes的後面：I believe so.
　　　　　 I'm looking forward to it.
　　　　　 If we hire more workers.
　　　　　 It's very nice.
　　　　　 I think it's wonderful.

我是這麼認為。
我很期待。
如果我們僱用更多職員。
這非常好。
我認為很精彩。

No的後面：It was canceled.
I have no time.
I've been too busy.
I don't think so.

那個被取消了。
我沒有時間。
我一直很忙。
我不這麼認為。

怪物講師的祕密

1 以Do you think開頭的句子，think後面的動詞部分當作核心詞彙。

2 若Yes後面加上No的附加說明，或No之後加上Yes的附加說明，就不是答案。

3 若三個選項當中只有一個包含Yes或No，該選項作為答案的機率更高。

《講師的補充說明》

一般、否定、附加疑問句的題型，在Part 2當中的出現率幾乎為三分之一。因此，與其帶著想一步登天的態度，不如持續記背考題與答案。有一般、否定、附加疑問句時，需注意疑問句的主詞在選項裡是否被變更或使用不對的時態。

Quiz

09-03.mp3

Q1 請邊聽邊填寫以下空欄。

(1) _____ you _____ with your computer software?

(2) _____ the shipment _____ yesterday?

(3) _____ you _____ these shirts in other colors?

(4) _____ you _____ at the sales meeting?

Q2 請聽問題之後選出適當的回答。

(1) ⓐ Yes, on 20th.   ⓑ That's a great idea.

(2) ⓐ This train does go fast.   ⓑ No, I'm really hungry.

(3) ⓐ In the cupboard, over the sink.   ⓑ I made it this morning.

▶ 答案在解析本第043頁

攻略法 18 回答否定、附加疑問句的方法

以Didn't、Isn't、Aren't等否定詞開頭的疑問句叫做否定疑問句。句子後面有尾巴的疑問句稱做附加疑問句。找否定、附加疑問句答案的原理與一般疑問句一樣。

🎧 09-04.mp3

第1階段：聽考題 將否定詞與尾巴先去掉不看再聽！

① 先去除否定詞與尾巴後，再聽句子的動詞部分！

② 動詞與時態都很重要！

③ 在考試裡常出現以Didn't、Isn't、Aren't開頭的否定疑問句。

否定、附加疑問句的主要例子

1）否定疑問句

Didn't you order some new microscopes last week?

Isn't the supervisor usually in the office on Wednesday?

Aren't you going to call Mr. Jones?

Weren't we supposed to meet at two?

Haven't you found your address book yet?

Hasn't the technician installed the software yet?

Don't you ever take a coffee break?

Won't the show be over by the time we get there?

2）附加疑問句

The presentation was a success, wasn't it?

You'll be available to check the documents, won't you?

We've been here before, haven't we?

It's cold in here, isn't it?

That's a restricted area, isn't it?

《講師的補充說明》

我們很容易混淆英語否定／附加疑問句的回答方式，原因在於我們的語言習慣。以「你昨天晚上沒有打電話給我嗎？」來看，我們會說「不，我打過」或「是，沒打」，回答與附加說明的敘述相反。但在英語裡Yes, I didn't. 或No, I did.的說法是不存在的。若打過電話就是Yes，若沒有打電話就要說No。

你上個星期沒有訂購顯微鏡嗎？
主管在星期三不是經常在辦公室嗎？
你不是要打電話給瓊斯先生嗎？
我們不是應該在兩點見面的嗎？
你還沒找到你的通訊錄嗎？
那位技師還沒安裝好軟體嗎？
你都不休息嗎？
我們到那裡的時候，表演不會已經結束了嗎？

這次的報告很成功，不是嗎？
你有空檢查那份文件，不是嗎？
我們以前來過這裡，不是嗎？
這裡很冷，不是嗎？
那裡是禁區，不是嗎？

對英語的否定、附加疑問句的回答方式，與對一般疑問句的回答方式一樣，以「動詞＋時態」的概念來表達。因此，否定詞或尾巴不能當作核心詞彙。

例如，上面否定疑問句的第一個例句，需要先將否定詞除掉之後再記得「訂購」的部分。而附加疑問句的第一個例句，需要先將尾巴除掉之後再記得「很成功」的部分。

在否定、附加疑問句裡常出現的說法

Didn't you go, Didn't you finish, Didn't you contact, Didn't you order

你沒有去嗎，你沒有完成嗎，你沒有聯絡嗎，你沒有訂購嗎

Don't you like, Don't you think, Haven't you heard, Haven't you found

你不喜歡嗎，你不覺得嗎，你沒聽過嗎，你還沒找到嗎

You've seen, You worked, You called, You visited, You ordered

你看過，你工作過，你打過電話，你訪問過，你訂購過

It's cold, That's a new （名詞）

很冷，那是新的（名詞）

🎧 09-05.mp3

第2階段：聽選項　選擇性地聽吧！

❶ 將否定詞與尾巴去掉，也注意時態！
❷ 肯定是Yes加附加說明的選項，否定是No加附加說明的選項。
❸ 對否定、附加疑問句而言，沒有Yes、No就直接出現附加說明的情形，比一般疑問句要來的少。

否定、附加疑問句題型主要出現的回答說法

Q：Isn't the supervisor usually in the office on Wednesday?
A：Yes, from 9:00 a.m. to 5:00 p.m.

將否定詞除掉之後，對於「經常在辦公室」以Yes與附加說明來回答！

Q：主管在星期三不是經常在辦公室嗎？
A：是，從早上九點到下午五點在。

Q：Haven't you found your address book yet?
A：No, and I looked everywhere.

將否定詞除掉之後，對於「找到」以No與附加說明來回答！

Q：你還沒找到你的通訊錄嗎？
A：不，而且我到處都看過了。

Q：Hasn't Ms. Daffi returned from her vacation?
A：I believe she has.

「我相信」是對於「回來」的肯定附加說明！Yes被省略了！

Q：達芬小姐還沒度假回來嗎？
A：我相信她回來了。

Q：Isn't the store closed?
A：It's open 24 hours a day.

「開著二十四小時」是對於「商店打烊」的否定附加說明！No被省略了！

Q：那家店不是打烊了嗎？
A：他們一天二十四小時開著。

Q：The presentation was a success, wasn't it?
A：It was very good.

附加疑問句也是一樣的原理。對於「成功」，是省略Yes以附加說明回答的！

Q：這次的報告很成功，不是嗎？
A：非常好。

Q：He was a magazine editor, wasn't he?
A：Yes, I think so.

對附加疑問句而言，也常出現「同意」的回答方式！

Q：他以前是雜誌編輯，不是嗎？
A：是，我也這麼認為。

找答案的原理與一般疑問句一樣。若動詞加時態的句意是肯定的就以Yes來回答，否定的話以No來回答，之後再加上附加說明。一部分的答案會以省略Yes或No，直接加附加說明的方式，這也和一般疑問句是一樣的，但其出現機率較低。

考試裡常出現的附加說明

肯定：I believe so, I think so, I thought so, That's what I'm planning, That's right, I'm looking forward to it

否定：Not yet, Not at all, Not very much, Not quite, I'm afraid I can't

我也這麼相信，我也這麼想，我也這麼想過，這就是我正在計劃的，沒錯，我很期待

還沒，完全不是，沒那麼多，沒有那麼，恐怕我不行

怪物講師的祕密

1 與一般疑問句一樣，說Yes之後加上No的附加說明，或說No之後加上Yes的附加說明，這樣的選項都不是答案。

2 變更主詞來回答的選項不是答案。
Will Ms. Perterson be back on Thursday?
不對：No, I'm arriving next week.

3 對附加疑問句而言，表達同意的回答(I think so. / I agree. / That's right.)常作為答案。

🎧 09-06.mp3

Quiz

Q3 請邊聽邊填寫以下空欄。

(1) Don't you _____ the book?

(2) Haven't you _____ to use that software?

(3) You've _____ for a while, haven't you?

(4) You _____ more stationary, didn't you?

Q4 請聽問題之後選出適當的回答。

(1) ⓐ Yes, it's a pleasant weather.　　ⓑ I'll turn on the air conditioner.

(2) ⓐ There used to be one.　　ⓑ I just bought some groceries.

(3) ⓐ She's getting them today.　　ⓑ Put them in his office.

▶ 答案在解析本第043頁

攻略法17　回答一般疑問句的方法

一般疑問句

一般疑問句裡，聽到動詞是最重要的。最好將Are you、Do you、Have you、Did you等發音記背下來。

一般疑問句的主要例子

Are you going to Ms. Chang's party on Saturday?

Do you think this article is well written?

Did you go to the seminar last night?

Have you heard about the rent increase in our building?

Will you speak at the sales meeting?

Should I give him your business card when he returns?

一般疑問句題型的主要答案

對一般疑問句而言，「動詞+時態」的句意若是肯定以Yes、否定以No來回答，之後再加附加說明。答案的30%是以不出現Yes、No而直接用附加說明來回答。

一般疑問句題型的主要回答方式

Yes, I put it on the table.

No, you'll need the exact amount.

I'll be a bit late, but I'll be there.

I've been too busy.

No, what's her new title?

I'll ask Dana.

攻略法18　回答否定、附加疑問句的方法

否定、附加疑問句

先將否定、附加疑問句的否定詞與尾巴除掉後，注意聽動詞為最重要。

否定、附加疑問句的主要例子

Didn't you order some new microscopes last week?

Aren't you going to call Mr. Jones?

Weren't we supposed to meet at two?

Haven't you found your address book yet?

You'll be available to check the documents, won't you?

We've been here before, haven't we?

It's cold in here, isn't it?

否定、附加疑問句題型的主要答案

否定、附加疑問句也是。

否定、附加疑問句題型的主要回答方式

Yes, from 9:00 a.m. to 5:00 p.m.

No, and I looked everywhere.

I believe she has.

It's open 24 hours a day.

It was very good.

Yes, I think so.

STEP 01 　若沒答對會後悔的考題　　　　請按照mp3錄音的指示進行以下的考題

例子

① 聽考題　　　　　　　　　　　　　　　　　**② 聽選項**

Did you go to the
seminar last night?

1 助動詞+主詞+動詞　Did you go

2 受詞與其他　to the seminar last night

Mark your answer.

(A)　(B)

1

1 助動詞+主詞+動詞

2 受詞與其他

Mark your answer.

(A)　(B)

2

1 助動詞+主詞+動詞

2 受詞與其他

Mark your answer.

(A)　(B)

3

1 助動詞+主詞+動詞

2 受詞與其他

Mark your answer.

(A)　(B)

4

1 動詞+形容詞

2 受詞與其他

Mark your answer.

(A)　(B)

5

1 主詞+助動詞+動詞

2 受詞與其他

Mark your answer.

(A)　(B)

▶ 答案在解析本第043頁

STEP 02　考題實戰練習　　　　請將以下部分當作真實考試，邊計時邊回答吧。

1　Mark your answer on your answer sheet.　　　　　(A)　(B)　(C)

高難度
2　Mark your answer on your answer sheet.　　　　　(A)　(B)　(C)

3　Mark your answer on your answer sheet.　　　　　(A)　(B)　(C)

4　Mark your answer on your answer sheet.　　　　　(A)　(B)　(C)

5　Mark your answer on your answer sheet.　　　　　(A)　(B)　(C)

6　Mark your answer on your answer sheet.　　　　　(A)　(B)　(C)

7　Mark your answer on your answer sheet.　　　　　(A)　(B)　(C)

重要
8　Mark your answer on your answer sheet.　　　　　(A)　(B)　(C)

重要
9　Mark your answer on your answer sheet.　　　　　(A)　(B)　(C)

10　Mark your answer on your answer sheet.　　　　　(A)　(B)　(C)

11　Mark your answer on your answer sheet.　　　　　(A)　(B)　(C)

12　Mark your answer on your answer sheet.　　　　　(A)　(B)　(C)

▶ 答案在解析本第044頁

Chapter 10

陳述句、間接疑問句
將考題與答案整套一起記下來！

Review Test

請回答以下的問題，也同時整理前面所學的內容。

1　一般疑問句的核心部分為何？　　　　　　　　　　　▶ ....

2　常出現的一般疑問句類型有哪些？　　　　　　　　　▶ ....

3　一般疑問句答案的30%是不出現Yes、No而直接以附加說明回答。　▶ ....

4　找出否定、附加疑問句答案的原理，與一般疑問句相同。　▶ ....

5　出現否定、附加疑問句時，先將否定詞與尾巴除掉後，注意聽動詞的部分。　　　　　　　　　　　　　　　　　　　　　▶ ....

6　常出現的否定疑問句的類型有哪些？　　　　　　　　▶ ....

7　對Didn't you find the report?而言，肯定的回答方式為何？　▶ ....

Preview

1 陳述句、間接疑問句考題的特色

在Part 2裡除了疑問句以外也會出現陳述句。因陳述句不是詢問問題，因此不知道會出現什麼樣的回答方式，所以在考試裡也很難預測可能有的回答方式。另外也有兩、三個月出現一次的間接疑問句，間接疑問句是在疑問句前面有Do you know或Can you tell me等說法的形式，對此的答題技巧與一般疑問句類似，但仍有些許差異。

2 出現陳述句、間接疑問句考題需考慮的重點

❶ 陳述句的語調往下掉。另外，陳述句以主詞開頭，且其中一半以上是以I開頭的。

I'd like to make a reservation this weekend.

I forgot to give you a morning call this morning.

❷ 陳述句考題當中也會出現表達主觀感覺的形容詞。

❸ 陳述句若聽到表達同意的選項，就是答案。

I think so.　　　I believe so.　　　That's right.

❹ 間接疑問句以Do you know或Can you tell me開頭。

Do you know when the sales report is due?

Can you tell me when the conference begins?

|答案|　1.動詞的部分　2. Are you , Do you , Have you　3.○　4.○　5.○　6. Didn't, Isn't, Aren't　7. Yes, I did.

回答陳述句的方法

陳述句的答案裡33%為反問句。但平時還是得多練習聽完考題的句子。

🎧 10-01.mp3

第1階段：聽考題 判斷為陳述句

❶ 沒有疑問詞，且以主詞開頭。（一半以上的主詞為I）

❷ 語調往下掉。

❸ 若為表達主觀想法的陳述句，聽I'd like、I (don't) like、I wish、I need、I think後面的動詞，或包含主觀感覺的形容詞。

❹ 若為表達客觀事實的陳述句，將常出現的句子記憶下來。

陳述句考題的難點在於：因為不是疑問句，所以得看情況有多種回答方式。因此，學習陳述句考題時，需要將考題與其答案一起記憶下來。例如，I'd like to（我想要…）類的陳述句裡，常出現「預訂、訂購、變更、取消」等的說法，而答案裡也常出現「叫什麼名字、有幾位、我去確認」等說法。

陳述句的主要例子

1）主觀陳述句（使用表達主觀想法的動詞）

I'd like to make a reservation.

I don't like to leave the office before 5 p.m.

I need a ride to the train station.

I thought you already left for Taipei.

I think the warranty on my oven expired last year.

我想訂位。
我不喜歡在五點前離開辦公室。
我需要有人載我到火車站。
我以為你已經往台北出發了。
我想我的烤箱的保固期限在去年過期了。

2）主觀陳述句（使用表達主觀感覺的形容詞）

It's so cold in this office.

I'm very impressed with your sales record this quarter.

The ideas presented in the proposal were very interesting.

Our coffee makers are perfect for offices.

這間辦公室裡很冷。
我很欣賞你這一季的銷售記錄。
那份企畫書裡提出的想法相當有趣。
我們的咖啡機對辦公室來說很完美。

3）客觀陳述句

I bought office supplies last week.

The concert starts at 8 o'clock.

Our vehicles come in five basic colors.

There's a phone call for you.

我上個星期買了辦公用品。
那場演唱會在八點開始。
我們的車輛有五種基本顏色。
有人來電找你。

陳述句以主詞開頭，其語調往下掉。一半以上的陳述句以I開頭，且聽到I'd like、I need、I think後面的動詞的話，大部分可以了解其內容。有時候若聽到主觀感覺的形容詞也能了解其內容。

但是若是表達客觀事實的陳述句，只聽到一部分還是很難了解內容，所以平時得記憶很多句子。

陳述句裡常出現主觀感覺的動詞與形容詞

動詞： think, seem, look, like, thought, believe, I'm not sure, need, wish, I'd like

形容詞：impressed, great, cooler, cold, excellent, finest, enough, easier, perfect, delicious, noisy, nice, hot, interesting, excited, busy

覺得，好像，看來，喜歡，以為，相信，我不確定，需要，希望，我想要

被感動的，極好的，更涼的，冷的，傑出的，最優質的，充分的，更容易的，完美的，好吃的，吵的，不錯的，熱的，有趣的，興奮的，忙的

🎧 10-02.mp3

第2階段：聽選項 選擇性地聽吧！

❶ 陳述句題型的答案中33%為反問句。
❷ 選項裡聽到向對方表達同意或傾向同意的說法，就是答案。
❸ 若陳述句包含「表達問題狀況的說法」，則「安慰／解決方法」為答案。
❹ 以單純的附加說明來回答的情形，最好將常出現的考題與答案一塊記憶下來。

- -

陳述句型題主要出現的回答說法

Q：I think the warranty on my oven expired last year.
A：Would you like me to check for you?
  若知道是陳述句，可以選擇佔答案的33%的反問句！

Q：我覺得我的烤箱的保固期限在去年過期了。
A：你要我幫你查看嗎？

Q：I don't like to leave the office before 5 p.m.
A：Neither do I.
  以向對方表達同意的說法來回答，就是答案！

Q：我不喜歡在五點以前離開辦公室。
A：我也不喜歡。

Q：I can't find my wallet anywhere.
A：Have you checked your pockets?
  提出問題狀況時，安慰或解決方法的說法為答案！

Q：在哪裡都找不到我的錢包。
A：你看過你的口袋嗎？

Q：I'll need some help moving these bookshelves.
A：I can help.
  對「需要幫助」類的內容而言，「我幫助你」這類的答案常出現！

Q：我需要有人幫我一起搬這些書架。
A：我可以幫忙。

Q：Mr. Johnston is standing right over there.
A：Thanks, I'll go introduce myself.
  由對方提供資訊時，「謝謝」這類的答案常出現！

Q：約翰斯頓先生就站在那邊。
A：謝謝。我會去自我介紹的。

Q：The new accountant will have the office next to yours.
A：I'll stop by to introduce myself.
  此為注意聽考題才能回答的情形，所以需要配對記憶！

Q：那位新會計師會用你旁邊的辦公室。
A：我會過去自我介紹的。

在陳述句考題的答案中，反問句佔33%，另外也會有以「You're right.」、「Neither do I.」等表達同意的說法來回答的答案。若陳述句考題為「故障了」等論及問題狀況的，那麼安慰或提供解決方法的說法為答案。

1 考試裡常出現表達同意的說法

I think so.	I believe so.	我是這麼想。
You're right.	I agree.	我是這麼相信。
That's right.	Neither do (did) I.	你是對的。
That's too bad.	I'm sorry to hear that.	我同意。
I thought it was delicious too.	Yes, he is very good at it.	正確。

我也不是。
太可惜了。
我很遺憾聽到那件事。
我也覺得很好吃。
是。他很擅長那件事。

2 在考試裡常出現論及問題狀況的說法，與對該問題的安慰／解決方法的說法

forgot → Do you remember...?

can't find → Have you checked（場所）?

cold → get your sweater

noisy → it should be finished soon

isn't working → call the technician

can't drive → I'll call 人 for a ride

burned out → call maintenance department

out of paper → I'll get some from（場所）

忘記了（你記得…嗎？）
無法找到（你找過〔某場所〕嗎？）
冷（拿你的毛衣）
吵（應該快結束了）
不運轉（打電話給技師）
無法開車（我打電話給〔某人〕要求搭便車）
燒掉了（打電話給維修部門）
紙張用完了（我去〔某場所〕拿）

怪物講師的祕密

1 陳述句常出現在容易降低專注力的考題後半段之間。

2 雖然答案選項不容易聽到，但非答案的選項都會用類似的發音，所以很容易排除。

3 除了反問句以外，若聽到「我幫忙你」、「對我很有幫助」、「謝謝」等，大部分是答案。

Quiz

🎧 10-03.mp3

Q1 請邊聽邊填寫以下空欄。

(1) _____ make a reservation.

(2) _____ you already left for Seoul.

(3) _____ a phone call for you.

(4) _____ I _____ my wallet.

Q2 請聽問題之後選出適當的回答。

(1) ⓐ Thanks, I'm glad you like it.   ⓑ What is your name?

(2) ⓐ I believe so.   ⓑ I read the sign.

(3) ⓐ I found it boring.   ⓑ Have you checked the conference room?

▶ 答案在解析本第047頁

攻略法

20

回答間接疑問句的方法

Do you know或Can you tell me等後面接著出現疑問詞的疑問句，叫做間接疑問句。對此回答方式與一般疑問句一樣，但唯一的差異是，對於間接疑問句的回答可以用Yes/No開頭。

🎧 10-04.mp3

第1階段：聽考題 **注意聽Do you know後面的疑問詞**

❶ 先聽Do you know或Can you tell me。

❷ 接著聽後面的疑問詞。

❸ 「疑問詞＋主詞＋should/will」可以縮略成「疑問詞 to」。

間接／準間接疑問句的主要例子

1）間接疑問句

Do you know <u>when</u> that report is due?

Can you please tell me <u>where</u> I can buy a train ticket?

Did Mr. Davis ask <u>why</u> the shipment of office supplies was late?

Can I tell Mrs. Jones <u>who's</u> calling?

Ms. Chow, could you tell us <u>how</u> you'd promote the magazine?

Do you know <u>how</u> to get to the movie theater?

Do you know <u>what</u> this week's meeting is about?

Have you decided <u>which</u> mobile phone to buy?

2）準間接疑問句

I don't know <u>how</u> to operate this camera.

I wonder <u>who</u> will be hired as the assistant manager.

你知道那份報告的應繳日期是什麼時候嗎？
你可以告訴我在哪裡能買到火車票嗎？
戴維斯先生有問過為什麼辦公用品晚出貨嗎？
我可以告訴瓊斯太太是誰打電話來嗎？
周小姐，你可以告訴我們你怎麼推銷那份雜誌嗎？
你知道如何去那個電影院嗎？
你知道這週的會議是有關什麼的嗎？
你決定要買哪種手機了嗎？

我不知道怎麼使用這台相機。
我很好奇誰會被雇用為副經理。

有間接疑問句考題時，聽到Do you know或Can you tell me後面的疑問詞為最重要。間接疑問句的疑問詞與一般疑問詞相比，很常有不易聽到的情形，所以得特別注意。

準間接疑問句是指看起來像陳述句，但其中包含疑問詞的句子。在此疑問詞仍然很重要。

當作間接疑問句句首的說法

Do you know, Can you tell me, Do you remember, Have you heard, Have you decided, Does anyone know, Did 人 say, Did 人 ask, I don't know, I wonder, I don't remember

你知道嗎,你可以告訴我嗎,你記得嗎,你聽過嗎,你決定了嗎,有人知道嗎,[人]說過嗎,[某人]問過嗎,我不知道,我在想,我不記得

🎧 10-05.mp3

第2階段:聽選項 **選擇性地聽吧!**

❶ 預測與一般疑問句一樣的回答方式。

❷ 即使以Yes、No開頭也沒有錯,所以得注意。

❸ 「不知道」、「還沒決定」這類間接迴避性的答案也常出現。

間接／準間接疑問句題型主要出現的回答說法

Q : Do you know when Ms. Jin will be back from her business trip?

A : On Tuesday, I think.
　　和When疑問句的回答方式一樣,以時間點介系詞片語回答!

Q:你知道金小姐什麼時候會出差回來嗎?
A:我想是星期二。

Q : Do you know where I can get a cup of coffee?

A : At the cafe just around the corner.
　　和Where疑問句的回答方式一樣,以場所介系詞片語回答!

Q:你知道我在哪兒可以買杯咖啡嗎?
A:在角落那家咖啡廳。

Q : Do you know why Ms. Soto called?

A : To schedule an appointment.
　　和Why疑問句的回答方式一樣,以「to動詞原形」回答!

Q:你知道索托小姐為什麼打電話來嗎?
A:為了約時間。

Q : Do you know who's responsible for this project?

A : Yes, Mr. Jack is.
　　和Who疑問句的回答方式一樣,以「人名」回答。也可以用Yes。

Q:你知道誰負責這份企畫案嗎?
A:是,傑克先生負責的。

Q : Do you know who was hired as the new program manager?

A : It hasn't been decided yet.
　　「還沒決定」是間接迴避性回答方式,通常都能作為答案!

Q:你知道誰被雇用為新計畫經理嗎?
A:還沒決定。

Q : I don't know how to operate this camera.

A : Let me show you.
　　準間接疑問句的回答,是和疑問詞的回答一樣的方式!

Q:我不知道怎麼使用這台相機。
A:讓我示範給你看。

對間接／準間接疑問句的回答方式與疑問詞疑問句一樣。但是疑問詞疑問句不可能有的Yes、No回答方式,在間接／準間接疑問句的回答仍然可以出現。與Part 2裡的別的疑問句相比,「我不太清楚」、「還沒決定」這類一聽就是答案的間接迴避性回答方式也更常出現。

考試裡常出現的間接迴避性回答

I don't know.	I have no idea.
Not that I know of.	I don't work here.
Not me.	I wish I knew.
Check with Janet.	I haven't heard about it.
They haven't decided it yet.	It's up in the air.
It depends on the situation.	It varies.

我不知道。
我完全不知道。
據我所知沒有。
我不在這裡上班。
不是我。
我希望我知道。
和珍妮特確認吧。
我沒聽過。
他們還沒決定。
什麼都不確定。
看情況而定。
可能性很多。

怪物講師的祕密

1 間接疑問句最常以Do you know開頭。

2 漏聽疑問詞的話，很有可能是Where。Where在間接疑問句裡不太容易聽到。

《講師的補充說明》

間接疑問句裡疑問句的語序變成陳述句的情形，例如：Whom will you meet?在間接疑問句裡變成Can you tell whom you will meet?。若是助動詞為do的情形，只要刪除該助動詞就好，例如：Whom do you like?變成Can you tell me who you like?的情形。不過疑問詞本身當作主詞的話，這種現象不會出現，例如：Who loves you?在間接疑問句裡還是Can you tell me who loves you?。

🎧 10-06.mp3

✏Quiz

Q3 請邊聽邊填寫以下空欄。

(1) _____ you bought your car?

(2) _____ the budget meeting was canceled?

(3) _____ computer to buy?

(4) _____ is supposed to water the plant.

Q4 請聽問題之後選出適當的回答。

(1) ⓐ Next week, perhaps.   ⓑ I can do it.

(2) ⓐ You can purchase it on the Internet.   ⓑ It does look plain.

(3) ⓐ Let me show you.   ⓑ With sugar, please.

攻略法19　回答陳述句的方法

陳述句

一半以上的陳述句以I開頭，且會聽到 I'd like、I (don't) like、I wish、I want、 I need、I think等包含動詞的說法或表達主觀感覺的形容詞。

陳述句的主要例子

I'd like to make a reservation.

I need a ride to the train station.

I thought you'd already left for Taipei.

It's so cold in this office.

I'm very impressed with your sales record this quarter.

I bought office supplies last week.

The concert starts at 8 o'clock.

陳述句題型的主要答案

陳述句題型的答案的33%為反問句。除此之外，若聽到向對方表達同意的選項，就是答案。有時也有安慰、解決方法（大部分是「我幫忙你」之類的內容）的說法，或因果關係的附加說明作為答案。

陳述句題型的主要回答方式

Would you like me to check for you?

Neither do I.

Have you checked your pocket?

I can help.

Thanks, I'll go introduce myself.

I'll stop by to introduce myself.

攻略法20　回答間接疑問句的方法

間接疑問句

聽到Do you know或Can you tell me後面的疑問詞為核心。Where疑問詞單獨出現時容易聽到，但在間接疑問句出現時可能不易聽到，所以得特別注意。

間接疑問句的主要例子

Do you know when that report is due?

Can you please tell me where I can buy a train ticket?

Did Mr. Davis ask why the shipment of office supplies was late?

Can I tell Mrs. Jones who's calling?

Ms. Chow, could you tell us how you'd promote the magazine?

I don't know how to operate this camera.

間接疑問句題型的主要答案

與疑問詞疑問句一樣的回答方式。但其差異為，可以用Yes或No來開始回答。「不太清楚」這類的間接迴避性答案也常出現。

間接疑問句題型的主要回答方式

On Tuesday, I think.

At the cafe just around the corner.

To schedule an appointment.

Yes, Mr. Jack is.

It hasn't been decided yet.

Let me show you.

STEP 01　若沒答對會後悔的考題

例子

① 聽考題

② 聽選項

Do you know when
the report is due?

1 決定類別的說法　　Do you know when

2 其他　　the report is due

Mark your answer.

(A)　(B)

1

1 決定類別的說法　...

2 其他　...

Mark your answer.

(A)　(B)

2

1 決定類別的說法　...

2 其他　...

Mark your answer.

(A)　(B)

3

1 決定類別的說法　...

2 其他　...

Mark your answer.

(A)　(B)

4

1 決定類別的說法　...

2 其他　...

Mark your answer.

(A)　(B)

5

1 決定類別的說法　...

2 其他　...

Mark your answer.

(A)　(B)

▶ 答案在解析本第048頁

STEP 02 考題實戰練習　　請將以下部分當作真實考試，邊計時邊回答吧。

1　Mark your answer on your answer sheet.　　　(A)　(B)　(C)

重要
2　Mark your answer on your answer sheet.　　　(A)　(B)　(C)

3　Mark your answer on your answer sheet.　　　(A)　(B)　(C)

4　Mark your answer on your answer sheet.　　　(A)　(B)　(C)

5　Mark your answer on your answer sheet.　　　(A)　(B)　(C)

6　Mark your answer on your answer sheet.　　　(A)　(B)　(C)

7　Mark your answer on your answer sheet.　　　(A)　(B)　(C)

8　Mark your answer on your answer sheet.　　　(A)　(B)　(C)

9　Mark your answer on your answer sheet.　　　(A)　(B)　(C)

10　Mark your answer on your answer sheet.　　　(A)　(B)　(C)

高難度
11　Mark your answer on your answer sheet.　　　(A)　(B)　(C)

重要
12　Mark your answer on your answer sheet.　　　(A)　(B)　(C)

▶ 答案在解析本第049頁

Part 3

短對話

概括性詢問的考題 I
只要聽到一個核心詞彙就好！

▶ 在Part 3得滿分的策略

在Part 3這部分是聽完十五到三十秒左右的對話後，回答考卷上的三個考題。這裡共有十三組對話，所以一共三十九個考題。考題與選項都印在考卷上，且配音員將對話與考題只唸一次。

1 若不看考題與選項，無法將三個考題都答對。因此一定要看考題然後再聽對話。針對於此，要反覆練習在固定時間之內先看考題再聽對話，這樣可以熟悉這部分的考試。

2 一般而言，在對話的第一行與最後一行會出現對第一個考題與最後一個考題答案的提示。尤其是最近在對話的最後部分將主要內容重述一次的情形很多。另外，考題的答案在對話裡面依序出現的情形為70%以上。

3 出現的考題、類型、詞彙都是固定的。因此請熟悉常出現的類型與考題，且將已出現過的考題與詞彙記背下來，也同時透過模擬考試來練習。

4 聽力考試全部結束了之後再填答案也不遲。在時間很緊迫的狀況下，不要一邊填答案浪費時間。

Preview

1 概括性詢問的考題的特色

Part 3的考題以「概括性詢問的考題」與「仔細詢問的考題」來分。「概括性詢問的考題」在任何對話之下都可以出現，而且無論是什麼對話，出現的考題都差不多一樣，而且聽完後大概都能找出答案，其提示的位置也比較明顯。出現概括性詢問的考題時，得注意考題的核心詞彙。

2 概括性詢問的考題需考慮的重點

❶ 若想知道是否為詢問主題的考題，看核心詞彙就好。
❷ 一般而言，在對話的前面聽得到對話的主題。
❸ 在對話裡與主題一起出現的說法幾乎是固定的。
❹ 若在考題裡出現where或who，可以知道是詢問場所與說話者的考題。聽到與場所與說話者直接相關的一、兩個核心詞彙，也可以判斷出是在什麼場所、誰在說話。

攻略法 **21** # 詢問對話主題的考題

英語對話是在前面出現主題，然後在後面附加敘述。因此，若有詢問主題的考題，得注意聽對話的前半段。

請記得英語對話是先講主題的，所以在對話的前半部分得特別專心。接著我們來學習一眼看出考題是否為詢問主題的方法，考卷上有考題和選項吧？在此請注意看考題，不需要把全部都翻譯，只要發現核心詞彙來判斷該考題是否為詢問主題的類型。

1 一般的對話

「在談什麼？」這類的考題就是詢問主題的。在短的對話裡不會發生多種問題，所以「有什麼問題？」這類的考題也是詢問主題的。

第1階段：看考卷 **透過核心詞彙來判斷考題的類別**

❶ 若考題裡看到以下的單字，就是詢問主題的！

topic, discussing, talking about, speakers doing, problem, concerned

> 主題，在討論，在談，說話者在做，問題，擔心的

❷ 對話的主題大部分在前面聽得到！

What is the woman's concern? ← 是詢問主題的考題！

(A) She cannot meet the deadline.

(B) She cannot meet Peter.

(C) She lost his briefcase.

(D) She lost the budget.

> 這個女生在擔心什麼？
> (A) 她無法在期限內完成。
> (B) 她無法和彼得見面。
> (C) 她把他的公事包弄丟了。
> (D) 她把預算案弄丟了。

1 What is the topic of this conversation?
出現topic，所以就是詢問主題的考題！答案應該在前面！

> 1 這段對話的主題是什麼？

2 What are the speakers mainly discussing?
discussing！就是詢問主題的呢！注意聽對話的前段！

> 2 這些說話者主要在談什麼？

3 What is the conversation mainly about?
詢問主要有關什麼？當然就是詢問主題的考題！

> 3 這段對話主要是有關什麼的？

4 What problem are the speakers discussing?
是什麼問題！就是詢問主題的考題！

> 4 這些說話者在討論什麼問題？

若想找到對話裡的主題，只要知道與其一起出現的說法就行。另外請記得，主題相關說法大部分在對話的前面出現！

🎧 11-01.mp3

第2階段：聽錄音 選擇性地聽答案！

主題與以下的說法一起出現！

I heard + 主題, Have you heard + 主題?

Have you seen + 主題?, I've got good news. + 主題

I'd like to + 主題, Would (Could) you + 主題?

I forgot to + 主題, I am pretty sure + 主題

我聽過+主題
你聽過+主題+嗎？
你看過+主題嗎？
我有好消息。+主題
我想要+主題
您可否+主題？
我忘了+主題
我肯定+主題

M: Hello, Jane. Have you seen Peter lately? ◄── 這就是主體！

W: Oh, he has gone to Paris last month. Didn't you know that?

男：珍，你好。你最近見過彼得嗎？
女：啊，他上個月去巴黎了。你不知道嗎？

1 I heard + 主題

Jin, I heard that the company website is going to be redesigned. I got an e-mail this morning about it.

公司網頁的變更（**預測答案**：updating a website）

1 金，我聽說公司的網頁要重新設計了。我今天早上收到有關這一點的電子郵件。

2 Have you seen + 主題？

Have you seen the new film directed by Richard Kim?

在談新的電影（**預測答案**：a recent movie release）

2 你看過理查·金所導演的新電影嗎？

3 I've got good news. + 主題

Mr. Lopez, I have good news. Office Caterer has agreed to provide excellent food during the convention.

有關外燴公司的消息（**預測答案**：plannnig an event）

3 洛佩茲先生，我有好消息。「辦公外燴」同意在會議期間當中提供頂級餐飲。

4 I'd like to + 主題

I'd like to make a reservation for dinner on Thursday around 6 o'clock. 訂位時間與日子為主題（**預測答案**：to make a reservation）

4 我想要訂星期四六點左右晚餐的位子。

5 Would you / Could you + 主題？

Could you check on the seating arrangements for the conference room? 詢問會議室的座位安排（**預測答案**：arrangements for the meeting）

5 您可以幫我確認會議室的座位安排嗎？

🎧 11-02.mp3

✏ Quiz

請聽對話之後選出適當的答案。

Q1 What is the conversation mainly about?

(A) A television program　　(B) A newly released film

Q2 What is the woman's problem?

(A) She can't find a seat available.　　(B) She can't see a movie with the man.

▶ 答案在解析本第052頁

2 電話上的對話

若有電話上的對話，常有「為什麼講電話？」或「通話的目的為何？」類的考題。這種考題就是詢問主題的。

第1階段：看考卷 透過核心詞彙來判斷考題的類別

若看到以下的單字，就是詢問通話內容主題的考題！
calling, purpose of the telephone call, contact 〈 在打電話，通話的目的，聯絡

- -

Why is the woman [calling]? ◄—— 就是詢問通話內容主題的考題！ 〈 這個女生為什麼在打電話？

(A) To reserve a room
(B) To promote a product
(C) To schedule a meeting
(D) To talk about a medicine

〈 這個女生為什麼在打電話？
(A) 為了訂房
(B) 為了推銷商品
(C) 為了約會議時間
(D) 為了談一種藥

---

1 Why is the woman <u>calling</u>?
　　為什麼打電話？就是詢問主題的考題！

〈 1 這個女生為什麼在打電話？

2 What is the <u>purpose of the telephone call</u>?
　　通話的目的？是詢問主題的考題！

2 這通電話的目的為何？

3 Why did the woman <u>contact</u> the man?
　　為什麼聯絡的？當然是為了談主題！

3 這個女生為什麼和這個男生聯絡？

4 What is the woman <u>calling</u> about?
　　打電話談什麼？也是詢問主題的考題！

4 這個女生在打電話談什麼？

關於通話主題的考題，也有把答案告訴你的對話模式。無論如何，你得抓住這一點且注意地聽。

第2階段：聽錄音 選擇性地聽答案！

以下模式的對話即是告訴你其主體為何！

I'm calling about + 主題（名詞）
I'm calling to + 主題（動詞原形）
Hi, my name is 人名, and I + 主題
This is 人名 from 公司名稱. + 主題

> 我打電話來談（主題）的
> 我為了（主題）打電話的
> 你好，我叫…，（主題）
> 我是…公司的…，（主題）

- -

A: Good morning. I'm calling to reserve a room for July 15th through the 17th. I'm attending the medical conference at your hotel.

　　　　　　　　　　這就是主體！

B: Certainly. Can I have your name?

> A: 早安。我打電話是為了訂七月十五號到十七號的房間。我會參加你們飯店的醫學會議。
> B: 沒問題的。我可以留下您的大名嗎？

1 I'm calling about + 主題（名詞）

Hi, I'm calling about a delivery of some factory equipment.

詢問工廠設備的運送（**預測答案**：to check on a delivery）

> 1 你好。我打電話來是有關一些工廠設備的運送。

2 I'm calling to + 主題（動詞原形）

Hello, I'm calling to find out how much it costs to send a package to Korea.

詢問價錢（**預測答案**：to inquire about the price）

> 2 你好。我打電話來是想了解寄一個包裹到韓國要多少錢。

3 Hi, my name is 人名, and I + 主題

Hi, my name is Janet Demarco, and I am calling about the fabrics that I ordered last week.

有關訂單打的電話（**預測答案**：to ask about the status of an order）

> 3 你好。我叫珍妮特‧馬克，我打電話來是有關我上週訂的布料。

4 This is 人名 from 公司名稱. + 主題

Hi, this is George Mercer from Fine Medical Supply. Dr. Kim requested some information on one of our examination tables.

有關資料的要求（**預測答案**：to provide some product information）

> 4 你好。我是「精密醫學用品」的喬治‧默瑟。金博士有要求過一些關於我們實驗桌的資料。

1 在考題裡找出詢問主題的核心詞彙，然後將此標記。← 考卷
2 預測錄音的前面會出現。← 考卷
3 專心聽主題與核心模式或說法。← 錄音
4 確認主題之後選出答案。← 考卷

🎧 11-04.mp3

✏ Quiz

請聽對話之後選出適當的答案。

Q3 What is the purpose of the call?

(A) To get a phone number (B) To send a package

Q4 Why is the man contacting the woman?

(A) To ask about exam results (B) To make an appointment

▶ 答案在解析本第052頁

攻略法
22

詢問對話的地點、說話者的考題

詢問對話的地點與說話者的職業的考題，以幾個單字決定答案。若聽到 check in（登記入住）、hotel（飯店），此為詢問對話的地點；若聽到 my store（我的店）、store owner（店主），此為詢問說話者的考題。

與詢問主題的考題相比，也有更容易預測到答案的考題。詢問對話地點與說話者職業或職稱的考題，就是屬於容易預測到答案的考題，這類考題的答案只要透過核心說法就能立刻看得出來。另外，詢問地點與說話者的考題大部分作為第一個提問。

1. 詢問地點的考題

> **第1階段：看考卷** **透過核心詞彙來判斷考題的類別**
>
> 若在第一題看到以下的單字，就是詢問地點的考題！
> Where... take place / Where... speakers
>
> --
>
> Where most likely are the speakers?
>
> 是詢問對話地點的考題呢！
>
> (A) In an office building
> (B) In a post office
> (C) In a factory
> (D) In a store

說話者很有可能在哪裡？
(A) 在辦公大樓
(B) 在郵局
(C) 在工廠
(D) 在商店

1 Where does the conversation (probably) take place?
詢問對話的地點的考題！

2 Where is the conversation (probably) taking place?
這是把第一題稍微改變的說法！也是詢問地點的考題！

3 Where does the conversation (most likely) occur?
不用 take place，而用了同義詞 occur！

4 Where (most likely) are the speakers?
說話者在哪裡？也是詢問地點的考題！

1 這段對話（可能）在哪裡發生的？

2 這段對話（可能）正在哪裡發生？

3 這段對話（很有可能）在哪裡發生的？

4 這些說話者（很有可能）在哪裡？

現在要看看在對話裡立刻聽得出來地點的方法。這很簡單！先熟知常出現的地點為何以及哪些說法是代表地點的就好。這些說法大部分在對話的前面出現，但有時候也會在對話裡平均分佈。

第2階段：聽錄音 只要聽到代表地點的兩個單字就行！

聽到了常出現的核心詞彙之後，要想到地點！

飯店：hotel, lobby, front desk, check in

商店：looking for, find, have 商品名稱 in stock

餐廳：table is ready, order, a glass of water, menu

醫院：doctor, patient, check-up, an eye exam

博物館：admission to the museum, exhibit, curator

飯店，大廳，服務台，登記入住

在找…，發現，（商品）有庫存

餐桌準備好，點餐，一杯水，菜單

醫生，患者，健康檢查，眼睛檢查

博物館入場，展覽，館長

A: Hello, what can I do for you?

B: Oh, yes. I'm <u>looking for</u> a present for my brother. I think he'd like one of these sweaters, but do you have any in blue?

—— 加底線的地方為線索！

A: 你好。需要什麼服務呢？
B: 啊，是。我正在找要給我哥哥的禮物。我覺得他可能會喜歡這些毛衣，不過你們有藍色的嗎？

1 飯店：hotel, lobby, front desk, check in

Excuse me. I want to buy a present for my brother's birthday. Is there a gift shop <u>here in the hotel</u>?

即使沒有全部聽到，還可以知道「在這間飯店」就是線索！

1 不好意思。我想買我弟弟的生日禮物。在這間飯店裡有禮品店嗎？

2 商店：looking for, find, have 商品名稱 in stock

Can I help you <u>find</u> anything? Everything in the back of the <u>store</u> is on sale.

「找」、「商店」等的說法就指「商店」為地點！

2 我可以幫你找些什麼嗎？商店裡後面的所有的東西都在打折。

3 餐廳：table is ready, order, a glass of water, menu

My friend recommended <u>eating here</u>. Everything on the <u>menu</u> looks really good.

「在這裡吃」、「菜單」等就指地點為「餐廳」！

3 我的朋友建議在這裡吃。菜單上所有的東西看起來都很好。

4 醫院：doctor, patient, check-up, an eye exam

Susan, could you reschedule my 9 o'clock <u>patient</u> tomorrow?

透過「病患」就知道地點為醫院、說話者為醫生！

4 蘇珊，你可以把我的明天九點鐘的病患重新安排時間嗎？

5 博物館：admission to the museum, exhibit, curator

Where can I find the floor plan of the <u>museum</u>? It's my <u>first time</u> here.

透過「博物館」、「第一次來的」等的說法就知道是「博物館」！

5 我在哪裡可以找到這博物館的平面圖？我第一次來這裡。

🎧 11-06.mp3

Quiz

請聽對話之後選出適當的答案。

Q5 Where most likely are the speakers?

(A) At a bank　　　　　　(B) At an accounting firm

Q6 Where most likely are the speakers?

(A) In a computer repair shop　　(B) In a car exhibition

2.詢問說話者是誰的考題

> **第1階段：看考卷** 透過核心詞彙來判斷考題的類別
>
> 若在第一個考題出現以下的單字，就是詢問說話者為誰的考題！
> Who is(are) the man/woman(speakers)
>
> --
>
> Who most likely are the speakers? ← 是詢問說話者為誰的考題！
>
> (A) New managers
> (B) Workshop presenters
> (C) Sales representatives
> (D) Job candidates

這些說話者們很有可能是誰？
(A) 新的經理們
(B) 工作坊發表者們
(C) 行銷人員們
(D) 求職者們

1 Who (most likely/probably) is the man?
　　　　　　　　　　這個男生是誰？男女的職業可能不同，所以將man標記！

這個男生（很有可能／可能）是誰？

2 Who (most likely/probably) are the speakers?
　　　　　　　　　　男女的職業一樣的情形。也是詢問說話者為誰的考題！

這些說話者們（很有可能／可能）是誰？

3 Who (most likely/probably) is the woman talking to?
　　　　　　　　　　男女之間對話內容為一般話題的情形。這是詢問該男生為誰的考題。

這個女生（很有可能／可能）在和誰說話？

4 Where does the man (most likely/probably) work?
　　　　　　　　　　詢問這個男生的職業的考題。對話的地點有時候提示說話者的職業。

這個男生（很有可能／可能）在哪工作？

這次，我們學習在對話裡立刻聽出說話者是什麼職業的方法吧。很簡單！先熟知哪些說話者常出現以及哪些說法與哪些說話者有直接相關就可以。這些相關提示通常出現在對話前面，所以必須掌握該部分。另外也有以對話地點來暗示說話者職業的情形，所以從對話的地點推測的話，有時也能找得出來說話者為誰。

第2階段：聽錄音 只要聽到代表說話者的兩個單字就行！

對話裡常出現的說話者以及提示說話者的說法

說話者：looking for（行銷人員或客人）、my photographs（攝影師）、my store（店主）、lead the tour（導遊）

地點：as a bank teller（銀行）、our factory（工廠）、our next show（畫廊）、play house（劇場）

正在找，我的照片，我的店，引導觀光

以出納員的身份，我們的工廠，我們下一場秀，劇場

- -

A : How did you like the workshop for new managers last Tuesday?

B : Well, it was pretty good. I'm glad they have workshops like that for less experienced managers like us.

←── 下底線的地方為線索！

A: 你覺得上週二為了新任經理開的講習會如何？
B: 嗯，相當好。我很高興他們為我們這些經驗不足的經理們開講習會。

詢問說話者為誰的考題類型

以下是詢問「說話者為誰？」的考題類型。這裡收集了最常出現的類型。

1 salesperson（行銷人員）

What kind of cameras are you looking for?

詢問「在找什麼樣的相機」的人是行銷人員！

1 你在找什麼樣的相機？

2 customer service representative（客服人員）

Hello, M&D Computers. Customer service department. This is Dan. How may I help you? 在打招呼的對話中論及自己的部門名稱，所以能猜測為客服人員！

2 你好。這裡是M&D電腦公司的客服中心。我是丹，需要什麼服務嗎？

3 receptionist（接待員）

Hi, I'm a guest here at this hotel. I want to make an international phone call, but I lost my mobile phone.

和飯店房客對話的人可能是接待員。

3 你好。我是這家飯店的房客。我想打國際電話，不過我把我的手機弄丟了。

詢問說話者的工作地點的考題類型

以下為詢問「說話者工作的地點」的類型。當然是詢問場所的。

1 at a store（商店）

That article should be good advertising for us. Not many other stores are selling that line of shoes yet.

透過「正在賣⋯的店沒有很多」這部分，可以猜測是在商店工作。

1 這篇文章對我們而言應該是很好的廣告。正在賣這系列鞋子的店還沒有很多。

2 at a bank（銀行）

For 5 years as a bank teller, I've never been late.

「做為出納員」？就能知道是在銀行上班的！

2 從事出納員的五年當中，我從來沒有遲到過。

3 at an office supply store（辦公用品店）

Hi, my name is Sandra Wilson, and I ordered some stationery from your store yesterday.

聽到這些話的人，應該是在「辦公用品店」上班的吧！

3 你好。我叫珊卓拉‧威爾森。我昨天在你們的店訂了一些辦公用品。

《不經過翻譯就能回答有關詢問地點/說話者的考題的方法！》

1 在考題當中確認詢問地點／說話者的核心詞彙，然後將此標記。

2 先看考題的選項，再聯想各種地點／說話者的核心詞彙。

3 特別專心聽提示地點／說話者的說法。

4 找出地點／說話者之後勾選答案。

🎧 11-08.mp3

✏ Quiz

請聽對話之後選出適當的答案。

Q7 Who probably do the speakers work for?

　　(A) A computer manufacturer　　(B) An advertising corporation

Q8 Who most likely is the man?

　　(A) A sales representative　　(B) An important client

攻略法21 詢問對話主題的考題

詢問主題的考題，核心詞彙為：

discussing, talking about, topic, purpose, call, contact, problem, concern

What is the **topic of** this conversation?

What are the speakers mainly **discussing**?

What is the conversation **mainly about**?

What **problem** are the speakers discussing?

立刻會聽出主題的核心模式：

I heard + 主題

Have you heard + 主題?

Have you seen + 主題?

I've got good news + 主題

I'd like to + 主題

Would[Could] you + 主題?

I forgot to + 主題

I am pretty sure + 主題

詢問通話內容主題的考題，核心詞彙為：

calling, purpose of the telephone call, contact

Why is the woman **calling**?

What is the **purpose of the telephone call**?

Why does the woman **contact the man**?

What is the woman **calling** about?

立刻會聽出通話內容主題的核心模式：

I'm calling about + 主題（名詞）

I'm calling to + 主題（動詞原形）

Hi, my name is 人名, **and I** + 主題

This is 人名 **from** 公司名稱. + 主題

攻略法22 詢問對話的地點、說話者的考題

若在第一個考題裡看到以下的單字，就是詢問地點的問題

Where... take place / Where... speakers

Where does the conversation (probably) take place?

Where is the conversation (probably) taking place?

Where does the conversation (most likely) occur?

Where (most likely) are the speakers?

當作地點相關提示的字詞：

飯店：hotel, lobby, front desk, check in

餐廳：table is ready, order, a glass of water, menu

醫院：doctor, patient, check-up, an eye exam

博物館：admission to the museum, exhibit, curator

若在第一個考題裡看到以下的單字，就是詢問說話者的問題

Who... is(are) the man/woman (speakers)

Who (most likely/probably) is **the man**?

Who (most likely/probably) are the **speakers**?

Who (most likely/probably) is the **woman talking to**?

Where does the man (most likely/probably) **work**?

當作說話者相關提示的字詞：

說話者：looking for（行銷人員或客人）、my photographs（攝影師）、my store（商店老闆）、lead the tour（導遊）

地點：as a bank teller（銀行）、our factory（工廠）、our next gallery show（畫廊）、play house（劇場）

例子

Why is the woman calling?

(A) To check on a delivery
(B) To ask about the prices

1 找出核心詞彙	calling
2 了解類型	詢問主題
3 看選項	配送或價格
4 聽錄音來確認答案	

▶ 請務必依照mp3的進行順序來學習。

---

1 What is the topic of this conversation?

(A) New parking regulations
(B) A city park

1 找出核心詞彙	
2 了解類型	
3 看選項	

2 What might be the problem?

(A) The phone is not working properly.
(B) The wrong model was sent.

1 找出核心詞彙	
2 了解類型	
3 看選項	

3 What are the speakers discussing?

(A) A sales presentation
(B) Lunch plans

1 找出核心詞彙	
2 了解類型	
3 看選項	

4 Why is the man calling the woman?

(A) He needs to send a package.
(B) His office needs repairs.

1 找出核心詞彙	
2 了解類型	
3 看選項	

▶ 答案在解析本第053頁

5　Where most likely are the speakers?

(A) At a post office
(B) At a gift shop

1　找出核心詞彙 ....

2　了解類型 ....

3　看選項 ....

6　Who most likely is the man?

(A) A computer technician
(B) A salesperson

1　找出核心詞彙 ....

2　了解類型 ....

3　看選項 ....

7　Where does the woman probably work?

(A) At an employment agency
(B) At a machinery company

1　找出核心詞彙 ....

2　了解類型 ....

3　看選項 ....

8　Where does the man most likely work?

(A) At an office supply store
(B) At a delivery company

1　找出核心詞彙 ....

2　了解類型 ....

3　看選項 ....

▶ 答案在解析本第054頁

9 Why is the man calling?

(A) To discuss a defective merchandise

(B) To report a lost item

(C) To ask for a receipt

1 找出核心詞彙	
2 了解類型	
3 看選項	
4 預測對話內容	1）產品故障而打電話給客服人員。
	2）需要收據而打電話給店主。

10 Who most likely is the woman?

(A) A store owner

(B) A mobile phone salesperson

(C) A customer service representative

---

11 What are the speakers discussing?

(A) The price of some instruments

(B) The location of the theater

(C) Preparations for an event

1 找出核心詞彙	
2 了解類型	
3 看選項	
4 預測對話內容	1）在樂器行詢問樂器的價格。
	2）在演奏廳準備表演。

12 Where most likely are the speakers?

(A) At a concert hall

(B) At a music shop

(C) On a road

---

13 Where does this conversation probably take place?

(A) In a meeting

(B) At a reception desk

(C) At an interview

1 找出核心詞彙	
2 了解類型	
3 看選項	
4 預測對話內容	1）求職者在服務台詢問面試地點。
	2）在面試求職者自我介紹。

14 Who most likely is the man?

(A) A delivery man

(B) A receptionist

(C) A job interviewee

▶ 答案在解析本第055頁

STEP 02 考題實戰練習　　請留意前面練習過的兩個階段，進行以下的考題 答對的題目數：＿＿＿＿＿＿

1　What are the speakers mainly discussing?

(A) An early meeting
(B) A way to get to work
(C) A problem with a mechanic
(D) A new work schedule

高難度
 2 What did the speakers agree to do?

(A) Stop by a repair shop
(B) Contact a client
(C) Share a taxi
(D) Go to work early

3　When will the speakers probably meet?

(A) In 10 minutes
(B) In 20 minutes
(C) In 30 minutes
(D) In 40 minutes

4　What most likely is the man's job?

(A) Warehouse worker
(B) Post office clerk
(C) Travel agent
(D) Telephone company operator

重要
 5 Why is the woman calling?

(A) To ask for a postal code
(B) To request driving directions
(C) To find some information about the tour
(D) To inquire about the price

6　What will the woman probably do next?

(A) Complete paperwork
(B) Weigh a package
(C) Mail some letters
(D) Purchase flight tickets

7　Where are the speakers?

(A) In a bank
(B) In a shopping center
(C) In a hotel
(D) In a restaurant

8　What does the woman want to do?

(A) Place an order
(B) Make a deposit
(C) Change her room
(D) Clean some clothes

9　When is the interview?

(A) This morning
(B) This afternoon
(C) Tomorrow morning
(D) Tomorrow afternoon

10　What is the conversation mainly about?

(A) Booking a movie ticket
(B) Booking a hotel room
(C) Booking a flight ticket
(D) Booking a dinner table

Flight number	Departure	Destination
CK 106	Taipei	Singapore
CK 381	Taipei	Sydney
CK 997	Taipei	Tokyo
CK 639	Taipei	Bangkok

 11　Look at the graphic, which flight will the man take?

(A) CK 106
(B) CK 381
(C) CK 997
(D) CK 639

12　How long will the man be away for?

(A) 3 days
(B) 5 days
(C) 7 days
(D) 10 days

▶ 答案在解析本第058頁

Review Test

Part 3概括性詢問的考題特色是，全部聽完回答也可以，而且有關任何錄音內容都可以出現。請看看以下的問題，溫習前面所學過的內容吧。

1 考題裡若出現discussing、topic、talking about，是問什麼的呢？ ▶ ....

2 若通話內容詢問「為什麼通話呢？」，是屬於哪類的考題？ ▶ ....

3 若論及某種問題的發生，會有幾個問題？ ▶ ....

4 Part 3的考題中，只聽到一兩個單字就能回答，
也是最容易的考題類型為何？ ▶ ....

5 詢問主題的考題，在前面、中間、後面其中哪裡有答案？ ▶ ....

6 詢問地點或說話者的考題，一般聽到幾個單字就會找到答案？ ▶ ....

Preview

1 概括性詢問的考題的特色

概括性詢問的考題中，除了詢問「主題、地點、說話者」的考題以外，也有詢問「要求事項」的考題（將Please或Why don't you後面的內容聽好就能回答的題目），以及詢問「下個行程」的考題（將I'll或Let me後面的提示聽好就能回答的題目）。這些考題都是聽完了才能回答，且在任何對話之下都可以出現。因此將這些考題歸類為「概括性詢問的考題」。

Part 3的考題為概括性詢問的考題或仔細詢問的考題，所以若學過到這個單元，對任何考題都會熟悉，也很容易找得出來對答案的提示藏在哪裡。

2 概括性詢問的考題需考慮的重點

❶ 是否為要求事項或建議的說法，由考題裡的核心詞彙來判斷。
❷ 要求事項大部分在對話的中間或後面出現。
❸ 若詢問下一個行程，其主要內容也會出現於對話的中間或後面。
❹ 詢問下一個行程的考題，未來時間點的單字成為找答案的線索。

|答案| 1.主題 2.主題 3.一個 4.地點或說話者的考題 5.前面 6.兩個單字

攻略法
23 詢問要求、建議事項的考題

為了找到詢問要求、建議、義務事項的考題的提示，請注意聽對話的中間與後面。在對話中，建議的說法（你可否…？、我會…。、需要…。）的前後會出現關於答案的提示。

強勢的建議變成要求，再強勢的要求變成義務。因此詢問要求、建議、義務事項的考題都歸成同一類，稱為「要求考題」。我們學學一眼就看出是否為要求考題的方法吧。

考卷上有考題與選項吧？在此請查看考題，不需要全部都翻譯，只要找到確認是否為要求考題的核心詞彙就好。接著我們看看這些核心詞彙吧。

第1階段：看考卷 透過核心詞彙來判斷考題的類別

① 考題裡看到以下的單字，就是詢問要求事項的！

ask, request, direct, want, need, offer, suggest, recommend, encourage

請，要求，指示，需要，有必要，提議，建議，推薦，鼓勵

② 要求事項在對話的中間或後面會聽到！

What does the man ask the woman to do?

— 是詢問要求事項的考題！

(A) Send him a message

(B) Read a report

(C) Submit an application

(D) Attend a conference

那個男生請那個女生做什麼？
(A) 傳簡訊給他
(B) 讀報告
(C) 提交申請書
(D) 參加會議

1 What does the man ask the woman to do?

有ask所以是詢問要求事項的考題！答案應該在建議的說法裡吧。

1 那個男生請那個女生做什麼？

2 What does the man request?

request也是「要求」的意思，所以是同一類的！

2 那個男生要求什麼？

3 What does the man offer to do?

提議的說法，所以是同一類的！

3 那個男生提議他要做什麼？

4 What does the man ask for?

不止要求某種行為，也可以要求某種名詞！

5 What does the man ask about?

詢問什麼？要求回答也算是一種要求！

現在要學習在對話錄音裡馬上聽出來是否為要求事項的方法。這很簡單！與要求考題裡的核心詞彙一樣，先知道經常接連一起出現的說法就好。

🎧 12-01.mp3

第2階段：聽錄音 選擇性地聽答案！

在對話錄音裡，要求事項會在以下的模式裡一起出現！

Why don't + 建議事項？／How about + 建議事項？

Would you + 要求事項？／Could you + 要求事項？

I'd like + 要求事項／Please + 要求事項

You have to + 要求事項／I recommend + 建議事項

W : Do you have time next Tuesday to interview someone with me for the marketing position?

M: I'll be attending a budget meeting on that day, but it should be finished by 11. **Please** send me an e-mail and tell me when the applicant is coming. ⌐ 這就是要求事項！

1 Why don't + **建議事項**

Why don't you come back in an hour?

建議晚一點回來（**預測答案**： come back later）

2 Could you + **要求事項**

Could you have a meeting with the sales team?

要求開行銷策略會議（**預測答案**： hold a meeting）

3 I recommend + **建議事項**

I recommend you visit our website to see samples of our past work.

建議參考網站（**預測答案**： refer to a website）

---

4 這個男生要什麼？

5 這個男生詢問什麼？

要不要（建議事項）？／（建議事項）如何？

你願意（要求事項）？／你可以（要求事項）？

我想要（要求事項）／請你（要求事項）

你必須（要求事項）／我建議（建議事項）

女：你下週二有空和我一起面試應徵行銷部門職位的一個人嗎？

男：那天我將參加預算會議，不過應該會在十一點的時候結束的。請寄給我電子郵件告訴我那位申請人什麼時候會來。

1 你何不隔一個小時再回來？

2 你可以和業務團隊一起開會嗎？

3 我建議你到我們的網站看我們過去工作的樣本。

📣 12-02.mp3

✏ Quiz

請聽對話之後選出適當的答案。

Q1　What does the woman ask the man to do?

(A) Mail a document　　　　　(B) Send a repairperson

Q2　What does the woman offer to do?

(A) Place an order for materials　　(B) Transfer the telephone call

攻略法 24

詢問下一個行程的考題

若對話錄音當中出現要求事項，則與執行相關的內容會在後面出現，且在後面通常以未來時態「我將會～」的形式作為線索。在考題裡也會包含未來時間點的說法，如：「明天」、「下週」等作為線索。

有關詢問說話者將會做什麼的考題，稱為「下一個行程」的考題。這類的考題種類不多，且透過核心詞彙馬上就能判別出來。「下一個行程」考題的另一個特色為，每組三個考題中，大部分出現在最後一題。

1. 沒有出現特定時間點的情形

若有do next或he(she) will do等線索，就在考驗對將要發生的事情猜測後找出答案的能力。

第1階段：看考卷 透過核心詞彙來判斷考題的類別

❶ 若第三個考題裡出現以下的單字，就是詢問下一個行程的考題！

do next, he(she) will do, going to do, planning to do

❷ 下一個行程在對話中間或後面會聽得到！

> 下次做，他（她）將會做的，即將要做，計劃要做

What will the woman probably do next? ◄──── 是詢問下一個行程的考題！

(A) Send a package

(B) Call the manufacturer

(C) Provide an address

(D) Fix a camera

> 這個女生接下來可能會做什麼？
> (A) 寄包裹
> (B) 打電話給製造業者
> (C) 提供地址
> (D) 修理相機

1 What will the man (most likely/probably) do next?

有do next，所以是下一個行程的考題。答案應該在未來時態吧。

> 1 這個男生接下來（很有可能／有可能）會做什麼？

2 What is the man going/planning to do?

有「即將／計劃」，所以也是下一個行程的考題。

> 2 這個男生即將／計劃做什麼？

3 What does the man say he will do?

也是下一個行程的考題。答案會出現在男生的話語當中未來時態的部分！

> 3 這個男生說他會做什麼？

這次看看在對話錄音裡如何立刻找出下一個行程是什麼的句子。很簡單！與「下一個行程」的考題裡找出的核心詞彙的方法一樣，只要知道一起出現的說法就好。

🎧 12-03.mp3

第2階段：聽錄音 選擇性地聽答案！

在對話當中與以下模式一起會出現下一個行程的線索！

I'll＋下一個行程／Let me＋下一個行程

Now, let's＋下一個行程／I'd better＋下一個行程

You'll have to＋下一個行程

> 我將會（下一個行程）／ 讓我（下一個行程）
> 那麼咱們（下一個行程）吧／我最好（下一個行程）
> 你將得（下一個行程）

M: My camera doesn't work. But I don't see any of your service centers in the area.

W: In that case, you can mail it directly to the manufacturer and they'll either repair or replace it. **I'll** give you the address to send it to. ◄—— 這就是下一個行程！

> 男：我的相機無法使用。不過我在這個地區看不到你們的服務中心。
> 女：這樣的話，你可以把它直接寄給製造廠。他們會修理或更換。我給你那裡的地址，你可以寄出去。

1 I'll + 下一個行程

I'll e-mail Tony now and see if he can help me.

預測給同事寄電子郵件（預測答案：Contact another colleague）

> 1 我現在寄給湯尼電子郵件看看他能不能幫忙我。

2 Let me + 下一個行程

Let me just put these books in the box.

預測將書放在箱子裡（預測答案：Pack some books）

> 2 讓我把這些書放在箱子裡。

3 You'll have to + 另一方的下一個行程

You'll have to go to the security office and get a new one.

預測在警衛室拿到新的東西（預測答案：Get a new pass card）

> 3 你必須到警衛室，然後拿新的。

🎧 12-04.mp3

Quiz

請聽對話之後選出適當的答案。

Q3 What is the woman most likely to do next?

(A) Repair the machine　　(B) Make a phone call

Q4 What does the woman say she will do?

(A) Look for a recruiting company　(B) Apply for a temporary job

▶ 答案在解析本第060頁

2. 出現特定時間點的情形

下一個行程的考題裡若出現未來時間點，除了 I'll... 的未來時態以外，像 tomorrow這類未來時間點，本身就是線索。

第1階段：看考卷 透過核心詞彙來判斷考題的類別

若在第三個考題裡出現以下的單字，就是詢問下一個行程的考題！
at 正確的時刻, this afternoon, tonight, later today,
on Monday, on December 10th, next week, in November

> 在正確的時刻，在今天下午，在今晚，在今天晚一點，在星期一，在十二月十日，在下個禮拜，在十一月

According to the conversation, what will happen next month?

(A) A new system will be installed.
(B) The display cases will be replaced.
(C) Workers will deliver water.
(D) Harvesting will begin.

出現特定時間點的，也就是詢問下一個行程的考題呢！

> 根據這段對話，下個月會發生什麼？
> (A) 有個新的系統會被安裝。
> (B) 顯示器外殼會被更換。
> (C) 工人會送水過來。
> (D) 收割會開始。

---

1 What does the woman say she will do tonight?

這是詢問下一個行程的考題，且在tonight前後會有答案！

> 1 這個女生說她今晚會做什麼？

2 What will the speakers do this afternoon?

this afternoon前後會有答案吧！

> 2 這些說話者今天下午會做什麼？

3 What is supposed to happen tomorrow morning?

「預訂會…」也是未來時態的說法。tomorrow morning的前後會有答案！

> 3 明天早上預計會發生什麼事？

4 According to the man, what will occur next week?

不是立刻，但next week也屬於近期未來的時間點！

> 4 根據這個男生所說的，下週會發生什麼事？

這次要學習在對話錄音裡立刻聽得出來下一個行程的句子的方法。很簡單！與在下一個行程考題裡找出核心詞彙的方法一樣，只要知道一起出現的說法就好。

第2階段：聽錄音 選擇性地聽答案！

在對話中，以下的模式裡會出現下一個行程的線索！

❶ 對話錄音的後段內容當中，未來時間點的前後

❷ not A until B（在B之前不發生A）的A部分

M: I think you'd find the new system worth the money. It saves time and reduces water use, and it should increase your yield. Don't you think you have a large crop this year?

W: Maybe. **We are going to** start harvesting **next month**. We'll know for sure then.

└─ 加底線的地方為線索！

> 男：我想你會發現那個新系統很有價值。它省時，且減少用水量，也應該會增加你的收穫量。你不覺得你今年有很多收穫嗎？
> 女：也許吧。我們下個月要開始收割了。我們到時候會確定。

1 下一個行程 + 未來時間點

I have a lot of work to do tonight to prepare for tomorrow's company banquet.

預測明天會準備宴會（預測答案：Contact another colleague）

> 1 為了準備明天的公司宴會，我今晚有很多事情要做。

2 not A until B的A部分

The conference table won't arrive until next week.

下週之前桌子不會到，就是在下週之後桌子會送達的意思。因此可以預測桌子會到。

（預測答案：The table will arrive.）

> 2 那張會議桌在下週之前不會到的。

《不經過翻譯而回答詢問下一個行程的考題的方法！》

1️⃣ 在考卷上確認詢問下一個行程的核心詞彙，將此標記。
2️⃣ 預測在對話錄音的後段會出現。
3️⃣ 注意聽出現下一個行程的未來時態或未來時間點。
4️⃣ 了解下一個行程後，選出答案。

Quiz

請聽對話之後選出適當的答案。

Q5 According to the man, what will probably happen in March?

(A) A new book will be released.　(B) A new editor will be hired.

Q6 What does the man say he will do this week?

(A) Go on a business trip　(B) Read a document

攻略法23　詢問要求、建議事項的考題

若以下的單字在考題裡出現，就是詢問要求、建議、義務事項的考題
ask, request, direct, want, need, offer, suggest, recommend, encourage

What does the man **ask** the woman to do?

What does the man **request**?
What does the man **offer to do**?
What does the man **ask** for?
What does the man **ask** about?

將會聽到要求事項的核心模式

Why don't + 建議事項？
How about + 建議事項？
Would you + 要求事項？
Could you + 要求事項？
I'd like + 要求事項
Please + 要求事項
You have to + 要求事項
I recommend + 建議事項

攻略法24　詢問下一個行程的考題

若在最後一個考題裡出現以下的單字，就是詢問下一個行程的考題
do next, he will do, going to do, planing to do

What will the man probably **do next**?
What is the man **going/planning to do**?
What does the man say he **will do**?

將會聽到下一個行程的核心模式

I'll（下一個行程）
Let me（下一個行程）
Now, let's（下一個行程）
I'd better（下一個行程）
You'll have to（對方的下一個行程）

若在最後一個考題裡出現以下的單字，就是詢問下一個行程的考題
at 2 p.m., this afternoon, tonight, later today, on Monday, on December 10th, next week, in November

What does the woman say she will do tonight?

What will the speakers do this afternoon?

What is supposed to happen tomorrow morning?

將會聽到下一個行程的核心模式

未來時態(I'll...)與未來時間點(at 2 p.m., this afternoon, tonight, on Monday, on December 10th, next week, in November) 之間

Not A until B的 A 部分

例子

What does the man ask the woman to do?

(A) Buy a new computer
(B) Hire more workers

1 找出核心詞彙	man ask
2 了解類型	詢問要求事項
3 看選項	購買電腦或僱用員工
4 聽錄音來確認答案	

---

1 What does the woman ask the man to do?

(A) Give her the correct address
(B) Tell her the order number

1 找出核心詞彙
2 了解類型
3 看選項

---

2 What does the woman request?

(A) A different appointment time
(B) Directions to an office

1 找出核心詞彙
2 了解類型
3 看選項

---

3 What does the woman suggest the man do?

(A) Use another copier
(B) Call a technician

1 找出核心詞彙
2 了解類型
3 看選項

---

4 What does the woman offer to do?

(A) Get a business card
(B) Move a bookshelf

1 找出核心詞彙
2 了解類型
3 看選項

▶ 答案在解析本第061頁

5 What will the woman probably do next?

(A) Issue a refund
(B) Bring some photos

1 找出核心詞彙
2 了解類型
3 看選項

6 What will the man probably do next?

(A) Complete a form
(B) Deliver supplies

1 找出核心詞彙
2 了解類型
3 看選項

7 What will the man do this afternoon?

(A) Give a presentation
(B) Prepare for a meeting

1 找出核心詞彙
2 了解類型
3 看選項

8 What will happen on Monday?

(A) An office will be closed.
(B) An employee will be introduced.

1 找出核心詞彙
2 了解類型
3 看選項

▶ 答案在解析本第062頁

9 What does the woman ask the man to do?

    (A) Check on a delivery
    (B) Order some equipment
    (C) Make repairs

1	找出核心詞彙	
2	了解類型	
3	看選項	
4	預測對話內容	1) 要求訂購之後查詢商品送達地址。
		2) 要求修理服務之後撥打電話確認細節。

10 What will the woman probably do next?

    (A) Make a telephone call
    (B) Return some merchandise
    (C) Find an address

---

11 What does the woman ask for?

    (A) A refund
    (B) A meal
    (C) A seat change

1	找出核心詞彙	
2	了解類型	
3	看選項	
4	預測對話內容	1) 要求座位變更之後與家人確認。
		2) 填寫要求退費的表格。

12 What will the woman do next?

    (A) Complete a form
    (B) Cancel a reservation
    (C) Talk to her sister

---

13 What does the woman ask the man to do?

    (A) Put some merchandise aside
    (B) Give the woman a receipt
    (C) Mail the woman her purchase

1	找出核心詞彙	
2	了解類型	
3	看選項	
4	預測對話內容	1) 要求保管商品之後填寫名字。
		2) 要求收據之後離開商店。

14 What will the woman probably do next?

    (A) Leave the store
    (B) Read the newspaper
    (C) Write something down

▶ 答案在解析本第064頁

STEP 02 考題實戰練習　請留意前面練習過的兩個階段，進行以下的考題 答對的題目數：＿＿＿＿＿

1　Where most likely are the speakers?

(A) At a construction area
(B) In a flower shop
(C) In a factory
(D) In a grocery store

2　What are the speakers talking about?

(A) A way to reduce costs on packaging
(B) The benefits of some new equipment
(C) The construction of a building
(D) A process for ordering goods

3　According to the conversation, what will happen next week?

(A) The old system will be inspected.
(B) The display cases will be replaced.
(C) Workers will work overtime.
(D) Orders will be placed.

4　Where does the woman work?

(A) At a museum.
(B) At a mall
(C) At a bookstore
(D) At a theater

Types of tickets	Per person	Remarks
Children	$ 750	Age 13 to 17
Adult regular	$ 1,000	Adult over 18
Adult special	$ 500	Handicap caregiver
Group ticket	$ 800	Starting group of 10

* 6 free wheelchair seats for each performance

5 Look at the graphic. How much money will the man need to pay?

(A) $ 1,000
(B) $ 1,500
(C) $ 2,000
(D) $ 2,500

6　What does the woman suggest the man do?

(A) Pay by credit card
(B) Allow time to be seated
(C) Pick up the tickets ahead of time
(D) Be a caretaker

7   What are the speakers discussing?

(A) Policies for returning goods
(B) Conflict in an appointment schedule
(C) Problems with accounting software
(D) Supplies for an upcoming event

重要

8   What does the woman ask the man to do?

(A) Attend a ceremony
(B) Organize a workshop
(C) Get a refund
(D) Make a delivery

9   What does the man ask about?

(A) A file folder
(B) An itinerary
(C) A receipt
(D) A photocopier

- -

10   What is the main topic of the conversation?

(A) An upcoming meeting
(B) Revised safety regulations
(C) A new website
(D) Internet shopping

高難度

11   According to the man, what can employees of the company now do?

(A) Get a free delivery
(B) Check e-mail away from the office
(C) Apply for travel brochures
(D) Sign up for an event online

12   What does the woman say she will do on Monday?

(A) Depart for a conference
(B) Order supplies online
(C) Get approval for the budget
(D) Update the website

▶ 答案在解析本第067頁

Review Test

請邊回答以下的問題，邊複習前面所學的內容。

1 若有詢問要求事項的考題，要注意聽對話錄音的中、後半部。 ▶ _____

2 請寫出與要求事項有關的單字。 ▶ _____

3 與建議事項一起出現的三個主要說法有哪些？ ▶ _____

4 詢問下一個行程的考題平常出現在哪裡？ ▶ _____

5 請寫出詢問下一個行程的考題裡常出現的主要說法。 ▶ _____

6 請寫出在對話錄音裡與下一個行程一起出現的說法。 ▶ _____

Preview

1 仔細詢問的考題的特色

詢問對話內容的考題當中，除了在任何對話情境中都會出現的「概括性詢問」考題以外，也有「仔細詢問」的考題。「仔細詢問」的考題有以下各種特色：在特殊對話之下才會出現的、按照不同對話有不同考題類型的、聽完對話錄音還是很難回答的、答案的線索為句子而不容易找出答案的等等。

依照選項的長短，這些考題可分為兩種。第一種為「簡短選項類」。這一類考題的選項是以簡短說法的形式，但因為所有的選項都出現於對話裡面，所以即使聽完對話還是很難判斷哪個選項為正確答案。第二種為「句子選項類」。該類考題的選項為句子形式，所以光是看考題與選項本身已經不容易了。

2 有仔細詢問的考題需考慮的重點

❶ 簡短選項類考題的核心詞彙，大部分出現在考題的後面。

❷ 需要先預測考題的核心詞彙會怎麼樣呈現於對話當中。
What is the man looking for? ▶ 預測在對話裡可能會聽到find。

❸ 若沒有掌握核心詞彙，得邊專心聽各選項裡出現的數字、日子、地名等，邊確認是否為答案。

❹ 仔細詢問的考題常常有句子選項類的，所以很不容易讀完。因此，有時候視狀況需求，而只看考題然後聽對話錄音，或在選項上劃底線來趕快了解核心詞彙。

❺ 大部分的考題依照對話的進行順序出現。

攻略法
25

簡短選項類的考題

若選項為簡短說法,必須針對某些目標來聽錄音。大部分考題的最後部分為核心詞彙,若核心詞彙為時間點,在對話裡會聽到其具體的時間,若非時間點,會聽到以不同方法來呈現的說法。

選項為簡短說法的考題叫做簡短選項類考題,也就是一眼看得出來其選項為以單字或片語形式的。以下看看簡短選項考題的類型吧。

第1階段:看考卷 了解考題類型與核心詞彙

❶ 先確認選項是否為簡短說法的以及考題是詢問什麼細項的,然後在核心詞彙劃底線。核心詞彙大部分出現於考題的後面。

對象:What is the woman looking for?

時間:When is the woman's appointment?

具體的地點:Where can the woman catch the bus?

具體的人物:Who are the workers waiting for?

方法:How will the woman submit her resume?

❷ 也預測考題的核心詞彙會怎麼樣呈現於對話當中!

When is the woman's |interview|? ◄── 選項為簡短說法。是詢問時間點的,
且其核心詞彙為interview!

(A) On Sunday

(B) On Monday

(C) On Tuesday

(D) On Wednesday

> 這個女人的面試是什麼時候?
> (A) 在星期天
> (B) 在星期一
> (C) 在星期二
> (D) 在星期三

---

1 What is the woman looking for?

詢問及物動詞的受詞,就是詢問對象的考題。looking for就是核心詞彙!在對話裡可能會聽到find!

> 1 這個女人在找什麼?

2 When is the woman's appointment?

選項反正都是時間點,所以核心詞彙不是when而是appointment!可能會聽到interview等具體的約定事項!

> 2 這個女人約定的時間是什麼時候?

3 Where can the woman catch the bus?

不是詢問對話的地點,而是詢問該女生可以搭上公車的地點的考題!

> 3 這個女人在哪裡可以搭上公車?

4 Who are the workers waiting for?

不是詢問說話者是誰,而是詢問這些工作人員在等的人是誰的考題!

> 4 這些工作人員在等誰?

5 How will the woman submit her resume?

詢問提交履歷表的方法，所以在對話裡submit可能會變成turn in或send in等來呈現吧！

我們看看如此找到的核心詞彙在對話當中會以什麼樣的方式來呈現吧。很簡單！選項裡的時間點、地名、人名在對話裡會出現同樣的，而其他類的選項會以同義詞或近似詞來呈現。

🎧 13-01.mp3

第2階段：聽錄音 **選擇性地聽答案！**

❶ 先聽在考題裡標記的核心詞彙或與核心詞彙相關意思的說法，再選答案。

❷ 若沒有找出核心詞彙，邊專心聽各選項裡出現的數字、日子、地名等，邊確認是否為答案。

W: Excuse me. I need to buy a business suit for my job interview next Wednesday. Would you recommend one for me?

└─ 這就是面試時間，所以是答案！

M: I'm sorry, but we are closing in a few minutes. We'll open on early Monday morning. Why don't you visit us then?

1 looking for（或find）+ 尋找的對象

I'm looking for a book for my son's birthday next week.

looking for後面聽到的「為了兒子生日的書」。書可以改成禮物來說。（**預測答案**：A present for his son）

2 appointment 前後的時間點

The doctor can see you tomorrow afternoon at 5:30.

將appointment改成「醫生可以跟你見面」來說的。其前後的時間點為答案。（**預測答案**：5:30）

3 catch the bus 前後的地點

The bus will pick up participants here in front of the tourist center.

將「搭上公車」改成「公車在這邊載」之後，在其後面聽到的地點為答案。（**預測答案**：At the tour center）

4 waiting for 前後的人物

We've been waiting for the maintenance company to fix it for a week.

將waiting for後面聽到的「維修公司」改成「維修人員」來回答。（**預測答案**：A repairperson）

5 submit one's resume 前後的方法

I could e-mail you my resume tomorrow if that would be more convenient.

將「提交履歷表」改成「透過電子郵件寄履歷表」。（**預測答案**：By e-mail）

---

5 這個女人會怎麼樣提交她的履歷表？

女：不好意思。我為了下週三的面試得買西裝。你可以幫我介紹一套嗎？
男：抱歉，我們在幾分鐘之內要打烊了。我們在星期一一大早會開門。你那時候來訪如何？

1 我在找一本書，為了下週我兒子的生日。

2 醫生在明天下午五點半可以跟你見面。

3 那台公車會在這邊遊客中心前面載參加者。

4 我們等維修公司來修理它等一個星期了。

5 如果這樣更方便的話，我可以明天把我的履歷表透過電子郵件給你。

1 透過考題的疑問詞以及選項的單字，來確認為簡短選項考題的哪一種。

2 確認考題當中的核心詞彙，將此標記。（大部分在考題的後面）

3 預測在核心詞彙或相關意思的說法前後會出現答案。

4 留意聽同時避開不是答案的選項。

🎧 13-02.mp3

✏️ Quiz

請聽對話之後選出適當的答案。

Q1 What did the woman receive this morning?

　　(A) An order　　　　　　　(B) An e-mail

Q2 When is the woman's appointment?

　　(A) At 4:00 p.m.　　　　　(B) At 4:30 p.m.

▶ 答案在解析本第069頁

攻略法

26

選項為句子的考題

句子選項類的考題，其答案的線索以句子的形式出現於對話裡，所以得以前、中、後區分來聽對話。也就是說，第一個考題是聽對話前段的句子，第二個考題是聽對話中間的，第三個考題是聽對話後段來找答案。

仔細詢問的考題當中也會出現一種題型是，因為選項為句子，因此很不容易先看考題與選項再聽對話錄音。這些考題叫做句子選項類的仔細詢問的考題。此時，得先看考題判斷為以下那種類型，然後再去找核心詞彙。與簡短選項的仔細詢問考題一樣，其核心詞彙大部分在考題對話的後段。

第1階段：看考卷 在三秒鐘之內看出類型、核心詞彙、
與第幾個考題的方法

❶ 先了解選項是否為句子類、什麼類型的、以及核心詞彙在哪兒，再劃底線。核心詞彙大部分在後面。

理由：Why does the man need to hurry?

意見：What does the man say about the computer?

行為：What did the man do last week?

陳述：What does the woman tell the man?

❷ 判斷為第幾個考題之後，預測在對話的前、中、後面的哪裡會出現其答案。

Why does the man need to hurry? ◄— 這是句子選項類的仔細詢問的考題，且其核心詞彙為need to hurry！若是最後一題，其答案可能在對話的後面出現吧！

(A) He is late for work.

(B) Someone is waiting for him.

(C) The business will close soon.

(D) It is going to rain.

這個男人為什麼必須快點？
(A) 他晚到公司。
(B) 有人正在等他。
(C) 這家店很快打烊了。
(D) 將要下雨了。

1 Why does the man need to hurry?

這是詢問理由的考題，且need to hurry為其核心詞彙！「快點」前後有答案！

1 這個男人為什麼必須快點？

2 What does the man say about the computer?

有say about，所以是詢問意見的考題。表達該男生對電腦的意見的句子為答案。

2 有關這台電腦，這個男人說什麼？

3 What did the man do last week?

有do，所以是詢問行為的考題，且last week為很好的線索。

3 這個男人上週做了什麼？

4 What does the woman tell the man?

找不出線索的最難的考題！答案可能在對話的前、中、後面。

與簡短選項考題一樣，找出來的核心詞彙若為時間點、地點、人名，在對話裡會以同樣的詞彙出現；若找出來是其他類的核心詞彙，會以類似的說法來出現。但是，萬一很不容易發現核心詞彙，就得在對話裡依照考題的順序搜尋答案。例如，是在第二個考題找不到核心詞彙，那麼這個題目的線索應該會在對話的中段。

🎧 13-03.mp3

第2階段：聽錄音 **選擇性地聽答案！**

❶ 針對各類型的核心詞彙或核心詞彙相關說法前後出現的理由、意見、行為等句子特別注意聽。

❷ 依照考題的順序來聽對話的前、中、後的部分。

- -

M : I'm looking for a place to withdraw some cash. Do you know if there's a bank nearby?

W : There's one on Lake Street, right across this street. But **you'll have to hurry** because it closes at 5:00 p.m.

└── 這個就是理由（need to hurry變化成you'll have to hurry，理由就是在其後面出現的內容。）

男：我正在找提款的地方。你知道這附近有沒有銀行？
女：雷克街上有一家，在這條馬路對面。不過你應該要快點，因為它在下午五點打烊。

---

1 need to hurry前後的理由

I'm in a rush because I'm running late for an important interview.

使用類似的說法in a rush之後，後面的「面試遲到」改成「有面試」來回答。
（預測答案：He has an interview.）

1 我在趕時間，因為一場很重要的面試快遲到了。

2 computer前後的意見

The computer isn't in stock, but I can do a special order for you.

將「沒有庫存，但可以下特別訂單」改成被動語態。（預測答案：It can be ordered.）

2 這台電腦不在庫存中，不過我可以為你下特別訂單。

3 last week前後的行為

How was your trip last week? You were visiting our office in Spain, weren't you?

若是有時間點，在對話和選項裡會出現一致的說法。將「訪問了我們的辦公室」改成「訪問了別的辦公室」來回答。（預測答案：Visited a different office）

3 上週你的旅行怎麼樣？你訪問了我們西班牙的辦公室，是吧？

4 一組（三個考題）當中的第三題，注意聽對話的後段

The food is excellent, but the service is very slow.

沒有核心詞彙，所以很難找出線索的考題。若是第三題，其線索可能在對話的後段。「服務很慢」的意思就是「服務很差」。（預測答案：The service is poor.）

4 食物無與倫比地好，但是服務很慢。

《不經過翻譯就能回答句子選項類仔細詢問的方法！》

1 透過考題的疑問詞及選項的句子，判斷為句子選項類仔細詢問的考題當中哪一型。

2 在考題當中找出核心詞彙，將此標記。（大部分在考題的後段）

3 預測該核心詞彙或相關意思說法的前後會出現答案。

4 依照考題的順序聽對話前、中、後的部分，選出答案。

🎧 13-04.mp3

✏️Quiz

請聽對話之後選出適當的答案。

Q3 Why should the woman hurry?

   (A) Someone is waiting for her.　　(B) The fruit will be out of stock soon.

Q4 What does the woman say about a registration fee?

   (A) It will be paid by the company.　(B) It is due in January.

▶ 答案在解析本第069頁

攻略法25 簡短選項類的考題

若選項為簡短說法,先得了解類型與核心詞彙,然後針對此聽核心詞彙或核心詞彙變化過的部分!

looking for, appointment, catch the bus, waiting for, submit his/her resume

在考題上先標記核心詞彙或與其核心詞彙意思相關的說法,然後針對此聽其前後內容。若找不出核心詞彙,專心聽並判斷在各選項裡出現的數字、日子、地點等是否為答案。

What is the woman looking for?(對象)

When is the woman's appointment?
(時間)

Where can the woman catch the bus?
(具體地點)

Who are the workers waiting for?
(具體人物)

How will the woman submit her resume?
(方法)

looking for + 尋找的對象

appointment 前後內容出現的時間點

catch the bus 前後內容出現的地點

waiting for 前後內容出現的人物

submit her resume 前後內容出現的方法

攻略法26　選項為句子的考題

若選項為句子，先得了解其類型與核心詞彙，然後針對核心詞彙或將核心詞彙變化的說法來聽。

針對核心詞彙或與核心詞彙意思相關的說法的前後內容來聽。但如果不太能找出核心詞彙的話，就要依照考題的順序，在對話前、中、後的部分找出各題的線索。

Why does the man need to hurry?
（理由）

need to hurry 前後內容出現的理由

What does the man say about the computer?（意見）

computer 前後內容出現的意見

What did the man do last week?（行為）

last week 前後內容出現的行為

What does the woman tell the man?
（陳述）

一組（三個考題）當中的第三題，注意聽對話的後段

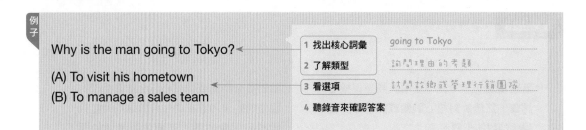

例子

Why is the man going to Tokyo?

(A) To visit his hometown
(B) To manage a sales team

1 找出核心詞彙 going to Tokyo
2 了解類型 詢問理由的考題
3 看選項 訪問故鄉或管理行銷團隊
4 聽錄音來確認答案

---

1 What does the woman say about the presentation?

(A) It was well done.
(B) It was sent to the company president.

1 找出核心詞彙 ......
2 了解類型 ......
3 看選項 ......

---

2 How will the woman most likely get to her destination?

(A) By taxi
(B) On foot

1 找出核心詞彙 ......
2 了解類型 ......
3 看選項 ......

---

3 What time will the speakers most likely leave work?

(A) At 6:00 p.m.
(B) At 7:00 p.m.

1 找出核心詞彙 ......
2 了解類型 ......
3 看選項 ......

---

4 Who is Mario Ortiz?

(A) A designer
(B) A manufacturer

1 找出核心詞彙 ......
2 了解類型 ......
3 看選項 ......

▶ 答案在解析本第070頁

5 Where is the woman planning to go on Saturday?

(A) To the opera
(B) To the art museum

1 找出核心詞彙 ....
2 了解類型 ....
3 看選項 ....

6 Why did the woman arrive late?

(A) She had the wrong schedule.
(B) Her flight was delayed.

1 找出核心詞彙 ....
2 了解類型 ....
3 看選項 ....

7 According to the woman, what must be completed?

(A) A training program
(B) Office renovations

1 找出核心詞彙 ....
2 了解類型 ....
3 看選項 ....

8 What does the woman say she did last week?

(A) Sent a large package
(B) Ordered software

1 找出核心詞彙 ....
2 了解類型 ....
3 看選項 ....

▶ 答案在解析本第071頁

9 Why is the woman surprised?

(A) There has been a schedule change.
(B) There are no seats left.
(C) There is no direct service.

10 How many tickets does the woman wish to purchase?

(A) One
(B) Two
(C) Six

1 找出核心詞彙	
2 了解類型	
3 看選項	
4 預測對話內容	1）訝異沒有直航班機，因此購買需轉機的機票。
	2）訝異沒有機位，因此購買別的時間的機票。

11 What is the president currently working on?

(A) A business merger
(B) A conference presentation
(C) A construction project

12 Why does the man thank the woman?

(A) For recommending him to the president
(B) For extending the deadline on his report
(C) For offering him some advice

1 找出核心詞彙	
2 了解類型	
3 看選項	
4 預測對話內容	1）老闆正在製作報告資料當中，幫忙了他而表達感謝。
	2）老闆正在進行建築個案當中，因為將他推薦給老闆而表達感謝。

13 Who are the workers waiting for?

(A) A business client
(B) An office manager
(C) A repairperson

14 How long have they been waiting?

(A) One hour
(B) Two hours
(C) Three hours

1 找出核心詞彙	
2 了解類型	
3 看選項	
4 預測對話內容	1）等客人等了一個小時。
	2）等修理工等了三個小時。

▶ 答案在解析本第072頁

STEP 02 考題實戰練習　請留意前面練習過的兩個階段，進行以下的考題　答對的題目數：＿＿＿＿＿

1　Why did Marsha request that the meeting be postponed?

(A) She is waiting for a client.
(B) She was out of the town.
(C) Some information was delayed.
(D) No meeting room was available.

重要
2　When will the meeting most likely be held?

(A) On Wednesday morning
(B) On Wednesday afternoon
(C) On Thursday morning
(D) On Thursday afternoon

3　What will the man most likely do next?

(A) Make a travel schedule
(B) Prepare a sales report
(C) Look for research data
(D) Try to contact Marsha

4　Which department needs a new manager?

(A) Personnel
(B) Customer service
(C) Accounting
(D) Marketing

5　What qualification does the man mention?

(A) Willingness to travel
(B) Strong references
(C) Relevant experience
(D) A university degree

6　What does the woman recommend?

(A) Contacting a possible candidate
(B) Transferring to another branch
(C) Placing an advertisement on the Internet
(D) Rescheduling some interviews

▶ 答案在解析本第074頁

7 Why does the woman want to talk to the man?

(A) To discuss customer satisfaction
(B) To request a transfer
(C) To ask for a recommendation
(D) To submit her resignation

8 Where do the speakers most likely work?

(A) At a travel agency
(B) At an advertising firm
(C) At a design school
(D) At a clothing company

9 What does the woman say about New York?

(A) Her family lives there.
(B) It has many tourist attractions.
(C) It has a lot of clothing stores.
(D) It has a school she wants to go to.

---

10 What has caused the delay?

(A) The restaurant is understaffed.
(B) The chef is late for work.
(C) The servers are chatting.
(D) The waiters are on strike.

新

11 Look at the graphic, which dish does the woman order?

(A) Chicken Teriyaki w / Rice
(B) Vegetable Yakisoba
(C) Tempura w / Rice
(D) California Roll

Yokoi Restaurant	
Lunch Specials	
1. Chicken Teriyaki w / Rice	$17
2. Vegetable Yakisoba	$15
3. Tempura w / Rice	$16
4. California Roll	$18

12 What does the woman imply about the restaurant?

(A) The waiters are always slow.
(B) It has a good reputation.
(C) Air conditioning is cold.
(D) The food isn't very good.

與公司相關的對話
有關公司會出現這些考題！

在Part 3裡，除了有在任何對話之下都會普遍出現的考題，也有關於特定對話仔細詢問的考題。這種仔細詢問的考題幾乎都不可能先聽完再回答，所以得邊找出核心詞彙邊看選項，然後有選擇性地找出答案。請進行以下的小考，再確認所學過的內容。

1 若選項以yesterday、today、tomorrow出現，這是什麼
　類型的考題？　　　　　　　　　　　　　　　　　▶ ....

2 若選項為長句，這是什麼類型的考題？　　　　　　▶ ....

3 簡短選項的仔細詢問考題總共有幾個類型？　　　　▶ ....

4 句子選項的仔細詢問考題總共有幾個類型？　　　　▶ ....

5 在 What does the man say about the book? 裡，核心
　語為哪個？　　　　　　　　　　　　　　　　　　▶ ....

6 在 Who are the workers waiting for? 裡，核心詞彙為哪個？　▶ ....

1 與公司相關對話的特色

Part 3的對話內容為與公司生活相關，以及和其他特定場所（例如商店、銀行、藥局、郵局、理髮店、飯店、修理廠）有關的對話。與公司相關的內容會出現公司外面的事情，如：訂票／開票、通勤／交通／搜尋、訂貨／配送、故障／修理／維修／改善等；以及公司內部的事情，如：會議／活動、僱傭／升遷、人事業務等與情相關的內容。

2 有與公司相關對話需考慮的重點

❶ Part 3的80%以上為與公司生活相關的對話。因為是一般很熟悉的主題，所以要習慣聽了對話的一部分後，就能預測到剩下的內容。

❷ 看考題與選項的話，大部分都能判斷是否為公司相關的主題。此時，邊看選項邊預測大約兩個答案比較有利做答。

❸ 在各種對話主題之下有其固定出現的核心詞彙。

❹ 學習與公司相關的對話內容，對之後Part 4獨白題的學習也會有幫助，因為其主題相似且出現的詞彙也接近，能更容易累積背景知識。

攻略法 **27**

與公司外面的事情相關的考題

對熟悉的主題會更容易聽得懂，這是理所當然的。但並不是聽完後才開始了解主題，而是在看考題與選項的時候先預測主題，然後再聽對話，就會更容易聽得懂。

與公司外面的事情相關的內容是指出差或產品有關的對話內容，透過考題也能知道對話主題會不會與公司外面的事情相關。若考題裡有 problem，在聽對話之前就可以預測到大部分是與「故障、修理、維修、改善」相關的主題。

第1階段：看考卷 邊看考題與選項，邊預測對話主題

❶ Why is the man calling the restaurant?
　Where is the woman's final destination?：「訂位、訂票」為主體

❷ How did the man get to work?
　What is the woman looking for?：「通勤、交通、搜尋」為主體

❸ Why was the shipment delayed?
　When is the delivery expected to arrive?：「訂貨、配送」為主體

❹ What problem does the woman describe?
　Where is the serial number located?：「故障、修理、維修、改善」為主體

- -

Why is the man calling the restaurant? ← 「訂票/開票」為主體！

(A) To deliver some groceries
(B) To make a reservation
(C) To complain about the service
(D) To change an appointment

---

1 How many tickets does the woman wish to purchase?
希望購買ticket，所以可能是有關「訂位、訂票」的主題！

2 Where is Mr. Tanaka's office located?
這是正在尋找田中先生辦公室的狀況！

3 When did the woman first notice a problem?
「察覺問題」，所以是因為什麼東西故障了，所以想要修理的內容！

4 What will the man do when he receives the woman's package?
「收包裹」，所以是有關「訂貨、配送」的內容！

右側註解：
這個男人為什麼打電話給這家餐廳？
這個女人的最終的目的地是哪裡？
這個男人怎麼去上班？
這個女人正在尋找什麼？
出貨為什麼被延遲的？
配送物預計什麼時候會到達？
這個女人描述了什麼問題？
那個編號位在哪裡？

這個男人為什麼打電話給這家餐廳？
(A) 為了配送一些食品
(B) 為了訂位
(C) 為了抱怨服務
(D) 為了變更預約的時間

1 這個女人希望購買幾張票？

2 田中先生的辦公室位於哪裡？

3 這個女人什麼時候第一次察覺問題的？

4 這個男人在收到這個女人的包裹的時候會做什麼？

若看著考題與選項已經似乎預測到了對話的主題，再透過各種主題之下的核心詞彙來聽對話，更有助於容易了解其內容。舉例來說，在主題為「訂票／開票」時，在對話裡常會聽到reservation、ticket、available等詞彙。若已經先知道了這些核心詞彙，就更容易了解對話內容。這些各種主題之下的核心詞彙也常出現於考題與選項中。

第2階段：聽錄音 **聽主題類別的核心詞彙後，再了解內容**

❶ 訂位、訂票
reservation, book, reserve, available, an aisle seat, cancellation

❷ 通勤、交通、搜尋
looking for, find, nearby, located, a five-minute walk

❸ 訂貨、配送
order, deliver, shipment, sent out, pick up, office supply

❹ 故障、修理、維修、改善
working, repair, fix, trouble, broken, out of paper

預訂，預訂，預訂，可用，靠走道的座位，取消
尋找，發現，附近，位於，步行五分鐘的距離
訂貨，配送，出貨，送出去，取貨，辦公用品
作業，維修，修理，問題，壞掉，缺紙

---

1 與訂位、訂票相關主題的對話範本

🎧 14-01.mp3

W: Hello, I'd like to make a reservation for dinner for tomorrow night.
M: Sure. How many people are you expecting?
W: There will be 10 people in our group. I wonder if you could put us down for 7 o'clock.
M: Let me check. I'm afraid we don't have any large table in the main dining area available at dinner time that day. You may call back tomorrow to see if there'll be any cancellations.

劃底線的部分是為幫助你了解「訂位、訂票」主題對話的核心詞彙！

女：您好。我想訂明天晚餐時的位置。
男：當然可以。你預估會有幾個人？
女：我們團裡會有十個人。我想知道你可否幫我們訂七點。
男：讓我看看。很抱歉我們在主餐廳區沒有任何那天晚餐可用的大餐桌。你可以明天回撥電話，看看有沒有別人取消。

若預測到了「訂位、訂票」為主體，能透過make a reservation、put 人 down for、available、large table、cancellation等詞彙，更容易了解內容！

2 與通勤、交通、尋找相關主題的對話範本

🎧 14-02.mp3

M: Excuse me. I'm looking for Allied Corporation. Is it close by?

W: No, it's on the other side of the town. It's about a 30-minute walk from here.

M: Oh, no. I have a job interview there starting in 15 minutes. I'm probably going to be late. Do you know if there's a bus I could take?

W: Well, we're not really near a bus route, but there is a nearby train station. That'll be the fastest way to get to the company. Just go three stops towards Center City.

男：不好意思。我正在找聯合公司。它在附近嗎？

女：不是。它在城市的另一邊。離這裡走路要三十分鐘。

男：啊，不行。我有一場求職面試是十五分鐘之內開始的。我可能會遲到。你知道我能搭什麼公車嗎？

女：我們其實不在公車路線附近，不過有很近的火車站。這應該是到那家公司的最快的方法。只要往中心都市的方向走三個紅綠燈吧。

若預測到了「通勤、交通、尋找」為主體，透過 looking for, 30 minute walk, bus, nearby, train station, fastest way, get to the company 等詞彙，能更容易了解對話內容！

3 與訂貨、配送相關主題的對話範本

🎧 14-03.mp3

W: Hi, my name is Lisa Barman. I am calling about a delivery from your store.

M: Let me check. According to our records, you ordered several office supplies. They are supposed to be delivered on April 4th.

W: But I can't pick them up on that day. I will be out of the town. I was told that they'd be here on the 2nd.

M: Let me tell my manager about this and get back to you right away.

女：您好，我的名字是麗莎・巴曼。我打電話來是有關從你們店裡來的配送。

男：讓我確認一下。根據我們的紀錄，您訂了一些事務用品。它們應該於四月四日被配送。

女：但是我無法在那天領取它們。我不會在城市內。我被告知它們會在二日的時候到這裡。

男：讓我告訴經理關於這件事，然後立刻回電給你。

若預測到了「訂貨、配送」為主體，透過 delivery, ordered, office supply, pick up 等詞彙，能更容易了解對話內容！

4 與故障、修理、維修、改善相關主題的對話範本

🎧 14-04.mp3

M: My laptop doesn't start. This is the fifth time it broke down. I think it has so many problems.

W: Why don't you call a technician to fix it?

M: I tried, but I think I should start looking for a new laptop. Do you know where I can get a good deal?

W: There's an excellent website you need to check out. The prices are reasonable, and it has a large collection of laptops.

男：我的筆記型電腦不能開機了。這是它第五次壞掉。我想它有非常多問題。

女：你為什麼不打電話給技師來修理它？

男：我試過了，但是我想我應該開始找一台新筆記型電腦。你知道我在哪裡可以買到好價錢的嗎？

女：有一個非常棒的網站你得去看看。價格很合理，而且它有很多種類的筆記型電腦。

若預測到了「故障、修理、維修、改善」為主體，透過 doesn't start, broke down, problems, technician, fix 等詞彙，能更容易了解對話內容！

與公司外面的事情相關的句子

🎧 14-05.mp3

1 Have you booked a place for our 50th anniversary party?
詢問訂位與否，所以是「訂位、訂票」類的主題呢！

你訂我們五十週年慶典的場地了嗎？

2 Could you give me a lift to Osaka for the regional sales meeting on Monday? 請別人開車送到特定地點，所以是「通勤、交通、尋找」為主體！

你星期一可以載我到大阪參加地區行銷會議嗎？

3 I'm expecting a package to be delivered here, but it hasn't arrived yet.
有要送過來的包裹的內容，所以是與「訂貨、配送」相關的！

我正在等包裹送到這裡，不過它還沒到達。

4 Hi, I've been having some difficulties accessing my e-mail.
進入電子郵件系統有問題，所以是與「故障、修理、維修、改善」相關的主題！

您好。我在登入我的電子郵件系統時有一些困難。

《不經過翻譯就能回答與公司外面事情相關的方法！》

1 看考題時確認是否有可以預測特定主題的說法。
2 看選項時更具體地想自己所預測的主題。
3 依照預測到的主題，選出兩個左右的預測答案。
4 聽對話時，透過各種主題之下的核心詞彙來提高理解程度。

🎧 14-06.mp3

✎ Quiz

請聽對話之後選出適當的答案。

Q1 Why are the speakers going to New York?

(A) To visit some attractions　　(B) To attend a conference

Q2 What problem does the man mention?

(A) Some workers have left early.　　(B) The projector is out of order.

▶ 答案在解析本第077頁

與公司外面事情相關的核心詞彙匯整

訂位、訂票

book / reserve 預訂
make a reservation 預訂
cancel the reservation 取消預訂
room rate 客房價錢
available （客房或場地等）可用的
be 2 miles away from 離～兩英里的距離
connecting flight 銜接航班
transfer 轉乘

round trip ticket 來回票
the rates vary 費用多樣化
private dinning room （餐廳的）個人用餐區
boarding pass 登機證
fit you in at 2 幫你訂位兩點
a window or an aisle seat 窗邊或走道邊的座位
regular rate 一般費用
timetable 時間表

通勤、交通、尋找

look for / find 尋找／找
give... a ride 載某人一程
missing 遺失的
locate 找到…的位置
Have you seen... ? 你看過…嗎？
leave... on his desk 將…留在他的桌上
misplace 放錯位置
running a little late 有一點延遲

try to reach 想要和…聯絡
a five-minute walk 五分鐘的步行
nearby 附近的
only a short distance to work 到公司很短的距離
The street is blocked. 道路封鎖。
the map says 根據地圖
just around the corner 就在轉角
be located 位於

訂貨、配送

mail the package 寄送包裹
deliver 配送
The shipment has arrived. 貨物到了。
order = place an order for 訂貨
the order 訂的東西
pick up 領取
have a lot of stops to make 有很多得停留的地方
on the way 在路上

office supply 辦公用品
printing company 印刷公司
send out 寄出去
The package is fragile. 這是易碎包裹。
delivery confirmation service 配送確認服務
process your order 處理你的訂單
check the status of the order 查看訂單的狀況
delivery in 2 business days 兩個工作天之內配送

故障、修理、維修、改善

trouble / difficult / hard time 問題／困難／不順的時候
user manual/ instruction 使用指南
online directions 線上指南
work properly 正常運作
repair technician 維修技師
take a look at / check it out （暫時）查看
fix = repair 修理
leaking 漏水的

broken / out of order 故障
break (down) 故障
replace the cracked headlight 更換龜裂的大燈
maintenance 維修
customer service department 客服部門
out of stock 沒有庫存的
warehouse 倉庫
install new software 安裝新的軟體

攻略法 28

與公司內部事情相關的主題

公司生活中除了有公司外面的業務，也有公司內部的事情。考題裡尤其常出現與會議相關的內容，例如：安排會議時間、會議前的準備、會議內容本身等等。

與公司內部事情相關內容是指會議或人事業務有關的。透過考題也能判斷是否為與公司內部的事情相關的主題。例如，若有interview一詞，在聽對話前也可以預測大部分是與「僱用、升遷、人事變動」相關的主題。

第1階段：看考卷 **看考題與選項時預測對話主題**

❶ When is the meeting scheduled to begin?
   Why will the meeting be postponed?：「準備會議、安排時間」為主題

❷ What does the woman plan to discuss at the meeting?
   What do they think about the meeting?：「會議內容」為主題

❸ How many applicants will be interviewed?
   What position is the woman applying for?：「僱用、升遷」為主題

❹ What should the man do to get reimbursed?
   Why has the payment been delayed?：「薪水、費用」為主題

> 會議預計什麼時候開始？
> 會議為什麼會延期？
> 這個女人在會議時計劃討論什麼？
> 他們對那場會議有什麼想法？
> 有幾個申請者要面試？
> 這個女人申請什麼職位？
> 為了退款這個男人該做什麼？
> 這次付款為什麼延遲？

- -

What position does the woman apply for? ←「僱用、升遷」為主題！

(A) A receptionist   (B) A nurse
(C) A hotel manager   (D) A housekeeper

> 這個女人申請什麼職位？
> (A) 接待員
> (B) 護士
> (C) 飯店管理者
> (D) 管家

---

1 When does Mr. Kentel want to meet with the woman?
   想安排會議時間的狀況，所以是「準備會議、安排時間」為主題！

2 What is the purpose of the meeting?
   詢問會議的目的的問題，所以是「會議內容」為主題！

3 How will the man most likely submit his resume?
   出現提交履歷表的說法，所以能知道「僱用、升遷」為主題！

4 When do they need the money?
   與錢相關的內容的話，可能是「薪水、費用」的主題吧！

> 1 肯特爾先生想要什麼時候和這個女人見面？
> 2 這場會議的目的是什麼？
> 3 這個男人很有可能如何提交他的履歷表？
> 4 他們什麼時候需要錢？

透過考題已經似乎預測到了主題，接著要想核心詞彙為何，因為各主題之下的核心詞彙大部分是固定的。先知道核心詞彙，看選項預測對話內容時會有幫助，而且更容易聽得懂對話。

第2階段：聽錄音 先聽各主題之下的核心詞彙，再去了解內容

❶ 準備會議、安排時間
meeting, arrange, make an appointment, caterer, extra seat

> 會議，安排，預約見面時間，外燴業者，多餘的座位

❷ 會議內容
agenda, take notes, strategy, instructor, presentation

> 會議事項，寫筆記，策略，講師，報告

❸ 僱用、升遷
interview, promote, transfer, application form, resume

> 面試，升遷，調職，申請表格，履歷表

❹ 薪水、費用
paycheck, budget, expense, reduce, reimburse, approve

> 薪水支票，預算，費用，減少，退費，許可

---

1 與準備會議、安排時間相關主題的對話範本

🎧 14-07.mp3

W: Do you know how many people we can comfortably seat in the conference room?

M: Usually that room is for twelve, but we can fit a few more people in there if necessary.

W: That's very good. Can you put in two more chairs? New recruits are expected to attend the meeting this time. So there'll be fourteen of us.

M: Sure. I'll ask for the extra seats right away.

> 女：你知道在這個會議室裡我們能舒服地容納多少人嗎？
> 男：通常那個房間是提供給十二個人的，但是如果有需要可以再多安置一點點人。
> 女：那太好了。你能多放兩張椅子嗎？新進人員將要參加這次的會議。所以我們將會有十四位。
> 男：當然。我將會立刻要求額外的座位。

若預測到以「準備會議、安排時間」為主體，透過 seat, conference room, chairs, attend the meeting, extra seats 等的詞彙，更容易了解對話內容！

2 與會議內容相關主題的對話範本

🎧 14-08.mp3

W: Hi, John. How was the <u>presentation</u> made by the sales director last Tuesday?

M: I found it <u>well-organized</u>. I learned a lot about how to attract potential customers efficiently and also about how to boost sales in both domestic and overseas market.

W: I liked it, but it was <u>a bit long</u>. He could have made it more <u>brief and to the point</u>.

M: That's true. I missed an important meeting because it ended much later than it was expected to.

女：您好，約翰。上週二銷售主管做的報告如何？

男：我覺得組織得很好。我學到很多關於如何有效吸引潛在客戶，以及如何在國內和海外市場大幅增加銷售量。

女：我喜歡這個，但是報告有點太久了。他其實可以讓它更簡短地說重點。

男：那是真的。因為它比原本預期的結束得更晚，我錯過了一場重要的會議。

若預測到了「會議內容」為主體，透過 presentaiton, well-organized, a bit long, brief and to the point 等的詞彙，更容易了解對話內容！

3 僱用、升遷相關主題的對話範本

🎧 14-09.mp3

M: Hi, this is John Franklin. I <u>applied for</u> a nursing <u>position</u> in Dr. Houston's office two weeks ago. Has someone been <u>hired</u> for the <u>position</u> yet?

W: No, Mr. Franklin. Actually, I was just about to call you for an <u>interview</u>. Can you come in this week, some time between Tuesday and Friday?

M: Sure, Wednesday works for me.

W: Okay. When you come in, just ask the receptionist where you can find the <u>hiring manager</u>, Mr. Lin.

男：您好，我是約翰‧法蘭克林。兩週前我申請了休士頓醫師辦公室的護士職位。這個職位已有人被僱用了嗎？

女：沒有，法蘭克林先生。有關於面試，我正要打電話給你。這週星期二到星期五之間你能過來嗎？

男：當然，星期三對我而言很好。

女：好。當你來的時候，只要問接待員在哪兒可以找到僱用經理林先生。

若預測到了「僱用、升遷」為主體，透過 applied for, position, hired, interview, hiring manager 等的詞彙，更容易了解對話內容！

4 與薪水、費用相關主題的對話範本

🎧 14-10.mp3

> M: Hello. This is Ronald Richards in the marketing department. I'm calling about my paycheck. I haven't received it for the last pay period.
>
> W: Let me see. Our records say it was sent to your home address last Friday. Haven't you received it yet?
>
> M: No, not yet. Is there anything I can do? A week has already passed.
>
> W: Well, in case of a delay like this, we can stop payment on the original check and issue a new one. You could pick it up in the payroll department later today.

若預測到了「薪水、費用」為主體，透過 paycheck, payment, payroll department 等詞彙，更容易了解對話內容！

男：您好。我是行銷部門的雷諾‧理查。我打電話來是有關於我的薪水支票。我沒有在上次的付款期收到它。

女：讓我看看。我們的紀錄是它上星期五已經寄到你的住家地址了。你還沒有收到嗎？

男：不，還沒。有任何事是我可以做的嗎？已經過了一週了。

女：好，假使像這樣的延遲，我們可以止付原來的支票，並且發出一張新的。今天稍晚你可以在支薪辦公室領取它。

與公司內部事情相關的句子

🎧 14-11.mp3

1 How many people have signed up for the seminar?
「為了研討會報名」，所以是「準備會議、安排時間」為主題！

2 Why do you think our new phone sales went down sharply last quarter?
透過「銷售量減少」，可以知道是「策略會議」的一部分內容！

3 According to your resume, you have a great deal of experience.
透過「履歷表」、「經驗」的核心詞彙，可以知道是「僱用、升遷」為主題！

4 Will the company reimburse me for my trip expenses this time?
看「付還出差費用」，就知道是「薪水、費用」的主題！

1 那場研討會有幾個人報名了？

2 你覺得我們新款電話的銷售量在上一季為什麼銳減？

3 根據你的履歷表，你有相當豐富的經驗。

4 這次公司會付還給我出差費用嗎？

1 將各主題之下的核心詞彙和句子範本全部都記下來。

2 熟悉各種考題的對話。

3 多看在Part 7常出現的電子郵件、信件、備忘錄等的文章，累積背景知識。

4 模擬或真實考試之後，自行分析對話內容且分類主題來學習。

🎧 14-12.mp3

✏️ Quiz

請聽對話之後選出適當的答案。

Q3 What is the purpose of the meeting?

(A) How to reduce expenses   (B) How to draw up a budget

Q4 What is stated about Ms. Sato?

(A) She's been promoted.   (B) She has been hired recently.

▶ 答案在解析本第077頁

與公司內部事情相關的核心詞彙總匯

準備會議、安排時間

seating arrangement 座位安排

add extra seat 增加額外的座位

sign up for / register for 報名

keynote speaker 主要演講者

auditorium 演講廳

performance 表演

set up a projector 安裝投影機

caterer 外燴業者

attend / participate / join 參加

The conference room is ready. 會議室準備好了。

have luck finding a place 運氣好找到場地

schedule a time 預訂時間

reschedule a meeting 重新預訂時間

confirm a day 確認日子

get to know each other 互相認識

make an appointment 預訂見面時間

會議內容

agenda 會議議程

take notes 做筆記

try a different sales strategy 嘗試一種不同的行銷策略

well-organized 井井有條的

instructor / speaker 講師／演講者

interesting / informative 有趣的／教育性的

boring / long 無聊的／漫長的

workshop for new managers 為了新任經理的講習

brief and to the point 簡短又中肯

wrap up a contract 完成合約

give a presentation 報告

report on 關於…報告

That's a good point. 這是個好論點。

pricing issue 價錢相關議題

sales went down 銷售量減少了

does not appeal to customers 不吸引消費者

僱用、升遷

personnel department 人事部門

human resources department 人力資源管理部門

orientation 歡迎會

(job) opening 職缺

job candidate 求職者

application form 申請表格

resume / reference letter 履歷表／推薦函

employ = hire = recruit 僱用

take the position 擔任職位

be promoted 被升遷

apply for a job 申請職位

start out 開始

schedule an interview 安排面試時間

conduct an interview 進行面試

expand the department 擴大部門

part-time position 臨時職位

薪水、費用

payroll department 薪資管理部門

expense 費用

reimburse 償還

travel allowance 旅行經費

overspent 超過消費的

stay within the budget 留在預算範圍之內

issue paychecks 發薪水支票

paid vacation 有薪休假

approve the budget 許可預算

benefits package 福利制度

work extended hours 加班

pay overtime 付加班費

cost reduction 費用減少

cut back on costs / spending 減少費用

expense report 開銷報表

limit travel expenses 限制旅行經費

攻略法27　與公司外面事情相關的考題

看考題與選項時預測對話的主題

Why is the man calling the restaurant?
Where is the woman's final destination?
- 「訂位、訂票」為主題

How did the man get to work?
What is the woman looking for?
- 「通勤、交通、搜尋」為主題

Why was the shipment delayed?
When is the delivery expected to arrive?
- 「訂貨、配送」為主題

What problem does the woman describe?
Where is the serial number located?
- 「故障、修理、維修、改善」為主題

透過各主題之下的核心詞彙，提高對公司外面事情相關對話的理解程度！

訂位、訂票：
reservation, book, reserve, available, an aisle seat, cancellation

通勤、交通／尋找：
looking for, find, nearby, located, a five-minute walk

訂貨、配送：
order, deliver, shipment, send out, pick up, office supplies

故障、修理、維修、改善：
working, repair, fix, trouble, broken, out of paper

攻略法28　與公司內部事情相關的考題

看考題與選項時預測對話的主題

When is the meeting scheduled to begin?
Why will the meeting be postponed?
- 「準備會議、安排時間」為主題

What does the woman plan to discuss at the meeting?
What do they think about the meeting?
- 「會議內容」為主題

How many applicants will be interviewed?
What position is the woman applying for?
- 「僱用、升遷」為主題

What should the man do to get reimbursed?
Why has the payment been delayed?
- 「薪水、費用」為主題

透過各主題之下的核心詞彙，提高對公司內部事情相關對話的理解程度！

準備會議、安排時間：
meeting, arrange, make an appointment, caterer, extra seat

會議內容：
agenda, take notes, strategy, instructor, presentation

僱用、升遷：
interview, promote, transfer, application form, resume

薪水、費用：
paycheck, budget, expense, reduce, reimburse, approve

例子

Why is the man calling the restaurant?

(A) To deliver some groceries
(B) To make a reservation

1 找出核心詞彙   calling the restaurant
2 了解類型   訂貨、配送
3 看選項   配送食物或訂位
4 聽錄音來確認答案

---

1 What does the man want to do?

(A) Purchase a round-trip ticket
(B) Order a travel book

1 找出核心詞彙
2 了解類型
3 看選項

---

2 Why was the man late to work?

(A) He was in a car accident.
(B) A road was closed.

1 找出核心詞彙
2 了解類型
3 看選項

---

3 What do the speakers suggest about
their products?

(A) They can be ordered online.
(B) They are reasonably priced.

1 找出核心詞彙
2 了解類型
3 看選項

---

4 What is the problem with the copier?

(A) The copies are too dark.
(B) It will not print on two sides.

1 找出核心詞彙
2 了解類型
3 看選項

▶ 答案在解析本第078頁

5　When is the meeting with the customers?

(A) Today
(B) Tomorrow

1　找出核心詞彙 ....

2　了解類型 ....

3　看選項 ....

6　What was the main topic of the seminar?

(A) Internet banking
(B) Advertising trends

1　找出核心詞彙 ....

2　了解類型 ....

3　看選項 ....

7　Why is Ms. Adler going to Hong Kong office?

(A) To visit a rival company
(B) To manage a sales team

1　找出核心詞彙 ....

2　了解類型 ....

3　看選項 ....

8　Why does the man want to talk to Ms. Sato?

(A) To discuss his employee benefits
(B) To discuss a pay raise

1　找出核心詞彙 ....

2　了解類型 ....

3　看選項 ....

9 Who most likely is the woman?

(A) A travel agent

(B) A ticket salesperson

(C) A security guard

10 What does the man want to do?

(A) See a movie

(B) Attend a performance

(C) Make travel arrangements

1 找出核心詞彙	
2 了解類型	
3 看選項	
4 預測對話內容	1）男人想買表演入場卷而和賣票的人對話。
	2）男人進去看電影時向警衛詢問路。

11 What are the speakers discussing?

(A) A shipping charge

(B) A damaged part

(C) The delivery of orders

12 What does the man say he will do immediately?

(A) Deliver a message

(B) Ship some merchandise

(C) Locate the missing item

1 找出核心詞彙	
2 了解類型	
3 看選項	
4 預測對話內容	1）說運費太貴，將此內容傳達給上面的人。
	2）配送上有問題，要求再次寄。

13 What position are the candidates applying for?

(A) Personnel manager

(B) Research analyst

(C) Assistant editor

14 How many applicants will be interviewed?

(A) One

(B) Two

(C) Three

1 找出核心詞彙	
2 了解類型	
3 看選項	
4 預測對話內容	1）申請人事部門的人總共有三位。
	2）申請編輯助理職位的人總共有兩位。

 **STEP 02** 考題實戰練習　請留意前面練習過的兩個階段，進行以下的考題 答對的題目數：_____

1　Where do they most likely work?

(A) A laundry
(B) A supermarket
(C) A bakery
(D) A law firm

	Items	Sets needed
1	Cartridges and toners	5
2	Folders and labels	15
3	Staplers and staples	8
4	Paper and envelopes	10

2　Why can't the woman make photocopies for the man?

(A) The copy machine is broken.
(B) She doesn't know how to operate the machine.
(C) The machine is out of cartridge.
(D) The man didn't ask in a polite manner.

 新
3　Look at the graphic. Which item would there likely be a change in?

(A) Cartridges and toners
(B) Folders and labels
(C) Staplers and staples
(D) Paper and envelopes

4　Where does the man probably work?

(A) At a post office
(B) At a delivery company
(C) At a repair shop
(D) At a bookstore

5　Why does the woman contact the man?

(A) To place an advertisement
(B) To pay a shipping charge
(C) To discuss a missing shipment
(D) To change a delivery address

 重要
6　What will the man do when he receives the woman's package?

(A) Keep it for pickup
(B) Provide a free delivery
(C) Schedule a new delivery time
(D) Issue her a refund

7   What department do the speakers most likely work in?

(A) Customer Service
(B) Technical Support
(C) Marketing
(D) Accounting

高難度
 What does the man say Jeff requested?

(A) Assistance with a project
(B) Approval to a marketing budget
(C) A different work schedule
(D) A transfer to another branch

9   What will the woman do next?

(A) Contact a co-worker
(B) Meet with some customers
(C) Attend a seminar
(D) Interview a job candidate

---

10   What does the man ask the woman for?

(A) How to get to another office
(B) Details about a meeting
(C) A list of advertisers
(D) Assistance with a sales proposal

高難度
 What have employees at the Hong Kong office done?

(A) Designed a new product
(B) Increased their sales
(C) Analyzed sales reports
(D) Finished their training

12   According to the woman, what will occur next week?

(A) A manager will retire.
(B) A customer will arrive.
(C) A company will be acquired.
(D) A meeting will be held.

▶ 答案在解析本第083頁

Chapter 15

與業餘活動、特定場所相關的考題
會出現與電影、表演、外食、興趣、度假計劃等相關的考題！

在Part 3裡的對話當中，與公司相關的主題佔百分之八十左右。這些與公司相關的主題是以公司外面與公司內部事情相關的主題來分類。請透過以下的小考，整理一下所學過的內容。

1 Why was the shipment delayed? 考題的對話主題為何？　▶ ....

2 Why will the meeting be postponed? 考題的對話主題為何？　▶ ....

3 若對話裡出現 interview, transfer, resume等說法，主題為何？　▶ ....

4 若對話裡出現 reservation, available, an aisle seat 等說法，主題為何？　▶ ....

5 為了準備公司生活相關的考題，多看Part 3的對話內容會有幫助。 ▶ ....

Preview

1 與業餘生活、特定場所相關對話的特色

Part 3裡的對話當中，除了公司生活相關的內容以外，也有業餘生活相關的。另外，也會出現特定場所裡發生的對話。多益考試的這些對話的說話者大部分是固定的。例如，在銀行進行對話的人，大多是行員與顧客。

2 有業餘生活、特定場所相關對話需考慮的重點

❶ 業餘生活相關的內容大部分是有關電影、表演、外食、興趣、度假計劃等。

❷ 透過考題裡面的核心詞彙，聽對話之前能有某種程度的預測到內容。

❸ 業餘生活相關的對話內容有獨特的進行方式。若先知道其順序與出現的詞彙，回答考題會很容易。

❹ 特定場所相關詞彙是固定的，且有不變的模式。只要理解這幾種模式，答題就變得很容易。

攻略法 29 回答業餘生活相關考題的方法

TOEIC是測驗在國際職場與他人用英文溝通能力的考試，但別以為只會有公司相關的主題，考試裡也會出業餘生活相關的內容。

業餘生活相關的內容大部分是有關電影、表演、外食、興趣、或度假計劃的。透過考題也能知道是否為與業餘活動相關的主題。若在考題或選項裡出現restaurant、review、performance等詞彙，就可以預測到是有關電影、表演、外食、興趣的對話主題。

第1階段：看考卷 邊看考題與選項，邊預測對話主題

❶ What are the speakers saying about the restaurant?

有關這家餐廳，說話者正在說什麼？

What does the man say about the plot?

有關故事大綱，這個男人說什麼？

Who will perform?：「電影、表演、外食、興趣」為主體

誰會表演？

❷ When is Jason leaving for his trip?

傑森什麼時候離開去旅行？

What is the man going to do this weekend?：「度假計劃」為主體

這個男人這個週末要做什麼？

What does the man say about the plot? ◄── 「電影、表演、外食、興趣」為主體！

有關故事大綱，這個男人說什麼？

(A) It was interesting.

(A) 很有趣。

(B) It was not innovative.

(B) 不創新。

(C) It was difficult to understand.

(C) 很難懂。

(D) It was unrealistic.

(D) 不夠實際。

---

1 Where will the event be held?

在別的考題裡出現了perform或ticket等詞彙，event是指表演活動的單字！

1 這場活動會在哪裡舉辦？

2 What will the local restaurants provide?

只看了考題就可以猜測為有關餐廳的對話！

2 這些當地的餐廳會提供什麼？

3 According to the conversation, what did the speaker see in the newspaper?

在報紙裡常出現對電影、舞台劇、或餐廳的評語。

3 根據這段對話，這個說話者在報紙裡看到了什麼？

4 How did Claire spend her vacation?

透過「休假怎麼過的」，可以知道「度假計劃」為主題！

4 克萊兒休假怎麼過的？

若看著考題與選項已經在某種程度上預測到了對話的主題,再透過各種主題之下的核心詞彙來聽對話,有助於更容易了解其內容。舉例來說,在主題為「電影、表演、外食、興趣」時,在對話裡會常聽到newly released、review、performance等的詞。若已經先知道了這些核心詞彙,會更容易了解其對話內容。這些各種主題之下的核心詞彙也會常出現於考題與選項裡。

第2階段:聽錄音 **聽主題類別之下核心詞彙之後再去了解內容**

❶ 電影、表演、外食、興趣
newly released film, review, new play, plot, movie theater, performance, sold out

> 最新上映的電影、評論、新的舞台劇、故事大綱、電影院、表演、售完

❷ 度假計劃
plan for the weekend, visiting, tourist attraction, vacation

> 週末計劃、拜訪、觀光景點、休假

---

1 與電影、表演、外食、興趣相關主題的對話範本

🎧 15-01.mp3

M: Julie, have you seen the newly released movie called 'Hanji'?
W: No. I love to go to the movies, but I haven't seen it yet. What did you think of it?
M: Well, the plot was a little weak, it was a kind of hard to follow the story, but I thought the sound effects of the movie were really good.
W: Hmm. I really want to see it this weekend, but I wonder if there's any ticket left for this weekend.

劃底線的部分是為了幫助你了解「電影、表演、外食、興趣」主題對話的核心詞彙!

> 男:茱莉,你看了那部最新上映叫作《漢記》的電影嗎?
> 女:沒有。我喜歡看電影,但我還沒看過它。你認為它如何呢?
> 男:嗯,結構有點弱,有點難懂這個故事,但是我認為這電影的音效真的很好。
> 女:嗯。我真的很想這週末去看。但是我不確定這個週末的票還有沒有。

若預測到「電影、表演、外食、興趣」為主體,透過 the newly released movie, go to the movies, plot, any ticket left 等詞彙,更容易了解其內容!

2 與度假計劃相關主題的對話範本

🎧 15-02.mp3

> W: John, what's your plan for this holiday? Will you visit your hometown this time, too?
>
> M: No, I'm going to Jiri Mountain with my close friend. We haven't seen each other since I moved here, and I want to do something fun with him.
>
> W: That sounds like fun! I wish I could get out of the city and enjoy some fresh air, but my sister is visiting me from New York this weekend. I'll have to take her to some tourist attractions.
>
> M: Hmm, then next time, why don't we go hiking together?

女：約翰，這個假日你的計畫是什麼？這次你也將會回你的家鄉去嗎？

男：不，我將和我的摯友去吉立山，自從我搬到這兒我們就沒見面了，我想和他一起去做些有趣的事。

女：那聽起來很有趣呢！我希望我可以離開這個城市，呼吸點新鮮空氣，但是我姊姊這週末要從紐約來拜訪我。我將要帶她去一些觀光景點。

男：嗯，那麼下一次我們何不一起去登山？

若預測到「度假計劃」為主體，透過 plan for this holiday, visit your hometown, get out of the city, visiting tourist attractions, go hiking 等的詞彙能更容易了解對話內容！

業餘生活主題相關的句子

🎧 15-03.mp3

1 I've wanted to eat there since I read the review about it in the newspaper. 「在報紙裡看過有關餐廳的評語」是指其主題為「電影、表演、外食、興趣」！

1 自從在報紙裡看過有關它的評語，我一直想在那邊用餐。

2 Have you seen the new play that just opened in town? 「剛剛開始演出的舞台劇」，所以「電影、表演、外食、興趣」為主體！

2 你看過在市區剛開始演出的新舞台劇嗎？

3 Do you have any plan for the long weekend? 透過「週末計劃」，可以知道其主題為「度假計劃」！

3 為了這次長週末你有什麼計劃嗎？

4 Hello. I'd like some information about the historic sites tour tomorrow. 「需要歷史遺址觀光資訊」，所以「度假計劃」為主題！

4 您好。有關明天的歷史遺址觀光，我需要一些資訊。

《不經過翻譯就能回答業餘生活相關主題對話的方法！》

1 論及電影或表演相關的話題。→ 引用報紙或各種媒體。→ 交換與話題相關的意見後，建議一起去看或購買門票。→ 接受建議或拒絕後提供理由。

2 大部分以疑問句開頭，如：「有什麼計劃？」或「計劃為什麼」、「聽說計劃為什麼」→ 說出自己的計劃後，建議對方一起參加。

其他核心詞彙總匯

電影、表演、外食、興趣

newly released film 新上映的電影	photography contest 攝影比賽
review 評語	audience 觀眾
new comedy show on TV 電視上的新的喜劇	movie theater 電影院
repeating the episode 重複一集	performance 表演
drawings and paintings 描繪與繪畫	reserve a ticket for 預訂…的門票
exhibition 展覽	sold out 售完的

度假計劃

be on vacation 休假當中	go on vacation 去度假
request for vacation time 休假時間申請	paid vacation 有薪假
time off 休息	vacation plan 度假計劃
pack up 打包	give an extension 延長
overseas 往國外	valid ticket 有效的票
suitcase 小型旅行箱	reserve a train ticket 預訂火車票

 15-04.mp3

 Quiz

請聽對話之後選出適當的答案。

Q1 According to the conversation, what did the man see in the newspaper?

(A) A critic's review　　　　(B) A job opening

Q2 What is the man going to do this weekend?

(A) Visit a city　　　　(B) Hold a party

攻略法

30 回答特定場所相關考題的方法

在Part 3裡會出現特定場所進行的對話。若看考題時預測對話場所，能知道該場所出現的說話者為誰、主題可能會是什麼，就能很容易回答考題。

透過看考題或選項，有時候能預測到對話的場所。例如，考題裡面有產品型號的話，這是在商店進行的對話、說話者為顧客或店員、其對話主題為詢問產品或交換產品的。

第1階段：看考卷 看考題與選項時預測對話場所

❶ What product does the man want to purchase?

What does the man say about model 700?：「商店」為主題

❷ Why did the man call the bank?

What document does the woman show?：「銀行」為主題

❸ What time will he be able to see his patient?

What can the doctor do later this evening?：「醫院」為主題

❹ What problem does the man mention?

When does the business close?：「修理站」為主題

- -

What does the man say about the book?

(A) It is on the shelf.

(B) It is currently on sale.

可以預測到商店為對話的場所、說話者為顧客或店員！

(C) It comes highly recommended.

(D) It can be ordered.

> 這個男人想購買什麼產品？
> 有關700型，這個男人說什麼？
> 這個男人為什麼打電話給這家銀行？
> 這個女人出示什麼文件？
> 他什麼時候能看到他的病患？
> 今天晚一點這個醫生可以做什麼？
> 這個男人論及什麼問題？
> 這家店什麼時候打烊？

> 有關這本書，這個男人說什麼？
> (A) 它在書架上。
> (B) 它正在銷售當中。
> (C) 它被強力推薦。
> (D) 它可以被訂購。

---

1 What does the woman want to buy?

透過考題裡的「想購買」，可以預測其對話的場所是商店、該女人是顧客。

2 What document does the woman show?

可以預測開戶頭或向想貸款的人要求出示身份證的狀況！

3 Why is the woman calling Dr. Perkin's office?

這是打電話給醫院的狀況，所以應該是「門診預約、詢問診察結果」的主題！

4 When does the business close?

可以預測為，狀況為將車子送修後，要決定回來取車的時間，因而詢問「店什麼時候打烊」的對話！

> 1 這個女人想買什麼？
>
> 2 這個女人出示什麼文件？
>
> 3 這個女人為什麼打電話給珀金醫生的辦公室？
>
> 4 這家店什麼時候打烊？

邊看選項邊預測場所的方法

Where most likely are the speakers?

(A) In a restaurant ◄─ 若是答案，可能會聽到table、ready、order等詞彙吧！

(B) In a store ◄─ 若是答案，可能會聽到looking for、product等詞彙吧！

(C) In a hotel ◄─ 若是答案，可能會聽到front desk、lobby、check in等詞彙吧！

(D) In a hospital ◄─ 若是答案，可能會聽到check up、medical、patient等詞彙吧！

說話者很有可能在哪裡？
(A) 在餐廳
(B) 在商店
(C) 在飯店
(D) 在醫院

若預測到了對話場所為醫院，透過patient、Dr.等的詞彙能更容易了解其對話內容，且能知道其對話者為接待人員與醫生！

在各種場所出現的核心詞彙是固定的。舉例來說，若是在商店，looking for、find、out of stock等詞彙常出現於對話與選項裡，所以能更容易預測到「購買商品或交換」為其主題，且在商店裡出現店員與購買者。

第2階段：聽錄音 先聽各種場所之下的核心詞彙，再去了解內容

❶ 商店／書店
looking for, find, models on display, out of stock, refund

尋找，找，陳列的型號，沒有庫存，退費

❷ 銀行
open a savings account, account number, apply for a loan

開儲蓄存款戶頭，帳號，申請貸款

❸ 醫院
see a doctor, prescription, check-up, medical file

看醫生，處方，診察，診療記錄

❹ 修理站
drop my car off, get a flat tire, touch up the paint

把我的車子留下來，輪胎爆胎，（汽車）補漆

---

1 與商店／書店相關主題的對話範本

🎧 15-05.mp3

W: Excuse me, I'm looking for the book by Arthur Chen called *Easy Spreadsheet*. But I can't find it anywhere.

M: Hmm, let me look it up on the computer. It seems like we have other books by Mr. Chen. But *Easy Spreadsheet* is out of stock. Why don't I place a special order for you?

W: Yes, that would be nice. When will it arrive?

M: That title may take about a week. If you could just give me your name and phone number, I'll call you when it arrives.

女：打擾一下，我在找亞瑟·陳寫的一本書叫做《簡單試算表》。但是我哪裡都找不到它。
男：嗯，讓我在電腦上看看。我們好像有陳先生寫的其他書。但是《簡單試算表》已經沒有庫存了。我要不要幫你下特別訂單呢？
女：好，那樣好。它會在什麼時候到呢？
男：那本書會需要大約一週。如果你能給我你的姓名和電話號碼，當它到達的時候我會打電話給你。

若預測到「商店或書店」為場所，透過 looking for, book, out of stock, place a special order, title 等詞彙，會更容易了解對話內容，且能知道其對話者為書店員工與購買者！

2　與銀行相關主題的對話範本

🎧 15-06.mp3

> M: Hello, I'd like to close my savings account. Can you help me?
> W: Certainly. I'll need your photo identification and a form. But may I ask why you are closing account with us?
> M: I've accepted a job in New York and will be moving there next week. I don't think your bank has a branch there.
> W: That's true. Okay, just fill out this form and give it back to me when you're finished. Meanwhile, I'll go and make a copy of your identification.

男：您好，我想要結束掉我的存款帳戶。你能幫我嗎？
女：當然。我需要你的大頭照身份證和一份表單。不過我可以請問您為什麼要結掉我們的帳戶嗎？
男：我接受了一份在紐約的新工作，而且下星期將將搬到那兒。我不認為你們銀行在那裡有分行。
女：對。好的，只要填這張表單並在完成後交回給我。在這個同時，我將會去影印你的身份證件。

若預測到「銀行」為場所，透過 close my savings account, photo identification, account, your bank 等詞彙，能更容易了解對話內容，且能知道其對話者為銀行員工與客戶！

3　醫院相關主題的對話範本

🎧 15-07.mp3

> M: Shannon, could you change the appointment with my 9 o'clock patient tomorrow? I need to attend my daughter's graduation.
> W: Sure, Dr. Miller. When is the earliest you could see him?
> M: The ceremony will end by 11, and I'll have lunch with my family, so 1 o'clock should be okay. I'll be in the office by then.
> W: Okay, I'll ask him to come in at 1.

男：香儂，你能變更我明天九點鐘病人的預約嗎？我需要去參加我女兒的畢業典禮。
女：當然，米勒醫生。你最早可以在什麼時候見他呢？
男：典禮會在十一點鐘結束，然後我要和我的家人吃午餐，所以一點鐘應該可以。那時我將會在辦公室。
女：好，我會要求他在一點鐘的時候過來。

若預測到「醫院」為場所，透過 patient, Dr. 等詞彙，能更容易了解對話內容，且能知道其對話者為接待人員與醫生！

4 汽車維修站相關主題的對話範本

🎧 15-08.mp3

M: Good morning. What can I do for you?

W: Yes. I'm having trouble with my car. The headlight seems to have cracked since I hit my car on a concrete post. Could you check it out for me?

M: Sure. It's not a difficult job to replace the headlight. But I need a couple of hours to get the replacement parts that are currently out of stock, so I expect your car won't be ready until noon.

W: Oh, that's fine. I'll be back here in the afternoon.

男：早安。有什麼我能為您做的嗎？

女：是的。我的車有了點問題。從我開車撞到一個水泥柱後，大燈就好像裂掉了。你能為我檢查一下嗎？

男：當然，換掉這個大燈不是困難的事。但是我需要幾個小時來拿到要替換的零件，因為現在沒有庫存，因此我預計你的車在中午前不會弄好。

女：噢，那好。我將會在下午時再回來這邊。

若預測到「修理站」為場所，透過 trouble, headlight, cracked, replace the headlight 等的詞彙能更容易了解對話內容，且能知道其對話者為修理工與客人！

《不經過翻譯就能容易回答特定場所相關考題的方法！》

1. 商店與書店：店員，客人──購買商品，交換商品
2. 銀行：行員，客戶──開戶，申請貸款，匯款
3. 醫院：醫生，接待員，病患──預約診療，詢問診療結果
4. 飯店：飯店接待員，房客──進房與退房手續，申請客房服務，飯店設施故障，申請早晨呼叫起床服務，在大廳見面，將商品或傳真送到飯店
5. 修理站：修理工，客戶──送修，取車
6. 圖書館：圖書館員工，客人──將借的書返還
7. 郵局：郵局員工，客人──詢問配送費用
8. 停車場：停車場管理員，客人──詢問停車費用

🎧 15-09.mp3

✎ Quiz

請聽對話之後選出適當的答案。

Q3 What is included in the purchase of the copier?

(A) Free installation　　(B) Free supplies

Q4 Why is the man calling Dr. Min's office?

(A) To schedule an appointment　　(B) To promote a product

▶ 答案在解析本第085頁

附加核心詞彙總匯

商店、書店

I'm looking for 正在尋找…	refund / receipt 退費／收據
models on display 展示的型號	warehouse 倉庫
prefer 比較喜歡	retail / wholesale 零售／批發
television set on sale 電視機在打折	shirt in blue 藍色的襯衫
have a few in stock 還有一些庫存	in a large size / in a medium size 大尺寸／中間尺寸
out of stock 沒有庫存	it costs 費用為…
free delivery 免費配送	extra fee 附加費用

銀行

open a savings account 開儲蓄戶頭	photo identification 大頭照身份證
close a savings account 取消儲蓄戶頭	picture ID 大頭照身份證
fill out an application form 填寫申請表格	driver's license 駕照
borrow some money 借一點錢	account number 帳號
loan officer 貸款專員	business loan 商務貸款
apply online 在網路上申請	annual income 年收入
accept... electronically 用網路的方式接收…	loan application form 貸款申請表格

醫院

medical file 醫療記錄	medical history form 病歷表格
doctor / patient 醫生／病患	physical exam / check-up 健康檢查
eye exam 視力檢查	cut back on one's exercise 減少運動量
make an appointment 預約見面時間	consult a doctor 詢問醫生
see a doctor 看醫生	flu 流感
symptom 症狀	general hospital 綜合醫院
prescription 處方	surgeon 外科醫生
clinic 診所	surgery 手術

汽車維修站

auto repair shop 汽車維修站	replace the headlight 更換大燈
garage 維修廠	touch up the paint （汽車）補漆
drop my car off for repairs 把我的車子留下來修理	ready to be picked up 已經可以取車
paint come off 烤漆掉下來	check it out 檢查
get a flat tire 輪胎爆胎	take a look at 看看

攻略法29　回答業餘生活相關考題的方法

看考題與選項時，預測對話主題為業餘生活的哪一種。

What are the speakers saying about the restaurant?
What does the man say about the plot?
Who will perform?

- 「電影／表演／外食／興趣」為主題

When is Jason leaving for his trip?
What is the man going to do this weekend?

- 「度假計劃」為主題

透過各主題之下的核心詞彙，提高對業餘生活相關對話內容的理解程度！

1）電影／表演／外食／興趣

newly released film, review, new play, plot, movie theater, performance, sold out

2）度假計劃

plan for the weekend, visiting, tourist attraction, vacation

攻略法30　回答特定場所相關考題的方法

看考題與選項時，預測對話場所為哪裡、在此場所會出現哪些說話者、且其主題為什麼。

What product does the man want to purchase?
商店／店員與客人／購買商品或交換

Why did the man call the bank?
銀行／行員與客戶／開戶，貸款，匯款

What time will he be able to see his patient?
醫院／醫生或接待人員、病患／預約診療，詢問診察結果

What problem does the man mention?
汽車維修站／修理工與客人／送修，取車

透過各場所裡可能有的核心詞彙，提高對對話內容的理解程度！

1）商店／書店

looking for, find, models on display, out of stock, refund

2）銀行

open a savings account, account number, apply for a loan

3）醫院

see a doctor, prescription, check-up, medical file

4）汽車維修站

drop my car off, get a flat tire, touch up the paint

例子

What does the man say about the plot?

(A) It was difficult to understand.
(B) It was unrealistic.

1 找出核心詞彙　　the plot
2 了解類型　　電影、表演、外食、興趣
3 看選項　　很難懂或不夠現實的
4 聽錄音來確認答案

---

1 Why is the woman going to Tokyo?

(A) To conduct a survey
(B) To visit a former co-worker

1 找出核心詞彙
2 了解類型
3 看選項

---

2 Why has the woman not yet gone to the event?

(A) She doesn't have much free time.
(B) She doesn't like the event.

1 找出核心詞彙
2 了解類型
3 看選項

---

3 Who is the woman shopping for?

(A) Her sister
(B) Her son

1 找出核心詞彙
2 了解類型
3 看選項

---

4 Where does this conversation most likely take place?

(A) A video rental store
(B) A car rental store

1 找出核心詞彙
2 了解類型
3 看選項

▶ 答案在解析本第086頁

5　Where are the speakers?

　(A) At a pharmacy
　(B) At a restaurant

1 找出核心詞彙	
2 了解類型	
3 看選項	

6　Why did the man call the bank?

　(A) To inquire about opening hours
　(B) To get information on opening an
　　　account

1 找出核心詞彙	
2 了解類型	
3 看選項	

7　Why is the mechanic not able to help
　the woman today?

　(A) He is unable to get parts.
　(B) He is too busy today.

1 找出核心詞彙	
2 了解類型	
3 看選項	

8　How much is the fee?

　(A) $5
　(B) $2

1 找出核心詞彙	
2 了解類型	
3 看選項	

9 What are the women mainly discussing?

   (A) A shopping complex
   (B) An apartment
   (C) The weather

1	找出核心詞彙	
2	了解類型	
3	看選項	
4	預測對話內容	1）討論在網路上也可以搜尋天氣預報。
		2）透過廣告得知新購物中心的相關消息。

10 What did the speaker see on the website?

   (A) An advertisement
   (B) A critic's review
   (C) The weather information

---

11 Where are the speakers?

   (A) In a clothing store
   (B) On a street corner
   (C) In a dry cleaner's

1	找出核心詞彙	
2	了解類型	
3	看選項	
4	預測對話內容	1）詢問有關服務快速的洗衣店。
		2）在路上詢問去劇場的方法。

12 What is the man's concern?

   (A) He needs a service finished quickly.
   (B) He needs directions to the theater.
   (C) He lost the ticket for the concert.

---

13 Where most likely are the speakers?

   (A) In a theater
   (B) In an office
   (C) In a museum

1	找出核心詞彙	
2	了解類型	
3	看選項	
4	預測對話內容	1）在辦公室的男人說他來雪梨參加會議。
		2）在博物館的男人說他正在雪梨度假。

14 Why is the man in Sydney?

   (A) He is attending a conference.
   (B) He is buying a house.
   (C) He is on a vacation.

▶ 答案在解析本第088頁

STEP 02 考題實戰練習　　請留意前面練習過的兩個階段，進行以下的考題　答對的題目數：＿＿＿＿＿

1　What did the man do recently?

(A) Move to a new apartment
(B) Manage a restaurant
(C) Apply for a position
(D) Take time off work

2　What does the woman suggest?

(A) Shopping at an outdoor market
(B) Going to a music performance
(C) Listening to a radio
(D) Consulting a travel guide

3　What will the local restaurants provide?

(A) Offer complimentary samples
(B) Remain open late
(C) Organize cooking classes
(D) Issue a gift certificate

4　Why is the man calling?

(A) To get directions to the store
(B) To inquire about the store's hours
(C) To ask for a delivery
(D) To cancel an order

5　What does the woman say about the store?

(A) It is relocating to a new area.
(B) It is about to close.
(C) It is short of some items.
(D) It has a job vacancy.

6　What does the woman ask the man to do?

(A) Consult a map
(B) Call back later
(C) Complete some work
(D) Visit the store tomorrow

7 Where is Dr. Johnson?

   (A) With a patient
   (B) At a conference
   (C) At a different office
   (D) On vacation

8 Why is the man calling Dr. Johnson's office?

   (A) To talk about a presentation
   (B) To schedule an appointment
   (C) To discuss a prescription
   (D) To ask about a bill

高難度

 What will the woman most likely do next?

   (A) Transfer the call
   (B) Contact Dr. Johnson
   (C) Make an appointment
   (D) Cancel an order

---

10 Where does this conversation take place?

   (A) At a burger shop
   (B) At a jewelry store
   (C) At a clothing store
   (D) At a souvenir shop

Items	Price
T-shirt	$100 / ea
Baseball hat	$50 / ea
Key chain	$10 / ea
Postcard	$5 / ea

11 What does the man think of buying to take home?

   (A) T-shirts
   (B) Hats
   (C) Sweat pants
   (D) Magnets

新

 Look at the graphic. How much money does the man need to pay?

   (A) $250
   (B) $300
   (C) $350
   (D) $400

▶ 答案在解析本第091頁

Review Test

在Part 3裡的對話當中，除了與公司相關的主題之外，也有與日常生活相關的，甚至是在特定場合裡才會出現的對話。在多益考試中，這些對話的人大多是固定的，如果是場合是銀行，那多為銀行行員與客戶的對話。

1 若考題或選項中出現何種詞彙，可預測是與電影、表演、外食、興趣有關的對話主題？　　　　　　　　　　　　▶

2 若對話場合是在商店，則說話者可能為何？對話內容可能為何？可能出現的關鍵字為何？　　　　　　　　　　　▶

3 若對話場合在餐廳，可能會聽到何種詞彙？　　　▶

4 若對話場合在醫院，可能會聽到何種詞彙？　　　▶

5 若對話場合在飯店，可能會聽到何種詞彙？　　　▶

Preview

1 三人對話或對話次數超過五次以上的對話特色

相較於對話次數四次的二人對話，不管是「三人對話」或是「對話次數超過五次以上的二人對話」，都使得要從對話中找到題目答案的複雜度提升。

雖然因為對話人物變多、對話長度變長，但對話的邏輯是一樣的，因此只要按照之前講述的攻略，按部就班地解題，就能夠破解此類題型。

2 有關三人對話或對話次數超過五次以上的注意重點

❶ 先看考卷上的題目，預測對話發生的場合與主題。
❷ 根據預測的主題，找尋對話中可能會出現的核心詞彙。
❸ 判斷題目答案會出現在對話中的位置。
❹ 依序解題。

|答案| 1. restaurant、review、performance　2. 顧客或店員、詢問產品或交換產品、looking for、find、out of stock　3. table、ready、order
4. check up、medical、patient　5. front desk、lobby、check in

面對三人對話考題的方法

這是TOEIC改制後的新題型，面對這樣的題型，三個人的角色關係要更注意。

由於在考卷上，看不出哪些題組是三人對話，通常是在聽對話的時候，才會發現原來這個題組為三人對話，此時考生可能會感到驚慌，而失去專注力，但這就喪失了得分的優勢。

基本上，兩人對話和三人對話的攻略要點一樣，兩者差別只在說話者變多了，對話變長了，答案的範圍更廣了。但其實解題順序、解題攻略……等等，是沒有改變的。

第1階段：看考卷　邊看考題與選項，邊預測對話主題

❶ Who is the man?：「詢問人物」為主題

❷ What is this conversation about?：「詢問對話主題」為主題

❸ When does the movie begin?：「電影、邀約」為主題

男子是誰？
此對話是關於什麼？
電影何時開始？

Why can't the woman go to the movie with the man?

(A) She doesn't like to see movies.

└─ 「電影邀約」為主題

(B) She has other plans.

(C) She has seen the movie already.

(D) She will have a day off on Friday.

為何女子不能和男子去看電影？
(A) 她不想看電影。
(B) 她有其它計畫。
(C) 她已經看過電影了。
(D) 她星期五休假。

第2階段：聽錄音　聽主題類別之下核心詞彙之後再去了解內容

1 以邀約電影對話範本

 16-01.mp3

W1: Thank God it's Friday. I've been looking forward to today for 5 days.

M: Why? Do you have any plans?

W1: Yes, I'm going to see the movie *The Day After*. Do you want to go with me? I have 2 free tickets.

M: I'd love to, but sorry I can't. I already have another pre-engagement. Maybe you can ask Clare.

W1: Are you free tonight, Clare? Do you want to go with me to the movie? It's an Oscar winning film.

W2: It seems like fun. A free movie, why not?

W1: Great! The movie is playing at the Sakura Theater starting 7:15. We can leave right after work.

W2: Sure. Since you are treating me a free movie, why don't I buy you a burger for dinner in return? We'll have a great time this evening.

畫底線的部分是為了幫助你了解「電影、邀約」主題對話的核心詞彙！

女1：太棒了！終於是星期五了！我等這天已經等了五天了！

男：為什麼？妳有什麼計畫嗎？

女1：是的。我要去看電影《明天過後》。你要不要跟我去？我有兩張免費票。

男：我很想，但是抱歉我不行耶。我已經有其他的約了。或許你可以問問克萊兒。

女1：克萊兒，你今晚有空嗎？你要不要和我去看電影？是一部奧斯卡得獎電影喔！

女2：好像蠻有趣的。免費電影，好啊？

女1：太棒了！電影七點十五分在櫻花戲院播放。我們可以下班後直接去。

女2：當然！你請我看免費電影，那何不我買個漢堡回請你當晚餐？我們會有個很棒的夜晚。

雖然對話角色變多，但對話的邏輯順序是一致的，可以看到上面的劃線地方（也就是「電影、邀約」主題的核心詞彙），只要抓到這些詞彙，就能回答以下問題。

1 Why can't the man go to the movie with the woman?
(A) He doesn't like to see movies.
(B) He has other plans.
(C) He has seen the movie already.
(D) He will have a day off on Friday.

2 When does the movie begin?
(A) 6:45
(B) 7:15
(C) 7:30
(D) 7:45

1 為何男子不能和女子去看電影？
(A) 他不想看電影。
(B) 他有其它計畫。
(C) 他已經看過電影了。
(D) 他星期五休假。

2 電影何時開始？
(A) 6:45
(B) 7:15
(C) 7:30
(D) 7:45

另外，有時候也會出現詢問說話者接下來行動的問題，此時就要留意對話的末端，例如第2名女子說「Sure. Since you are treating me a free movie, why don't I buy you a burger for dinner in return? We'll have a great time this evening.」，其中的這句「... I buy you a burger for dinner...」便可回答下面的這個問題：

1 What will Clare do for the woman in return?
   (A) Take her out for movie next week.
   (B) Treat her a burger for dinner.
   (C) Give her a free ride home.
   (D) Buy her a beer.

1 克萊兒會回報女子什麼？
   (A) 下週帶她去看電影。
   (B) 請她晚餐吃漢堡。
   (C) 讓她搭便車回家。
   (D) 買啤酒請她。

面對對話次數超過五次以上考題的方法

這是TOEIC改制後的新題型，考生聆聽對話時的專注度、找尋答案位置的方法，更顯重要。

面對這樣的題型，基本上沒有太多特殊的攻略，它與之前對話次數差不多三四次的對話內容，也沒有太大的差異。只是因為對話內容變多，就代表答案的分布範圍變廣了，因此需要更加熟悉之前的攻略法，才能夠更快找到正確答案。

第1階段：看考卷 邊看考題與選項，邊預測對話主題

❶ When will the event finally take place?
What is offered at the exhibition?：「表演、展覽」為主題

❷ When will the woman leave?
How will the man fly?：「飛行、旅行」為主題

❸ When is the meeting scheduled to begin?
Why will the meeting be postponed?：「會議」為主題

❹ What do they think about the meeting?：「會議內容」為主題

- -

Where does the man plan to go ?

「旅行、外出計畫」為主題

(A) Vancouver

(B) Los Angeles

(C) Toronto

(D) San Francisco

> 這活動最後會在何時舉行？
> 展覽提供什麼？
> 女子將於何時離開？
> 男子將如何飛行？
> 會議預定何時開始？
> 會議為何延後？
> 他們對那場會議有什麼想法？

> 男子計畫去哪裡？
> (A) 溫哥華
> (B) 洛杉磯
> (C) 多倫多
> (D) 舊金山

若看考題與選項已經大概預測到對話的主題，便可應用之前學過的攻略技巧，在對話中找尋各種主題之下會出現的核心詞彙，會有助於更容易了解對話內容。

記得，因為對話的次數變多了，所以要更記得對話語氣的轉折、時間點、期間、關鍵字……等重點。

第2階段：聽錄音 聽主題類別之下核心詞彙之後再去了解內容

1 以安排飛機航班為主題的對話範本

🎧 16-02.mp3

W: Sir, let's see... To fly to Toronto from Taipei, you can change flight at Los Angeles.

M: Isn't there a direct flight from Taipei to Toronto?

W: No, I'm sorry, Sir. There is no direct flight between these two cities. OR, maybe you can change planes in Vancouver. It will save you almost an hour's time. And this way, you don't need a visa for the US.

M: That's better. Can you book me a round-trip ticket to and from Toronto, please? I plan to leave latest by tomorrow afternoon.

W: There is an 11:00 o'clock flight tomorrow morning. Is it all right?

M: Good. I'll take it.

畫底線的部分是為了幫助你了解「飛機、航班、旅行」主題對話的核心詞彙！

女：先生！我幫您看看……從台北飛多倫多，您可以在洛杉磯轉機。

男：從台北飛多倫多沒有直航班機嗎？

女：沒有耶，對不起，先生。這兩個城市間沒有直航班機。或者，或許您可以在溫哥華轉機，您將節省快一個小時的時間。而且這樣的話，您也不需要飛美國的簽證。

男：這樣比較好。可以幫我訂一張到多倫多的來回機票嗎？我計劃最晚明天下午就要出發。

女：明天早上十一點有一個班次。可以嗎？

男：好！我訂下來。

2 以餐廳訂位為主題的對話範本

🎧 16-03.mp3

M: Hi, I need to make a reservation for tomorrow evening, seven PM.

W: Sure, may I have your name and number of your guests, please?

M: It's Shaw. We need a table for eight. There will be six adults and two children.

W: I'm sorry, seven PM is all booked. But we'll have a table available at seven thirty. Would it be all right with you, Mr. Shaw?

M: Well, it's better than nothing.

畫底線的部分是為了幫助你了解「用餐、訂位」主題對話的核心詞彙！

男：嗨！我需要預約明天傍晚，七點。

女：沒問題。麻煩可以有您的大名及來賓人數嗎？

男：我叫蕭。我們需要一張八人的桌子。將會有六個大人及兩個小孩。

女：抱歉，七點都訂滿了。不過我們七點半有一張桌子會空出。這樣您可以嗎？蕭先生。

男：好吧！總比沒有好。

攻略法31	面對三人對話考題的方法

第1階段：看題目

1. 預測題目發生的場合、對話主題
2. 找尋該主題會出現的核心詞彙
3. 判斷題目答案會出現在對話中的位置

第2階段：聽錄音

1. 確認與預測的場合、主題是否一致
2. 確認核心詞彙
3. 依照對話順序解題
4. 釐清三人對話的角色

攻略法32	面對對話次數超過五次以上考題的方法

第1階段：看題目

1. 預測題目發生的場合、對話主題
2. 找尋該主題會出現的核心詞彙
3. 判斷題目答案會出現在對話中的位置

第2階段：聽錄音

1. 確認與預測的場合、主題是否一致
2. 確認核心詞彙
3. 依照對話順序解題

例子

What does the man say about the
advertising department? ◄

(A) It will hire new employees.
(B) It will move to third floor.

1 找出核心詞彙   advertising department
2 了解類型   職場、公司、部門
3 看選項   詢問部門的政策
4 聽錄音來確認答案

---

1 Why did the man reject the woman's request?

(A) Because he was sleeping.
(B) Because he was about to go out.
(C) Because he was working.
(D) Because he was on a phone.

1 找出核心詞彙
2 了解類型
3 看選項

---

2 What's purpose of the man's call?

(A) Book a table
(B) Book a ticket
(C) Book a room
(D) Book a flight

1 找出核心詞彙
2 了解類型
3 看選項

---

3 Where does the woman work at?

(A) An airline company
(B) A European government
(C) A travel agency
(D) A tourist spot

1 找出核心詞彙
2 了解類型
3 看選項

---

4 What is the man thinking about doing?

(A) Getting married
(B) Buying a car
(C) Starting a business
(D) Buying a house

1 找出核心詞彙
2 了解類型
3 看選項

▶ 答案在解析本第093頁

5 Where does the dialogue take place?

    (A) In the waiting room
    (B) On the train
    (C) At the ticket office
    (D) At the platform

    1 找出核心詞彙
    2 了解類型
    3 看選項

6 What is the woman complaining about?

    (A) The company is too far from home.
    (B) The salary has not been paid out.
    (C) The accounts are too confusing.
    (D) The accounts are missing.

    1 找出核心詞彙
    2 了解類型
    3 看選項

7 What type of business does the woman work for?

    (A) A medical institution
    (B) A magazine publisher
    (C) An accounting firm
    (D) A shipping company

    1 找出核心詞彙
    2 了解類型
    3 看選項

8 What does the man inquire about?

    (A) The address of a building
    (B) The password to the archives
    (C) The architect's contact information
    (D) The location of some documents

    1 找出核心詞彙
    2 了解類型
    3 看選項

▶ 答案在解析本第094頁

1　What's the first woman's suggestion?

(A) To lower the price
(B) To increase the price
(C) To intensify publicity
(D) To increase the quality

2　Which one is correct about the thoughts of the three people?

(A) They have the same thought.
(B) Only two people have the same thought.
(C) Everyone has a different thought.
(D) Only two people came up with thoughts.

3　What does the second woman mean by saying "I still stick to my idea"?

(A) She is so stubborn.
(B) She thinks her thought is the best.
(C) She strongly disagreed with the third person's idea.
(D) She will give in.

- -

4　What are these women doing?

(A) Reserving the air tickets
(B) Buying the air tickets
(C) Boarding the plane
(D) Meeting someone at the airport

5　What does Mr. Smith mean by saying "but I'm going to meet your manager after a while"?

(A) He has no time to go to the hotel to have a rest.
(B) He can't check in the hotel.
(C) He doesn't want to go to the hotel.
(D) He doesn't have to go to the hotel.

6　Which one is not true according to the dialogue?

(A) Mr. Smith stayed on the plane for twelve hours.
(B) Mr. Smith accepted their suggestion.
(C) Mr. Smith refused to let them to meet him.
(D) Mr. Smith is glad that they came to meet him.

▶ 答案在解析本第095頁

Review Test

Part 3的對話主題，一般可分為與公司相關、與日常生活相關的主題，多半可以從題目中預測與判斷對話場合。不管對話的長度、對話人物的多寡，其對話的邏輯都是一樣的。

1 若題目在詢問人物的身分，可從對話中的哪裡找到答案？　▶ ....

2 若題目詢問人物接下來的行為，可從對話中的哪裡找到答案？　▶ ....

3 若題目出現time、schedule、meeting等詞彙，
可能是哪種對話主題？　▶ ....

4 若題目出現book、reservation、available等詞彙，
可能是哪種對話主題？　▶ ....

5 若對話出現but、however等詞彙，表示什麼意思？　▶ ....

Preview

1 會在Part 3對話題搭配出現的圖表類型

❶ 時刻表
與各種交通工具、電影、表演……等有關。
可能出現的題目為搭乘時間（或班次）、表演時間（或場次）……等。

❷ 價目表
與商品、票券、房間、餐點……等有關。
可能出現的題目為支付金額。

❸ 優惠券
與商品購買、優惠折扣……等有關。
可能出現的題目為折扣方式、折扣期限、折扣金額……等。

❹ 地圖
與樓層平面圖、大樓樓層圖、地圖……等有關。
可能出現的題目為確認某公司或建築物的位置、詢問某人或某公司的所在位置……等。

|答案|　1. 對話內容的前段　2. 對話內容的後段　3. 會議時間安排　4. 餐廳訂位　5. 語氣的轉折

攻略法

33 破解圖表題的方法

這是TOEIC改制後的新題型，面對這樣的題型，要先看懂圖表的內容，才能準確掌握對話主題、對話中的關鍵內容。

多益改制之後，在Part 3新增圖表題。對話會搭配圖表，三個題目為一題組，其中一題一定會與圖表的內容有關，這類的題目旨在測驗考生聽力、閱讀的能力。

圖表的內容基本上包括：表格、時間表、價目表、優惠券、地圖、樓層圖、樓層平面圖……等等。只要看得懂圖表內容，就會知道對話的主題，如果圖表與「地圖、樓層圖、樓層平面圖」相關，那對話的內容大致上就是在討論公司的位置、職員的座位等；如果圖表是各種保險方案的比較，那對話的內容就會是討論保險內容，對話角色則為保險業務員與客戶。

第1階段：看考卷 邊看考題與圖表時，邊預測對話主題

Dishes	Price / per person
Entrée: pork / chicken	$100
Noodle	$50
Soup: vegetable / seafood	$30
Drink and salad	$30
Combo	$180

Look at the graphic. How much money does the woman need to pay for lunch?

　　　　　　└ 與圖表有關，「餐廳用餐」為主題

(A) $180

(B) $150

(C) $210

(D) $160

請看此圖。女子需要付多少錢買午餐？
(A) 180元
(B) 150元
(C) 210元
(D) 160 元

觀看表格，可發現表格主題為餐點的內容與費用。

餐點	每人價格
主菜：豬肉／雞肉	$100
麵	$50
湯：蔬菜／海鮮	$30
飲料和沙拉	$30
套餐價	**$180**

再看題目是在詢問女子購買午餐需要支付的費用，因此可以推斷對話的主角為餐廳員工與顧客，女子為顧客，會向店員述說點餐的內容，因此要仔細聆聽，並搭配圖表的價錢，便可知道女子所需支付的午餐費。

有時候多益題目會設計「顧客詢問產品→店員回覆並轉推薦其他產品→顧客選購」或是「顧客請店員推薦→店員推薦→顧客選購」這樣的對話流程，不斷出現的產品，會讓考生感到混淆，此時應特別注意顧客的回應（例如：that sounds great、ok、I'll pick that one……等），才能夠判斷選購的內容、支付的費用。

第2階段：看圖表 看圖表並聽錄音，找尋核心詞彙

❶ 商品價目
price, $, dollar, discount, coupon, voucher

❷ 銷售報告
sale, rise, down, monthly, yearly, report

❸ 會議時間
meeting, conference, schedule, time

❹ 度假計畫
flight, vacation, hotel, book, reserve

❺ 地理位置
map, beside, front, right, left, across, opposite

接下來，我們來看幾個常在Part 3出現的圖表類型。

1 與商品比較相關的圖表與對話範本

🎧 17-01.mp3

Room Types	Rates / Night
2 singles	$1,800
1 double	$2,000
2 doubles	$2,500
1 double + 2 singles	$3,000

畫底線的部分是為了幫助你了解更快找到關鍵訊息！

M: Good evening. Thank you for calling Royal Hotel. This is Ted speaking, how may I help you?

W: Hi, I'm making a reservation for a double room on June 16th.

M: Thank you, ma'am. We have two rooms. One with a double bed, and the other with two single beds.

W: I'll chose the two single beds.

畫底線的部分是為了幫助你了解「飯店訂房」主題對話的核心詞彙！

男：晚安！感謝您致電皇家飯店。我是泰德，很高興為您服務。

女：你好，我想要預定六月十六日，一間雙人房。

男：謝謝您，那天剩兩間房，一間提供一張雙人床，另一間則是兩張單人床。

女：我要選兩張單人床。

這個圖表搭配的問題可能為：

Look at the graphic, how much will the woman pay for her room?
(A) $1,800
(B) $2,000
(C) $2,500
(D) $3,000

女子將為房間付多少費用？
(A) 1,800元
(B) 2,000元
(C) 2,500元
(D) 3,000元

看到題目便可知道這是與「訂房」有關的對話主題，對話角色為飯店人員與顧客，可預測對話中會出現兩種以上的房間選項，顧客最後會選擇其中一種。掌握這樣的對話邏輯，再搭配表格內容，便能順利找出答案。

房型	價格／每晚
單人床2張	1,800元
雙人床1張	2,000元
雙人床2張	2,500元
雙人床1張＋單人床2張	3,000元

2 與優惠券相關的圖表與對話範本

 17-02.mp3

```
Duke Department Store
        Coupon
         $100

Valid through May 31ˢᵗ
```

畫底線的部分是為了幫助你了解更快找到關鍵訊息！

W: Sir, it'll come up to $375 dollars in total, cash or charge, please?

M: Oh, I'll pay by cash, and I have a $100-dollar-coupon. Here you go!

W: Let me see. I'm sorry, Sir, The activity ended last month. This coupon is no longer valid.

M: That's too bad!

畫底線的部分是為了幫助你了解「優惠券使用」主題對話的核心詞彙！

女：先生，總共是$375元。您要付現還是刷卡？。

男：喔！我付現，另外，我有一張一百元的優惠券。給你！

女：讓我看看。先生抱歉。這個活動上個月結束，優惠券已經失效了。

男：真糟糕！

這個圖表搭配的問題可能為：

Look at the graphic. What month is it when the speakers are talking?
(A) May
(B) June
(C) April
(D) July

請看此圖。講者說話的月份是何時？
(A) 五月
(B) 六月
(C) 四月
(D) 七月

先看到題目，題目問「哪一個月」，表示答案大約有85%的機率不會是 May，而這個題目與優惠券有關，日期又不是優惠券上的日期，可推測對話主題的事件為「優惠券過期」。再看到優惠券的內容為：

```
公爵百貨公司
   優待券
    $100

有效至5月31日
```

接下來只要再留意對話中出現與時間相關、期限過期的核心詞彙即可。

除此之外，可能會搭配優惠券出現的題目還有「詢問價錢」，此時只要留意對話中講述的商品總額，再扣除優惠券上的數字即可。例如：

Look at the graphic. How much money does the man need to pay?
(A) $ 375
(B) $ 334
(C) $ 406
(D) $ 275

請看此圖。男子需要付多少錢？
(A) 375元
(B) 334元
(C) 406元
(D) 275元

3 與時刻表相關的圖表與對話範本

🎧 17-03.mp3

Leaving First Street	Arriving at Second Street
8:30	9:00
8:55	9:25
9:20	9:50
9:45	10:15

畫底線的部分是為了幫助你了解更快找到關鍵訊息！

W: Can you come this Sunday to decorate the exhibition?

M: Okay, what time should I arrive?

W: Can you arrive at the gallery in the morning at about 9:30? We need to get everything ready at 11:30.

M: 9:30? No problem. The gallery is on Second Street, right? I can take the bus from First Street.

W: Correct.

畫底線的部分是為了幫助你了解「交通時刻」主題對話的核心詞彙！

女：你這個星期天能來布置展覽會場嗎？

男：好，我應該幾點抵達呢？

女：你可以大概九點半到畫廊嗎？我們需要在十一點半前將所有東西就緒。

男：九點半？沒問題。畫廊在第二街，對吧？我可以從第一街搭公車。

女：正確。

這個圖表搭配的問題可能為：

Look at the graphic, what time will the man get on the bus?
(A) 8:30
(B) 9:00
(C) 8:55
(D) 9:20

請看此圖，男子何時會搭上公車？
(A) 8:30
(B) 9:00
(C) 8:55
(D) 9:20

先看到題目，再問男子搭車的時間，因此可以推論對話中，會出現希望男子抵達的時間，根據對話中的訊息，再搭配公車時刻表，便可推論出男子的搭車時間。

第一街出發	抵達第二街
8:30	9:00
8:55	9:25
9:20	9:50
9:45	10:15

對話中，女子希望男子九點半左右到，觀看公車時刻表，可知男子最適合搭乘的公車班次為八點五十五分從第一街出發、九點二十五分抵達第二街的這班公車，順利找出答案。

此外，看到這類的時刻表，除了注意時間之外，也要留意搭車與下車的地點，以免看錯內容，白白喪失得分的好機會。

4 與樓層平面圖相關的圖表與對話範本

🎧 17-04.mp3

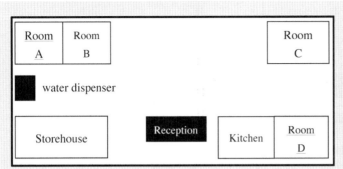

畫底線的部分是為了幫助你了解更快找到關鍵訊息！

M: Lisa, where can I find David? I need to discuss some matters with him.

W: His office is <u>next to</u> the water dispenser. Wait... he is in the meeting room right now. He said he wants to prepare the meeting tomorrow morning.

M: Which meeting room?

W: The one <u>next to</u> the kitchen.

M: Ok, thanks a lot.

畫底線的部分是為了幫助你了解「平面圖、地圖」主題對話的核心詞彙！

男：麗莎，我可以在哪裡找到大衛？我有幾件事情要和他討論。

女：他的辦公室在飲水機旁。等一下……他現在正在會議室，他說他想要準備明天早上的會議。

男：哪間會議室？

女：在廚房旁邊的那間。

男：好的，謝謝。

這個圖表搭配的問題可能為：

Look at the graphic. Where will the man find David?
(A) In Room A
(B) In Room B
(C) In Room C
(D) In Room D

請看圖表，男子將會在哪個房間找到大衛？
(A) 房間A
(B) 房間B
(C) 房間C
(D) 房間D

看到這個圖表，就要留意各種與位置相關的核心詞彙，例如：right、left、next to、across from等等。平面圖上標示了八個地點，其中有四個地點為選項，剩餘的water dispenser、storehouse、reception、kitchen作為標示說明使用。例如：最靠近飲水機的房間、倉庫的對面房間、接待處的右手邊、廚房的旁邊……等等。

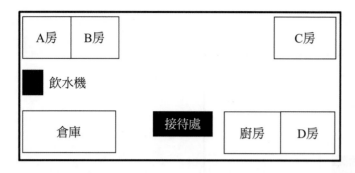

先大略掌握樓層平面圖之後，觀看題目，發現是在詢問可以在哪間房間找到大衛。這類的題目通常不會直接告訴你正確位置，通常會「先告訴你第一個位置，然後再告訴你第二個位置」，然後要搭配對話中的其他訊息，請考生判斷正確答案。碰到這種題目，考生除了要有高度的專注度之外，若能稍微有點位置概念，就能更容易找出正確答案。

攻略法33　破解圖表題的方法

第1階段：看題目與圖表

1. 預測題目發生的場合、對話主題
2. 找尋該主題會出現的核心詞彙
3. 判斷對話的邏輯，找尋圖表與對話的連結點
4. 判斷題目答案會出現在對話中的位置

第2階段：聽錄音

1. 確認與預測的場合、主題是否一致
2. 確認核心詞彙
3. 依照對話順序解題
4. 確認圖表與對話的對應處

與商品資訊有關的圖表與主題

price, $, dollar（產品價目）

sale, rise, down, monthly, yearly, report（報告相關）

與優惠券有關的圖表與主題

discount, coupon, voucher（折扣優惠）

與時刻表有關的圖表與主題

meeting, conference, schedule, time（會議時間）

flight, timetable, departure, arrive（交通時刻）

與樓層平面圖或地圖有關的圖表與主題

map, beside, front, right, left, across, opposite （地圖位置）

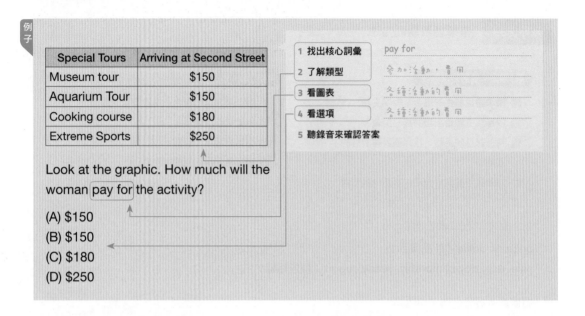

STEP 01　若沒答對會後悔的考題

請按照mp3錄音而先填寫右邊的空欄，再進行以下的考題

例子

Special Tours	Arriving at Second Street
Museum tour	$150
Aquarium Tour	$150
Cooking course	$180
Extreme Sports	$250

1 找出核心詞彙 　　pay for
2 了解類型 　　參加活動，費用
3 看圖表 　　各種活動的費用
4 看選項 　　各種活動的費用
5 聽錄音來確認答案

Look at the graphic. How much will the woman pay for the activity?

(A) $150
(B) $150
(C) $180
(D) $250

1

Floor	Tenants
5	P & R Accounting
4	Princess Orthopedics
3	Champion Software
2	Positive Advertisement
1	Castel Real Estate

1 找出核心詞彙
2 了解類型
3 看圖表
4 看選項
5 聽錄音來確認答案

Look at the graphic. What floor should the woman go to?

(A) Floor 2
(B) Floor 3
(C) Floor 4
(D) Floor 5

▶ 答案在解析本第096頁

1　What's the man want to do?

(A) Negotiating with the woman
(B) Coming to pick up the office supplies
(C) Helping the woman with the order
(D) Bargaining with the woman

Order	NO. 86425
Items / quantity	Unit price
Highlighter / 200	0.5 dollar
Duplicating paper / 200 boxes	30 dollars / box
Stapler / 20	15 dollars

2　How much should the man pay for staplers according to the woman?

(A) 300 dollars
(B) 255 dollars
(C) 345 dollars
(D) 200 dollars

3　What do the man's last words mean?

(A) He would cancel the order.
(B) He would give up buying the stapler.
(C) He would buy all the duplicating paper.
(D) He would buy fewer staplers.

4　What are they talking about?

(A) About the employee numbers
(B) About the training time
(C) About the interview results
(D) About the interview time

Interview Notice

• All applicants are requested to come to our company for an interview at ten a.m. next Monday.

• The interview is divided into three rounds and will be completed within a week.

• Candidates should be formally dressed.

6 June, 2017

5　How many candidates are there in all?

(A) 20
(B) 22
(C) 18
(D) 23

6　When will the interview be held?

(A) Next month
(B) This Friday
(C) Next week
(D) The week after next

▶ 答案在解析本第097頁

7　Will the woman go to see a science fiction movie with the man?

(A) Yes, she will.
(B) No, she won't.
(C) Not mentioned.
(D) Yes, she'd love to.

The Names of The Film	Time	Price
Love and Other Drugs	7:30	35 dollars
Love Actually	8:00	40 dollars
Midnight in Paris	8:30	35 dollars
The Holiday	9:00	35 dollars
The Painted Veil	9:30	40 dollars

8　Which love movie would they choose?

(A) *Love and Other Drugs*
(B) *Midnight in Paris*
(C) *The Painted Veil*
(D) *The Holiday*

9　What can we learn from the dialogue?

(A) They are lovers.
(B) The man likes to watch science fiction movies very much.
(C) The woman doesn't like to watch science fiction movies.
(D) The man respects the woman's choice.

10　What time did the man go to see the musical?

(A) Six twenty
(B) Twenty to seven
(C) Seven twenty
(D) Seven forty

Broadway musical *The Sound of Music*

Time: forty past six in the evening of May 6, 2018
Venue: Art Gallery
Seat: Row 25, No. 6
Fare: 890 dollars
Ticket No.: 22852582

11　Does the man like pop music?

(A) No, he doesn't. He likes jazz and country music.
(B) No, he doesn't. He likes all the music except pop music.
(C) Yes, he does. He likes all kinds of music
(D) Yes, he does. He likes all kinds of music besides jazz and country music.

12　Which of the following is correct?

(A) They both like pop music
(B) The man only likes jazz and country music
(C) The man watched the country music concert.
(D) They are in the same city now.

▶ 答案在解析本第098頁

Part 4
說明文

電話錄音
注意聽撥電話者的身份、目的、要求事項！

▶ **Part 4滿分策略**

Part 4總共有十個錄音、帶有三十個考題。這部份是聽每一段二十五到三十五秒鐘左右的錄音之後，回答考卷上三個問題。考題與選項會在考卷上顯示，但錄音的內容不會出現在考卷上，是由錄音員將錄音內容與考題唸一次。比起Part 3的對話內容，其錄音較長，所以若不熟悉解題技巧會覺得Part 4比Part 3更難。

1 和Part 3一樣會在考卷上顯示考題與選項，所以聽錄音之前，先看考題與選項是最重要的。此時最好將所看過的考題記憶下來。

2 不要逐字翻譯考題，而應該將此當作一個單位來處理；出現的考題大部分是固定的，所以得先熟知常出現的類型，並且要練習一看就馬上認出考題的方法。

3 在錄音當中，核心內容大部分在開頭與結尾的部分。而且如同Part 3，答案依照考題的順序來出現的機率為70%以上。因此在開頭的地方若是沒有聽清楚，作答第二題、第三題也會很辛苦。

Preview

1 **電話錄音類考題的特色**

電話錄音類型是指機構、公司的自動錄音系統訊息或個人的答錄機留言，大部分是以約二十五秒鐘左右的獨白形式出現。因為每月最少兩個、最多三個會出現，所以可以說是最重要的類型。其中，嗶聲後個人留話的答錄機留言是每月出現的，且機構、公司的自動語音系統錄音，每兩、三個月就出現一個。

2 **電話錄音類考題需考慮的重點**

❶ 若考題裡看到message、caller、reached、listeners、open、dial、press，就是電話錄音類考題。

❷ 若是機構的語音系統錄音類型的考題，得先看三個考題之後確認其類別！

攻略法 34 個人留話的答錄機留言

聽到了「現在無法接聽，請留言」，嗶聲後在答錄機裡留言。答錄機留言的順序為「我是～」、「我撥電話的理由為…」、「請你…」。

三個考題當中若有message、call、caller、calling等的單字，就是電話錄音類。該類中，若預測是答錄機留言，就得想到「說話者→主題、具體事項→要求事項」的留言順序，且應該預測在錄音內容的前、中、後當中哪裡有各個考題相關的線索。

《講師的建議》

平時得仔細學習電話錄音各階段的核心說法，而在考試時基於這些核心說法注意聽錄音的前、中、後的部分。此時邊聽錄音，邊在預測的答案位置標記。因此，若已有兩個左右的預測答案，聽錄音時會更容易找出答案。

第1階段：看考卷 **透過考題與選項來判斷錄音的類型！**

❶ 若考題裡看到以下的單字，就是個人電話留言類！

❷ 邊想「說話者→主題、具體事項→要求事項」的留言順序，邊預測答案的位置。

Why is the woman **calling?** ◀── 這是電話錄音類，且答案的線索可能會在前、中的部分！

(A) To schedule an appointment

(B) To place an ad in the paper

(C) To report a problem

(D) To announce an event

> 這個女人為什麼打電話？
> (A) 為了預約見面時間
> (B) 為了在報紙上登廣告
> (C) 為了報告一個問題
> (D) 為了公告一場活動

1 Who most likely is the caller?

有caller，所以是電話錄音類的考題。在問說話者為誰，所以其線索在錄音的前面！

> 1 打電話來的人很有可能是誰？

2 What is the purpose of the message?

也是透過message就能判斷其類型。這是詢問主題的，所以其線索應該在錄音的前面。

> 2 這項留言的目的是什麼？

3 Why does the woman request the phone call?

也是電話錄音類。「要求回撥」是在錄音後面出現的，所以其線索也在該部分。

> 3 這個女人為什麼要求電話回覆？

4 When is the listener asked to return the phone call?

就是電話錄音類。應該注意聽錄音後段的數字吧！！

> 4 這接聽者被要求什麼時候回撥電話？

首先在錄音的前段論及自己的名字、公司名稱、部門名稱，之後簡單說明撥電話的目的（訂貨、預約、詢問行程、請求建議、作業完成、報告問題、診察結果、修理完成等等）。接下來會出現詳細說明撥電話目的的部分，此時大部分為發生問題的情形（庫存不足、無法出席等等）。最後部分為「請確認後通知我」、「請回撥給我」之類的要求事項以及結語。

🎧 18-01.mp3

第2階段：聽錄音 播放錄音時聽核心詞彙前後的內容尋找答案！

❶ 透過電話錄音各階段的核心說法，了解錄音內容的順序。

說話者：This is 說話者 calling from 公司名稱

主題／具體內容：I'm calling about 主題 / Unfortunately...

要求事項：Please, Could you, I'd like

❷ 錄音內容進行到有關預測的答案時，決定是否為正確答案。

> 我是（公司名稱）的（說話者）。
> 我打電話來是有關（主題）／很不幸地…
> 請你…，您可否…，我想要…

Hi, this message is for Ms. Prechal. My name is Sara Jang. I'm the hiring manager for BNT accounting office.

I received your application, and I'm calling to schedule an interview with you for next week. However, I will be out of town this week and won't be back until this Sunday.

So, please call my assistant and let her know when you will be available. I look forward to meeting you.

I'm calling to為表示主題的核心說法。預約面試日期就是主題呢！

> 您好，這是給普契先生的留言。我的名字是莎拉·張。我是BNT會計事務所的招聘經理。
> 我收到你的申請而打電話來安排您下星期的面試時間。然而，我這週將要出差，並且在週日前不會回來。
> 因此，請打電話給我的助理，並讓她知道什麼時候可以來。我期待見到您。

1 說話者的自我介紹

Hi, John. This is Kanish Isida from Natural Interiors.

透過from後面的Interiors，能預測說話者為interior designer！

> 1 約翰您好。我是自然室內設計的卡尼許·伊斯達。

2 打電話的目的／具體內容

I'm calling about the bookcase you ordered from us last week. Unfortunately, the item you ordered was out of stock.

電話的目的為討論書架，可以預測配送上有問題！

> 2 我打電話來是有關你上週和我們訂的書架。很不幸地，你訂的貨沒有庫存。

3 要求事項／結語

Please call me and let me know if Monday works for you to come to meet me?

Please後面應該會出現要求事項。這是要求回撥電話的內容呢！

> 3 請給我電話，讓我知道星期一你是否方便和我見面。

1. 先看三個考題之後，判斷是否為個人電話留言類！← 考卷
2. 按照個人電話留言的進行順序來預測各個考題的答案的位置。← 考卷
3. 透過個人電話留言各階段的核心詞彙，了解錄音內容。← 錄音
4. 根據線索找出答案。← 考卷

個人電話留言的核心詞彙
Hi, 接聽者
I'm calling from 公司名稱
I'd like to leave a message for 聽話者
I'm calling about 主題 ／
I'm calling to 主題
I need to speak with you about 主題
Unfortunately / However, 論及問題
There have been difficulties 論及問題
So, please 要求事項／
I need to 要求事項
Thank / Hope you / Again 結語

Quiz

🎧 18-02.mp3

請聽錄音之後選出適當的答案。

Q1 What is the purpose of this message?

　　(A) To invite a guest speaker 　　(B) To confirm an appointment

Q2 What is the interviewee asked to bring?

　　(A) A photo identification 　　(B) A copy of a document

▶ 答案在解析本第100頁

攻略法

35 機構的自動語音系統錄音內容

打電話到公司或某些機構時，有時候會聽到自動語音系統的錄音回答。自動語音系統錄音是以「機構名稱」、「自動語音回答的理由」、「營業時間等公告事項」、「各項資訊」的順序而進行。

三個考題當中若有message、caller、reached、listeners、open、dial、press等單字，就是電話錄音當中的機構、公司的自動語音系統錄音。此時就得要想到「公司名稱／自動語音回答的理由→營業時間／公告事項→各項資訊」的錄音進行順序，然後預測各個考題的線索在錄音的前、中、後段的哪裡。

第1階段：看考卷 透過考題與選項來判斷錄音的類型！

❶ 若考題裡出現以下的單字，就是自動語音系統的錄音！

❷ 想「公司名稱／自動語音回答的理由→營業時間／公告事項→各項資訊」的錄音進行順序，之後預測答案的位置。

What type of business has the caller reached ?

(A) A medical office
(B) A restaurant
(C) A movie theater
(D) A fitness center

> 這是自動語音系統錄音類型，且其答案應該在錄音的前面部分！

這個人打電話到什麼樣的營業場所？
(A) 診療所
(B) 餐廳
(C) 電影院
(D) 健身中心

1 What type of business has the caller reached?

「聯絡到什麼樣的營業場所」，就是自動語音系統錄音類型！

1 這個人打電話到什麼樣的營業場所？

2 Who is this message intended for?

這是有關聽話者的。若聯絡到的地方為醫院，其聽話者應該是病患吧！

2 這個留言是給誰的？

3 When will the office open tomorrow?

這是自動語音系統錄音類型當中詢問營業時間的考題！其答案在錄音的中間部分！

3 這間辦公室明天什麼時候開始？

4 Why would the caller press '9'?

也是一樣的類型。在錄音後段部分提供資訊的時候，數字9附近應該有答案！

4 這個人為什麼會按「9」？

在開頭的部分會出現「您聯絡到了某營業場所（電力公司、電影院、觀光局、工廠、牙科診所、百貨公司的服務單位、火車站、銀行、圖書館）」的錄音內容，然後說明為什麼以自動語音系統錄音來回答（由於是國慶日、天氣不佳、星期天的關係），或直接提供該營業場所的介紹。接下來會出現具體的公告事項，此時大部分會論及營業時間等。

在最後的部分，以「若需要…，請您…」等的模式提供各個號碼的說明，然後以「謝謝您來電」等的說法來結語。

🎧 18-03.mp3

第2階段：聽錄音 播放錄音時，聽核心詞彙前後的內容尋找答案

❶ 透過自動語音系統錄音的各階段別核心詞彙，了解內容順序。

營業場所名稱，自動語音系統回答的理由：
You have reached 營業場所名稱
Our office is currently closed due to 理由
營業時間，公告事項：Our office hours are 營業時間
資訊/要求事項：If... / To... / For... , please... 資訊／要求事項

您聯絡到（營業場所名稱）
我們辦公室由於（理由）而目前休息
我們辦公室的營業時間為（營業時間）
如果…／為了…／為了…，請您（資訊／要求實行）

❷ 錄音內容進行到有關預測的答案時，決定是否為正確答案。

Thank you for calling Dr. Peterson's office. We're sorry we are not here to take your call due to the national holiday.

Thank you for calling是告訴營業場所名稱的核心說法。
Dr. Peterson's office是指診所，所以顯示這一點的選項就是答案！

Our regular office hours are 10 a.m. to 7 p.m. from Monday to Friday and 9 a.m. to 3 p.m. on Saturday. The office is closed on Sundays and holidays.

To make an appointment with Dr. Peterson, please call back during our regular business hours. We will reopen tomorrow morning, June 15th at 10 o'clock. Thank you, and have a nice day.

感謝您致電彼德森醫師辦公室。由於目前是國定假日，我們很抱歉無法在此接聽您的來電。
我們一般上班時間是從週一到週五的上午十點到下午七點，以及週六的上午九點到下午三點。週日及假日不上班。
要和彼德森醫師預約，請在我們平常上班時間來電。我們將會在明天早上六月十五日的十點再開始營業。謝謝您，並祝您有美好的一天。

1 營業場所名稱／自動語音系統回答的理由
You have reached Dr. Collins' Office. Our office is currently closed due to the national holiday.
You have reached、due to等告訴你「醫院」、「由於是國慶日」為答案！

1 您聯絡到了科林斯醫生的辦公室。由於是國慶日，我們辦公室目前不上班。

2 營業時間／公告事項
Our office hours are from 8 a.m. to 5 p.m. on weekdays.
從八點至五點為營業時間！

2 平日我們的辦公時間為早上八點至下午五點。

3 資訊／要求事項
For more information, please press 9.
按9的話，可能會得到附加資訊吧！

3 若需要更多資訊，請按9。

1 先看過三個考題，判斷是否為自動語音系統錄音類！← 考卷
2 按照自動語音系統錄音進行順序，來預測各個考題的答案的位置。← 考卷
3 透過自動語音系統錄音各階段的核心詞彙，了解錄音內容。← 錄音
4 根據線索找出答案。← 考卷

《講師的建議》

自動語音系統錄音的核心詞彙
You have reached 營業場所名稱
Our office is currently closed due to 自動系統回答的理由
Our office hours / business hours / hours of operation are 營業時間
However, please be aware that 公告事項
Members should be aware that 公告事項
For... , please 要求／資訊事項
To... , please 要求／資訊事項
If... , please 要求／資訊事項
Thank / Hope you / Again 結語

🔊 18-04.mp3

✏ Quiz

請聽錄音之後選出適當的答案。

Q3 Who is the caller trying to reach?

(A) An electric company   (B) An Internet service provider

Q4 Why would the caller press '1'?

(A) To make a reservation   (B) To leave a message

▶ 答案在解析本第101頁

| 攻略法34 | 個人留話的答錄機留言 |

聽錄音之前

邊看考題，邊判斷電話錄音的類型
Who most likely is the caller?
Why is the woman calling?
What does the woman ask the listener to do?
Why is the listener asked to arrive early?

依照個人電話留言的進行順序，預測錄音裡答案的位置
前面：自我介紹，簡單的主題
中間：主題具體事項，論及問題
後面：要求事項，結語

聽錄音時

若出現以下的核心詞彙，就會出現答案！
詢問撥電話的人或接電話人物身份的考題
Hi, 打電話對象人物. I'm calling from 營業場所名稱
I'd like to leave a message for 打電話對象人物

詢問主題或問題是什麼的考題
I'm calling about 主題
I'm calling to 主題
I need to speak with you about 主題
Unfortunately / However, 論及問題
There have been difficulties 論及問題

詢問要求事項的考題
So, please 要求事項, I need to 要求事項
Thank, Hope you, Again 結語

攻略法35　機構的自動語音系統錄音內容

聽錄音之前

邊看考題，邊判斷電話錄音的類型

What is the main purpose of the message?

Who is the caller trying to reach?

Who is this message intended for?

Why is the office currently closed?

When will the office open tomorrow?

Why would the caller press '9'?

依照自動語音系統錄音的進行順序，預測錄音裡答案的位置

前面：營業場所名稱，以自動系統錄音回答的理由

中間：營業時間，公告事項

後面：要求，資訊事項

聽錄音時

若出現以下的核心詞彙，就會出現答案！

詢問聯絡的營業場所名稱，或為何以自動語音系統回答的考題

You have reached 營業場所名稱

Our office is currently closed due to 自動系統回答的理由

詢問營業時間或公告事項是什麼的考題

Our office hours/ business hours / hours of operation are 營業時間

However, please be aware that 公告事項

Members should be aware that 公告事項

詢問要求事項或資訊事項的考題

For... / To... / If... , please 要求／資訊事項

Thank / Hope you / Again 結語

1 What's the purpose of the message?

(A) To reschedule a game
(B) To join a sports club

1 找出核心詞彙
2 類型與答案的位置
3 看選項

2 What type of company has the caller reached?

(A) A bank
(B) An embassy

1 找出核心詞彙
2 類型與答案的位置
3 看選項

3 What department does the speaker work in?

(A) Accounting
(B) Marketing

1 找出核心詞彙
2 類型與答案的位置
3 看選項

4 Who is this message intended for?

(A) Hotel employees
(B) Hotel customers

1 找出核心詞彙
2 類型與答案的位置
3 看選項

▶ 答案在解析本第101頁

5 What is the problem?

    (A) An item is not available.

    (B) Payment has been made.

1 找出核心詞彙 ....

2 類型與答案的位置 ....

3 看選項 ....

6 Why is the office currently closed?

    (A) Due to renovations

    (B) Due to a national holiday

1 找出核心詞彙 ....

2 類型與答案 ....

3 看選項 ....

7 What does the caller suggest the listener do?

    (A) Return the phone call

    (B) Visit the store

1 找出核心詞彙 ....

2 類型與答案 ....

3 看選項 ....

8 What does the speaker ask callers to do?

    (A) Stay on the line

    (B) Press '1'

1 找出核心詞彙 ....

2 類型與答案 ....

3 看選項 ....

▶ 答案在解析本第102頁

9 What kind of business is this?

   (A) A restaurant
   (B) A movie theater
   (C) An office supply store

1 找出核心詞彙

2 類型與答案的位置

3 看選項

4 預測對話內容　1）聯絡到了餐廳，但星期一為公休。

2）聯絡到了辦公用品店，但週末休息。

10 When is the store closed?

   (A) On Monday
   (B) On Friday
   (C) On Sunday

---

11 Why is the man calling?

   (A) To deliver a message
   (B) To reschedule a meeting
   (C) To get a co-worker's phone number

1 找出核心詞彙

2 類型與答案的位置

3 看選項

4 預測對話內容　1）為了通知晚發電話的人，然後要求回電。

2）為了詢問同事的電話號碼，而被要求來到行銷部門。

12 What does the man ask the listener to do?

   (A) Come to marketing department
   (B) Make a phone call
   (C) Catch an early flight

---

13 What is the caller's complaint?

   (A) The order arrived damaged.
   (B) The order hasn't arrived yet.
   (C) The wrong item was delivered.

1 找出核心詞彙

2 類型與答案的位置

3 看選項

4 預測對話內容　1）訂購的商品尚未到達，而要求回電。

2）訂購的商品有損，而要求退書。

14 What does the caller ask the company to do?

   (A) Refund the amount paid
   (B) Make a phone call
   (C) Deliver the order right away

▶ 答案在解析本第103頁

STEP 02 考題實戰練習　請留意前面練習過的兩個階段，進行以下的考題 答對的題目數：＿＿＿＿＿＿

1　Who is the caller?

(A) An accountant
(B) A clothing maker
(C) A sales manager
(D) A fashion designer

2　What is the problem?

(A) An item is not available.
(B) Some documents are missing.
(C) Some products were damaged.
(D) The delivery is late.

重要
 3 What does the caller need to know from Erica?

(A) The type of model she wants
(B) The time she will return to the office
(C) The cost of a specially ordered item
(D) The expected arrival time of delivery

4　Where does the speaker work?

(A) A travel agency
(B) A car rental company
(C) An insurance agency
(D) A pharmacy

Payment method	Rate charged
Annual payment	$179,671
Semi-annual payment	$93,429
Quarterly payment	$47,074
Monthly payment	$15,811

新
 5 Look at the graphic, how much will the listener pay each time after application?

(A) $179,671
(B) $93,429
(C) $47,074
(D) $15,811

6　What is the listener required to do for the change?

(A) He needs to submit an application form.
(B) He needs to make an online request.
(C) He needs to write a letter of apology.
(D) He needs to talk to a sales rep.

▶ 答案在解析本第105頁

以下為與真實考試同一類型和難易度的考題。請當作真實考試，邊計時邊回答吧。

高難度

 7 What is the purpose of the message?

(A) To order an electronics product
(B) To apply for a job opening
(C) To follow up on an application
(D) To get information about a company

8 What does the caller say about himself?

(A) He worked for a newspaper.
(B) He has relevant experience.
(C) He has heard a lot about the company.
(D) He has recently moved to the area.

9 What does the man say he will do?

(A) Stop by the office
(B) Show a contract
(C) Call back next week
(D) Submit a resume

---

10 What type of company probably has the caller reached?

(A) An Internet service provider
(B) A movie theater
(C) An auto repair shop
(D) A computer company

11 How long will the caller need to wait?

(A) 1 minute
(B) 2 minutes
(C) 5 minutes
(D) 10 minutes

重要

 Why would the listener press 2?

(A) To have the phone call returned
(B) To reserve a ticket
(C) To ask about products
(D) To know about payment options

▶ 答案在解析本第106頁

Review Test

請透過以下的小考確認前面所學過的內容。

1 個人電話留言的進行順序為何？　　　　　　　　　　　▶ ....
2 I'm calling about或I'm calling to後面出現的內容大部分為何？　▶ ....
3 在個人電話留言裡常出現的要求事項為何？　　　　　　▶ ....
4 機構／營業場所的自動語音系統錄音的中間部分，常出現的內容為何？▶ ....
5 若考題或選項裡有dial、press等單字，是哪種類型的？　▶ ....

Preview

1 **正式公告 I 類考題的特色**

正式公告是將正式場合上出現的「公告、通知」、「演說、演講」等都包括在內，且每個月出現四個錄音的重要類型。「公告、通知」當中最常出現的為「會議上的公告」，也就是在會議上主持人向出席者做的公告。其他各種場合（公司、購物中心、電影院、機場、交通工具等之內）的公告，大部分是由廣播系統播出的。

另外，活動開始之前做的活動相關說明與要求事項相關公告，特別分類稱之為「活動前公告」。此外，一個人講話的類型叫做「演說、演講」，這是截取講者的演講、演說內容的一部分的形式。

2 **正式公告 I 類考題需考慮的重點**

❶ 若考題裡有changes、go into effect、happen（時間點）、announce、new等說法，就是「會議上的公告」類型。

❷ 聯想「感言、主題→公告背景→要求事項、結語」的進行順序時，也預測答案的位置。

❸ 在「會議上的公告」其前段部分會出現「說話者」、「會議出席者」、「公告的主題」等。在中間部分會出現「問題的具體事項」，或者是提供充分理由來使「聽話者得到了解」的內容。在後段部分是以「結語」、「建議事項」或「下一場會議」構成。

❹ 在各種場所上的公告，要聯想「引起注意、主題→公告的背景→要求事項、結語」的進行順序，也同時預測答案的位置。

❺ 若有以上兩種類型，當錄音播放到含有答案的內容時，得同時決定答案選項。

|答案| 1.說話者→主題／具體事項→要求事項　2.電話錄音的主題　3.請回撥電話　4.營業時間/公告事項　5.機構／營業場所的自動語音系統錄音

攻略法

36

會議上的公告

在會議上，主持人向出席者傳達公告事項的類型叫做「會議上的公告」。以「向出席者發表的感言」、「關於某事因為什麼背景而公告」、「請如何如何做」的形式進行。

若在三個考題當中有changes、go into effect、happen（時間點）、announce、new等的說法，就是「會議上的公告」類型。此時聯想基本的進行順序「感言、主題→公告背景→要求事項、結語」，之後得預測各個考題的線索會在錄音內容的前、中、後的哪裡。

《講師的建議》

在公司開會的主要理由是什麼呢？為了討論政策上的變化、業績、策略，將新的員工介紹給大家，向大家公告即將退休的人是誰，或為了將工作進行的情況與大家分享等等。這些內容就是「會議上公告」的主題

第1階段：看考卷 透過考題與選項來判斷錄音的類型！

❶ 若考題裡看到以下的單字，就是「會議上的公告」類！

changes, go into effect, happen（時間點）, announce, new

❷ 邊想「感言、主題→公告背景→要求事項、結語」的順序，邊預測答案的位置。

What will happen next Friday? ← 這是「會議上公告」類型，答案可能在中間的部分！

(A) Computers will be replaced.

(B) An office will resume operation.

(C) Employees will register for a seminar.

(D) A demonstration will be held.

下個星期五會發生什麼事情？
(A) 電腦會被更換。
(B) 辦公室會重新辦公。
(C) 員工們會報名參加一場研討會。
(D) 展示會會被舉辦。

---

1 What is being changed?

有changed，所以可能是「會議上的公告」類型。線索應該在前面的部分吧！

1 什麼東西被變更？

2 What is the main purpose of the talk?

詢問演講主題的考題。在這種情形之下，若選項裡有change或announce，大部分就是答案！

2 這場演講的主要目的是什麼？

3 Who most likely is the speaker?

說話者大部分是manager等屬於能主持會議的地位的人。聽眾大部分是公司員工或行銷人員。

3 說話者很有可能是誰？

4 What will happen in July?

「在七月會發生什麼事情，所以得做什麼」類的內容順序。答案在中間的部分。

4 在七月會發生什麼事？

5 What does the speaker ask the listeners to do?

在「會議上的公告」的後面的部分會出現要求事項或下一個行程！答案是在後面的部分！

5 演講者要求聽眾做什麼？

錄音的前面部分會出現「謝謝來到某會議場所出席」這類的感言，之後再論及說話者、會議出席者、公告主題（業績／策略、公司政策、新進員工介紹、活動之前的準備事項、目前工作進行情況分享、維修工程通知等等）。

在錄音中間部分，論及「問題的具體事項」，或者是提供充分理由來使「聽話者得到了解」的內容等，這些內容可稱之為「公告背景」。另外，若是介紹新進人物，也會出現該人物的經歷與將要做的事情。

在錄音後段，以具體的要求事項以及「有疑問嗎？」、「有些建議嗎？」、「謝謝」等結語，或有關下一場會議的內容構成。

🎧 19-01.mp3

第2階段：聽錄音 播放錄音時，聽核心詞彙前後的內容尋找答案！

❶ 透過「會議上的公告」各階段的核心說法了解錄音內容的順序。

感言／主題： I'd like to tell you about 主題

公告背景： as you know/since S V/as you can see/first…

要求事項： make sure/please/you must 要求事項

❷ 錄音內容進行到有關預測的答案時，決定是否為正確答案。

Before we end today's meeting, I want to inform everyone about the new software that will be installed on all payroll department computers.

This software will help us process employee's paychecks much more efficiently. Next Friday, tech support will demonstrate how to use this software.

若還記得核心詞彙Next Friday，該說法後面聽到的「會示範」的部分為答案！

Please register for the demonstration on the company website by the end of this week. Any questions?

有關（主題）我想告訴你們
據你們所知／由於S V／如你們可以看到的／首先…
確認／請你／你得（要求事項）

在我們結束今天的會議之前，我想通知各位有關我們將會在發薪部門的所有電腦上安裝新軟體。這個軟體將幫助我們更加有效率地處理員工的薪水支票。下星期五，技術支援部門將會來示範如何使用這個軟體。
請在本週結束前，上公司的網頁報名這場示範會。有任何疑問嗎？

---

1 感言／主題

The next item on today's meeting agenda is our new recycling procedure.　可以知道這場會議是為了討論回收程序的。

1 今天議程當中下一個議題為我們全新的回收程序。

2 公告的背景原因

As you know, the cafeteria will undergo renovation as of this Friday.
As you know的後面會出現在談要求事項前，先說明背景的內容。

2 如你們所知道，這個星期五自助餐廳會進行整修。

3 要求事項／結語

Make sure to pick up coupons from several restaurants in the administrative office.　這場會議的公告事項為「請收取禮券」

3 請記得在行政辦公室領取幾張餐廳禮券。

1 「會議上公告」類型當中，若以人物介紹為主體，在前面部分一定會出現introduce
   或introduction。此時如果聽到new、newly等的單字，是在介紹新進人物的，則聽到
   retire、retirement等單字，就是介紹即將退休的人物的內容。

2 「會議上公告」類型考題裡面常出現以下的詞彙！

   on short notice（在很短的時間內）

   call a meeting（召開會議）

   meeting agenda（會議議題）

   make it to 活動名稱（參加…活動）

   give a reminder of（有關…提醒）

   give a brief overview（提供概況）

   implement a new policy（執行新的政策）

《講師的建議》

「會議上公告」類型的核心詞彙

I'd like to announce / talk about
clarify 主題
I'd like to introduce 人物
as you know, since S V, as you
can see, first 公告背景
I've just received 資訊／報告
So, please 要求事項
Make sure that 要求事項
Remember 要求事項
You must 要求事項

🎧 19-02.mp3

 Quiz

請聽錄音之後選出適當的答案。

Q1　What is the main purpose of the talk?

　　(A) To announce maintenance work　　(B) To recruit volunteers for the work

Q2　What does the speaker ask the listeners to do?

　　(A) Brainstorm ideas for improvement　　(B) Draw up quarterly sales data

▶ 答案在解析本第108頁

各種場合上的公告

廣播公告的各種場所包括：公司，公共場所（機場、火車站、表演廳、購物中心、書店、足球場等等），交通工具（飛機或火車等）

若三個考題當中有announcement，很有可能是各種場合上的公告。看到close或departure time等的話，其公告場所可能是購物中心、圖書館、機場等。如果看到employees、department等，很有可能是公司內部的公告。

一旦知道了公告類型之後，聯想「引起主題、主題→公告背景→要求事項、結語」的進行順序，然後得想各個考題的線索在錄音內容的前、中、後面的哪個部分。

《講師的建議》

「公告背景」是在談到要求事項之前，先提供背景理由的部分。這樣聽眾才會容易同意並一起行動。舉例來說，突然公告説「將所有的電腦關機，且儲存資料」的話，聽眾會感到訝異。因此，説「從三點開始會停電」的內容作為背景理由。

第1階段：看考卷 透過考題與選項來判斷錄音的類別！

❶ 若考題裡出現以下的單字，就是各種場合上的公告類！
announcement, employees, instructed, asked, suggested,
go into effect, close, departure time

❷ 想「引起主題、主題→公告背景→要求事項、結語」的進行順序，之後預測答案的位置。

公告，職員，被指示的，被要求的，被建議的，生效，關閉，出發時間

- -

What is the new departure time? ← 這是交通場所的公告，答案可能在中、後面部分！

(A) 1 p.m.　　(B) 2 p.m.　　(C) 3 p.m.　　(D) 4 p.m.

新的出發時間為何？
(A) 下午一點
(B) 下午兩點
(C) 下午三點
(D) 下午四點

1 Where most likely is the announcement being made?
裡面有announcement，所以是「公告」類型。將要仔細觀察剩下的兩個考題，猜測出來是哪一種場所的公告！

1 這個公告很有可能是在什麼場所的？

2 Who would most likely be making this announcement?
公告的人大部分是人事部門／管理部門／各場所的manager、飛機機長、火車車長、航空公司員工等等！

2 很有可能是誰在發出這個公告？

3 What are the passengers asked to have ready?
這是關於要求事項的考題。裡面出現「乘客」，所以是機場、飛機、車輛等裡面播出的公告！

3 乘客們被要求將什麼準備好？

4 What are employees advised to do?
出現「員工」，所以是「公司內公告」類型，且其答案可能在後面部分！

4 員工們被建議做什麼？

第2階段：聽錄音 播放錄音時，聽核心詞彙前後的內容尋找答案

① 透過各種場合公告的各階段別核心詞彙，了解內容順序。

引起注意、主題：Attention 聽眾

This is 說話者 from 部門

I have an announcement (reminders) about 主題

公告背景：due to 問題的原因

as you know 公告背景

要求事項、結語： Our office hours are 營業時間

② 錄音內容進行到有關預測的答案時，決定是否為正確答案。

Attention, passengers traveling on Flight 462 to Sydney.

Due to the bad weather, the airplane to this airport has been delayed in New York and has just arrived right here in Chicago. The flight is now scheduled to depart at 3 p.m.

———這是機場內的公告。出現問題的原因，也會提出全新的出發時間！

Please stay near the gate so that you can hear the announcements to board. We sincerely apologize for the delay and thank you for your cooperation.

搭乘462班機飛往雪梨的乘客請注意。
由於天候不佳，要到本機場的這班飛機在紐約被延誤，剛剛才到達芝加哥這邊。班機目前預訂的出發時間是下午三點。
請您待在登機口附近，才能聽到登機的通知。關於這個延誤，我們誠摯地致歉並感謝您的合作。

「公司／公共場所內公告」類型的進行順序

開頭的部分會出現公告的對象（員工、購物的民眾、乘客等等）。接著有可能會出現大略的公告主題：如果是公司內的話，常出現維修相關主題；若是其他場所，以營業時間或搭乘時間變更相關內容為主題。在中間部分將主題更仔細地說明或提供問題的原因。

最後部分以各種要求事項（請留在登機口附近、請使用頭上方的置物櫃、請在收銀台結帳、請準備離開、表演當中禁止喧嘩、錄音、攝影等等）以及「感到遺憾」、「謝謝合作」等的說法結語。

《講師的建議》

各種場合上公告類型的核心詞彙
Attention 聽眾 / This is 説話者 from 部門
I'm sorry to announce that 主題
This is just a reminder 主題
Welcome aboard 航班名稱
As you know 公告背景
Due to 問題的原因
Please 要求事項
Make sure 要求事項
Don't forget 要求事項

「車內公告」類型的進行順序

錄音開頭的地方會提示在哪一種交通工具（大部分是飛機上，偶爾是火車上）做的公告，也會論及聽眾、說話者、簡單的主題。中間部分會出現現在的氣象狀況、出發與到達時間、以及即將發生的事情（提供簡餐、電影播放等等）。若發生過問題，也會出現問題的具體內容或解決狀況。

在後面部分的話，以附加資訊（如果有疑問請按鈕）或要求事項（請留在位子上、請準備票等等）、以及「謝謝合作」等的說法來結語。

1　引起主題、主題

Attention, shoppers. The store will be closing in ten minutes.

出現attention，所以是公告。「即將打烊」為主題。

> **1** 請大家注意。這家店在十分鐘之內將打烊。

2　公告事項

Unfortunately, there was a disabled train ahead of us that had to be moved off the tracks.

透過「有拋錨的火車」可以知道火車進站的時間會延遲！

> **2** 很不幸地，在我們之前有一輛拋錨的火車得被搬離鐵軌。

3　要求事項、結語

So, please shut down your computer and cover it with plastic or other water-proof material.

有「請將電腦蓋起來」，所以是「公司內公告」類型。另外，由please能知道這是要求事項！

> **3** 因此，請把電腦關機，然後將它用塑膠或防水材質的東西蓋起來。

1 車內以及公司內公告的出現率不高，甚至也有都不出現的時候（平均三、四個月出現一段錄音）。但因為其錄音內容進行順序與考題很明確，所以一定得把三個考題全部都答對。

2 各種場合上公告類型裡，常出現以下的說法！

Welcome aboard.（歡迎搭乘。）

This is the captain speaking.（我是機長。）

seat belt signs[lights]（安全帶指示燈）

change in our departure time（我們出發時間的變更）

inclement weather conditions（險惡的氣象狀況）

perform annual maintenance checks（執行一年一次的維修）

 19-04.mp3

Quiz

請聽錄音之後選出適當的答案。

Q3 Where most likely is this announcement being made?

    (A) In a stadium   (B) In a store

Q4 What does the speaker suggest customers do?

    (A) Go to the checkout lane   (B) Check with the manager

▶ 答案在解析本第108頁

攻略法36　會議上的公告

聽錄音之前

邊看考題，邊判斷是否為「公司內公告」

Where most likely is the announcement being made?

Who would most likely be making this announcement?

What are employees advised to do?

依照「公司內公告」的進行順序，預測答案的位置
前段：感言／主題
中間：公告背景
後段：要求事項／結語

聽錄音時

若出現以下的核心詞彙，就會出現答案！
詢問「公司內公告」的主題、說話者、聽眾為何的考題

I'd like to announce/talk about 主題
I'd like to introduce 人物

詢問公告背景為何的考題

as you know, since S V, as you can see, first 公告背景
I've just received 資訊／報告

詢問要求事項的考題

So, please 要求事項
Make sure that 要求事項
Remember 要求事項
You must 要求事項

攻略法37　各種場合上的公告

聽錄音之前

邊看考題，邊判斷「各種場合上公告」的類型

Where most likely is the announcement being made?

Who would most likely be making this announcement?

What are the passengers asked to have ready?

依照「各種場合上公告」的進行順序，預測答案的位置
前段：引起注意／主題
中間：公告背景
後段：要求事項／結語

聽錄音時

若出現以下的核心詞彙，就會出現答案！
詢問「各場合上公告」的主題、說話者、聽眾為何的考題

Attention 聽眾 / This is 說話者 from 部門
I'm sorry to announce that 主題
This is just a reminder 主題
Welcome aboard 航班名稱

詢問公告背景為何的考題

As you know 公告背景
Due to 問題的原因

詢問要求事項為何的考題

Please 要求事項
Make sure 要求事項
Don't forget 要求事項
You must 要求事項

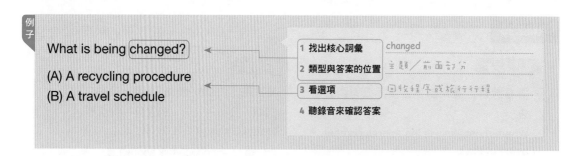

1 What kind of business does the speaker work for?

(A) A coffee shop chain
(B) An employment agency

    1 找出核心詞彙
    2 類型與答案的位置
    3 看選項

2 What is the purpose of the talk?

(A) To discuss plans to raise money
(B) To introduce a new staff member

    1 找出核心詞彙
    2 類型與答案的位置
    3 看選項

3 What does the speaker ask the listeners to do?

(A) Submit a certain request to personnel
(B) Report problems immediately

    1 找出核心詞彙
    2 類型與答案的位置
    3 看選項

4 What are the listeners asked to check for?

(A) Work schedules
(B) Daily announcements

    1 找出核心詞彙
    2 類型與答案的位置
    3 看選項

▶ 答案在解析本第108頁

5 What is the topic of the meeting?

(A) Riding in taxis
(B) Office expenses

1 找出核心詞彙 ....
2 類型與答案的位置 ....
3 看選項 ....

6 Where is the announcement being made?

(A) On an airplane
(B) On a train

1 找出核心詞彙 ....
2 類型與答案的位置 ....
3 看選項 ....

7 What event is taking place?

(A) A play
(B) A reception

1 找出核心詞彙 ....
2 類型與答案的位置 ....
3 看選項 ....

8 What are the employees asked to do?

(A) Test the alarm
(B) Do their routine work

1 找出核心詞彙 ....
2 類型與答案的位置 ....
3 看選項 ....

9 What does the survey report say?

   (A) An advertisement was successful.
   (B) The customers are satisfied.
   (C) Sales have declined.

1 找出核心詞彙	
2 類型與答案的位置	
3 看選項	
4 預測對話內容	1）因銷售量減少，公司發表解決方案。
	2）意見調查表示顧客滿意，所以另外討論。

10 According to the talk, what will happen next?

   (A) The group will make a presentation.
   (B) Response cards will be given out.
   (C) The survey results will be discussed.

---

11 Who is this announcement for?

   (A) Employees
   (B) Shoppers
   (C) Visitors

1 找出核心詞彙	
2 類型與答案的位置	
3 看選項	
4 預測對話內容	1）向員工公告：請確認是否遺失什麼東西。
	2）向客人公告：請填寫表格。

12 What are the listeners asked to do?

   (A) Fill out a form
   (B) Talk to the security manager
   (C) Check for missing items

---

13 Where most likely is this announcement being made?

   (A) In a parking lot
   (B) In an office
   (C) In a shopping mall

1 找出核心詞彙	
2 類型與答案的位置	
3 看選項	
4 預測對話內容	1）在辦公室停車相關的公告。
	2）在購物中心停車相關的公告。

14 Where should the listeners park until the garage is completed?

   (A) On the street
   (B) Around the corner
   (C) In a shopping center parking lot

▶ 答案在解析本第111頁

STEP 02 考題實戰練習　　請留意前面練習過的兩個階段，進行以下的考題 答對的題目數：＿＿＿＿＿＿

1　Why was the departure rescheduled?

(A) A piece of equipment was broken.
(B) There was a malfunctioning train.
(C) Some tracks were not repaired.
(D) The railway was closed.

2　When is the train scheduled to depart?

(A) At 4:30 p.m.
(B) At 5:45 p.m.
(C) At 6:15 p.m.
(D) At 8:30 p.m.

重要

3　What are passengers asked to do?

(A) Board according to the group number
(B) Look at a guidebook
(C) Check their seat assignments
(D) Stay near a departure gate

- -

4　Who is the speaker?

(A) A sales manager
(B) A maintenance worker
(C) A software designer
(D) A repair technician

重要

5　What will happen in July?

(A) A company will stop its operation.
(B) Renovations on a new building will begin.
(C) The speaker will transfer to a new city.
(D) A presentation will be made at a meeting.

6　What does the speaker ask the listeners to consider?

(A) Meeting a project deadline
(B) Moving to a different office
(C) Recruiting more employees
(D) Modifying a building design

▶ 答案在解析本第112頁

以下為與真實考試同一類型和難易度的考題。請當作真實考試，邊計時邊回答吧。

7　What is the main objective for the listeners to attend the seminar today?

(A) Learn about government policy
(B) Childcare and parenting
(C) Learn how to learn English as an adult
(D) How to earn 1 million dollars in a year.

Schedule	
Morning	
09:00~10:30 Bill Shun	Shadowing and speaking
11:00~12:30 Jessie Chen	Improve listening through TED talk
Lunch break	
Afternoon	
02:00~03:30 Marie Lin	Read between the lines
04:00~05:30 Debbie Chang	How to build up your writing skills?

新
8　Look at the graphic. Which speech will be given first?

(A) Shadowing and speaking
(B) Improve listening through TED talk
(C) Read between the lines
(D) How to build up your writing skills?

9　What was NOT mentioned by the host?

(A) Be back to seats on time
(B) Mute the cell phone
(C) No recording without permission
(D) Do not drink water

10　What is the main purpose of the announcement?

(A) To inform new safety procedures
(B) To announce the closing of the store
(C) To introduce payment options
(D) To advertise meat prices

11　Where are customers with questions directed to go?

(A) To the manager
(B) To the checkout lane
(C) To information center
(D) To customer service desk

高難度
12　Who can use the express checkout lanes?

(A) People who buy vegetables
(B) People who buy fewer than 15 items
(C) People who wait for over 20 minutes
(D) People who signed a survey form

正式公告 II
注意聽公告的場所、目的、要求事項！

Review Test

請透過以下的小考確認前面所學過的內容。

1 若考題裡有 changes、go into effect、happen、announce、new
是哪種類型？　　　　　　　　　　　　　　　　　　▶ ....

2 「會議上公告」類型的主要進行順序為何？　　　　　▶ ....

3 「會議上公告」類型之下，若選項裡有 change、announce是不
是答案？　　　　　　　　　　　　　　　　　　　　▶ ....

4 在公告當中，說明要求事項理由的部分叫做什麼？　　▶ ....

5 Please或make sure等的說法後面常出現的內容為何？　▶ ....

Preview

1 正式公告 II 類考題的特色

正式公告是將正式場合上出現的「公告、通知」、「演說、演講」等都包括在內的概
念，且每個月出現四個錄音的重要類型。「公告、通知」當中最常出現的為「會議上的
公告」，也就是在會議上主持人向出席者做的公告。其他各種場合上（公司、購物中
心、電影院、機場、交通工具等之內）的公告，大部分是由廣播系統播出的。

另外，活動開始之前做的活動相關說明與要求事項相關的公告，特別分類稱之為「活動
前公告」。活動相關說明之外，一個人講話的類型叫做「演說、演講」，這是截取講師
的演講、演說內容一部分的形式。

2 正式公告 II 類考題需考慮的重點

❶ Speech、schedule change、audience、give a talk、recently done、announcement、invited
to do等說法，若出現於三個考題裡，就是「活動前公告」類型。

❷ 若有「活動前公告」類型，先聯想「活動名稱、活動背景→活動內容、具體事項→要
求事項、後續行程、結語」的進行順序，再預測答案的位置。

❸ Audience、speaker、topic of the talk、field、speaker work、how many years、profession
等說法若出現於考題，就是「演說、演講」類型。

❹ 若有「演說、演講」類型，先聯想「自我介紹、主題→具體說明1→具體說明2、結
語」的進行順序，再預測答案的位置。

[答案] 1.會議上公告的類型　2.感言/主題→公告背景→要求事項、結語　3.答案　4.公告背景　5.要求事項

攻略法

38 回答活動前公告考題的方法

活動開始時主持人論及活動大概的順序或領獎者的類型。需要聽到在前面部分出現的活動名稱、說話者、聽眾，也一定得聽到包括後續行程的要求事項。

若在三個考題當中有speech、schedule、change、audience、give a talk、（人物）recently done、announcement、invited to do等的說法，就是「活動前公告」的類型。此時聯想基本的進行順序「活動名稱、活動背景→活動內容、具體事項→要求事項、後續行程、結語」，之後得預測各個考題的線索在錄音內容的前、中、後的哪裡。

第1階段：看考卷 透過考題與選項來判斷錄音的類型

① speech, audience, give a talk,（人物）recently done, invited to do, changes, go into effect, happen（時間點）, announce, new

② 邊想「活動名稱/活動背景→活動內容／具體事項→要求事項／後續行程／結語」的順序，邊預測答案的位置。

According to the speaker, what has Mr. Kim recently done?

這是「活動前公告」類型，答案可能在中間的部分！

(A) Got a contract
(B) Taught at a university
(C) Published a book
(D) Educated senior citizens

1 What is the purpose of the speech?

這是「活動前公告」類型，且其線索應該在前面部分。大部分的答案為「為了頒獎」等的選項。

2 Who is the audience?

有「聽眾」，所以很有可能是演講或演說前的公告。聽眾相關考題的話，其答案總是在前段部分出現！

3 Who is David Grandfield?

很有可能是領獎者或被邀請來的講師，且主持人在介紹當中會論及該人是誰。答案可能在前段或中間部分吧！

4 Why has there been a schedule change?

「活動前公告」裡常出現通知行程上突然的變化的情況！答案在中間部分！

《講師的建議》

在考試裡最常出現，大型會議（conference）前總主持人論及活動順序的情況。在頒獎典禮上主持人介紹領獎人，或公開演講上主持人介紹講師的也是屬於「活動前公告」。也有在展覽開幕時博物館長做開幕演說，或公司郊遊時公司的代表演說的情況。因此「活動前公告」裡，大部分以職位高的人作為説話者。

根據説話者，金先生最近做了什麼？
(A) 拿到合約了
(B) 在一所大學教書了
(C) 出版了一本書
(D) 教長輩們

1 這場演説的目的為何？

2 聽眾是誰？

3 大衛格蘭菲是誰？

4 為什麼有行程上的變化？

5 What does the speaker invite the audience to do after the presentation?

5 說話者邀請聽眾在報告之後做什麼？

介紹活動的具體事項之後，在最後的部分會說「報告之後有某事，所以請你們做～」形式的簡單要求事項。答案就在後面部分！

前段部分會出現「謝謝來參加活動／歡迎」類的說法，之後論及說話者、活動參加者、活動名稱（大部分是conference、頒獎典禮、演講／教育訓練、展覽會／博物館開幕典禮、示範活動、電影／表演、公司郊遊／宴會、退休典禮、新進員工歡迎會、博覽會、工廠開工典禮等等）。

在中間部分會介紹大概的活動順序或領獎者／演說者的經歷，有時候也會出現順序、場地、演講者的變更相關的內容。

後段部分以包括簡單要求事項（請你們參加…、請你們訪問…等等）的後續行程，與「謝謝」、「請你們享受吧」類的結語構成。

🎧 20-01.mp3

第2階段：聽錄音 播放錄音時，聽核心詞彙前後的內容尋找答案

❶ 透過「活動前公告」各階段的核心說法了解錄音內容的順序。

活動名稱/活動背景：Welcome to 活動名稱 / I'll be leading 活動名稱

活動內容/具體事項：First / Tonight / This evening 具體事項

要求事項/後續行程：Now, I'd like to invite you to 要求事項／後續行程

❷ 錄音內容進行到有關預測的答案時，決定是否為正確答案。

歡迎來到（活動名稱）／我將要主持（活動名稱）
首先／今晚／今晚（具體事項）
現在我想邀請你們（要求事項／後續行程）

Good evening, ladies and gentlemen. Tonight I'm pleased to present this year's award for effective management to Mr. Na-hoon Kim.

Mr. Kim is the president of GW Education, which is recognized as a global leader in the field of early childhood education. He recently published a book, *How to Improve Work Morale*, and it's receiving positive feedback among both critics and readers.

└─「活動前公告」類型的中間部分為介紹領獎人或演說者的經歷的內容，一般常出現「寫了什麼書」之類的話。

Tonight, we will learn from some of his experiences. Now I'm happy to introduce Mr. Na-hoon Kim.

各位女士各位先生，晚安。今晚我很榮幸將年度有效管理獎頒給金納宏先生。
金先生是早期幼兒教育領域裡被公認為世界領先的高威教育的總裁。他近期出版的書「如何改善士氣」，收到評論家和讀者群很正面的回應。
今晚，我們將從他的經驗當中來學習。現在我很高興介紹金納宏先生。

1 活動名稱／活動背景

Good morning, ladies and gentlemen, and <u>welcome to</u> the Association of Accountants' Annual Conference.

「活動前公告」類型裡，welcome的後面會出現活動名稱！

1 各位先生女士早安。歡迎來到會計師協會年度會議。

2 活動內容／具體事項

The first hour of this evening's program will feature guest conductor David Coulter, and <u>will be followed</u> by a 15-minute intermission.

這是介紹活動的大概程序的部分。答案應該在中間部分吧！

2 今晚活動的第一場客座指揮大衛考特即將演出，然後會有十五分鐘的休息時間。

3 要求事項／後續行程／結語

After lunch, <u>don't forget to</u> attend the keynote speech, titled "Effective Money Managemaent."

「活動前公告」類型的後面部分，會論及即將發生的事情或簡單的要求事項！答案應該在後面部分！

3 午餐之後，請別忘記參加主要演講「有效的金錢管理」。

《有關「活動前公告」類的考題一定得記得的說法！》

1 以Welcome開頭之後出現活動名稱的話，很有可能是「活動前公告」類型。「活動前公告」是由職位高的人（CEO、chairman、president等）來當作說話者的情形為多。被介紹的領獎者或演說者大部分接著簡單地演說。

2 「活動前公告」裡常出現的活動名稱為如下！

opening（開幕典禮）

employee appreciation's ceremony（慶功宴）

awards banquet（頒獎宴會）

fashion show（時裝秀）

new employee orientation（新進員工歡迎會）

new product review（新產品評估會議）

training seminar（訓練課程）

clients appreciation dinner（顧客感恩晚宴）

focus group session（小組討論時間）

《講師的建議》

「活動前公告」類型的核心詞彙

Ladies and gentlemen. Welcome to 活動名稱

I'll be leading 活動名稱

Welcome 聽眾

As 職稱

As you know, I'm 職稱

In just a minute 具體行程

First, 具體行程

Tonight 具體行程

This evening 具體行程

After lunch, don't forget 要求事項／後續行程

Afterward 後續行程

Now, I'd like to invite you to 要求事項／後續行程

Okay, let's start with 後續行程

🎧 20-02.mp3

✏️ Quiz

請聽錄音之後選出適當的答案。

Q1 Where most likely are the listeners?

(A) At an employee orientation (B) At an award banquet

Q2 What will the listeners do in the afternoon?

(A) Meet with managers (B) Take pictures for ID

▶ 答案在解析本第116頁

攻略法 39 回答演說、演講類考題的方法

這是說話者以講師或演說者的身份自己說話的類型，不同於「活動前公告」裡說話者以主持人身份介紹活動全體的程序。

若三個考題裡有 speaker、audience、topic of the talk、field、speaker work、how many years、profession 等的單字，就是「演說、演講」類型。此時得聯想「自我介紹、主題→具體說明1→具體說明2、結語」的進行順序，然後得預測各個考題的線索在錄音內容的前、中、後面的哪裡。

《講師的建議》

「演說、演講」類型的話，一不小心可能會與「活動前公告」混淆，但其最大的區別在於說話者以主持人身份介紹當日活動全體的行程，或是以講師或演說者的身份說自己的話。該類型的焦點不是在於全體的順序或行程上。

第1階段：看考卷 透過考題與選項來判斷錄音的類別！

❶ 若考題裡出現以下的單字，就是「演說、演講」類型！
audience, speaker, topic of the talk, field, speaker work,
how many years, profession

聽眾，演講者，演講的主題，領域，演講者從事，幾年，專業

❷ 想「自我介紹、主題→具體說明1→具體說明2、結語」的進行順序，之後預測答案的位置。

Where is this speech most likely taking place?
←── 這是詢問演說場地的。答案可能在前面部分！
(A) At an employee orientation　(B) At an awards ceremony
(C) At a job interview　(D) At a sales conference

這場演說很有可能在哪裡進行？
(A) 在一場員工歡迎會上
(B) 在一場頒獎典禮上
(C) 在一場面試上
(D) 在一場行銷會議上

1 What is the purpose of the speech?
這是詢問演說主題的考題。「演說、演講」類型的主題也是在前面部分出現。「領獎之後，為了表達感謝」為答案！

1 這場演講的目的為何？

2 Who is the speaker?
這是詢問說話者、也就是演說者或演講者為誰的考題。答案也是在前段部分！

2 這個演講者為誰？

3 Where is this speech most likely taking place?
這是演講/演講地點為何的考題。答案在前段或中間部分！

3 這場演講很有可能在哪裡進行的？

4 Who most likely is the audience for the speech?
職業類別出現在選項上的話，就是「活動前公告」或「演說、演講」類型，且其答案在前段部分。

4 這場演說的聽眾很有可能是誰？

5 What will the speaker do next?
這是詢問演說者的下一個行程的考題。也是「演講、演講」類型，且其答案在後段部分！

5 這個演講者接下來將做什麼？

在錄音前段部分，會出現「謝謝、歡迎」類的迎接詞與活動名稱（大部分是演講／教育訓練或研討會、求職面試、頒獎典禮、訪問分公司後的演講、講習會），然後說話者會介紹自己的身份。在此與「活動前公告」不同的一點，就是說話者即為演講者或演說者。

中間部分是以說話者本身仔細、具體的故事構成，而大部分為「在哪裡、幾年當中、做了什麼」類的過去經歷。

在錄音後段部分，講包括後續行程的具體事項之後，以「謝謝」等說法結語。

🎧 20-03.mp3

第2階段：聽錄音 播放錄音時，聽核心詞彙前後的內容尋找答案

❶ 透過「演講、演說」類型的各階段別核心詞彙，了解內容順序。

　自我介紹、主題：Welcome to 活動名稱, I'm 說話者, As 說話者
　　　　　　　　　　 I'd like to thank you for 主題

　具體內容1：I recently 經歷, I have been 經歷

　具體內容2、結語：I'd recommend 要求事項, Finally 後續行程
　　　　　　　　　　 Now let me 後續行程, Now please 要求事項、後續行程

❷ 錄音內容進行到有關預測的答案時，決定是否為正確答案。

歡迎來到（活動名稱），我是（說話者），以（說話者）的身份，有關（主題）我想表達謝意
我最近（經歷），我（經歷）了
我推薦（要求事項），最後（後續行程）
現在讓我（後續行程），現在請你們（要求事項、後續行程）

- -

Thank you for giving me the opportunity [to tell you more about my qualifications for this position.]

「因得到機會說自己的資格背景而感謝」可以視之為面試當中的speech！

I worked as a financial consultant for over 12 years. In those 12 years, I worked with many different types of small companies, like yours, helping them to expand their financial base.

I also have the necessary training for this job with my degree in business administration. And I'm currently taking some coursework to familiarize myself with the biotechnology industry.

感謝您給我這個機會來告訴您針對這個職位我的資格條件。
我做財務顧問已超過十二年。在這十二年當中，我和許多像你們一樣的不同類型的小公司一起工作，幫助他們開展他們的財務基礎。
為了這個工作，我也在企管學方面受了必須的訓練。同時為了讓我熟悉生物科技產業，我目前在修一些課程。

1 自我介紹、主題

Thank you for this award. I'm pleased to be here tonight in the company of my fellow science writers.

說話者為領獎者，其主題為領獎後表達的感想！

1 我對於這份獎賞非常感謝。我很高興今晚在這裡和我的科學文章作者同仁們在一起。

2 具體內容1

I have been a news reporter with the Korea Times over the past 10 years. 中間部分是有關自己的具體內容，且大部分有數字在內！

2 我在韓國時報當新聞記者當了十年多了。

3 具體內容2、結語

Now, please direct your attention to the screen at the front of the room. 出現包括後續行程的結語。這是後段部分的內容！

3 現在請你們注意看房間前方的螢幕。

《有關「演說、演講」類的考題一定得記得的說法！》

1 在Part 4裡，專業名稱不太會作為答案。舉例來說，若詢問聽眾為誰的考題的選項裡有 patients（病患）、doctors（醫生）、nurses（護士）、pharmacists（藥師），其答案可能是非專業人士的patients。但「演說、演講」類型，反而會以專業人士作為答案。詢問聽眾為誰的考題的答案，線索大部分在錄音的前段部分。

2 「演講、演說」類型裡常出現以下的說法！

qualifications for this position（這個職位的資格條件）

invited to speak（被邀請演說）

direct your attention to the screen（請注意看螢幕）

as I got older, I realized that S V（在我成長過程當中覺悟了…）

my greatest ambition（我最大的抱負）

《講師的建議》

「演講、演說」類型的核心詞彙

Welcome to 活動名稱
I'd like to thank you for 主題
I'm 說話者 / As 說話者
I recently 經歷
I have been 經歷
I'd recommend 要求事項
Finally 後續行程
Now let me 後續行程
Now please 要求事項、後續行程

🎧 20-04.mp3

🖊 Quiz

請聽錄音之後選出適當的答案。

Q3 Who most likely is the audience for the speech?

(A) Students (B) Teachers

Q4 Who is Steven Reynolds?

(A) A financial consultant (B) A radio host

▶ 答案在解析本第116頁

攻略法38　回答活動前公告考題的方法

聽錄音之前

邊看考題，邊判斷是否為「活動前公告」

What is the purpose of the speech?
Who is the audience?
Who is David Grandfield?
Why has there been a schedule change?
What does the speaker invite the audience to do after the presentation?

依照「活動前公告」的進行順序，預測答案的位置
前面：活動名稱／活動背景
中間：活動內容／具體事項
後面：要求事項／後續行程／結語

聽錄音時

若出現以下的核心詞彙，就會出現答案！
詢問活動前公告的主題、說話者、聽眾為何的考題

Welcome to 活動名稱
I'll be leading 活動名稱
Welcome 聽眾
as 職稱
as you know, I'm 職稱

詢問具體行程的考題

In just a minute 具體行程
First, ... 具體行程
Tonight... 具體行程
This evening... 具體行程

詢問要求事項或後續行程的考題

After lunch, don't forget 要求事項、後續行程
Afterward 後續行程
Now, I'd like to invite you to 要求事項、後續行程
Okay, let's start with 後續行程

攻略法39　回答演說、演講類考題的方法

聽錄音之前

邊看考題，邊判斷是否為「演說、演講」類型

What is the purpose of the speech?

Who is the speaker?

Where is this speech most likely taking place?

Who most likely is the audience for the speech?

What will the speaker do next?

依照「演說、演講」類型的進行順序，預測答案的位置
前段：自我介紹／主題
中間：具體說明1
後段：具體說明2／結語

聽錄音時

若出現以下的核心詞彙，就會出現答案！
詢問「演說、演講」的主題、說話者、聽眾為何的考題

Welcome to 活動名稱

I'd like to thank you for 主題

I'm 說話者 / as 說話者

詢問說話者的經歷的考題

I recently 經歷

I have been 經歷

詢問要求事項或後續行程的考題

I'd recommend 要求事項

Finally 後續行程

Now let me 後續行程

Now please 要求事項／後續行程

例子

Why has there been a [schedule change]?

(A) A guest speaker has arrived late.
(B) A room is unavailable.

1 找出核心詞彙　　　schedule change
2 類型與答案的位置　具體內容／中間部分
3 看選項　　　　　　被邀請的演說者遲到
4 聽錄音來確認答案　或沒有可用的房間

---

1 What are the listeners asked to do?

(A) Look at a schedule
(B) Register at the conference hall

1 找出核心詞彙
2 類型與答案的位置
3 看選項

2 What has been changed?

(A) The presenter
(B) The workshop schedule

1 找出核心詞彙
2 類型與答案的位置
3 看選項

3 What will the listeners do in the afternoon?

(A) Meet with department managers
(B) Become familiar with customer issues

1 找出核心詞彙
2 類型與答案的位置
3 看選項

4 Who is the speaker?

(A) A chief executive officer
(B) A software engineer

1 找出核心詞彙
2 類型與答案的位置
3 看選項

▶ 答案在解析本第116頁

5 What does the speaker invite the
   listeners to do after the lecture?

   (A) Sign up for future lectures
   (B) Attend a reception

1 找出核心詞彙
2 類型與答案的位置
3 看選項

6 What did the speaker want to be when
   he was young?

   (A) A teacher
   (B) A scientist

1 找出核心詞彙
2 類型與答案的位置
3 看選項

7 What is the purpose of the speech?

   (A) To express appreciation for an award
   (B) To explain company regulation

1 找出核心詞彙
2 類型與答案的位置
3 看選項

8 What is the speaker giving out to the
   participants?

   (A) Presentation notes
   (B) Software

1 找出核心詞彙
2 類型與答案的位置
3 看選項

9 Where is the speaker?

(A) In a banquet hall
(B) In a conference room
(C) In a bookstore

10 What did Sofia Russo do?

(A) She worked for a hospital.
(B) She published a book.
(C) She developed a medical drug.

1	找出核心詞彙	
2	類型與答案的位置	
3	看選項	
4	預測對話內容	1) 在會議室面試當中，且介紹經歷。
		2) 在宴會介紹演講者的經歷。

11 In what field does the speaker work?

(A) Computer programing
(B) Accounting
(C) Journalism

12 What does the speaker say about his previous work experience?

(A) It helped him learn how to perform various tasks.
(B) It doesn't cover the new task.
(C) He often went abroad on business.

1	找出核心詞彙	
2	類型與答案的位置	
3	看選項	
4	預測對話內容	1) 說話者在面試當中說明自己足夠的經歷。
		2) 新進員工說明自己經歷與新的工作沒有關聯。

13 What is the purpose of the talk?

(A) To introduce a guest speaker
(B) To announce the opening of a hotel
(C) To explain travel itinerary

14 What will most likely happen after the speech?

(A) There will be a short intermission.
(B) A question and answer session will be followed.
(C) Video footage will be played.

1	找出核心詞彙	
2	類型與答案的位置	
3	看選項	
4	預測對話內容	1) 說明旅遊行程之後暫時休息。
		2) 介紹演講者之後有提問時間。

▶ 答案在解析本第119頁

STEP 02 考題實戰練習　　請留意前面練習過的兩個階段，進行以下的考題　答對的題目數：＿＿＿＿＿

1　What is the main topic of the conference?

(A) Community health
(B) Presentation methods
(C) Software design
(D) Medical tools

2　What does the speaker say about the small group sessions?

(A) They will be held in various locations.
(B) They are not included in the program.
(C) They require prior registration.
(D) They are a part of product demonstrations.

重要
3　According to the speaker, what can the listeners find on the conference website?

(A) Survey reports
(B) An estimate
(C) Registration confirmation
(D) A program list

- -

4　Why is the announcement being made?

(A) To honor an employee
(B) To introduce several new dishes
(C) To announce schedule change
(D) To celebrate a company's success

5　Where will the lunch be served?

(A) In the main meeting room
(B) In the Red River Room
(C) In the Blue Mountain Room
(D) In the cafeteria

6　What does the speaker suggest the listeners do in the evening?

(A) Have dinner with close friends
(B) Attend a presentation
(C) Pick up questionaires
(D) Get a signed book

以下為與真實考試同一類型和難易度的考題。請當作真實考試，邊計時邊回答吧。

7   According to the speaker,
    what problem has there been?

    (A) An electric shut down
    (B) A memory lost
    (C) A traffic jam
    (D) An earthquake

8   Look at the graphic. Which session
    will take place else where?

    (A) The history of the disease
    (B) The early symptoms of the disease
    (C) Lunch break
    (D) Gene screening

9   What are the listeners warned NOT to do?

    (A) Touching the power switches
    (B) Climbing the stairs
    (C) Taking the elevators
    (D) Taking the shuttle bus

New Dawn to Alzheimer's Disease
May 25 – Grand Conference Hall
The history of the disease .... 9:00~10:20
The early symptoms of the disease .... 10:30~11:50
Lunch break
Gene screening .... 14:00~15:20
Q & A .... 15:30~16:50

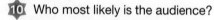

高難度
10 Who most likely is the audience?

    (A) Managers of a company
    (B) Members of a farmer's association
    (C) Customers at a computer store
    (D) Employees at a restaurant

11 What was recently developed?

    (A) Potential customers
    (B) A software system
    (C) Office supplies
    (D) A medical device

12 What will the speaker do next?

    (A) Show an audiovisual presentation
    (B) Guide a tour of a facility
    (C) Introduce a company director
    (D) Purchase a software system

Review Test

請透過以下的小考確認前面所學過的內容。

1 「活動前公告」類型裡得注意聽哪些內容？　▶ ....

2 「活動前公告」類型的基本進行順序為何？　▶ ....

3 「活動前公告」類型的中間部分會出現什麼內容？　▶ ....

4 暗示為「演說、演講」類型的單字有哪些？　▶ ....

5 「演說、演講」類型的基本進行順序為何？　▶ ....

6 在錄音裡，與後續行程內容一起出現的說法有哪些？　▶ ....

Preview

1 「廣播節目」類考題的特色

該類錄音是指在廣播裡播出的路況報導、天氣預報、受訪節目、新聞報導等，每個月出現一、兩個。路況報導與天氣預報的類型相似，且內容進行順序很明確，所以若熟知典型的類型與核心說法，很容易回答考題。但是路況報導與天氣預報在兩個月中出現不到一個。

受訪節目是主持人與來賓談話的內容，在三個月當中出現一個錄音左右。在考試裡最常出現的是「一般報導」類型，但內容本身很難且進行順序不固定，是屬於高難度的考題。

2 「廣播節目」類考題需考慮的重點

❶ 若考題裡有 hear next、suggest、recommend、advise、weather、traffic 等說法，就是「路況報導、天氣預報」類型。

❷ 「路況報導、天氣預報」的進行順序為「節目種類、目前狀況→論及問題→有用資訊、下次報導時程」。

❸ 在「路況報導、天氣預報」裡，交通或氣象狀況大部分在前段部分出現。

❹ 若考題裡有 announced、construction、project、business report、hear next 等說法，就是「一般報導」類型。

❺ 「一般報導」類型大部分顯示「節目種類→具體內容1→具體內容2、結語」的進行順序。

回答路況報導、天氣預報類型考題的方法

路況報導與天氣預報的類型相似。兩個類型都常常論及問題狀況，要注意聽問題以及其原因為何、有用的資訊為何、下一次報導是什麼時候、後續的節目是什麼等等。

若在三個考題當中有report或hear next，就是「廣播節目」類型。尤其是如果裡面有suggest、recommend、advise等，就是「路況報導、天氣預報」類型。此時，也可以透過weather、delay on（路名）或closed、traffic等的說法來區別「天氣預報」還是「路況報導」。

有該類型時，要先想基本的進行順序「節目種類、目前狀況→論及問題→有用資訊、下一次報導時程」，之後得預測各個考題的線索在錄音內容的前、中、後的哪裡。

第1階段：看考卷 透過考題與選項而判斷錄音的類型

① 若考題裡出現以下的說法，就是「路況報導、天氣預報」類型！
② 先聯想「節目種類、目前狀況→論及問題→有用資訊、下一次報導時程」的順序，再預測答案的位置。

When is the weather report most likely being given?
◄── 這是「天氣預報」類型，答案可能在前面部分！

(A) In the morning　　(B) At noon
(C) At 4 p.m.　　(D) In the evening

1 What does the report mainly concern?
這是詢問廣播節目類型的考題。透過剩下的兩個考題能預測是否為「路況報導」還是「天氣預報」。另外，聽錄音的前面部分也能判斷廣播節目的類型！

2 Who is this report probably for?
因為是「廣播」類型，所以能猜測其聽話者為聽眾！不聽錄音還是能回答考題！

3 According to the speaker, what is causing a problem?
因為是「廣播」類型，所以能猜測其聽話者為聽眾！不聽錄音還是能回答考題！

4 What does the speaker recommend listeners do this evening?
「路況報導/天氣預報」裡不止論及問題狀況，也會提供對此有用的資訊。這是詢問有用資訊的考題。答案在中間或後段部分！

《講師的建議》

「廣播節目」類型裡，除了「路況報導、天氣預報」以外，也有「一般報導」類型，還有「受訪節目」類型。其中「受訪節目」類型，除了前段部分的「這是…節目」以外，都很接近「活動前公告」或「會議上公告」類型中介紹人物的內容：錄音前段部分論及受訪人物為誰，接著在中間部分介紹人物的經歷，在最後部分介紹受訪者將要說什麼。

這次天氣預報很有可能是什麼時候提供的？
(A) 在早上
(B) 在中午十二點
(C) 在下午四點
(D) 在晚上

1 這篇報導主要是有關什麼？

2 這篇報導可能是為了誰的？

3 根據這個說話者，什麼造成問題？

4 這個說話者建議聽眾今晚做什麼？

5 When is the next traffic report?

這是「路況報導」類型。若在後段部分聽到數字，這就是答案的線索！

5 下一次的路況報導是什麼時候？

在錄音前段部分可以聽到問候語與主持人介紹，也能判斷是否為路況報導還是天氣預報。接著會出現目前的路況或氣象狀況報導。

中間部分會出現問題的原因以及結果。如果是「路況報導」，會聽到基於故障車輛、鄰近活動、道路施工、氣象條件惡化（降雪、起霧等）、水管破裂等塞車狀況；若是「天氣預報」，會聽到低雲、嚴重霧氣、炎熱、氣溫下降、豪雨、暴雪、打雷、閃電等問題狀況。

如此說明了問題狀況之後，在錄音後段部分會提供有用資訊（請使用大眾運輸、開車慢行、將外套留在家裡出門、到戶外去、別到戶外去、多喝水、記得帶外套、往別的道路繞去、帶著雨傘出去等等），接著介紹下一次報導時程後結束。

🎧 21-01.mp3

第2階段：聽錄音 播放錄音時，聽核心詞彙前後的內容尋找答案

❶ 透過「路況報導/天氣預報」各階段的核心說法了解錄音內容的順序。

節目種類、目前狀況： Good morning. This is 主持人名字 with your traffic / weather report.

論及問題狀況：However 論及問題 / 問題的原因 caused 問題的結果

有用資訊/下一次報導時程： Be sure/ Make sure 有用資訊

❷ 錄音內容進行到有關預測的答案時，決定是否為正確答案。

早安，我是路況報導/天氣預報的（主持人名字）。

然而（論及問題）／（問題的原因）造成（問題的結果）
請你確實（有用資訊）

Good evening, this is Jim Carter with your weather update. We are enjoying a beautiful and mild Wednesday evening.

前面部分介紹節目種類時也論及什麼時候的節目！(D)為答案！

However, this is going to change. We'll have rain tonight, and starting midnight, temperatures will drop dramatically, and there will be a snowfall in some areas along with some gusty winds.

So when you go out tomorrow morning, be sure to take a coat or a sweater. I'll be back in 30 minutes with another weather update.

晚安，我是吉姆‧卡爾特，為您做氣象更新。我們正享受著美好又溫暖的週三傍晚。

然而，即將要有變化了。今天晚上將會下雨，且從午夜開始氣溫會劇烈下降。有些地區將會下雪和伴隨著陣風。

因此當您明天早上外出的時候，要確定帶著外套或毛衣。我將在三十分鐘後回來做另一次的氣象更新。

1 廣播節目種類、目前狀況

And now for the latest GWF Radio's traffic report. Traffic is moving smoothly this afternoon.

在前面部分會出現問候語之後，也有主持人、節目種類、目前狀況等相關的線索！

1 那麼現在是GWF電台的路況報導時間。今天下午的車流移動得很順暢。

2 論及問題

However, after the rain stopped the temperatures fell.

「路況報導、天氣預報」的話，一定在中間部分論及問題，且其前後也可能會有該問題的原因！

3 有用資訊、下一次報導時程

Don't forget to take an umbrella with you.

報導「將下雨」的問題狀況，也應該提供有用資訊。Make sure或Don't等說法後面會有答案，接著在有用資訊的後面會說明下次報導是什麼時候！

2 但是，雨停了之後溫度會下降。

3 請別忘記帶雨傘。

《有關「路況報導、天氣預報」類的考題一定得記得的說法！》

1 是「路況報導」還是「天氣預報」，透過考題可以很容易判斷，或是由錄音前段部分也能聽得出來。只要是「路況報導、天氣預報」，大部分的聽眾為駕駛人。塞車的原因大部分是交通事故或道路施工。

2 「路況報導、天氣預報」類型裡常出現的問題狀況或原因相關說法！

paving（鋪路）	break down（拋錨）
congestion（停滯）	repair work（維修工程）
be backed up（塞車）	be closed to traffic（關閉無法通行）
heavy fog（濃霧）	freezing temperatures（結冰的溫度）
gusty winds（陣風）	excessive heat（嚴重的熱氣）
high humidity（高濕度）	

《講師的建議》

「路況報導、天氣預報」類型的核心詞彙

Good morning. This is 主持人名字 with your

We're happy to report that today 目前氣象狀況
I'm happy to announce that 目前路況
However, 問題狀況
Bad news 問題狀況
Due to 問題的原因
問題的原因 caused 問題狀況
I suggest 有用資訊
You should 有用資訊
We recommend 有用資訊
Be sure / Make sure 有用資訊
You may want 有用資訊

🎧 21-02.mp3

✏Quiz

請聽錄音之後選出適當的答案。

Q1 Who most likely is the speaker?

    (A) A radio reporter   (B) A hotel manager

Q2 What does the speaker suggest the listeners do?

    (A) Take an alternate route   (B) Drive slowly

▶ 答案在解析本第124頁

攻略法
41

回答一般報導類型考題的方法

「一般報導」是截取一部分新聞報導的形式，其內容很難。先找出主題可以幫助了解全體的脈絡。主題可以在錄音前段部分決定。接著出現的具體事項的話，先看考題之後再聽比較容易了解。

若是三個考題裡有report或hear next等，就是「廣播節目」類型。如果不是「路況報導、天氣預報」或「受訪節目」，就是「一般報導」類型，尤其是裡面有construction、project、business report等說法的時候。

此時要先聯想「廣播節目類型、主題→具體內容1→具體內容2、結語」的進行順序，然後預測各個考題的線索在錄音內容的前、中、後的哪裡。

《講師的建議》

「一般報導」的考題類型很多樣化，因此透過考題與選項有時候不容易判斷類型。但透過report可以得知是「廣播節目」類型，如果不是其他廣播節目類（路況報導、天氣預報、受訪節目），就可以判斷成「一般報導」類型；例如，聽到news report或business report，就要知道是「一般報導」類型。

第1階段：看考卷 透過考題與選項來判斷錄音的類別！

❶ 若考題裡出現以下的單字，就是「一般報導」類型！

report, announced, construction, project, business report, hear next

❷ 想「廣播節目類型、主題→具體內容1→具體內容2、結語」的進行順序之後，預測答案的位置。

報導，發表，施工，計劃，商務新聞報導，下次聽

What was announced by the city transportation authority?
　　　　透過announced、construction等可以知道是「一般報導」類型！
　　　　這是詢問主題的考題，所以答案是在前段部分！

(A) A proposal to fix the city's street
(B) A plan to reduce air pollution
(C) The opening of a website
(D) Approval for a construction project

城市交通局發表了什麼？
(A) 城市道路維修案
(B) 空氣污染減少計劃
(C) 網站開設
(D) 施工案許可

1 What is the subject of this business report?
告訴你這是「廣播節目」中「一般報導」類型的考題。答案的線索在前段部分！

2 What construction project is the announcement about?
「一般報導」的主題常為建築或施工，需要聽清楚是哪一種。其答案在前段部分。

3 Who most likely is the speaker?
若透過另外兩個考題預測到了「一般報導」，那麼這題就是以newscaster（新聞報導主持人）作為答案的考題！

1 這個商務新聞報導的主題為何？

2 這個發表是有關什麼施工計劃的？

3 這個說話者很有可能是誰？

4 How long will the project take?

「一般報導」類型裡project或construction常常出現！在中間部分說明具體內容時可能會找出答案。

5 What do some people expect will happen?

具體內容在錄音後段部分再次深入說明。先有了某一件事情，再深入說明該事情，所以答案很有可能在後段部分。

4 這個案子將要持續多久？

5 有些人預測將發生什麼事？

在錄音前段部分會出現問候語與廣播節目的種類（商業新聞、地區新聞、特定節目介紹等等），接著會聽到說話者自我介紹和主題（公司併購/合併、學校建設方案許可、施工開始、高速公路開通、道路維修計劃、特定公司的工廠建設、土地採購等等）。

在中間部分會針對已論及的主題，透過數字、日期等來說明具體內容。

在錄音後段部分是用轉換說法（however、so、in addition等）提供更多附加的具體內容，然後以廣播節目種類、附加資訊應該參考什麼資源、下一個節目（大部分是天氣預報）是什麼等說法來結束。

🎧 21-03.mp3

第2階段：聽錄音 播放錄音時，聽核心詞彙前後的內容尋找答案

❶ 透過「一般報導」類型的各階段別核心詞彙，了解內容順序。

廣播節目種類/主題：Now for 節目名稱 / In local news today 主題 / announced/decided/approved 主題

具體內容1： however, so, in addition 附加具體內容

具體內容2、結語： So be sure to tune in 下一個節目時程

❷ 錄音內容進行到有關預測的答案時，決定是否為正確答案。

現在是（節目名稱）的時間／今天的地區新聞為（主題）／發表／決定／許可（主題）
然而，所以，此外（附加具體內容）
因此請你們確實收聽（下一個節目時程）

Now for the local news. The city transportation authority finally approved the plan to build the highway connecting the border and the capital city.

「一般報導」類型的主題都在前面部分決定。將「許可高速公路建設計劃」加以變化的(D)為答案！

Long distance commuters and other travelers have always complained about the length of time they spend driving from the border to the capital city by taking local roads.

If the construction is successfully completed by next year as planned, it is expected that taking the new highway will reduce commuting time to two hours. Drivers taking the highway will pay a toll of $5.

現在是地區新聞時間，都市交通當局終於通過了興建聯結邊境和首都的高速公路的計畫。
長距離通勤者和其他旅行者總是抱怨他們要花長時間駕駛於邊境和首都的地區道路。
若這項建設照計畫在明年成功完成，預計利用新的高速公路會將通勤時間減少成兩個小時。使用這條高速公路的駕駛人將要付五元通行費。

1 廣播節目種類／主題

In local news today, the city planning committee today announced they will expand regional sports complex.

這是「地區新聞」，且其主題應該為為「區域運動場地的建設」。

2 具體內容1

The school, which will be completed in 3 years, will hold about 500 students from 1st to 6th grade.

中間部分是對主題加以具體說明的部分，且常包含數字！

3 具體內容 2、結語

However, planning the center took quite a while due to the city's limited budget.

多說明附加具體內容的部分，也就是後段部分的內容。

1 關於地區新聞。城市計劃委員會今天公佈他們將擴大區域運動設施。

2 將在三年之內完工的這所學校會容納從一年級到六年級的五百個學生。

3 但是，由於城市有限的預算，這個中心的規劃經過了相當長的時間。

《有關「一般報導」類的考題一定得記得的說法！》

1 「一般報導」類型的主題在前段部分出現。但若沒聽到也無妨，先認為是「併購、合併」或「建設、施工」，然後只要在中間部分注意聽數字、事情的原因、結果、影響範圍、主要人物等，大部分都能找出答案。

2 「一般報導」類型裡常出現以下的說法！

acquisition（併購）、merger（合併）、plan（計劃）、opening（開幕）、proposal（提案）、construction（建設）、committee（委員會）、expand（擴大）、add（增加）、result（結果）、take place（發生）、due to（由於）、concern（憂慮）、in the next few years（接下來幾年之內）、cost 1.5 million dollars（需要一千五百萬美金）、approximately 200 local workers（大概兩百個當地工人）、soon（即將）、several months（幾個月）、meet next week（下週見）、finish（結束）、be completed（完成）、reduce traffic congestion（減少交通堵塞）、be scheduled to start（預期開始）、be encouraged（被鼓勵）

《講師的建議》

「一般報導」類型的核心詞彙

主持人名字 from 電台名稱
Now for 節目名稱
In local news today 主題
Announce/decided/approved 主題
However, so, in addition 附加具體內容
OK, that's it for today. Tune in 下一個節目時程 for the interview with 人名
So be sure to tune in 下一個節目時程
Now back to 人名 in the studio

🎧 21-04.mp3

✏️Quiz

請聽錄音之後選出適當的答案。

Q3 Who most likely is Sandra Johnson?

(A) A news reporter   (B) A corporate head

Q4 How long will the project take?

(A) Two months   (B) Four months

▶ 答案在解析本第124頁

攻略法40 回答路況報導、天氣預報類型考題的方法

聽錄音之前

邊看考題,邊判斷是否為「路況報導、天氣預報」

What does the report mainly concern?

Who is this report probably for?

According to the speaker, what is causing a problem?

What does the speaker recommend listeners do this evening?

When is the next traffic report?

依照「路況報導、天氣預報」的進行順序,預測答案的位置

前面:節目種類、目前狀況

中間:論及問題

後面:有用資訊、下一次報導時程

聽錄音時

若出現以下的核心詞彙,就會出現答案!

詢問「路況報導、天氣預報」類型的說話者、聽眾、主題、目前狀況為何的考題

Good morning. This is 主持人名字
with your traffic/weather report.
I'm happy to announce that 目前路況

詢問問題狀況或原因的考題

However, 論及問題

bad news 論及問題

Due to 問題的原因

問題的原因 caused 問題的結果

詢問有用資訊或下一次報導時程的考題

I suggest 有用資訊

You should 有用資訊

We recommend 有用資訊

Be sure/ Make sure 有用資訊

攻略法41　回答一般報導類型考題的方法

聽錄音之前

邊看考題，邊判斷是否為「一般報導」類型

What is the subject of this business report?

What construction project is the announcement about?

Who most likely is the speaker?

How long will the project take?

What do some people expect will happen?

依照「一般報導」類型的進行順序，預測答案的位置

前段：節目種類／主題

中間：具體說明1

後段：具體說明2、結語

聽錄音時

若出現以下的核心詞彙，就會出現答案！

詢問「一般報導」類型的說話者、聽眾、主題為何的考題

This is 主持人名字 from 電台名稱

Now for 電台名稱

In local news today 主題

詢問「一般報導」類型的具體內容的考題

however, so, in addition 附加具體內容

詢問「一般報導」類型的具體內容以及下一個節目的考題

OK, that's it for today. Tune in 下一個節目的時程

for the interview with 人名

Now, back to 人名 in the studio.

例子

What is the subject of this business report?

(A) A business merger
(B) Road repairs

1 找出核心詞彙   subject of the business report
2 類型與答案的位置   主題／前面部分
3 看選項   公司合併或道路修理
4 聽錄音來確認答案

---

1 What is the reason of the delay?

(A) A car accident
(B) Road repairs

1 找出核心詞彙
2 類型與答案的位置
3 看選項

---

2 What are the listeners asked to do?

(A) Turn up the radio
(B) Keep listening to the radio

1 找出核心詞彙
2 類型與答案的位置
3 看選項

---

3 What does the report mainly concern?

(A) Weather
(B) Traffic

1 找出核心詞彙
2 類型與答案的位置
3 看選項

---

4 According to the speaker, what will be needed in the morning?

(A) A heavy coat
(B) An umbrella

1 找出核心詞彙
2 類型與答案的位置
3 看選項

▶ 答案在解析本第124頁

5 What does the speaker recommend the listeners do this afternoon?

(A) Drive carefully
(B) Take an umbrella

1 找出核心詞彙
2 類型與答案的位置
3 看選項

6 Who is Mr. Chen?

(A) A company president
(B) A broadcaster

1 找出核心詞彙
2 類型與答案的位置
3 看選項

7 What is the report mainly about?

(A) A business aquisition
(B) A construction project

1 找出核心詞彙
2 類型與答案的位置
3 看選項

8 What will happen at noon?

(A) There will be a commercial break.
(B) Listeners will call the radio station.

1 找出核心詞彙
2 類型與答案的位置
3 看選項

9 Who most likely is talking?

(A) A pilot
(B) A weather forecaster
(C) A travel agent

1 找出核心詞彙	
2 類型與答案的位置	
3 看選項	
4 預測對話內容	1）旅行社員工說明天是陰天。
	2）氣象預報員說明天是晴天。

10 What's the weather going to be like tomorrow?

(A) Rainy
(B) Sunny
(C) Cloudy

---

11 What is the subject of the report?

(A) A business merger
(B) A marketing campaign
(C) The release of a new computer

1 找出核心詞彙	
2 類型與答案的位置	
3 看選項	
4 預測對話內容	1）新電腦將在兩週之內上市的新聞。
	2）因為新行銷策略，從今天起開始販賣產品。

12 When will the new product arrive in stores?

(A) Today
(B) Within two weeks
(C) Within three weeks

---

13 What does the speaker recommend?

(A) Take public transportation
(B) Drive slower than usual
(C) Take an alternate route

1 找出核心詞彙	
2 類型與答案的位置	
3 看選項	
4 預測對話內容	1）請使用大眾運輸。下一次路況報導在五分鐘之後。
	2）請走別的道路。下一次路況報導在十五分鐘之後。

14 When is the next traffic report?

(A) In 5 minutes
(B) In 10 minutes
(C) In 15 minutes

▶ 答案在解析本第127頁

 **STEP 02** 考題實戰練習　請留意前面練習過的兩個階段，進行以下的考題　答對的題目數：＿＿＿＿＿

1　Who is the announcement for?

(A) Drivers
(B) Pilots
(C) News reporters
(D) Police officers

2　What is the problem on Route 4?

(A) There is construction.
(B) There was a helicopter crash.
(C) There was an accident.
(D) There are too many travelers.

3　Where is the speaker?

(A) In a news studio
(B) In a car
(C) On the ground
(D) In a helicopter

 重要
4　Who is this talk directed to?

(A) Radio station employees
(B) Public servants
(C) Government officials
(D) Residents

 重要
5　What are the listeners asked to avoid?

(A) Water plants
(B) Swim in the pool
(C) Take a walk
(D) Throw garbage

6　What can be found at the website mentioned by the speaker?

(A) A map of current weather information
(B) A list of ways to conserve energy
(C) Addresses of government officials
(D) A price list for gardening tools

7   Why did the city residents lose electric power?

(A) There was a big storm.
(B) There are too many residents in the city.
(C) Work crews are installing a new system.
(D) The Power Company employees are on strike.

8   What makes it difficult for workers to work?

(A) Strong winds
(B) Low temperatures
(C) Foggy conditions
(D) Heavy rains

9   When will the entire city have power?

(A) This afternoon
(B) This evening
(C) Tonight
(D) Tomorrow morning

10 Who is the special guest today?

(A) Gracie Hunter
(B) Jennie Chen
(C) Claire Jenson
(D) Emma Newton

	The name of the dish
1	Appetizer
2	Fruit Salad
3	Steamed fish
4	Stewed beef

新

11 Look at the graphic. What dish is most likely to be introduced on the show?

(A) Appetizer
(B) Fruit Salad
(C) Steamed fish
(D) Stewed beef

12 What's the name of the book given out as a gift?

(A) How to Bake Delicious Cakes
(B) Best Lunch Boxes for Children
(C) Don't Nuke, Let's Stew
(D) Roast Beef and Sea Salt

Review Test

我們在前面學過「廣播節目」類型。請透過以下的小考確認前面所學過的內容。

1 「路況報導、天氣預報」類型裡常出現哪些單字？　▶ ....

2 「路況報導、天氣預報」類型的前面部分常出現什麼內容？　▶ ....

3 「路況報導、天氣預報」類型的主要進行順序為何？　▶ ....

4 「一般報導」類型裡常出現的單字有哪些？　▶ ....

5 「一般報導」類型的主要進行順序為何？　▶ ....

Preview

1 「廣告、參觀、觀光」類考題的特色

「廣告」類型大部分是廣播或電視廣告的一部分，先簡單說明廣告商品之後，會再說明購買方法、優惠等。該類型很明確，且每月一定出現最少一次。

「參觀、觀光」類型是一種帶著「公告」色彩的錄音內容。該類型具有在參觀/觀光地點說明全體行程以及注意事項的內容特色，且每兩個月出現一次。「廣告」類型與「參觀/觀光」類型的內容順序或形式很明確，所以比起別的類型，考題及答案位置更明顯、也很容易回答問題。

2 「廣告、參觀、觀光」類考題需考慮的重點

❶ 若考題裡有 advertised、advertisement、offered、benefit、featured、discount、provided、advantage 等單字，就是「廣告」類型。

❷ 「廣告」類型的主要進行順序為「引起注意、廣告產品→優點→購買方法、優惠、期間」。

❸ 「廣告」錄音的後段部分大部分出現購買方法、優惠、優惠期間，然後以催促的話語結束。

❹ 若考題裡有 tour、tourist、later in the day、come to see、exhibit、group 等，就是「參觀、觀光」類型。

❺ 「參觀、觀光」類型大部分的進行順序為「參觀地點、背景知識→參觀行程→注意事項、勸導話、許可、以及後續行程」。

[答案] 1. report, hear next, suggest, recommend, advise, weather, traffic　2.問候語，主持人介紹，節目種類，目前路況或氣象　3.節目種類/目前狀況→論及問題→有用資訊/下一次報導時程　4. report, announced, construction, project, business report, hear next　5.節目種類/主題→具體內容1→具體內容2、結語

回答廣告類型考題的方法

「廣告」錄音以疑問句開頭，且在考題裡也常出現「廣告」一詞。請注意聽廣告的商品、優點、優惠是什麼，以及為了得到附加資訊該做什麼。

若考題裡有advertise或advertisement，就是「廣告」類型。另外，offered、benefit、featured、discount、provided、advantage等單字也常出現。一旦知道錄音類型，接著要想到基本的進行順序「引起注意、廣告產品→優點→購買方法、優惠、期間」，之後得預測各個考題的線索在錄音內容的前、中、後的哪裡。

《講師的建議》

「廣告」類型的開頭的地方與別的錄音有很明顯的區別性。其特色為大部分以「不是需要…嗎？」、「想要…嗎？」等的疑問句開始。另外，根據「請別忘記」、「請別錯過」、「請不要再猶豫」等催促的話語的出現也很容易判別其類型。

第1階段：看考卷 透過考題與選項來判斷錄音的類型

❶ 若考題裡出現以下的單字，就是「廣告」類型！

advertised, advertisement, offered, benefit, featured, discount, provided, advantage

❷ 「引起注意、廣告產品→優點→購買方法、優惠、期間」

- -

What is being advertised? ◄── 這是「廣告」類型，而且是詢問廣告的商品為何的考題，所以其答案可能在錄音前段或中間部分！

(A) Insulation　　(B) Electrical supplies
(C) Furniture　　(D) Appliances

正在廣告什麼？
(A) 絕緣體
(B) 電器零件
(C) 家具
(D) 家電器具

---

1 What is being advertised?
這是詢問廣告商品為何的考題。在前面部分的疑問句後面就有答案。

1 什麼正在被廣告？

2 Who most likely is the intended audience for the advertisement?
這是詢問「廣告」的聽眾為誰的考題。思考廣告商品為何，可以猜測到答案。

2 這項廣告的預設聽眾很有可能是誰？

3 How is the company different from its competitors?
這是詢問廣告商品的優點的考題。優點大部分出現於前面或中間部分，而答案可能在那兒裡。

3 這家公司如何不同於競爭對手？

4 According to the advertisement, how can someone purchase the product?
這是「廣告」類型的詢問購買方法的考題！答案的一半以上是「請撥電話」。

4 根據這項廣告，人們要如何購買該商品？

5 According to the speaker, why should people visit the website?
在結語附近提供提供附加資訊的地方。到訪網站的理由大部分是為了得到附加資訊。

5 根據該說話者，民眾為什麼要到訪網站？

在錄音的前段部分會出現疑問句以及對廣告商品的暗示。接著會聽到廣告商品（大部分是餐廳、旅行社、商店打折活動、表演、課程等）。中間部分是陳述廣告商品的優點的地方，例如「給折扣」、「增加了什麼服務項目」、「歷史悠久了」、「可以量身定做」等與別的商品之間的區別。

在錄音後段部分會說明購買方法（撥電話、到門市、至網頁）與優惠（折扣、免費贈送、免費配送、安裝服務等），以及該優惠的期間，然後以催促的話語（請趕快購買、請別錯過、請到門市、請撥電話、希望你如何等）來結束。

🎧 22-01.mp3

第2階段：聽錄音 播放錄音時，聽核心詞彙前後的內容尋找答案

❶ 透過「廣告」類型各階段的核心說法了解錄音內容的順序。

引起注意、廣告商品：(Are you) looking for 引起注意

It's time 廣告商品 / 公司名稱 will be offering 廣告商品

We've 優點：We've now added 優點 / specialize in 優點

購買方法/優惠/期間：If... / In order to... / To... , 購買方法

Visit / Call / hurry to 公司名稱

❷ 錄音內容進行到有關預測的答案時，決定是否為正確答案。

你正在找…嗎？（引起注意）
現在是（廣告商品）的時間／（公司名稱）將提供（廣告商品）
我們目前增加了（優點）／專門（優點）
如果…／為了…／為了…（購買方法）
請到／撥電話／趕快（公司名稱）

Do you want a house that is more environmentally-friendly?
If so, Forest in Your Home is the answer.

↑ 在前面部分會出現大概的線索，接著會聽到廣告什麼商品的。(C)為答案！

We provide a variety of furniture such as sofas, chairs and tables and decoration materials, all of which are made of natural and safe materials.

And this week only, we'll give you a 40% discount on all hand-made furniture in our store. As usual, we cover finance charges for 6 months. Call us today at 503-555-0167 to find the store near you and enjoy a healthy and natural life.

你希望擁有一棟更環保的房子嗎？如果是這樣，「森林在你家」就是答案。
我們提供各種家具，如沙發、椅子和桌子以及裝潢材料，全都是以天然安全的材料製成的。
僅限於本週，對於我們店裡所有的手工家具，我們將給您百分之四十的折扣。和平時一樣，我們負擔六個月以內的融資手續費。今天就打電話503-555-0167給我們，找到距離您最近的商店，並享受健康自然的生活。

---

1 引起注意、廣告商品

Are you looking for an exciting job? If so, consider joining the Oakfield wait staff. 以疑問句開始的話，就是廣告類型！可以知道是徵人廣告！

1 你正在找有趣的工作嗎？如果是的話，請考慮參加「橡木園」的服務團隊。

2 優點

Unlike other renowned restaurants, we have been specifically designed for families. 在中間部分會陳述兩、三個優點！

2 有別於其他知名餐廳，我們是特別為家庭單位客人準備的。

3 購買方法、優惠、期間

<u>Stop by</u> any of our locations near you to take advantage of this offer. 答案的50%為「請撥電話」，25%為「請到門市」，而其他為「請至網頁」類。

3 為了利用這項優惠，請去到你們附近的門市即可。

《有關「廣告」類的考題一定得記得的說法！》

1 「廣告」類型的95%以上以疑問句開始，而且商品一定會在前段部分出現。廣告內容當中先說明優點，之後再提供購買方法，其中一半以上為「請撥電話」、「請到門市」或「請至網頁」等。

2 「廣告」類型裡常出現以下的說法！

state-of-the-art（最先進的）
authentic（正統的）
customized（量身定做的）
next day installation service（隔日安裝服務）
rated as best for three years in a row（三年連續被評審為最好的）
the sale runs（販賣持續）
This offer is only good until（僅提供到某期限）
Availability is limited.（貨量有限）

《講師的建議》

「廣告」類型的核心詞彙
(Are you) looking for / (Are you) interested in / Do you need to 引起注意
It's time 廣告商品
公司名稱 will be offering 廣告商品
Visit/Try 公司名稱
We've now added 優點
Specialize in 優點
Not only that, but 優點
Specially 優點
Unlike 優點
If... / In order to... / To... 購買方法
Visit / Call / hurry to 公司名稱
For more information, 附加資訊
Don't miss / hope / looking forward to 結語

22-02.mp3

✎ Quiz

請聽錄音之後選出適當的答案。

Q1 What type of business is being advertised?

(A) A training institute (B) A computer store

Q2 According to the advertisement, why would the listeners call the number?

(A) To get a consultation (B) To see a doctor

▶ 答案在解析本第131頁

回答參觀、觀光類型考題的方法

若tour或tourist常出現，就是「參觀/觀光」類型。有該類型的話，注意聽參觀地點、全體行程、注意事項、集合地點、第一個參觀地點是什麼地點就行。

若三個考題以及選項裡有 tour、tourist、later in the day、come to see、group 等單字，很有可能是「參觀、觀光」類型。此時得聯想「參觀地點、背景說明→參觀行程→注意事項、勸導、許可、以及後續行程」的進行順序，然後得預測各個考題的線索在錄音內容的前、中、後的哪裡。

《講師的建議》

以概括的觀點來看，「參觀、觀光」類型也是一種「公告（announcement）」。但是有別於其他公告類型，「參觀、觀光」類型很明確地傳達特定地點的參觀行程或參觀注意事項，因此要另外分類出來。還有，這類的考題以及選項大部分有tour或tourist，且錄音內容通常以「Welcome+場所名稱」來開始，所以能很容易判別出類型。

第1階段：看考卷 透過考題與選項來判斷錄音的類型

❶ 若考題／選項裡出現以下的單字，就是「參觀、觀光」類型！
❷ 想「參觀地點、背景說明→參觀行程→注意事項、勸導、許可、以及後續行程」的進行順序，之後預測答案的位置。

- -

Who most likely is the speaker?

(A) A sales manager

(B) A photographer

(C) A ticket agent

(D) A tour guide ← 選項裡有tour guide的考題，基本上就是「參觀/觀光」類型！

這個說話者很有可能是誰？
(A) 行銷主管
(B) 攝影師
(C) 售票員
(D) 導遊

---

1 Who most likely is the speaker?
若選項裡有tour或tour guide，在考題上很有可能是「參觀、觀光」類型！

1 這個說話者很有可能是誰？

2 Where is the announcement being made?
「參觀/觀光」類型的話，welcome錄音後段就有答案。

2 這項公告正在哪裡公布的？

3 What does the speaker recommend to the listeners?
「參觀/觀光」類型裡會出現注意、勸導、許可事項！答案可能在中間、後段部分！

3 這個說話者要給聽話者什麼建議？

4 Where are people asked to return?
與參觀行程相關，這是詢問集合地點的考題。中間或後段部分應該會有答案！

4 民眾被要求回到哪裡？

5 What will most likely happen next?

將所有的行程與注意/勸導/許可事項說明後，介紹後續行程時會出現答案！線索應該在錄音後段吧！

錄音前段部分以「歡迎」類的問候語開始，之後會出現參觀地點（古蹟、博物館、工廠、動物園、城市、國家公園等等），然後說話者自我介紹為導遊。接下來會出現參觀地點的背景知識，此時為了說明歷史與規模常聽到數字。

中間部分會簡單說明參觀所需時間、具體的參觀地點等。

錄音後段部分會出現注意事項（禁止拍照、攝影，禁止帶入食物、禁止離席、準時集合、小心步行、禁止依靠窗戶、禁止餵食動物、禁止丟棄垃圾）與勸導、許可事項（去禮品店、在飛機上慢行、戴保護鏡、拍照、多喝水、提問等等），最後出現「好，若準備好，請跟我來」、「開始吧」等即將要發生的事情的暗示與結語。

🎧 22-03.mp3

第2階段：聽錄音 播放錄音時，聽核心詞彙前後的內容尋找答案

❶ 透過「參觀/觀光」類型的各階段別核心詞彙，了解內容順序。

參觀地點、背景知識：Welcome to 參觀地點 / My name is 導遊名字

參觀行程： Our tour will start with 參觀行程

注意/勸導/許可事項以及後續行程：Please / Be sure 注意/勸導事項

Now / Let's begin / Please follow me

後續行程

❷ 錄音內容進行到有關預測的答案時，決定是否為正確答案。

- -

Welcome to the Sakamoto Art Museum. My name is Miyuki, and I'll be your guide. This big museum was built 100 years ago, and the number of daily visitors here reaches 1,000.

透過「Welcome+地點名稱」可以知道是為「參觀/觀光」類型，而其說話者為tour guide！

The museum has many different art collections, but our tour here lasts only 1 hour because our time is limited. We'll begin our tour at the contemporary art wing and end up back here in the restaurant.

Photography is not allowed in any of the galleries, so please remember not to take pictures on the tour. All right. Everyone ready? Follow me!

5 接下來很有可能會發生什麼事？

歡迎來到（參觀地點）／我叫（導遊名字）
我們的旅遊以（參觀行程）開始
請你／請務必（注意/勸導事項）
現在／我們開始／請跟我來（後續行程）

歡迎來到坂本藝術博物館。我的名字是美雪，我將是你們的導遊。這個大型博物館建造於一百年前，每日到這兒的遊客量達到一千人。

這個博物館有很多不同的藝術收藏品，但是由於我們時間的限制，今天在這進行的參觀只有一小時。我們將從現代藝術廳開始我們的參觀，然後回到這邊的餐廳結束。

在任何展覽廳都不允許拍照，因此請記得參觀中不要照相。好。每個人都準備好了嗎？跟我來！

1 參觀地點、背景知識

Welcome to Jiri Mt. National Park. My name is John, and I will be your tour guide.

這是「參觀/觀光」類型，且其參觀地點為國家公園、其說話者為tour guide！

2 參觀行程

Our tour lasts approximately 2 hours and ends back here at the souvenir shop.

這是說明參觀行程的部分，也是錄音的中間部分。有時候會論及多個參觀地點！

3 注意、勸導、許可事項以及後續行程

Be sure that you drink water frequently throughout the tour. Now let's begin our tour.

「請多喝水」為注意或勸導事項，也能知道參觀即將開始了。

1 歡迎來到智力山國家公園。我的名字叫約翰，我將是你們的導遊。

2 我們的旅遊需要大概兩個小時，然後回到禮品店這兒結束。

3 請你們在旅遊行程中務必常喝水。現在我們開始旅遊吧。

《有關「參觀/觀光」類的考題一定得記得的說法！》

1 錄音開頭的地方聽到Welcome的類型只有「活動開始公告」與「參觀、觀光」類型。若接著聽到地點名稱就是「參觀、觀光」，而說話者為「導遊」，參觀地點大部分為「古蹟、博物館、工廠、城市、動物園」等。

2 「參觀、觀光」類型裡常出現以下的說法！

sites and attractions（遺址與景點）
restored to its original condition（恢復為其原狀的）
take several short breaks（多次短暫休息）
proceed from the gift shop（從禮品店繼續前進）
slippery（滑的）
uneven（不均勻的）
contemporary art wing（當代藝術廳）
main feature（主要特點）

《講師的建議》

「參觀、觀光」類型的核心詞彙

Welcome to 參觀地點 / My name is 導遊名字
I'll be showing you 參觀地點
We'll start the tour of 參觀地點
Our tour will last approximately 所需時間
Our tour will start with 參觀行程
Please / Be sure 注意/勸導事項
I recommend 注意/勸導事項
Now / Let's begin / Let's get started / Please follow me 後續行程

🎧 22-04.mp3

✏ Quiz

請聽錄音之後選出適當的答案。

Q3 Where is the announcement being made?

(A) In a factory   (B) In a sales meeting

Q4 What will most likely happen next?

(A) A tour will begin.   (B) A movie will be shown.

▶ 答案在解析本第132頁

攻略法42 回答廣告類型考題的方法

聽錄音之前

邊看考題，邊判斷是否為「廣告」類型
What is being advertised?

Who most likely is the intended audience for the advertisement?

How is the company different from its competitors?

According to the advertisement, how can someone purchase the product?

According to the speaker, why should people visit the website?

依照「廣告」類型的進行順序，預測答案的位置
前段：引起注意、廣告商品
中間：優點
後段：購買方法、優惠、期間

聽錄音時

若出現以下的核心詞彙，就會出現答案！
詢問「廣告」類型的主題、說話者、聽眾的考題

(Are you) looking for / (Are you) interested in / Do you need to 引起注意
It's time 廣告商品
公司名稱 will be offering 廣告商品
Visit / Try 公司名稱

詢問廣告商品的優點的考題
We've now added 優點
specialize in 優點
Not only that, but 優點
specially 優點
unlike ~ 優點

詢問購買方法、優惠、附加資訊的考題
If... / In order to... / To... 購買方法
Visit / Call / hurry to 公司名稱
For more information 附加資訊
don't miss / hope / looking forward to 結語

攻略法43　回答參觀、觀光類型考題的方法

聽錄音之前

邊看考題，邊判斷是否為「參觀、觀光」類型

Who most likely is the speaker?

Where is the announcement being made?

What does the speaker recommend to the listeners?

Where are people asked to return?

What will most likely happen next?

依照「參觀、觀光」類型的進行順序，預測答案的位置

前段：參觀地點、背景知識

中間：參觀行程

後段：注意、勸導、許可事項以及後續行程

聽錄音時

若出現以下的核心詞彙，就會出現答案！

詢問「參觀」類型的說話者、聽眾、地點為何的考題

Welcome to 參觀地點 / My name is 導遊名字

I'll be showing you 參觀地點

We'll start the tour of 參觀地點

詢問參觀行程等具體內容的考題

Our tour will last approximately 所需時間

Our tour will start with 參觀行程

詢問注意、勸導、許可事項以及後續行程的考題

Please/ Be sure 注意、勸導事項

I recommend 注意、勸導事項

Now / Let's begin / Let's get started / Please follow me 後續行程

例子

How long is the tour expected to last?

(A) One hour
(B) Two hours

1 找出核心詞彙   tour expected to last
2 類型與答案的位置   具體內容（旅遊行程）／前面部分
3 看選項   一個小時或兩個小時
4 聽錄音來確認答案

---

1 What is being advertised?

(A) A magazine
(B) A TV program

1 找出核心詞彙
2 類型與答案的位置
3 看選項

---

2 What is true about the restaurant?

(A) It offers free dessert.
(B) Seafood is its specialty.

1 找出核心詞彙
2 類型與答案的位置
3 看選項

---

3 Who is the speaker?

(A) A tour guide
(B) A security guard

1 找出核心詞彙
2 類型與答案的位置
3 看選項

---

4 How long will they stay at the Wilson House?

(A) Half an hour
(B) One hour

1 找出核心詞彙
2 類型與答案的位置
3 看選項

▶ 答案在解析本第132頁

5　Why is the business offering discounts?

(A) To celebrate its anniversary
(B) To close its business

1　找出核心詞彙
2　類型與答案的位置
3　看選項

6　How can someone use the service?

(A) By giving a call
(B) By visiting a website

1　找出核心詞彙
2　類型與答案的位置
3　看選項

7　What will customers receive if they call now?

(A) Free shipping
(B) Free installation

1　找出核心詞彙
2　類型與答案的位置
3　看選項

8　What are the tourists asked to do?

(A) Stay quiet
(B) Carry their garbage

1　找出核心詞彙
2　類型與答案的位置
3　看選項

▶ 答案在解析本第133頁

9 What service is being offered to the customers?

   (A) Complimentary gift wrapping
   (B) Free delivery
   (C) Installation without charge

10 When does the sale start?

   (A) On Monday
   (B) On Friday
   (C) On Sunday

1 找出核心詞彙
2 類型與答案的位置
3 看選項
4 預測對話內容

1）免費配送的優惠在星期五開始。

2）免費安裝的優惠在星期一開始。

---

11 What has the audience come to see?

   (A) An art museum
   (B) A historic site
   (C) An automobile factory

12 Where are people asked to return?

   (A) To an airport
   (B) To a bus
   (C) To a gift shop

1 找出核心詞彙
2 類型與答案的位置
3 看選項
4 預測對話內容

1）參觀古蹟的民眾在公車上集合。

2）參觀美術館的民眾在禮品店集合。

---

13 What is convenient about the product?

   (A) It can be easily carried.
   (B) It can be folded.
   (C) It's very lightweight.

14 Where can the listeners find the product?

   (A) In a department store
   (B) In a hair salon
   (C) At a supermarket

1 找出核心詞彙
2 類型與答案的位置
3 看選項
4 預測對話內容

1）商品很輕。在百貨公司有貨。

2）商品很容易搬運。在超市有貨。

▶ 答案在解析本第134頁

STEP 02 考題實戰練習　請留意前面練習過的兩個階段，進行以下的考題 答對的題目數：_____

1　What type of business is being advertised?

(A) A train
(B) An Internet service
(C) A moving company
(D) A hotel

重要
2　What change has the business made recently?
(A) It has hired more staff.
(B) It has expanded into a new market.
(C) It has updated its websites.
(D) It has added a service.

3　According to the speaker, who will receive a discount this month?
(A) First-time customers
(B) Patrons
(C) Local residents
(D) Contest winner

- -

4　Who is Marie-Clare Cooper?

(A) A teacher
(B) A tour guide
(C) A sculptor
(D) A gardener

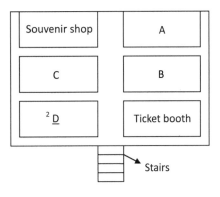

新
5　Look at the graphic. Where is the coatroom?

(A) A
(B) B
(C) C
(D) D

6　Which artworks are NOT being displayed?

(A) Paintings
(B) Sculptures
(C) Potted plants
(D) Photographs

▶ 答案在解析本第136頁

7   Where most likely is the announcement being heard?

(A) On a bus
(B) On a ship
(C) On a train
(D) In an airplane

8   Why will they take a few stops in the morning?

(A) To purchase some food
(B) To take pictures
(C) To take a rest
(D) To pick up other groups

重要
 9 What does the speaker encourage people to do?

(A) Drink water
(B) Feed the animals
(C) Speak quietly
(D) Carry their trash with them

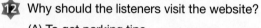

10 Who most likely is the speaker?

(A) A movie director
(B) A tour guide
(C) A restaurant manager
(D) A mayor

11 What is included as part of the special package?

(A) Tickets to a museum
(B) A discount at the gift shop
(C) A city tour
(D) A guidebook

高難度
12 Why should the listeners visit the website?

(A) To get parking tips
(B) To see a list of current performances
(C) To register for an event package
(D) To learn more about city attractions

▶ 答案在解析本第137頁

Review Test

Part 4的獨白主題，一般可分為錄音、公告、廣播、廣告……等，這些獨白題的破解重點在前面都講過。透過下面的小測驗，看看前面Chapter講述的內容，你是否都理解了。

1 若獨白是「廣告」類型，預測答案出現的順序為何？ ▶ ....

2 在廣告類型的獨白中，與講述產品優點相關的核心詞彙有哪些？ ▶ ....

3 若獨白是「廣告」類型，預測答案出現的順序為何？ ▶ ....

4 若題目出現be sure..., I recommend, let's begin, please follow... ，
可能是哪種獨白主題？搭配的問題可能為何？ ▶ ....

Preview

1 會在Part 4獨白題搭配出現的圖表類型

❶ 時間表

與各種議程、課程時間表……等有關。

可能出現的題目為會議時間或議程變更、選購課程……等。

❷ 報告

與銷售報告、調查報告……等有關。

可能出現的題目為根據報告衍生的討論項目。

❸ 產品資訊

與商品購買、產品價格……等有關。

可能出現的題目為產品選購、訂購產品的變更……等。

❹ 地圖

與樓層平面圖、地圖……等有關。

可能出現的題目為確認某公司或建築物的位置、找尋某公司或建築物的所在位置……
等。

|答案| 1. 前段：引起注意、廣告商品；中間：產品優點；後段：購買方法、優惠、期間 2. we've now added, specialize in, not only, but, specially, unlike 3. 前段：參觀地點、背景知識；中間：參觀行程；後段：注意、勸導、許可事項、後續行程 4. 參觀或觀光類型，與注意、勸導、許可事項、後續行程有關的題目

攻略法 44
破解圖表題的方法

這是TOEIC改制後的新題型，面對這樣的題型，要先看懂圖表的內容，才能準確掌握獨白主題、獨白中的關鍵內容。

2018年的多益改制，除了在Part 3新增圖表題之外，Part 4也新增獨白搭配圖表的新型題組。獨白搭配圖表，三個題目為一題組，其中一題一定會與圖表的內容有關，主要在測驗考生聽力、閱讀的能力。

和Part 3的圖表內容差不多，基本上包括：表格、時間表、價目表、優惠券、地圖、樓層平面圖……等等。只要看得懂圖表內容，就會推斷出獨白的主題。假設圖表是與會議的時程表有關的話，那說話者可能是會議的司儀，宣布會議的注意事項、時程變動；如果獨白是價目表的話，那說話者可能為銷售人員或公司的工作人員，透過電話留言提供商品價目資訊、確認訂購資訊……等等。

第1階段：看考卷 邊看考題與圖表時，邊預測獨白主題

Agenda of the annual meeting
New recruit training
Oversea expansion
Market trend
Budgetary reduction

Look at the graphic . Which topic will be discussed first ?

(A) New recruit training
(B) Oversea expansion ── 與圖表有關，「會議時程」為主題 ──
(C) Market trend
(D) Budgetary reduction

請看此圖，哪一個主題會先討論？
(A) 新進人員訓練
(B) 海外拓展
(C) 市場趨勢
(D) 預算刪減

觀看表格，可發現表格主題為會議時間，

年會會議議程表
新進人員訓練
海外拓展
市場趨勢
預算刪減

再看題目是在詢問會議中，先進行討論的議程主題為何，因此可以推斷說話者為會議的司儀或是主持人。這類的題目，需要搭配圖表與獨白一起作答，若只看題目與圖表，答案會是(A) New recruit training，但多益考試不會這麼簡單，通常在獨白中會講述基於某原因而造成議程有所變動，所以要搭配獨白的內容進行作答。

第2階段：看圖表 **看圖表並聽錄音，找尋核心詞彙**

① 會議時間
講者名、序數、start, change, switch

② 銷售報告
sale, rise, down, monthly, yearly, report

③ 產品資訊
price, number, discount, cancel, order

④ 地理位置
map, beside, front, right, left, across, opposite

接下來，我們來看幾個常在Part 4出現的圖表類型。

1　與會議時間相關的圖表與獨白範本

🎧 23-01.mp3

Program	
Speaker	**Time**
Mr. Chambers	1:30-2:00
Ms. Jones	2:10-2:40
BREAK	2:40-3:00
Mr. Black	3:00-3:30
Ms. Albom	3:40-4:10
Q & A	4:10-4:30

畫底線的部分是為了幫助你了解更快找到關鍵訊息！

We're happy to see you all this afternoon. We will start in 10 minutes. Please note that there's an error in your printed program: there will be a change—a switch—in times for the first two speakers. Mr. Chambers will arrive at 2:00, due to the plane delay.

我們很高興在今天下午見到各位，我們將在十分鐘內開始。請注意，您手上的議程表中有誤：報告順序稍作調整，前兩個講者的順序對調。因為班機延誤，錢伯斯先生將在兩點抵達。

畫底線的部分是為了幫助你了解「會議時間」主題獨白的核心詞彙！

這個圖表搭配的問題可能為：

Look at the graphic, who will be the first speaker?
(A) Mr. Chambers
(B) Ms. Jones
(C) Mr. Black
(D) Ms. Albom

請看圖表。誰將是第一位講者？
(A) 錢伯斯先生
(B) 瓊斯女士
(C) 布萊克先生
(D) 艾爾邦女士

看到題目便可知道這是與「會議時間」有關的獨白主題，獨白的說話者是會議的主持人，可預測獨白的內容會是「歡迎詞→會議的注意事項宣布→講者或是議程順序的變動」。而題目考的通常就是「講者或是議程順序的變動地方」。只要掌握這樣的獨白邏輯，再搭配表格內容，便能順利找出答案。

議程表	
講者	**時間**
錢伯斯先生	1:30-2:00
瓊斯女士	2:10-2:40
休息時間	2:40-3:00
布萊克先生	3:00-3:30
艾爾邦女士	3:40-4:10
Q & A	4:10-4:30

2 與報表相關的圖表與獨白範本

🎧 23-02.mp3

畫底線的部分是為了幫助你了解更快找到關鍵訊息！

About the customer satisfaction, you can see the <u>results</u> of the customer satisfaction survey. I'm glad to announce that customers are satisfied with our service and food. About the item that received the <u>lowest</u> satisfaction rating, that's what I'd like to discuss at this meeting. Please talk in pairs or groups of three.

關於客戶滿意度，你們可以看到客戶滿意度的調查結果。我很高興宣布客戶對於我們的服務與食物感到滿意。至於滿意度最低的項目，是我想在今天會議討論的內容。請兩人或三人一組進行討論。

畫底線的部分是為了幫助你了解「報表」主題獨白的核心詞彙！

這個圖表搭配的問題可能為：

Look at the graphic. What does the speaker ask the listeners to discuss?
(A) Food variety
(B) Wi-Fi connection
(C) Space
(D) Service

根據圖表，說話者要求聽眾討論什麼？
(A) 餐點的多樣性
(B) 無線網路的連接
(C) 空間
(D) 服務

圖表為報表，報表的內容可能為銷售報告、成本報告、調查報告……等，因此可以預測獨白的內容為發表報告、講解報告內容。考生可以先看到題目，題目問「說話者請聽眾討論什麼」，表示圖表中有一項內容會需要請聽眾進行討論，一般來說，會需要進行討論的會是表現較差的項目，再搭配獨白內容進行確認，便可知道答案。

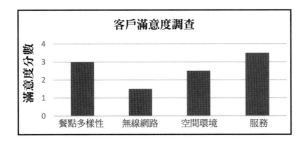

🎧 23-03.mp3

Order number: A171119	
Binder	20
Calculator	10
Ink Cartridge	5
Laptop	4

畫底線的部分是為了幫助你了解更快找到關鍵訊息！

Hi, Theresa... I turned in an order for office supplies yesterday afternoon, but I hope you haven't processed it yet. I was just informed that we'll be having three new employees arriving next Monday, so we have to add another three laptops to the list. The rest of the order seems fine as it is. Please call me back to confirm whether you can make these adjustments. Thanks.

畫底線的部分是為了幫助你了解「商品資訊」主題獨白的核心詞彙！

嗨，泰瑞莎，我昨天下午送了一張辦公用品的訂單，但我希望妳還沒有處理，我剛剛才得知我們下周一將有三名新員工到職，所以我們必須在清單上增加三台筆電。訂單的其他部分沒有問題。請回電給我，以確認是否能夠進行這些變更，謝謝。

這個圖表搭配的問題可能為：

Look at the graphic. How many laptops does the company need in total?
(A) 4
(B) 7
(C) 8
(D) 10

請看此圖，公司總共需要幾台筆記電腦？
(A) 4台
(B) 7台
(C) 8台
(D) 10台

圖表的內容是訂購單，可預測獨白的內容有兩種：
①訂購者針對訂單有所調整。
②接受訂單的人，針對訂單提出疑問。
在這個獨白的情況，是訂購者基於某些原因，需要新增訂購的數量。只要掌握到獨白中的關鍵訊息「add another three laptops」，便可得出答案為(B) 7。

訂單編號：A171119	
活頁夾	20
計算機	10
墨水匣	5
筆記型電腦	4

這類商品訂購單的圖表，除了產品的數量之外，也有可能會出現商品的價格。此時的獨白內容可能為多半為確認產品訂購的內容。例如：

Product	Price
Cooking Lesson	$ 800
Language Lesson	$ 700
Diving Lesson	$ 750
Dancing Lesson	$ 650

此時可能搭配的題目為：

Look at the graphic. How much money does Ms. Moyes need to pay?
(A) $ 800
(B) $ 700
(C) $ 750
(D) $ 650

請看圖表。莫伊斯女士需要付多少錢？
(A) 800元
(B) 700元
(C) 750元
(D) 650元

產品	價錢
烹飪課	800元
語言課	700元
潛水課	750元
舞蹈課	650元

🎧 23-04.mp3

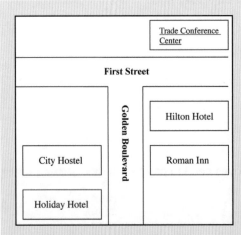

畫底線的部分是為了幫助你了解更快找到關鍵訊息！

Hi, Liza. I am going to New York for an academic seminar next week, and please help me to book a room. As far as I know, the seminar will be held at the Trade Conference Center. For convenience of travel, please book me a room at a hotel as close to the center as possible. Thanks.

畫底線的部分是為了幫助你了解「平面圖、地圖」主題對話的核心詞彙！

嗨，麗莎，我下周要去紐約參加學術研討會，請幫我訂一間房間。據我所知，研討會在貿易會議中心舉辦。為了交通方便，請盡可能幫我在靠近會場的飯店訂一間房間。

這個圖表搭配的問題可能為：

Look at the graphic. Which hotel would the speaker choose?
(A) Hilton Hotel
(B) Roman Inn
(C) City Hostel
(D) Holiday Hotel

請看圖表，講者會選擇哪間旅館？
(A) 希爾頓飯店
(B) 羅馬旅館
(C) 城市青年旅館
(D) 假日飯店

地圖類的圖表，除了樓層平面圖之外，也會看見像這樣的地圖。碰到這類地圖，要掌握的是各項建築物的位置關係。

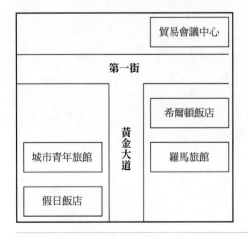

這類圖表搭配的獨白內容，通常是說話者想要請聽者去某個地方，在獨白中講述各個地點的相互關係，而搭配的問題通常都是詢問地點位置。像這個題目中，只要掌握說話者說的「as close to the center as possible」，就可以得知答案是(A) Hilton Hotel。

這類圖表也有可能會出現這種題目：

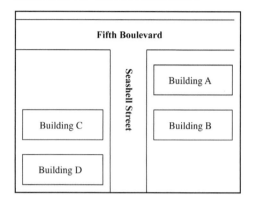

此時可能搭配的題目為：

Look at the graphic. Where is the company?
(A) Building A
(B) Building B
(C) Building C
(D) Building D

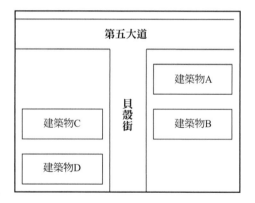

請看圖表。公司在哪裡？
(A) 建築物A
(B) 建築物B
(C) 建築物C
(D) 建築物D

攻略法44　破解圖表題的方法

第1階段：看題目與圖表

1. 預測獨白主題、與講述的場合
2. 找尋該主題會出現的核心詞彙
3. 判斷對話的邏輯，找尋圖表與獨白的連結點
4. 判斷題目答案會出現在獨白中的位置

第2階段：聽錄音

1. 確認與預測的場合、主題是否一致
2. 確認核心詞彙
3. 依照獨白順序解題
4. 確認圖表與獨白的對應處

與會議時間有關的圖表與主題

講者名、序數、start, change, switch

→多半搭配會議時間、議程變更……等題目

與銷售報告有關的圖表與主題

sale, rise, down, monthly, yearly, report

→多半搭配討論重點、銷售預測……等題目

與產品資訊有關的圖表與主題

price, number, discount, cancel, order

→多半搭配訂購商品變更、商品選購……等題目

與地圖有關的圖表與主題

map, beside, front, right, left, across, opposite

→多半搭配判斷建築物位置、找尋地點……等題目

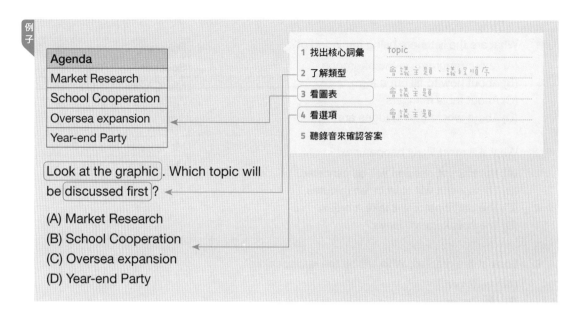

STEP 01 若沒答對會後悔的考題　請按照mp3錄音而先填寫右邊的空欄，再進行以下的考題

例子

Agenda
Market Research
School Cooperation
Oversea expansion
Year-end Party

Look at the graphic. Which topic will be discussed first?

(A) Market Research
(B) School Cooperation
(C) Oversea expansion
(D) Year-end Party

1 找出核心詞彙　　topic
2 了解類型　　會議主題、議程順序
3 看圖表　　會議主題
4 看選項　　會議主題
5 聽錄音來確認答案

1

Furniture	
Royal Series	$12,500
Renaissance Series	$11,200
Minimalism Series	$9,700
Country Series	$9,500

Look at the graphic. What furniture unit will Mr. Black order?

(A) Royal Series
(B) Renaissance Series
(C) Minimalism Series
(D) Country Series

1 找出核心詞彙
2 了解類型
3 看圖表
4 看選項
5 聽錄音來確認答案

1　What are the listeners being reminded of?

(A) About programs in the afternoon
(B) About how to fill out a form
(C) About table manners
(D) About where their badges are

2　What will most likely happen next?

(A) The training session will be canceled.
(B) The speech will start in ten minutes.
(C) The participator will take a break.
(D) The speakers will leave.

3　Look at the graphic. Who will be the last speaker?

(A) Ms. Green
(B) Mr. Crews
(C) Mr. Tropper
(D) Ms. Davies

Program	
Speaker	**Time**
Ms. Green	1:00-1:45
Mr. Crews	1:50-2:35
BREAK	2:35-3:00
Mr. Tropper	3:00-3:45
Ms. Davies	3:50-4:35

4　What kind of training does the school offer?

(A) Foreign languages
(B) Computer skills
(C) Public speaking
(D) Industrial design

5　Look at the graphic. What is being advertised?

(A) Web Design
(B) Computer Programming
(C) Industrial Design
(D) Computer Skills

6　How long will the training be?

(A) 1 month
(B) 2 months
(C) 3 months
(D) 4 months

	Weekday	Weekend
Morning	Web Design	Computer Skills
Afternoon	Computer Programming	Computer Skills
Evening	Software Design	X

▶ 答案在解析本第140頁

7   Where is the announcement being made?

(A) In a museum
(B) In a factory
(C) In a station
(D) In a meeting

```
                  +----------+    +----------+
                  |  Room B  |    |   Café   |
        +---------+----------+    +----------+--------+
        | Room A  |                              Room D|
        |         +----------+    +----------+        |
        |         |  Room C  |    |Information|        |
        |         |          |    |  Center   |        |
        +---------+----------+    +----------+--------+
```

8   What will most likely happen next?

(A) A movie will be shown.
(B) A shop will be open.
(C) A tour will begin.
(D) A museum will close.

9   Look at the graphic. Where is the gift shop?

(A) Room A
(B) Room B
(C) Room C
(D) Room D

---

10   Where does the speaker work?

(A) A travel agency
(B) A car dealer
(C) A gallery
(D) A movie theater

Leader Program	Copper Program	Dulcet Program
- on the First Floor - with French windows - 7-day lease period	- on the First Floor - without French windows - 14-day lease period	- on the Second Floor - 30-day lease period

11   What information was given to the listener by email?

(A) A picture of artwork.
(B) A quote on site rental.
(C) An apologetic letter.
(D) A sales report.

12   Look at the graphic. Which program is the most expensive?

(A) Leader Program
(B) Copper Program
(C) Dulcet Program
(D) They are the same price.

模擬練習

LISTENING TEST

In the listening test, you will be asked to demonstrate how well you understand spoken English. The entire listening test will last approximately 45 minutes. There are four parts, and directions are given for each part. You must mark your answers on the separate answer sheet. Do not write your answers in the test book.

PART 1

Directions: For each question in this part, you will hear four statements about a picture in your test book. When you hear the statements, you must select the one statement that best describes what you see in the picture. Then find the number of the question on your answer sheet and mark your answer. The statements will not be printed in your test book and will be spoken only one time.

Example   **Sample Answer**

Statement (B), "He's making a presentation," is the best description of the picture, so you should select answer (B) and mark it on your answer sheet.

1.

2.

▶ ▶ ▶GO ON TO THE NEXT PAGE

3.

4.

5.

6.

▶ ▶ ▶ GO ON TO THE NEXT PAGE

PART 2

Directions: You will hear a question or statement and three responses spoken in English. They will not be printed in your text book and will be spoken only one time. Select the best response to the question or statement and mark the letter (A), (B), or (C) on your answer sheet.

For Example

You will hear :   Where is the meeting room?
You will also hear :   (A) To meet the new director.
                        (B) It's the first room on the right.
                        (C) Yes, it's 2 o'clock.

Sample Answer
Ⓐ ● Ⓒ

The best response to the question "Where is the meeting room?" is choice (B), "It's the first room on the right." So (B) is the correct answer. You should mark answer (B) on your answer sheet.

7. Mark your answer on your answer sheet.

8. Mark your answer on your answer sheet.

9. Mark your answer on your answer sheet.

10. Mark your answer on your answer sheet.

11. Mark your answer on your answer sheet.

12. Mark your answer on your answer sheet.

13. Mark your answer on your answer sheet.

14. Mark your answer on your answer sheet.

15. Mark your answer on your answer sheet.

16. Mark your answer on your answer sheet.

17. Mark your answer on your answer sheet.

18. Mark your answer on your answer sheet.

19. Mark your answer on your answer sheet.

20. Mark your answer on your answer sheet.

21. Mark your answer on your answer sheet.

22. Mark your answer on your answer sheet.

23. Mark your answer on your answer sheet.

24. Mark your answer on your answer sheet.

25. Mark your answer on your answer sheet.

26. Mark your answer on your answer sheet.

27. Mark your answer on your answer sheet.

28. Mark your answer on your answer sheet.

29. Mark your answer on your answer sheet.

30. Mark your answer on your answer sheet.

31. Mark your answer on your answer sheet.

PART 3

Directions: You will hear some conversations between two people. You will be asked to answer three questions about what the speakers say in each conversation. Select the best response to each question and mark the letter (A), (B), (C), or (D) on your answer sheet. The conversations will not be printed in your test book and will be spoken only one time.

32. Where does the man plan to go?

(A) Vancouver
(B) Los Angeles
(C) Toronto
(D) San Francisco

33. How will he fly?

(A) Direct flight to Toronto
(B) Change flight in Taipei
(C) Change flight in Los Angeles
(D) Change flight in Vancouver

34. When will he leave?

(A) 11:00 tonight
(B) 11:00 tomorrow morning
(C) 10:00 tomorrow night
(D) 10:00 tomorrow morning

35. Where does the conversation take place?

(A) In a car dealer
(B) On a bus
(C) At a hospital
(D) In a supermarket

36. What most likely is the speakers' relationship?

(A) Neighbors
(B) Teacher and student
(C) Old colleagues
(D) Relatives

37. What will the man most likely do next?

(A) Go to the hospital with the woman.
(B) Go to see his dentist.
(C) Go and buy candies.
(D) Go home.

▶ ▶ ▶GO ON TO THE NEXT PAGE

38. What is likely to be the woman's
    occupation?
    (A) A doctor
    (B) A manager
    (C) A teacher
    (D) A preacher

39. What is the main purpose of the man's
    call?
    (A) He would like to inquire about the
        cost of rooms.
    (B) He would like to negotiate on price.
    (C) He would like to get a discount.
    (D) He would like to pay a visit to the
        hotel.

40. What will the woman do tomorrow?
    (A) She will be on a business trip.
    (B) She will meet the man.
    (C) She will send a quote to the man.
    (D) She will ask for a leave.

41. What are the speakers doing?
    (A) Ordering office supplies
    (B) Working on a roof
    (C) Storing building materials
    (D) Fixing a truck

42. What have the speakers lost?
    (A) Brushes
    (B) Automobile parts
    (C) Some paintings
    (D) A work schedule

43. When most likely will the job be
    finished?
    (A) This morning
    (B) This afternoon
    (C) Tomorrow morning
    (D) Tomorrow evening

44. What is the main topic of the
    conversation?
    (A) A job opening
    (B) A product price
    (C) A group presentation
    (D) A restaurant reservation

45. What does the man recommend?
    (A) Returning his phone call later
    (B) Talking to a manager
    (C) Sending in some references
    (D) Coming at a different time

46. What information does the woman
    provide?
    (A) Her name
    (B) Her order number
    (C) Her home address
    (D) Her phone number

47. Why was the woman late today?
    (A) She slept in.
    (B) She had an accident.
    (C) She got on the wrong bus.
    (D) She got caught in bad traffic.

48. Why does the woman prefer taking the
    bus over the MRT?
    (A) It doesn't cost her a penny.
    (B) The bus is more convenient.
    (C) The MRT station is stuffy.
    (D) She doesn't like to climb stairs.

49. How old most likely is the woman?
    (A) 52
    (B) 59
    (C) 63
    (D) 68

50. What does the man want to do?

(A) Buy an automobile
(B) Change to a different job
(C) Rent an apartment
(D) Photograph a car

51. What does the man say about his preference?

(A) He wants an expensive car.
(B) Reliability is important.
(C) He likes a company that pays more.
(D) He usually uses public transportation.

52. What will the woman probably do next?

(A) Sign a contract
(B) Check the computer
(C) Give a discount
(D) Install some equipment

53. Why is the woman calling?

(A) To cancel a meeting
(B) To schedule an appointment
(C) To request service
(D) To inquire about an order

54. What will happen tomorrow afternoon?

(A) A new accountant will be hired.
(B) A product will be delivered.
(C) A contract will be signed.
(D) A reservation will be canceled.

55. According to Jenny, what can employees do in the accounting department?

(A) Access salary information
(B) Use a new copier
(C) Pick up office supplies
(D) Print out some documents

56. What does the man want to do?

(A) Mail a letter
(B) Withdraw some money
(C) Eat lunch
(D) Buy some ice cream

57. Why does the woman tell the man to hurry?

(A) The restaurant is far away.
(B) The bank is almost closed.
(C) The chef will soon take a break.
(D) The clock almost stops.

58. What time is it now?

(A) 08:37
(B) 11:55
(C) 13:36
(D) 14:40

59. Why did the man go to the restaurant?

(A) To apply for a position
(B) To meet a colleague for dinner
(C) To deliver an order
(D) To arrange an event

60. What is the problem?

(A) All rooms are fully booked.
(B) The manager is not available.
(C) The restaurant is closed due to the holiday.
(D) A customer has complained about the service.

61. What does the woman recommend?

(A) Going to a different restaurant
(B) Calling the following day
(C) Consulting the website
(D) Coming back with a friend

▶ ▶ ▶ GO ON TO THE NEXT PAGE

Dishes	Price / per person
Entrée: fish / chicken	$ 100
Rice	$ 50
Soup: corn / tomato	$ 50
Coffee and cake	$ 50
Combo	$ 200

62. Where does this conversation take place?

(A) At a theater
(B) At a supermarket
(C) At a restaurant
(D) At a laundry

63. What is the entrée that the woman wants to order?

(A) Chicken
(B) Pork
(C) Beef
(D) Fish

64. Look at the graphic. How much money does the woman need to pay for lunch?

(A) $ 100
(B) $ 150
(C) $ 200
(D) $ 250

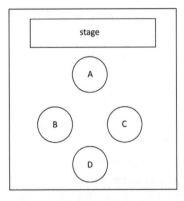

65. What is the conversation mainly about?

(A) About a conference meeting
(B) About a welcoming banquet
(C) About a trip to LA
(D) About a talent show

66. Look at the graphic. Where will Dr. Hamilton sit?

(A) Table A
(B) Table B
(C) Table C
(D) Table D

67. What kind of entertainment will be arranged?

(A) Ballet dancing
(B) Magic show
(C) Singing and band
(D) Street dance

68. What is likely to be the woman's job?

(A) A store manager
(B) A sales rep
(C) A cashier
(D) A chairman

69. Look at the graphic. What month is it when the speakers are talking?

(A) February
(B) March
(C) April
(D) May

70. What is NOT implied about the conversation?

(A) The man needs to pay $265 today.
(B) His $50 coupon expired.
(C) The man will pay by cash, not credit card.
(D) He can get 10% off his purchase today.

▶ ▶ ▶GO ON TO THE NEXT PAGE

PART 4

Directions: You will hear some short talks given by a single speaker. You will be asked to answer three questions about what the speaker says in each short talk. Select the best response to each question and mark the letter (A), (B), (C), or (D) on your answer sheet. The talks will not be printed in your test book and will be spoken only one time.

71. Where does the speaker work?

    (A) A cafeteria
    (B) A clinic
    (C) A bank
    (D) A grocery store

72. What is needed to apply for the small loan?

    (A) A diploma
    (B) A financial statement
    (C) A medical record
    (D) A marriage certificate

73. What does the speaker recommend the listener to do?

    (A) Come to see him anytime.
    (B) Call small loan office for appointment.
    (C) Apply for a new credit card.
    (D) Check online for more information.

74. What is being announced?

    (A) A new hiring procedure
    (B) A survey on employee satisfaction
    (C) A conference date
    (D) A software installation

75. What will happen next Friday?

    (A) A budget will be reviewed.
    (B) Survey results will be announced.
    (C) Computers will be replaced.
    (D) Employees will be trained.

76. What are the listeners asked to do by the end of the week?

    (A) Submit the expense report
    (B) Call the personnel department
    (C) Meet with their managers
    (D) Register for a training session

77. Why has the highway traffic decreased?

   (A) Recent road construction has been completed.
   (B) The weather conditions have been unfavorable.
   (C) The citizens are on holiday.
   (D) Train service has improved.

78. What is causing a delay on Highway 100?

   (A) An overturned vehicle
   (B) A broken traffic sign
   (C) Slippery road conditions
   (D) Road repairs

79. When will the next report occur?

   (A) In 5 minutes
   (B) In 10 minutes
   (C) In 15 minutes
   (D) In 30 minutes

80. Who is Tracy Bowe?

   (A) A new manager
   (B) A new sales rep
   (C) A new accountant
   (D) A new assistant

81. What is NOT required for the listener to bring on Monday?

   (A) A copy of TOEIC certificate
   (B) A copy of ID
   (C) A copy of diploma
   (D) A copy of transcript

82. What activity will there be on Monday?

   (A) Anniversary
   (B) Celebration party
   (C) Leisure activity
   (D) Year-end banquet

83. What is the speaker calling to talk about?

   (A) A recent inquiry
   (B) A new regulation
   (C) A canceled reservation
   (D) Reduced rents

84. What does the speaker say about the two-bedroom apartment?

   (A) It has been occupied.
   (B) It is very expensive.
   (C) It is undergoing renovation.
   (D) It is popular among senior citizens.

85. What does the speaker suggest the listener do?

   (A) Compare the prices of two apartments
   (B) Check the floor plan
   (C) Retain a rental contract
   (D) Call for a tour of an apartment

86. Who is the guest speaker tonight?

   (A) Danny Luke
   (B) Jamie Blake
   (C) Laurie Springfield
   (D) Jenny Black

87. What was the guest speaker's occupation before?

   (A) A lawyer
   (B) A singer
   (C) A doctor
   (D) A teacher

88. What can the audience do to the guide dog?

   (A) Pat it
   (B) Feed it
   (C) Watch it
   (D) Play with it

▶ ▶ ▶GO ON TO THE NEXT PAGE

89. Who are the listeners most likely?

   (A) Students
   (B) Tourists
   (C) Employees
   (D) Clients

90. What is implied by the speaker?

   (A) Some employees will be laid off.
   (B) It has been a rough year.
   (C) People are selfish.
   (D) The company has potential.

91. Which benefit is NOT mentioned in the talk?

   (A) Business trip
   (B) Company trip
   (C) Health check-up
   (D) Stock bonus

92. What is the purpose of the talk?

   (A) To discuss a customer complaint
   (B) To announce a policy change
   (C) To introduce a new employee
   (D) To brainstorm new advertising strategies

93. Who most likely is the speaker talking to?

   (A) Accountants
   (B) Warehouse supervisors
   (C) Customer service representatives
   (D) Travel agents

94. What does the speaker ask the listeners to do?

   (A) Make phone calls frequently
   (B) Provide a reference number
   (C) Come up with an idea
   (D) Record phone calls

Agenda of the semiannual meeting
Market trend
New recruit training
Oversea expansion
Budgetary reduction

95. Why can't Lucy come to the meeting on time?

   (A) She is making a slide.
   (B) She is copying material.
   (C) She is talking on the phone.
   (D) She is absent from work.

96. How often does the staff have this type of meeting?

   (A) Once a month
   (B) Once a year
   (C) Twice a month
   (D) Twice a year

97. Look at the graphic. Which topic will be discussed first?

   (A) Market trend
   (B) New recruit training
   (C) Oversea expansion
   (D) Budgetary reduction

Dr. Anderson's appointment chart					
	Mon	Tue	Wed	Thu	Fri
5:30		A		C	
6:30			B		
7:30					
8:30					D

98. Who is Dr. Anderson?

(A) A lawyer
(B) A dentist
(C) A surgeon
(D) A professor

99. Look at the graphic. Which is the appointment time being offered?

(A) A
(B) B
(C) C
(D) D

100. What is the listener suggested to do?

(A) Explain a problem
(B) Provide a report
(C) Return a call
(D) Submit a resume

聽寫練習

Part 2 說出以下的對話   請邊聽邊寫下內容，每題各聽三次

01 Who should I .... help?
    (A) No, I don't .... you.
    (B) You can ask the ....
    (C) She is the ....

02 What is this .... about?
    (A) It's about a .... living in ....
    (B) It .... about .... dollars.
    (C) ...., I really like it.

03 .... are the .... they've been ....?
    (A) .... 'll go to the .... tomorrow.
    (B) ....
    (C) .... it might spoil.

04 .... the ....?
    (A) ....
    (B) ....
    (C) .... 're on the top shelf.

05 .... will be .... the ....?
    (A) 5 .... so far.
    (B) ...., I have a job interview today.
    (C) .... Ms. Shimamura ....

06 .... will you .... from your business trip?
    (A) You can .... me .... weekend.
    (B) .... left on the next ....
    (C) ....

▶ 翻譯在下一頁

01 我應該向誰求助呢？
　　(A) 不，我不同意你的意見。
　　(B) 你可以問前台服務員。
　　(C) 她是總裁祕書。

02 這本書在講什麼？
　　(A) 是關於一個住在日本的外國人。
　　(B) 它花費約十美元。
　　(C) 是，我非常喜歡。

03 蔬菜被摘完後儲存在哪裡？
　　(A) 他明天將去商店。
　　(B) 在冷藏保管容器裡。
　　(C) 因為它可能會腐壞。

04 我在哪裡可以找到廠長？
　　(A) 晚上十點。
　　(B) 往左邊第二道門去。
　　(C) 它們在貨架最上層。

05 誰即將和申請者面談？
　　(A) 到目前為止五位申請者。
　　(B) 是，今天我有求職面試。
　　(C) 我會請島村女士來做。

06 你何時出差回來？
　　(A) 你可以預計我下個週末回來。
　　(B) 下個街角左轉。
　　(C) 八年了。

▶ 對話在前一頁

Part 2 說出以下的對話　　　　　　　　　請邊聽邊寫下內容，每題各聽三次

07 _____ the _____ that _____?
    (A) _____ .
    (B) They're _____ .
    (C) They're made of _____ .

08 _____ 's _____ to _____ the _____ ?
    (A) It _____ at five.
    (B) Dr. Sheppard _____ .
    (C) I love _____ .

09 _____ is the supply cabinet?
    (A) You can find _____ in the _____ .
    (B) On the _____ floor.
    (C) Food supply is running _____ .

10 _____ do you _____ the _____ ?
    (A) _____ over there.
    (B) _____ afternoon.
    (C) Our past _____ are no longer available.

11 _____ don't you take a _____ ?
    (A) _____ , I'll _____ 10 minutes.
    (B) No, he is very _____ .
    (C) I _____ my leg.

12 _____ should I _____ for our customers?
    (A) They were impressed by the _____ .
    (B) _____ .
    (C) _____ the ABC bank.

▶ 翻譯在下一頁

07 你把昨天送達的機器零件貨運放在哪？
   (A) 這是事實。
   (B) 它們在儲藏室。
   (C) 它們以金屬製成。

08 誰能為閉幕演講？
   (A) 它在五點關閉。
   (B) 雪帕德博士可以。
   (C) 我愛桃子。

09 文具櫃在哪裡？
   (A) 你可以在抽屜裡找到新的信封。
   (B) 在二樓。
   (C) 食物供給快要短缺了。

10 你把會議記錄歸檔在哪？
   (A) 在那邊的櫃子。
   (B) 每個星期五下午。
   (C) 我們之前的記錄已不能用了。

11 你何不休息一下呢？
   (A) 好，我休息十分鐘。
   (B) 不，他很高。
   (C) 我摔斷腿了。

12 我該去哪買給我們客戶的禮物？
   (A) 他們對於介紹感到印象深刻。
   (B) 約二十元。
   (C) 試試去 ABC 銀行附近的百貨公司。

▶ 對話在前一頁

Part 2 　說出以下的對話　　　　　　　　請邊聽邊寫下內容，每題各聽三次

01 _____ an _____ with Dr. Yang?
  (A) _____ .
  (B) _____ after 4:00 p.m.
  (C) _____, please?

02 _____ ?
  (A) Do you know where he _____ ?
  (B) _____, I wake up _____ .
  (C) _____ for the meeting.

03 How _____ meetings do we have _____ ?
  (A) There _____ .
  (B) Call me _____ you get home.
  (C) I don't have much _____ left.

04 _____ the _____ ?
  (A) _____ it last week.
  (B) You can't use the _____ until 3 p.m.
  (C) _____ .

05 Do you know that all _____ are _____ ?
  (A) That's _____ I _____ .
  (B) The salesman is very _____ .
  (C) _____, no one _____ the final exam.

06 _____ to Tokyo?
  (A) _____, it _____ pretty well.
  (B) _____ .
  (C) _____, it's within _____ distance.

▶ 翻譯在下一頁

01 我什麼時候能約楊博士？
(A) 從這裡步行十分鐘。
(B) 下午四點後的任何時間。
(C) 可否麻煩您？

02 你為何這麼早離開？
(A) 你知道他住哪裡嗎？
(B) 是的，我很早起床。
(C) 我開會遲到了。

03 我們下個月有幾個會議？
(A) 總共有三個。
(B) 你一到家就打電話給我。
(C) 我所剩的時間不多了。

04 你什麼時候完成這個計畫的？
(A) 他上週完成了。
(B) 你不能使用投影機，直到下午三點。
(C) 我仍在處理當中。

05 你知道所有的銷售都是不能退換貨的嗎？
(A) 我是這麼聽說的。
(B) 那個銷售員很沒禮貌。
(C) 不，沒有人通過期末考。

06 你何時到東京出差？
(A) 是的，它相當地好。
(B) 下週五。
(C) 不，它在步行距離之內。

▶ 對話在前一頁

Part 2   說出以下的對話

07 _____ the _____?
(A) _____, I think.
(B) _____ the _____.
(C) I'll have it _____.

08 _____ you like to have _____ or _____?
(A) Actually, I would _____ a _____ meal.
(B) _____, you made a mistake.
(C) I see some _____ on the _____ table.

09 _____ the _____?
(A) _____, _____.
(B) _____, that's a good one.
(C) There are five _____.

10 _____ the _____?
(A) _____, I'm too _____.
(B) I'll make an _____.
(C) _____ Mr. Tanaka _____.

11 _____ you _____ to _____?
(A) _____ 'll be out of the town today.
(B) _____.
(C) _____.

12 How about going for a _____ tonight?
(A) _____.
(B) That _____ be great.
(C) I lost sleep for two _____.

▶ 翻譯在下一頁

07 為什麼新的地毯還沒到呢？
(A) 我認為是搭火車。
(B) 我會打電話給快遞公司。
(C) 我會把它乾洗。

08 你要牛排還是海鮮？
(A) 其實，我比較想要輕食。
(B) 不，你弄錯了。
(C) 我在餐桌上看到一些食物。

09 下一場舞台劇何時開始？
(A) 今晚七點三十分。
(B) 是的，這個不錯。
(C) 那有五名球員。

10 行程為什麼改變？
(A) 很抱歉，我太忙了。
(B) 我將會預約。
(C) 因為田中先生那時不能在這裡。

11 你什麼時候回到你的家鄉？
(A) 他今天將出城。
(B) 在城市。
(C) 在一個星期內。

12 今晚去看場電影如何？
(A) 我們還不能搬家。
(B) 那太棒了。
(C) 我失眠兩個晚上了。

▶ 對話在前一頁

Part 2　說出以下的對話　　　　　　　　　　

01 ＿＿＿＿＿＿＿＿＿＿ you think the ＿＿＿＿＿＿＿＿＿ is terrible?
(A) Yes, I completely ＿＿＿＿＿＿＿＿ you.
(B) ＿＿＿＿＿＿＿＿＿＿＿＿＿＿＿＿＿＿＿.
(C) My ＿＿＿＿＿＿＿＿＿ number is 403.

02 ＿＿＿＿＿＿＿＿＿＿＿＿＿＿＿ on Tuesday?
(A) ＿＿＿＿＿＿＿＿＿＿＿＿＿＿＿.
(B) ＿＿＿＿＿, let's speak then.
(C) ＿＿＿＿＿＿ I haven't seen them.

03 ＿＿＿＿＿ have you ＿＿＿＿ at ＿＿＿＿＿＿＿＿＿?
(A) About ＿＿＿ kilometers from here.
(B) ＿＿＿＿＿＿＿＿＿＿＿＿＿＿＿＿＿.
(C) It doesn't ＿＿＿＿ properly.

04 ＿＿＿＿＿＿＿＿＿ is your birthday?
(A) It is ＿＿＿＿＿＿＿＿＿＿＿＿ 18.
(B) I'm ＿＿＿＿＿＿ you have the ＿＿＿＿＿ number.
(C) That's ＿＿＿＿＿ my ＿＿＿＿＿.

05 ＿＿＿＿＿＿ are you ＿＿＿＿ the wall?
(A) ＿＿＿＿＿＿＿＿, I think.
(B) ＿＿＿＿＿＿＿＿ from now.
(C) The ＿＿＿＿'s over there.

06 ＿＿＿＿＿ are the ＿＿＿＿ to ＿＿＿＿＿?
(A) About ＿＿＿＿＿.
(B) ＿＿＿＿＿＿＿＿＿.
(C) Bikes aren't ＿＿＿＿ in this area.

▶ 翻譯在下一頁

01 你不覺得交通太擁擠了嗎？
(A) 是，我完全同意你的看法。
(B) 綠色的就好。
(C) 我公寓號碼是403。

02 我週二需要攜帶哪些文件？
(A) 我辦公桌上的。
(B) 是的，我們到時說吧。
(C) 因為我還沒有看見他們。

03 你在貴公司工作多久了？
(A) 從這兒起約四公里。
(B) 到下個月就三年了。
(C) 它不能正常運作。

04 你的生日是什麼時候？
(A) 是在二月十八日。
(B) 你打錯了。
(C) 那不是我的尺寸。

05 你用什麼顏色來油漆牆壁？
(A) 我打算用淺棕色。
(B) 從現在起三個星期。
(C) 冷卻器在那兒。

06 這個博物館的入場費多少錢？
(A) 大約一小時。
(B) 只要五元。
(C) 在這個地區不准帶腳踏車進來。

▶ 對話在前一頁

Part 2　說出以下的對話　

07 _____ 's the _____ to _____ ?
(A) I can't _____ .
(B) About _____ .
(C) _____ .

08 _____ ?
(A) I'm still _____ how.
(B) _____ .
(C) About _____ .

09 Would you _____ the _____ , please?
(A) _____ , here you are.
(B) I _____ like _____ in my coffee.
(C) Paper is getting _____ these years.

10 _____ 's Mr. Thomas _____ ?
(A) _____ , I think he's in today.
(B) _____ .
(C) He _____ far away.

11 _____ are smart phones so _____ ?
(A) Because they are _____ products.
(B) Yes, my students are all very _____ .
(C) _____ can expand your _____ .

12 _____ ?
(A) It's _____ .
(B) _____ , thanks.
(C) Thanks for the _____ .

▶ 翻譯在下一頁

07 聯繫到你老闆最好的方式是甚麼？
(A) 我無法到達。
(B) 約十公斤。
(C) 試試致電她的手機。

08 你怎麼知道這個工作的？
(A) 我現在仍然在學。
(B) 我在報紙上讀到它。
(C) 大約一個月前。

09 麻煩你遞一下胡椒，好嗎？
(A) 沒問題，拿去。
(B) 我咖啡裡不喜歡加糖。
(C) 這些年，紙張越來越便宜。

10 湯瑪士先生在他的休假期間要做甚麼呢？
(A) 不，我想他今天會在。
(B) 他在社區活動中心參加課程。
(C) 他住得很遠。

11 智慧型手機為什麼這麼貴？
(A) 因為他們是高科技產品。
(B) 對，我的學生都很聰明。
(C) 有趣的旅遊能拓展你的視野。

12 這個冰淇淋如何？
(A) 相當好。
(B) 我感到好些了，謝謝。
(C) 謝謝你的好意。

▶ 對話在前一頁

Part 2　說出以下的對話　　　　　　　　請邊聽邊寫下內容，每題各聽三次

01 _____ the _____ when I finish?
(A) No, can you _____ it?
(B) _____ . _____ .
(C) Yes, I'd love to _____ .

02 _____ developed the _____ ?
(A) The _____ sales department did.
(B) You can _____ in the _____ .
(C) The _____ was _____ into a park.

03 _____ instead?
(A) It isn't that _____ .
(B) _____ ?
(C) _____ .

04 _____ your _____ or your _____ for _____ .
(A) _____ , I _____ .
(B) Leave your _____ here.
(C) Oh, I don't have _____ .

05 _____ is the _____ to _____ ? Islington Road or the _____ ?
(A) You can _____ in the garage.
(B) _____ .
(C) To _____ .

06 _____ a _____ to the _____ ?
(A) _____ .
(B) I'm not sure I can _____ this box alone.
(C) I enjoy their _____ , too.

▶ 翻譯在下一頁

01 當我看完後，你想閱讀這本雜誌嗎？
(A) 不，你可以修好它嗎？
(B) 不，謝謝。我已經買了一份。
(C) 是的，我很喜歡帶領他人。

02 誰開發了這個銷售計畫？
(A) 出口銷售部門做的。
(B) 你可以在院子裡種樹。
(C) 這片土地被開發成公園。

03 你想換成這件襯衫試試看嗎？
(A) 它不是那麼短。
(B) 它的尺寸是多少？
(C) 是的，我們有。

04 我們需要檢查您的護照或駕駛執照來確認身份。
(A) 是，我是。
(B) 把你的車留在這兒。
(C) 噢，我任何一個都沒有。

05 哪個是到銀行最快的方法呢？伊斯林頓路還是高速公路？
(A) 你可以把車停在車庫。
(B) 它們兩個都差不多。
(C) 為了兌現一張支票。

06 要不要載你去聚會？
(A) 謝謝你。
(B) 我不確定我能否獨自舉起這個箱子。
(C) 我也喜歡他們的談話。

▶ 對話在前一頁

Part 2　說出以下的對話　　

07 ＿＿＿＿＿＿ did you put my ＿＿＿＿＿＿?
(A) They'll ＿＿＿＿＿ the case with me.
(B) It is really ＿＿＿＿＿ for you.
(C) In the ＿＿＿＿＿ down the ＿＿＿＿＿.

08 ＿＿＿＿＿ would you like to ＿＿＿＿＿?
(A) ＿＿＿＿ is at 7 p.m.
(B) ＿＿＿＿＿＿?
(C) ＿＿＿, it's quite good.

09 Have ＿＿＿＿ the ＿＿＿＿, or do you want ＿＿＿＿?
(A) Is that your ＿＿＿＿?
(B) ＿＿＿＿＿. Do you?
(C) No, ＿＿＿＿ yet.

10 ＿＿＿＿＿＿＿?
(A) Thanks, I'll ＿＿＿ some, please.
(B) No, I'd like to ＿＿＿.
(C) No, I ＿＿＿ to him this morning.

11 ＿＿＿＿ do you ＿＿＿＿ your email?
(A) About ＿＿＿ a day.
(B) We have about ten ＿＿＿.
(C) Email is a convenient ＿＿＿.

12 ＿＿＿＿＿＿.
(A) ＿＿＿＿＿.
(B) That's the ＿＿＿＿.
(C) To ＿＿＿ a new convention hall.

▶ 翻譯在下一頁

07 你把我的皮箱放在哪裡了？
(A) 他們會和我討論這個案子。
(B) 這真的很適合你。
(C) 在走廊那邊的衣櫥裡。

08 哪家餐廳是你想推薦的？
(A) 晚餐在晚上7點。
(B) 韓式餐廳如何？
(C) 是的，它相當不錯。

09 你和旅行社聯繫了沒？還是由我來打電話給他們？
(A) 那是你的電話號碼嗎？
(B) 我沒有時間。你有嗎？
(C) 不，我目前沒有很多。

10 難道你不想搭計程車嗎？
(A) 謝謝，我取用一些吧。
(B) 不，我想走路。
(C) 不，我今天上午告訴過他。

11 你多常查看你的電子信箱？
(A) 大概一天兩次。
(B) 我有大約十個訊息。
(C) 電子郵件是一項很便利的發明。

12 下週到工地去一下吧。
(A) 我下週將要出城。
(B) 那是居民的公寓。
(C) 為建立一個新的會議廳。

▶ 對話在前一頁

Part 2 說出以下的對話 　　　　　　　　　　請邊聽邊寫下內容，每題各聽三次

01 _____ chairs are there in the room?
(A) The room number is _____ .
(B) _____ .
(C) Cheers! _____ our _____ living room.

02 _____ you _____ the doctor _____ ?
(A) _____ .
(B) I _____ about twice a month.
(C) _____ .

03 The _____ at 9 o'clock, doesn't it?
(A) That's the _____ .
(B) _____ .
(C) I found the _____ better.

04 Excuse me. Is this the _____ to Taipei?
(A) Yes, it goes _____ .
(B) You _____ leave now.
(C) _____ at the Taipei Main Station.

05 _____ for today's _____ ?
(A) It's probably the most _____ skill.
(B) _____ .
(C) You must present your _____ .

06 _____ at the science _____ ?
(A) _____ , _____ .
(B) That's good _____ .
(C) Yes, to build a _____ .

▶ 翻譯在下一頁

01 房間裡有幾張椅子？
(A) 房間號碼是808。
(B) 有十二張。
(C) 為我們的新客廳，乾杯！

02 你今天下午不打電話給醫生嗎？
(A) 在我們最後一次的會議。
(B) 我大約每月去兩次。
(C) 我今天上午給他打過電話了。

03 演唱會在9點鐘開始，不是嗎？
(A) 那是間唱片店。
(B) 我想入場票上應該有時間。
(C) 我認為結局的部分好一些。

04 不好意思，這是到台北的火車嗎？
(A) 對，這車子北上。
(B) 你可以走了。
(C) 在台北車站下車。

05 有今天舞台劇的任何門票嗎？
(A) 它可能是最具價值的技術。
(B) 恐怕已經都賣完了。
(C) 你必須出示你的票。

06 你去過在科學博物館的新展覽會嗎?
(A) 不，但我打算下週去。
(B) 這真是個好消息。
(C) 是的，為了蓋新的博物館。

▶ 對話在前一頁

Part 2　說出以下的對話　

07 ＿＿＿＿＿＿＿ Ms. Johnson ＿＿＿＿＿ the ＿＿＿＿＿＿＿＿＿＿＿＿＿＿＿＿＿＿ ?
(A) ＿＿＿＿＿＿＿＿＿＿＿ .
(B) The ＿＿＿＿＿＿ arrived ＿＿＿＿＿＿＿＿＿＿＿ .
(C) The ＿＿＿＿＿＿＿＿＿＿＿＿＿＿＿＿ .

08 Jacob ＿＿＿＿＿＿＿＿＿＿＿＿＿＿＿ the ＿＿＿＿＿＿＿＿＿＿＿ , won't he?
(A) Yes, he's just been ＿＿＿＿＿＿＿＿＿ .
(B) ＿＿＿＿＿＿ , ＿＿＿＿＿＿＿＿＿＿＿＿＿＿＿＿＿＿ .
(C) ＿＿＿＿＿＿＿＿＿＿＿＿＿＿＿ .

09 Did you turn ＿＿＿＿＿＿＿＿＿＿ the ＿＿＿＿＿＿＿＿＿＿＿ ?
(A) Yes, ＿＿＿＿＿＿＿＿＿＿＿＿＿＿ at the corner.
(B) It is not ＿＿＿＿＿＿＿＿＿ . It's very ＿＿＿＿＿＿＿＿＿＿＿ .
(C) No, I ＿＿＿＿＿＿＿＿＿ leave it ＿＿＿＿＿＿＿＿＿ .

10 ＿＿＿＿＿＿＿＿＿＿＿＿＿＿＿＿＿＿＿＿＿＿＿＿＿ ?
(A) ＿＿＿＿＿＿＿＿＿＿＿＿＿＿＿＿＿＿＿ .
(B) No, it ＿＿＿＿＿＿ a ＿＿＿＿＿＿＿＿＿＿＿ .
(C) I put the ＿＿＿＿＿＿ by the window.

11 Isn't that ＿＿＿＿＿＿＿＿＿＿＿ to ＿＿＿＿＿＿＿＿＿ ?
(A) ＿＿＿＿＿＿＿＿＿ , ＿＿＿＿＿＿＿＿＿＿＿＿＿＿ .
(B) No, the ＿＿＿＿＿＿＿＿＿ departs at 5:03.
(C) I believe it's ＿＿＿＿＿＿＿＿ .

12 This plant was ＿＿＿＿＿＿＿＿＿＿＿＿＿＿＿ , wasn't it?
(A) Yes, ＿＿＿＿＿＿＿＿＿＿＿ .
(B) Was the result ＿＿＿＿＿＿＿＿＿ ?
(C) It ＿＿＿＿＿＿＿＿＿ a good plan.

▶ 翻譯在下一頁

07 強生女士上週沒有將保險文件歸檔嗎？
(A) 我將會問她。
(B) 昨天瓷磚到了。
(C) 塑膠的那個更好看。

08 雅各將能重新安排這個約會，不是嗎？
(A) 是的，他剛被任命。
(B) 是的，他會馬上做的。
(C) 太多次了。

09 你有關燈嗎？
(A) 對，到街角右轉。
(B) 這不輕，很重的。
(C) 沒有，我一直都讓它開著。

10 這個週末你有任何計劃嗎？
(A) 我們週六將要去健行。
(B) 不，這是一個導覽旅遊。
(C) 我把植物放在窗邊。

11 培訓課不是預定為兩個小時嗎？
(A) 是的，它會準時結束。
(B) 不，火車在5:03出發。
(C) 我相信它是你的。

12 這家工廠是大約兩年前建造的，不是嗎？
(A) 是的，我認為那是對的。
(B) 結果令人滿意嗎？
(C) 它看起來像是個好計劃。

▶ 對話在前一頁

Part 2　說出以下的對話　

01 ....
    (A) I thought we needed two lights.
    (B) .... ?
    (C) Several ....

02 .... Ms. Wagner ....
    (A) I haven't .... it yet.
    (B) .... , ...
    (C) .... in today.

03 Where is your .... ?
    (A) We .... in New York City.
    (B) His .... is by the ....
    (C) It is .... from the ....

04 .... for ....
    (A) .... ?
    (B) .... only.
    (C) Let's .... for a while.

05 What .... is the phone number .... ?
    (A) Did you check .... the sofa?
    (B) It is at .... page four.
    (C) It is ....

06 .... to .... Mr. Tang's .... ?
    (A) ....
    (B) .... yet.
    (C) .... it this morning.

▶ 翻譯在下一頁

01 我認為這本小冊子的圖片太淡了。
　　(A) 我以為我們需要兩個燈。
　　(B) 它有可能被加深嗎？
　　(C) 幾張彩色照片。

02 我以為華格納女士將會領導這個工作坊。
　　(A) 我還沒有讀過。
　　(B) 不，她在休假中。
　　(C) 它在今天進來。

03 你老闆坐在哪裡？
　　(A) 我們住在紐約市。
　　(B) 他的位子靠窗。
　　(C) 它懸掛在天花板。

04 我想預訂今晚晚餐的座位。
　　(A) 請告訴我您的大名。
　　(B) 只有兩晚。
　　(C) 我們休息一會兒吧。

05 電話號碼在哪一頁？
　　(A) 妳有沒有查看沙發底下？
　　(B) 在第四頁的上方。
　　(C) 是0933-909-876。

06 你可以告訴我湯先生的辦公室在哪兒嗎？
　　(A) 他在隔壁大樓工作。
　　(B) 我們還沒有被預約。
　　(C) 她今天上午發現的。

▶ 對話在前一頁

Part 2 說出以下的對話 請邊聽邊寫下內容，每題各聽三次

07 _____.

    (A) It's _____.

    (B) _____?

    (C) We projected _____ sales.

08 _____ did you buy your car?

    (A) No, I _____ a _____ here.

    (B) It _____ me a lot of _____.

    (C) _____ I got married last year.

09 _____ for this project?

    (A) Yes, the _____ is.

    (B) Yes, it's _____.

    (C) About new _____.

10 The _____.

    (A) _____.

    (B) _____.

    (C) The _____ is next to the _____.

11 _____.

    (A) _____.

    (B) Our new _____ goals.

    (C) _____.

12 _____ will he _____?

    (A) He _____ the book _____.

    (B) He'll be _____ after spring _____.

    (C) Please make a _____ here.

▶ 翻譯在下一頁

07 我已經聘請了兩名軟體工程師。
(A) 它很難用。
(B) 他們將在這週內開始嗎？
(C) 我們計畫更高的銷量。

08 你何時買你的車子？
(A) 沒有，我是騎U-bike來的。
(B) 它花費我很多錢。
(C) 我去年結婚的時候。

09 你知道誰負責這個計畫嗎？
(A) 是的，是行銷經理。
(B) 是的，在下週一。
(C) 有關於新產品。

10 禮堂的麥克風壞掉了。
(A) 今天上午某個時候。
(B) 我會去找技師。
(C) 那張桌子在電腦旁。

11 我們上一季的銷售額下降了百分之十。
(A) 需求下降是主要的原因。
(B) 我們的新的銷售目標。
(C) 我習慣於這種天氣。

12 他什麼時候回來？
(A) 他昨天還書。
(B) 他春假以後會回來。
(C) 請在這裡右轉。

▶ 對話在前一頁

Part 3 說出以下的對話　　　　　　　請邊聽邊寫下內容，每題各聽三次

Questions 1~3

W1: Hi, Maria. It's Joanna. _____ to _____ this morning? My car _____

_____ late last night, and it's _____ in the _____ .

W2: I'd be _____ to, but I _____ go into work early to _____ an important

meeting. Do you _____ leaving 30 minutes _____ ?

W1: Not at all. I will be _____ in 10 minutes.

W2: You can _____ . I _____ to _____ before

_____ _____ .

Questions 4-6

M: Welcome to the _____ . May I have your tickets, please?

W1: There you go. There are the _____ of us.

M: Sure. Please enter through the _____ door. There is a locker room at the very

end of the _____ floor. Please check your coats, hats, and bags.

W2: Can we carry our _____ ?

M: _____ are allowed, but no _____ or _____ ,

please.

W1: You'd better finish drinking your _____ now.

W2: All right. Give me a minute. Is there a tour _____ for the _____ ?

M: Unfortunately not. But we do offer the _____ service machines that

include _____ system.

▶ 翻譯在下一頁

Questions 1~3

女1：嗨，瑪麗亞，我是喬安娜。今天早上你能否載我一程去上班？昨天深夜我的車壞了，它正在修車廠被維修。

女2：我很樂意，但我得很早去上班，為了要準備一個重要會議。你介不介意比平常提早三十分鐘出門？

女1：完全不介意，我會在十分鐘內準備好。

女2：你可以有二十分鐘。外出前，我需要一些時間穿衣服。

Questions 4~6

男：歡迎來展覽。請問可以給我您的門票嗎？

女1：在這裡。我們有兩個人。

男：當然。請由前門進入。一樓的最裡面有間置物間。請寄放您的外套、帽子、還有包包。

女2：我們可以帶手機嗎？

男：手機可以，但是食物和飲料不行。

女1：妳最好現在就把果汁喝完。

女2：好吧！給我一分鐘。展覽有沒有導覽員？

男：很抱歉沒有。不過我們有提供多語系統的語音導覽服務器。

▶ 對話在前一頁

Part 3 說出以下的對話

Questions 7~9

W: Can you please fix my red _____ for me? It _____ work.

M: I am _____ with my speech _____. Can't you fix it by yourself? Or you can use the blue _____ in the _____. That one should work.

W: That one is too _____. I am _____ to move it alone without your help. I think this _____ better. Can you repair it for me, please? I can wait!

M: All right. Give me a minute. I'll take a _____ for you.

Questions 10~12

W: _____ Star Travel Service. _____?

M: Hello, _____ Antonio Chang _____ G&W corporation. I'm _____ to _____ a _____ this weekend. I'd like to _____ New York tomorrow night and _____ on Sunday morning.

W: Let me check. You can leave for 8 p.m. tomorrow, but all the _____ have been _____ for Sunday morning. _____ return Sunday afternoon or _____ sit in a _____.

M: Well, _____ on a business class. I have a _____ that afternoon. So, I _____ before the meeting.

▶ 翻譯在下一頁

Questions 7~9

女：你可不可以幫我修紅色的檯燈？它壞掉了。

男：我在忙我明天的演講。你不能自己修一下嗎？或是你可以用車庫裡的藍檯燈。那台應該沒壞掉吧。

女：那台太重了。沒有你幫忙我無法獨自移動它。我覺得這台紅色檯燈比較好用。你能幫我修理嗎？拜託！我可以等！

男：好吧！給我一分鐘。我會幫你看一下。

Questions 10~12

女：謝謝您來電星光旅遊服務，需要什麼服務嗎？

男：哈囉，我是G＆W的安東尼奧張，我打算本週末去出差。我想明晚往紐約出發，並且在星期天早上返回。

女：請讓我確認一下。您可以在明天晚上八點離開，不過星期天早上所有經濟艙座位都已訂滿。您可以在週日下午返回，不然您要在上午搭商務艙返回。

男：嗯，那麼我訂商務艙，我那天下午有一個會議。所以我必須在會議之前回來。

▶ 對話在前一頁

Part 3　說出以下的對話　

Questions 1~3

M:　Good evening, Marie. How's _____ going with your _____ ? I was in the area and thought I'd _____ to see how the new _____ is _____ .

W:　Oh, I find that the _____ is _____ . It's a lot more _____ to _____ the bread dough shaped and baked _____ .

M:　I am sure it is _____ . It _____ and _____ flour use, and it should _____ your _____ . Does it seem that you _____ more bread this month?

W:　Hopefully. We are _____ large orders next week, and I'm sure we can _____ this time.

Questions 4~6

M:　Hi, I need to make a _____ for tomorrow _____ , _____ PM.

W:　Sure, may I have your _____ and _____ of guests, please?

M:　It's Shaw. We need a table for _____ . There will be _____ and _____ children.

W:　I'm sorry, seven PM is all _____ . But we'll have a table _____ at seven thirty. Would it be all right with you, Mr. Shaw?

M:　Well, it's better than nothing.

▶ 翻譯在下一頁

Questions 1~3

男：晚安，瑪麗。你的麵包工廠營運得如何？我在這個地區，我想是否能了解一下新烘烤系統運作得如何。

女：哦，我認為你賣給我們的系統太棒了。它非常方便於使生麵成型和自動烘烤。

男：我確信它值得花那筆錢，這樣可以節省時間和減少麵粉的使用，並增加您的產量。你覺得這個月生產了更多麵包嗎？

女：希望是。下週我們期待有大訂單，現在我敢確定我們能在截止日期前完成。

Questions 4~6

男：嗨！我需要預約明天傍晚，七點。

女：沒問題。麻煩可以有您的大名及來賓人數嗎？

男：我叫肖。我們需要一張八人的桌子。將會有六個大人及兩個小孩。

女：抱歉，七點都訂滿了。不過我們七點半有一張桌子會空出。這樣您可以嗎？肖先生。

男：好吧！總比沒有好。

▶ 對話在前一頁

Part 3　說出以下的對話　　

Questions 7~9

M: Ms. Waldron? ＿＿＿＿＿＿＿＿ the ＿＿＿＿＿＿＿＿ for the company ＿＿＿＿＿＿＿＿?

W: Yes, I did. Could you ＿＿＿＿＿＿ and ＿＿＿＿＿＿ to the ＿＿＿＿＿＿ this Friday by 2:00? One truck ＿＿＿＿＿＿ be enough. And please don't ＿＿＿＿＿＿ to ＿＿＿＿ the ＿＿＿＿＿＿ the accounting department when you're ＿＿＿＿＿＿.

M: ＿＿＿＿＿＿. Don't you need a ＿＿＿＿＿＿ of it for your ＿＿＿＿＿＿?

W: Yes, I do. Please copy and give it to my ＿＿＿＿＿＿ to ＿＿＿＿＿＿.

Questions 10~12

M: Good morning, Mary. You are ＿＿＿＿＿＿ today.

W1: Yes, have you met Lucy? Lucy, this is John, our ＿＿＿＿＿＿. John, this is Lucy, the new ＿＿＿＿＿＿ in the sales department.

M: Nice to meet you, Lucy.

W2: Nice to meet you, John.

M: Hi, you look ＿＿＿＿＿＿ young, Lucy. Are you still a student?

W2: Yes, I just ＿＿＿＿＿＿ from ＿＿＿＿＿＿ School last month. And will be admitted to night school of local ＿＿＿＿＿＿ from September.

W1: All right, Lucy, why don't we ＿＿＿＿＿＿ the ＿＿＿＿＿＿ now? I'll show you ＿＿＿＿＿＿ and let's meet more ＿＿＿＿＿＿ from the company.

W2 ＿＿＿＿＿＿. Talk to you ＿＿＿＿＿＿, John.

▶ 翻譯在下一頁

Questions 7~9

男：沃爾倫女士，妳有聽到妳幫公司頒獎典禮訂的裝飾品剛剛到達了嗎？

女：是的，我知道。你能取貨，並在這週五兩點前把他們送到大廳嗎？一台卡車應該就夠了。當你完成時，請別忘了將收據給會計部。

男：當然。妳不需要一份影本做記錄嗎？

女：是的，我要。請複印，並把它拿給我的助理歸檔。

Questions 10~12

男：瑪莉，早安。妳今天來早了！

女1：是啊。你有見過露西了嗎？露西，這是約翰，我們的產品工程師。約翰，這是露西，新進業務助理。

男：很高興認識妳，露西。

女2：很高興認識你，約翰。

男：嗨！妳看起來真年輕。露西。妳還是學生嗎？

女2：是的。我上個月剛從高中畢業。從九月起，會入學當地大學念夜間部。

女1：好吧！露西。我們開始員工培訓吧。我帶妳四處看看，再去見見其它的公司同事！

女2：好的！約翰，我們回頭再聊。

▶ 對話在前一頁

Part 3 說出以下的對話

Questions 1~3

W: Good morning. _____ Marsha about _____ the _____ on Tuesday?

M: She just _____. The _____ expected to _____ yesterday only _____ this morning. She needs to _____, so she _____ we could _____ for Wednesday.

W: Well, I'm _____ a business trip _____, but I can make myself _____ for an early morning meeting. Would you call her and reschedule the meeting?

M: Sure. _____.

Questions 4~6

W: Becker, how's the _____? Did you _____ anyone who is a _____?

M: No. The _____ department _____ down the applications to two, but _____ to be _____. We're _____ young _____ in the clothing _____. We need _____ who has experience in the _____ field.

W: I have a _____ who is really qualified for the job. He's been with a _____ company for _____. Why don't you contact him to see if he's _____?

▶ 翻譯在下一頁

Questions 1~3

女：早安，你有和瑪莎談到關於在星期二安排銷售會議嗎？

男：她剛剛打電話來。預估昨天要到的季度銷售報告，在今天早上才來。她需要分析所有的數據，所以她要求我們是否能重新安排會議在星期三。

女：嗯，那天我要出差，但我能儘量參加晨間會議。你可以打電話聯繫她，並重新安排會議嗎？

男：當然，我會盡可能快點聯繫到她。

Questions 4~6

女：貝克，尋求行銷經理的事情進行得如何？你有找到任何不錯適合的人嗎？

男：沒有。人事部門縮小應徵者範圍到兩位，但似乎沒有一個具有資格。我們的目標是服裝市場的年輕消費者，我們需要一位在相關領域有豐富經驗的人。

女：我有一個朋友相當有資格來做這個工作。他在一家服裝公司幾十年了。你何不聯絡他，看看他有沒有興趣？

▶ 對話在前一頁

Part 3 說出以下的對話

Questions 7~9

W1: Excuse me, we'd like to know if you offer any _____ for _____.

M: Let me see. Yes, we have a course for people who are _____ in becoming _____ tour guides or tour managers.

W1: Is it for Japanese division?

M: I'm sorry. We used to offer _____ for the _____, but now we only have _____ left.

W2: Why is that? I thought the _____ market _____ to be quite big in our country.

M: Well, don't know why. But if not _____ people _____ for the _____, we will stop _____ new students. Then gradually the class will be _____.

W2: Lorena, if we can't find a _____ we need here, _____ we have to check with _____ schools.

W1: That's the only thing to _____ now!

Questions 10~12

W: Excuse me, _____ our table be _____? It's _____ a half an hour _____.

M: Well, _____ right away. But you _____ a table for only 4 people, but now _____. We have tables that can _____ only 4 people _____.

W: I'm sorry the _____ decided to join us _____ leaving the office. We have to _____ for a meeting at 2 o'clock. And it's already 1 o'clock now, so _____ sitting in two _____ tables.

M: Oh, that _____. The _____ in the _____ seems to be _____ soon. _____ and _____ for you.

▶ 翻譯在下一頁

Questions 7~9

女1：不好意思，我們想知道你們是否有開任何導遊的訓練課程。

男：我看看。有的！我們有一門課專為有興趣從事專業導遊或領隊的人所開設。

女1：是給日文組的嗎？

男：抱歉！我們曾經提供課程給日文組，但是我們現在只剩下英文組了。

女2：為什麼呢？我以為日文市場在我們國家應該蠻大的。

男：嗯，不知道為什麼。但是若沒有足夠的人註冊課程，我們會停止招新生。那漸漸地，課程就會終止了。

女2：洛蕾娜，若我們無法在此找到我們需要的課程，或許我們必須查查其他學校。

女1：現在只好這樣了。

Questions 10~12

女：打擾一下，我們的桌次什麼時候可以準備好？我們已經到這兒半小時了。

男：嗯，我也希望我能馬上給您座位。但為您保留的是四人桌，而現在您的團體有八位。我們現有的桌子只能容納四位。

女：我很抱歉，我們正要離開辦公室前，其他人才決定加入。我們得回去工作，開兩點鐘的會。現在已經快一點了，所以我們不介意分坐在兩張桌子。

男：噢，不需要那樣。在後面房間好像有一大群團體正準備要離開。我去為你們確認一下。

▶ 對話在前一頁

Part 3 說出以下的對話　　　　　　請邊聽邊寫下內容，每題各聽三次

Questions 1~3

W: David, ＿＿＿＿＿＿＿＿＿＿＿＿ from King Corporation.
＿＿＿＿＿ a ＿＿＿＿＿＿＿＿＿ for their ＿＿＿＿＿＿ this weekend. Did
you ＿＿＿＿＿ that?

M: Well, let me check. Yes, I've given them ＿＿＿＿＿＿＿＿＿ on the second floor
for Friday and Saturday night and ＿＿＿＿＿＿＿＿＿＿ for Saturday
afternoon. Is that ＿＿＿＿＿＿？

W: ＿＿＿＿＿, you ＿＿＿＿＿＿ one thing. They ＿＿＿＿＿＿ to reserve a
hall for ＿＿＿＿＿＿ on Friday night, too.

M: Oh, I ＿＿＿＿＿＿＿＿＿＿. I'll book a banquet hall as well as prepare a
＿＿＿＿＿＿＿＿＿, so ＿＿＿＿＿＿＿ fax it to them right away.

Questions 4~6

W: Hi, my name is Sara Wilson, and I ＿＿＿＿＿＿＿＿＿＿＿＿ from your store
yesterday. ＿＿＿＿＿＿＿, I don't think I will be home next week to ＿＿＿＿＿ the
＿＿＿＿＿＿. Can you have the package ＿＿＿＿＿ to my office, ＿＿＿？

M: I'm ＿＿＿＿＿ we've already ＿＿＿＿＿＿＿＿＿, Ms. Wilson. If no one
＿＿＿＿＿＿ the ＿＿＿＿＿ of the delivery, the package will be ＿＿＿＿＿ to
us. Then, we will call you to set up a new ＿＿＿＿＿＿＿.

W: Then should I ＿＿＿＿＿ an ＿＿＿＿＿ to get it?

M: ＿＿＿＿＿, yes, you should. There will be an ＿＿＿＿＿＿ charge.

▶ 翻譯在下一頁

Questions 1~3

女：大衛，我接到從金氏企業來的電話。為了這週末的預訂，他們要我傳真確認函。你有處理了嗎？

男：嗯，我確認一下。是的，我給了他們週五和週六晚上在二樓所有的單人房間，並在週六下午預訂了一間會議室。這樣對嗎？

女：事實上，你漏掉了一件事。他們也要求保留在週五晚上晚餐的宴會廳。

男：噢，我忘了那個。我會預訂好宴會廳以及準備書面確認，讓你可以立刻傳真給他們。

Questions 4~6

女：嗨，我的名字是莎拉・威爾遜，我昨天從您的商店訂購一些書籍。但是，我想我下週不會待在家收到投遞。你可以把包裹改送到我的辦公室嗎？

男：恐怕我們已經送出您的訂單了，莎拉・威爾遜女士。如果沒有人確認簽收，包裹將被退還給我們。之後，我們會打電話給您安排新的寄送日期。

女：那我該付額外的費用嗎？

男：實際上來說，是的，您應該是。這將有一筆額外的收費。

▶ 對話在前一頁

Part 3 說出以下的對話　　　　　　　　　請邊聽邊寫下內容，每題各聽三次

Questions 7~9

M: Rachel, can you _____ Jeff with the work on _____ our _____ _____ ice cream? Jeff asked me to find _____ .

W: _____ ? We _____ collaborate before, and the _____ were _____ successful.

M: Yes, that's why Jeff _____ working with you. He is _____ that you're _____ in _____ ice cream, so he needs your _____ .

W: Okay, _____ to see if he can _____ today. I want to _____ .

Questions 10~12

W: Hi, Mr. Jefferson. This is Miramar _____ Agency. We are sorry to _____ you that your flight to Paris on Friday has _____ been _____ due to a local _____ .

M: That's terrible. I have been _____ to spend the _____ there with my wife celebrating our _____ .

W: We're very sorry. But it's really not something we can _____ . May I _____ another tourist _____ for you? Do you prefer _____ cities?

M: _____ it. We chose _____ because it was where we first met 30 years ago. It won't be the same _____ it anywhere else.

▶ 翻譯在下一頁

Questions 7~9

男：瑞琪爾，有關於如何向市場推出我們新的冰淇淋，你能夠幫忙傑夫嗎？傑夫要我找人和他一起做。

女：有何不可？我們之前曾經合作過，結果總是很成功。

男：對了，這就是為什麼傑夫提議與你一起工作。他很清楚你在行銷冰淇淋上有經驗，所以他需要你的意見。

女：沒問題，讓我打電話給他看看他是否可以今天開始這個計畫。我想盡快開始。

Questions 10~12

女：嗨，傑弗森先生。這裡是美麗華旅行社。我們很抱歉要通知您，由於一場當地的罷工，你星期五飛巴黎的班機突然被取消了。

男：太糟糕了！我一直在期待和我太太在那兒度假慶祝我們的週年紀念。

女：我們非常地抱歉。但是這真的不是我們所能控制。我可以為您推薦另一個旅遊景點嗎？您比較喜歡歐洲城市嗎？

男：算了！我們選擇巴黎，是因為它是我們三十年前最初見面的地方。到別的地方慶祝感覺就不一樣了。

▶ 對話在前一頁

Part 3　說出以下的對話　　　　　　　請邊聽邊寫下內容，每題各聽三次

Questions 1~3

W1: _____ it's Friday! I've been looking _____ to today for 5 days!

M:　Why? Do you have any _____?

W1: Yes, I'm going to see the movie 'The Day After'. Do you _____ to go with me? I have 2 _____ tickets.

M:　I'd love to, but _____ I can't. I already have another _____. Maybe you can ask Clare.

W1: Are you _____ tonight, Clare? Do you want to go with me to the movie? It's an Oscar _____ film.

W2: It _____ like fun. A free movie, _____?

W1: Great! The movie is playing at the Sakura _____ starting _____. We can leave right after work.

W2: Sure. _____ you are treating me a free movie, why don't I buy you a _____ for dinner in return? We'll have a _____ this evening.

Questions 4~6

W:　Thank you for _____ Ellen Jay Bookstore. _____?

M:　Hello, _____ a newly _____ book, Back To Nature, _____ in today's _____. But I don't remember how _____. Is it on 14th street or 16th street? I'm going to _____ your store _____.

W:　_____. _____ near 17th Street, and you need to walk _____. However, _____ in five minutes. _____ come tomorrow, _____. We're open at 9 a.m.

▶ 翻譯在下一頁

Questions 1~3

女1：太棒了！終於是星期五了！我等這天已經等了五天了！

男：為什麼？你有什麼計畫嗎？

女1：是的。我要去看電影「明天過後」。妳要不要跟我去？我有兩張免費票。

男：我很想，但是抱歉我不行耶。我已經有其他的約了。或許你可以問問克萊兒。

女1：克萊兒，你今晚有空嗎？你要不要和我去看電影？是一部奧斯卡得獎電影喔！

女2：好像蠻有趣的。免費電影，好啊（為什麼不）？

女1：太棒了！電影七點十五分在櫻花戲院播放。我們可以下班後直接去。

女2：當然！你請我看免費電影，那何不我買個漢堡回請你當晚餐？我們會有個很棒的夜晚。

Questions 4~6

女：感謝您來電艾倫傑書店。我能為您做些什麼嗎？

男：哈囉，我想購買在今天的報上受評論的新上市的書「回歸自然」。但我不記得怎麼去你的店。是在第十四街還是十六街？我要在我回家的途中順便到你的商店。

女：都不是。我們位於第十七街附近，你需要往下走三個街區。但是我們在五分鐘內將打烊。您得明天再來，我們在上午九點營業。

▶ 對話在前一頁

Part 3 說出以下的對話　　　　請邊聽邊寫下內容，每題各聽三次

Questions 7~9

M: _____ Dr. Johnson's office. _____ ?

W: Hello, my name is David Wilson, one of Dr. Johnson's _____ . _____ the _____ he _____ . I want to change it to _____ .

M: I'm _____ Dr. Johnson is _____ to _____ . Since it _____ to be an _____ , let me _____ to Dr. Lee's office. She's been _____ .

Questions 10~12

M: I am thinking about _____ my job and _____ a business on my own. Being your own _____ can give you more freedom, more _____ , and most of all, more money. What do you think?

W: Mmm... all these _____ might come true if you _____ in this _____ market. And _____ , you need a lot of _____ to get started. Do you have the _____ ?

M: Well, I can get a _____ from the _____ . Or have you heard of the Government Business _____ Loan? Most of them are pretty good _____ .

W: There is no _____ giving it a _____ . But I suggest you not _____ your job yet before you _____ more information on it.

▶ 翻譯在下一頁

Questions 7~9

男：謝謝您來電強生醫生辦公室。我能提供什麼幫助嗎？

女：哈囉，我的名字是大衛威爾遜，是強生醫生的病人之一，我打電話來是有關他開給我的藥。
　　我想改換成另一種。

男：恐怕強生醫生剛好離開辦公室去參加一場醫學會議了。既然這事似乎不緊急，我把你的電話
　　轉接到李醫生的辦公室。他不在時，一向是由她代他的工作。

Questions 10~12

男：我在想，我想辭去工作自己創業。作自己的老闆可以給你較多的自由、較多的尊嚴，還有最
　　重要的是較多的錢。妳覺得呢？

女：嗯，所有這些優點或許可以成真，如果你在這多變的市場成功的話。此外，你需要很多錢才
　　能開始。你有資金嗎？

男：喔，我可以從銀行貸款。或者妳有沒有聽說過政府創業貸款？他們大部分都是蠻好的優惠。

女：試試看是無妨啦。不過我建議你在蒐集較多資訊以前，還是先別辭職。

▶ 對話在前一頁

Part 4　說出以下的對話　　　　　請邊聽邊寫下內容，每題各聽三次

Questions 1~3

Hi, Erica. This is Madison Morton _____ Westwood Furniture _____ , and I'm a _____ . I'm _____ the _____ you _____ from us _____ . _____ , the second type model _____ is _____ . We can _____ a _____ for it, but _____ we can get it _____ two months. _____ , we have the third type model now. So _____ whether you want to order the third type model or _____ wait for the _____ . _____ for the day _____ six, so _____ as soon as you get this _____ . Thank you.

Questions 4~6

Thanks for calling THBC _____ . Our _____ are all busy at the moment. Please do not hang up and stay on the line, the next _____ available will _____ your call as soon as possible. If it is an emergency, please dial 0, our _____ will take your call right away. Or if you know the extension number of the bank clerk you are looking for, please dial the _____ now. We can also be _____ at our webpage www.thbc.com Our office hours are 9 AM to 5 PM, Mondays to Fridays, and we are _____ on Saturdays and Sundays. Thank you again for calling THBC bank. Your _____ is very important to us.

▶ 翻譯在下一頁

Questions 1~3

嗨，艾瑞卡。這是西木家具店麥迪森摩頓的留言，我是銷售經理。我是因上週您和我們訂購的衣架而來電的。很不巧地，您選的第二款沒有庫存。我們可以下特別訂單，但我不認為我們能在兩個月之內拿到。然而，我們目前有第三款可提供。所以我想知道您是否要訂購第三款，或寧願等第二款。我今天六點左右會離開，所以當您聽到這個留言，請儘快回電給我。謝謝！

Questions 4~6

感謝您來電THBC銀行。我們的電話線現在都在忙線中。請不要掛斷並留在電話線上，下一位有空的代表將會儘速接聽您的電話。若這是緊急情況，請撥0，我們的總機將立即回覆您。或者若是您知道您要找的銀行員分機號碼，請現在就撥打分機。也可以透過網頁www.thbc.com與我們聯絡。我們的辦公時間是星期一到星期五，上午九點到下午五點，星期六及星期日公休。再次感謝您來電THBC銀行。您的滿意度對我們非常重要。

▶ 對話在前一頁

Part 4　說出以下的對話　　　請邊聽邊寫下內容，每題各聽三次

Questions 7~9

Hello, this _____ is for Mr. Jefferson. My name is John Franklin. I'm _____ the electronic engineering _____ in today's _____. I'm _____ that I am an _____ for the _____. I have over 5 years of _____ working for an _____. I designed circuit layouts for _____ electronic _____. Also, I was the _____ of my team for the last 2 years. I will be visiting near your _____ next week, so I was _____ I could _____ my _____ work _____. _____ a copy of my _____ this afternoon. I hope to _____ from you soon. Thanks, and _____.

Questions 10~12

_____ Countway Computers. We _____ your call. All of our lines are _____ now. If you want to _____ our computer products, _____ and dial 222-3456. _____ speak to a _____, please _____ and _____. Right now _____ a wait of _____ five minutes. _____, please _____ a brief voice mail _____ with your name and telephone number by _____. Your call will be _____ by our next _____ customer service representative. Thank you.

▶ 翻譯在下一頁

Questions 7~9

哈囉，這是給傑佛森先生的留言。我的名字是約翰富蘭克林。我打電話是因注意到今天報紙上刊登的電子工程師職位。我肯定我會是這個職位出色的候選人。我在一家電子公司工作已經有超過五年的經驗。我為多種電子產品設計電路佈局。而在過去兩年我也是團隊的領導者。下週我會在你們市中心辦公室的附近，所以我在想，那時是否能給你們看我以前設計的電路佈局。今天下午我會寄出我的簡歷給您。希望能很快得到您的回覆。謝謝，祝您有美好的一天。

Questions 10~12

您已連接至康威電腦。我們重視您來電。目前所有線路均忙線中。如果你想詢問我們的電腦產品，請掛斷電話，並撥打222-3456。如果您希望與服務人員通話，請在線上等候，您的電話將被依序應答。目前大約要等候五分鐘。或是您可以按二，留下您的姓名和電話號碼的語音訊息。我們下一位服務人員將回撥給您。謝謝您。

▶ 對話在前一頁

Part 4　說出以下的對話　　　　　　　　　　請邊聽邊寫下內容，每題各聽三次

Questions 1~3

Do you want to _____ your _____ skills and earn more money?
Hi-Q _____ training school will help you attain your goal. We offer courses that
are up to date and market _____. All our teachers are _____ trained
and well _____. We guarantee you will learn what you need to know in a time of
three months. Job hunting service is also _____ for all _____.
Our courses are offered in the evenings and on weekends for someone who still holds a day job
just like you. What are you waiting for? Call now and _____!

Questions 4~6

_____, our network _____ sales _____.
We _____ that sales will _____, so we're _____ to
_____ a _____ in Busan in _____. I've been
_____ the sales department in Busan, so I will be _____ my _____ as
_____. _____ will be _____ to
the _____. All of you are _____ the
_____ of transferring to Busan. Please give us some _____ within next few weeks if
you're _____ in _____.

▶ 翻譯在下一頁

Questions 1~3

您想要提升您的職業技能，並且賺更多的金錢嗎？Hi-Q電腦訓練學校將幫助您實現您的目標。我們提供最新而且市場導向的課程。所有我們的老師都有學術訓練並有合格證書。我們保證您將在三個月的期間內學習您所需要知道的技能。求職服務也被提供給所有的學員。我們提供的課程是在傍晚和周末，為了像您一樣仍有白天工作的人。您還在等什麼？現在就來電註冊吧！

Questions 4~6

如同大家所知道的，我們的網絡設備銷售量上升了。我們期待銷售量將繼續增加，所以我們計劃在八月初開始在釜山開設新的分公司。我被安排帶領釜山銷售部門，所以我會在七月離開銷售經理的職位。將有幾位新員工被雇用來處理增加的業務，當然，同樣的機會也會給予公司內經驗豐富的銷售代表們。請大家考慮轉換到釜山的可能性。若您對此一變動有興趣，請在未來幾週之內給我們回應。

▶ 對話在前一頁

Part 4 說出以下的對話　　　請邊聽邊寫下內容，每題各聽三次

Questions 7~9

Dear Ms. Jefferson, this is Melody Jones calling from Caves Art ....
My colleague left me a note saying that you called to .... about the site
.... matters. Our gallery has three different spaces ....
to the public. Two of them are on the .... floors of the building. They are
.... and has a .... lease period. There is also one on
the first floor which has a .... lease term of seven days. But the
.... is this .... has French windows and .... walking by can
see your .... works from outside the building. The rental
for this room is higher, but the .... performance is rather ....
I will send you an email with a quote on these room types. If you have any questions, please
give me a call .... again. Thanks.

Questions 10~12

.... Our .... will be .... in twenty minutes.
Please make your final .... and .... the .... lane.
.... to .... the .... for today's ....
.... fresh .... and .... fruit .... , but
.... a few more minutes. The .... counter is now .... Please
.... to the manager .... Shoppers
.... fifteen or .... can use .... Just
.... to the express lanes at the .... Thank you for
.... with us, and .... seeing you ....

▶ 翻譯在下一頁

Questions 7~9

親愛的傑佛遜女士，我是敦煌藝術美術館的美樂蒂·瓊恩斯。我的同事留紙條給我說您來電詢問場地租借的事宜。我們的美術館有三個不同的空間供大眾租借。其中兩個是在建物較高的樓層。它們比較便宜，而且租期較長。還有一個在一樓，有七天的限制租期。但是好處是這個展覽室有落地窗，路過的行人能從建物外面看見您的展品。這間展覽室的租金較高，但是廣告效益頗令人滿意。我將給您一封有房型報價的電郵。如果您有任何問題，請再給我來電，謝謝！

Questions 10~12

顧客們請注意。我們的商店將在二十分鐘內打烊。請完成您的選購並前往結帳通道。別忘了於農產品部看看今天的特價品。有新鮮的蔬菜和多種水果在拍賣，但只限最後這幾分鐘。目前客戶服務櫃檯已關閉。所有的問題請直接向值班經理洽詢。購買十五個或更少物品可以使用快速結帳通道。只需依照店前方的紅色標誌前往快速結帳通道。感謝您來店購物，我們期待再次見到您。

▶ 對話在前一頁

Part 4 說出以下的對話　　請邊聽邊寫下內容，每題各聽三次

Questions 1~3

_____ everyone to _____'s Global Conference on Community Health. We're _____ have _____ 200 _____ who work in _____ of community health programs _____ give _____. Our presenters will be _____, survey _____, and ideas for providing _____ to _____ of the world. Before I _____ our _____, I have an _____ about the small group sessions on the program. Because of limited space, you need to _____ the sessions _____. Your tickets _____ in your _____ for each _____ you sign up for. _____, check our website to _____ that you are really registered.

Questions 4~6

Welcome to our _____. Before we _____ with this morning's _____, I'd like to _____ the _____. Our first group _____ her _____ thirty minutes later than _____. She _____ at 9:15, _____ at _____, in our _____. At twelve o'clock, _____ in the Red River Room _____ the Blue Mountain Room, which will _____. This evening, _____ in your _____, don't _____ to _____ our keynote speaker's presentation. Thank you.

▶ 翻譯在下一頁

Questions 1~3

歡迎大家來到今年的社區衛生服務全球會議。我們很高興能有超過兩百名工作於世界各地社區衛生計畫多樣領域的專業人員來演講。我們的發表者將分享他們為世界公民提供醫療的經驗、調查結果和想法。在介紹今天的主講人之前，有關於程序當中的小團體會議，我有一項重要的公告。因空間有限，這個會議您需要預先登記。每一場您登記的會議門票應該在您邀請卡上。如果沒有，請於我們的網站確認您是否已真正註冊。

Questions 4~6

歡迎來到我們的年度會議。在我們開始今天上午的程序前，有關時間表我想做個重要的公告。我們第一組的演講者將比原本預定的時間晚三十分鐘開始她的演講。現在她將於九點十五分，而不是八點四十五分，在大會議室演講。十二點鐘時，午餐將在紅河室，而不是將用於晚餐的藍山室。今晚，如同印好的時間表所列，別忘了參加我們主講人的演講。感謝您。

▶ 對話在前一頁

Part 4　說出以下的對話　

Questions 7~9

Welcome, everyone, to today's ＿＿＿＿＿＿＿＿＿＿. Our ＿＿＿＿＿＿＿＿＿＿ today is Mr.
John Park, once the ＿＿＿＿＿＿＿＿ of the Stock Analyst Association. He is ＿＿＿＿＿ an
＿＿＿＿＿＿＿＿＿＿＿ of "Secrets of a Millionaire." Mr. Park will read
from his book and ＿＿＿＿＿＿＿＿＿＿ from the ＿＿＿＿＿＿＿. ＿＿＿＿＿＿＿, he
will be ＿＿＿＿＿＿ to sign ＿＿＿＿＿ of his book. You can ＿＿＿＿＿ the book at
the ＿＿＿＿＿ of the ＿＿＿＿＿＿ for twenty-five dollars. To get more
on his ＿＿＿＿＿＿＿＿＿, you may ＿＿＿＿＿ the ＿＿＿＿＿ available ＿＿＿＿＿＿.
Now, let's ＿＿＿＿＿＿＿＿＿＿＿＿ to Mr. John Park.

Questions 10~12

Hi, Jessie, this is Mary calling from the ＿＿＿＿＿＿＿＿＿＿＿ department. The
officers are holding an ＿＿＿＿＿＿＿＿＿ training at 3 o'clock tomorrow afternoon, and we
need a conference room ＿＿＿＿＿＿＿＿＿ 15 people. The only room big enough is
＿＿＿＿＿＿＿＿＿＿ room A, yet as I know that the sales department will have the
monthly meeting in room A at the same time. ＿＿＿＿＿＿＿＿＿ I am calling to see if it is
＿＿＿＿＿＿＿＿＿ for your meeting to be moved to conference room B, which is also fully
＿＿＿＿＿＿＿＿＿ and can hold as many as 10 people. Would you please give me a call
back as soon as possible to see if there can be a ＿＿＿＿＿＿＿＿ in ＿＿＿＿＿＿＿＿＿?
Thanks.

▶ 翻譯在下一頁

Questions 7~9

歡迎大家來到今天的系列講座。我們今天的特別演講者，是曾為股票分析協會主席的約翰帕爾可先生。他也是《百萬富翁先生的祕密》的獲獎作者。帕爾可先生將讀出他書中的摘要和回答聽眾的問題。之後，他將會為他的書簽名。您可於觀眾席後面以二十五美元購買這本書。若想知道有關於他其他書籍的更多資訊，您可以參考這邊提供的小冊子。現在，請給予約翰帕爾可先生熱烈的歡迎。

Questions 10~12

嗨！潔西，我是物流部門的瑪莉。物流人員將在明天下午三點召開一場在職訓練，我們需要一個能容納十五人的會議室。唯一夠大的房間是A會議室，但就我所知業務部門將於同時段在A會議室召開例行性的月會。所以我來電想看看是否你們的會議可以挪到B會議室，它一樣也是配備齊全，而且能容納多達十人。麻煩請盡快回電給我，看看是否能做安排上的改變？謝謝！

▶ 對話在前一頁

Part 4 說出以下的對話　　　　　　　請邊聽邊寫下內容，每題各聽三次

Questions 1~3

Good morning, everyone. I have an _____ to make. Our IT department will have

a _____ next Monday. Tina Gomez will work as our new _____.

She has been in the industry for 12 years and is very _____ in dealing with

different _____ languages. She is also one of the _____ in

designing the famous Janova case. We are very happy to have her _____ our

team. On _____, Jessie Shun will give her an _____, showing her

around the _____ departments of the company, the staff _____,

and most _____ our computer systems and our _____ for handling

_____.

Questions 4~6

The _____ is a _____, brought you by Radio

ABC. _____ the _____, _____ are _____ all

city _____ to _____. _____ are _____ not to _____

their _____ or _____ their _____. Right

now, the _____ is asking _____ to do this on a _____,

_____ if the _____ becomes _____, it is _____ that _____ will

be _____. _____, _____ energy conservation

at our website at www.energytips.or.uk.

▶ 翻譯在下一頁

Questions 1~3

大家早。我有一個公告要宣布。下週一我們的資訊部將有一位新成員。Tina Gomez將擔任我們的新系統分析師。她在業界已經十二年，而且處理不同程式語言的技術很好。她也是設計著名的Janova案的其中一位參與者。我們很高興有她加入團隊。在星期一，Jessie Shun將幫她做職前訓練，帶她看看公司的不同部門、員工餐廳，最重要的是我們的電腦系統，還有處理技術零件的程序。

Questions 4~6

以下由ABC電台為您帶來一則公共服務公告。由於乾旱，政府官員要求各城市的居民節省用水。直到進一步通知前，居民被要求不在游泳池注水或花園澆水。此刻，政府要求居民基於自願來做這些事，但如果情況變嚴重，有可能會加以罰款。有關訊息，請在我們網站www.energytips.or.uk.搜尋節能小建議。

▶ 對話在前一頁

Part 4　說出以下的對話　　　　　　請邊聽邊寫下內容，每題各聽三次

Questions 7~9

_____ this afternoon's _____. _____ of Melton

city are still _____. The _____ and strong winds _____ the

county _____ and _____ power lines. _____, 150,000 residents

are _____. _____ have been

_____, but the winds, which

strong, are _____. The Power Company _____ that

the _____ will be _____ to

this evening, but the rest of the city will _____ have

_____.

Questions 10~12

Good evening, this is Joe Butler, host of the Butler Live. _____

Mary Stein, _____. She

will _____ useful tips from her _____, "10 Steps to Effective

Communication" _____ on the _____ of

_____ for more than 6 weeks. _____ the interview, Ms. Stein has

_____ from our _____. If you have

for Ms. Stein, _____ at 555-4343, and _____

_____.

▶ 翻譯在下一頁

Questions 7~9

現在是今天下午頭條新聞。梅爾頓市的居民依然沒有電力。昨晚大雨和強風席捲該市，同時摧毀了電力線，導致十五萬居民到今天下午無電使用。施工團隊盡全力恢復供電，但仍強的風勢使他們的工作困難。電力公司預計今天傍晚該城西部將能夠開燈，但城市其餘地區若到明天早上供電就算是幸運的。

Questions 10~12

晚安，我是巴特勒實況秀的主持人喬巴特勒。今天我將訪問國家領導級的溝通專家之一，瑪麗斯坦。她將談到在大部分主流報紙中名列最佳銷售超過六週，她的新書《有效溝通的十個步驟》裡的有用建議。在訪談的最後，瑪麗斯坦女士同意接聽由我們聽眾打來的電話。若您想問瑪麗斯坦女士任何問題，請致電555-4343，我們會盡力在節目中接通。

▶ 對話在前一頁

Part 4　說出以下的對話　　　　　　　　請邊聽邊寫下內容，每題各聽三次

Questions 1~3

_____ been _____ for an _____

bad weather or _____? _____ a _____ to get to your

_____? Then _____ Koreana Railways. Koreana Railways

has _____ to every major business destination _____, and

_____ customers' business _____, we've just _____ providing

_____ Internet service _____, so you can get on the Internet _____

to your destination. _____, we are _____ special _____ for

_____. This offer will be _____ the end of the month. _____

_____, _____ at www.koreanrailway.com. We look forward to

you _____ at Koreana Railways.

Questions 4~6

Thank you. I hope you've all _____ the _____ half of our program

this morning. I'd like to _____ you that there will be another training

_____ given in the afternoon. Our _____ speaker, Dr. Harvey from

The Harvard Consultation Center is going to give a _____ right after the lunch

break. There will be more _____ coming for the afternoon _____,

so the event will be held in the bigger _____ next door. We are going to give out

lunch boxes to _____ who signed up for the whole day session. Please get them

from the _____ in yellow vests. Let's take a break for one hour, and please show

your badge for _____. Thank you.

▶ 翻譯在下一頁

Questions 1~3

你曾因惡劣的天氣或繁忙的交通而在重要會議中遲到嗎？在尋找一種舒適的方式讓您準時到達目的地嗎？那麼看看可麗安納鐵路吧。可麗安納鐵路有到全國各地每一個主要商業區的列車，同時為了更符合於客戶的需求，我們開始於車上提供無線上網服務，因此您能在移動到目的地的時候上網。此外，我們也提供特別折扣給新客戶。這項優惠將持續到本月底。有關更多訊息，請至我們的網站www.koreanrailway.com。我們期待很快與您在可麗安納鐵路相見。

Questions 4~6

謝謝！我希望大家都喜歡今天上午我們前半段的課程。我想提醒大家下午有另外一場培訓課程。特邀講師哈佛諮詢中心的哈維博士將在午休過後為我們上課。因為下午有較多的學員來參加這堂課，所以課程將於隔壁的大禮堂舉行。我們將給登記上全天課的學員便當。請向穿著黃背心的工作人員領取。我們休息一個小時，請出示名牌重新進場。謝謝！

▶ 對話在前一頁

Part 4　說出以下的對話　　　　　　　請邊聽邊寫下內容，每題各聽三次

Questions 7~9

Hello, everyone, welcome to Big Mountain National Park. My name is George, and I'll be your guide ＿＿＿＿＿＿. I have a few ＿＿＿＿＿＿ before ＿＿＿＿＿＿. This morning, we will have a 90 minute ＿＿＿＿＿ to the Big Waterfalls. On the way, ＿＿＿＿＿＿. We will ＿＿＿＿ a few times ＿＿＿＿＿, so that ＿＿＿＿＿＿ if you want. However, please don't attempt to ＿＿＿＿＿＿. Also, it's ＿＿＿＿＿＿. It is ＿＿＿＿ to ＿＿＿＿＿. After ＿＿＿＿ an hour at the Big Waterfalls, we will have ＿＿＿＿ for one hour at the Jinsan Restaurant ＿＿＿＿＿ our bus will be ＿＿＿＿ for us to ＿＿＿ the ＿＿＿＿＿.

Questions 10~12

Dear passengers, may I have your ＿＿＿＿＿＿, please. This is your train conductor speaking. We are ＿＿＿＿＿＿ Karate Station and will be making a pause there due to ＿＿＿＿＿ to the track after a car ＿＿＿＿＿＿. Passengers are ＿＿＿＿＿＿ to get off the train there and ＿＿＿＿＿ by shuttle buses to your ＿＿＿＿＿. The train is being ＿＿＿＿＿ now and hopefully will ＿＿＿＿＿ working state tomorrow morning. For passengers who need to transfer to the shuttle bus, please get a free transfer ticket from the desk. Sorry about the ＿＿＿＿＿＿.

▶ 翻譯在下一頁

Questions 7~9

哈囉，大家好，歡迎來到巨山國家公園。我的名字是喬治，我將是你今天的導遊。在我們開始行程之前我有幾項提醒。今天上午，我們將開90分鐘車程去大瀑布。在路上，我們將看到很多動物。沿路上我們會停車幾次，因此如果您願意，您可以拍照。不過，請不要企圖餵食動物。另外，今天如此溫暖，我們建議您經常補充水份。在大瀑布待一小時之後，我們將在津森餐廳用餐一小時，我們的巴士將在那兒等候我們移動到下一站。

Questions 10~12

親愛的乘客，請注意。這是你們的火車列車長報告。我們即將要接近空手道站，並會在該站暫停，因為一場車禍後鐵軌有毀損。乘客必須在該站暫停，並轉搭接駁車到您的目的地。火車正在搶修當中，並希望明天早上就能恢復通車。需轉搭接駁車的乘客，請在服務台領取免費轉乘車票。造成不便請見諒。

▶ 對話在前一頁

聽寫練習解答

01 Who should I ask for help?
(A) No, I don't agree with you.
(B) You can ask the receptionist.
(C) She is the CEO's secretary.

02 What is this book about?
(A) It's about a foreigner living in Japan.
(B) It costs about 10 dollars.
(C) Yes, I really like it.

03 Where are the vegetables stored after they've been picked?
(A) He'll go to the store tomorrow.
(B) In refrigerated storage containers.
(C) Because it might spoil.

04 Where can I find the factory manager?
(A) At 10 p.m.
(B) Go to the second door on the left.
(C) They're on the top shelf.

05 Who will be interviewing the applicants?
(A) 5 applicants so far.
(B) Yes, I have a job interview today.
(C) I'll ask Ms. Shimamura to do it.

06 When will you return from your business trip?
(A) You can expect me next weekend.
(B) Turn left on the next corner.
(C) For eight years.

07 Where did you put the shipment of machine parts that arrived yesterday?
(A) It's a fact.
(B) They're in the store room.
(C) They're made of metal.

08 Who's available to give the closing speech?
(A) It closes at five.
(B) Dr. Sheppard can do it.
(C) I love peaches.

09 Where is the supply cabinet?
(A) You can find new envelopes in the drawer.
(B) On the second floor.
(C) Food supply is running short.

10 Where do you file the meeting records?
(A) In the cabinet over there.
(B) Every Friday afternoon.
(C) Our past records are no longer available.

11 Why don't you take a short break?
(A) All right, I'll rest for 10 minutes.
(B) No, he is very tall.
(C) I broke my leg.

12 Where should I go to buy some presents for our customers?
(A) They were impressed by the presentation.
(B) About twenty dollars.
(C) Try the department store near the ABC bank.

P. 367-370

01 When can I schedule an appointment with Dr. Yang?
(A) A ten-minute walk from here.
(B) Any time after 4:00 p.m.
(C) Could you, please?

02 Why are you leaving so early?
(A) Do you know where he lives?
(B) Yes, I wake up early.
(C) I'm running late for the meeting.

03 How many meetings do we have next month?
(A) There are three in total.
(B) Call me as soon as you get home.
(C) I don't have much time left.

04 When did you finish the project?
(A) He finished it last week.
(B) You can't use the projector until 3 p.m.
(C) I'm still working on it.

05 Do you know that all sales are final?
(A) That's what I heard.
(B) The salesman is very impolite.
(C) No, no one passed the final exam.

06 When's your business trip to Tokyo?
(A) Yes, it went pretty well.
(B) Next Friday.
(C) No, it's within walking distance.

07 Why hasn't the new carpet arrived yet?
(A) By train, I think.
(B) I'll call the delivery company.
(C) I'll have it dry-cleaned.

08 Would you like to have steak or seafood?
(A) Actually, I would prefer a light meal.
(B) No, you made a mistake.
(C) I see some food on the dining table.

09 When is the next play going to start?
(A) Tonight, at 7:30.
(B) Yes, that's a good one.
(C) There are five players.

10 Why was the itinerary changed?
(A) Sorry, I'm too busy.
(B) I'll make an appointment.
(C) Because Mr. Tanaka couldn't be here then.

11 When will you return to your hometown?
(A) He'll be out of the town today.
(B) In the city.
(C) Within a week.

12 How about going for a movie tonight?
(A) We can't move yet.
(B) That would be great.
(C) I lost sleep for two nights.

01 Don't you think the traffic is terrible?
   (A) Yes, I completely agree with you.
   (B) Green would be nice.
   (C) My apartment number is 403.

02 What files do I need to bring on
   Tuesday?
   (A) The ones on my desk.
   (B) Yes, let's speak then.
   (C) Because I haven't seen them.

03 How long have you worked at your
   company?
   (A) About 4 kilometers from here.
   (B) It will be three years next month.
   (C) It doesn't work properly.

04 When is your birthday?
   (A) It is on February 18.
   (B) I'm afraid you have the wrong
       number.
   (C) That's not my size.

05 What color are you painting the wall?
   (A) Light brown, I think.
   (B) Three weeks from now.
   (C) The cooler's over there.

06 How much are the admission to this
   museum?
   (A) About an hour.
   (B) Only 5 dollars.
   (C) Bikes aren't allowed in this area.

07 What's the best way to reach your
   employer?
   (A) I can't reach it.
   (B) About ten kilograms.
   (C) Try calling her mobile phone.

08 How did you learn about this job?
   (A) I'm still learning how.
   (B) I read about it in the newspaper.
   (C) About a month ago.

09 Would you pass the pepper, please?
   (A) Of course, here you are.
   (B) I don't like sugar in my coffee.
   (C) Paper is getting cheaper these
       years.

10 What's Mr. Thomas doing during his
   leave of absence?
   (A) No, I think he's in today.
   (B) He's taking courses at the
       community center.
   (C) He lives far away.

11 Why are smart phones so expensive?
   (A) Because they are high-tech
       products.
   (B) Yes, my students are all very smart.
   (C) Fun trips can expand your horizon.

12 How's the ice cream?
   (A) It's quite good.
   (B) I'm feeling better, thanks.
   (C) Thanks for the favor.

01 Would you like to read the magazine when I finish?
  (A) No, can you repair it?
  (B) No, thanks. I already bought a copy.
  (C) Yes, I'd love to lead.

02 Who developed the sales plan?
  (A) The export sales department did.
  (B) You can plant trees in the yard.
  (C) The land was developed into a park.

03 Would you like to try this shirt on instead?
  (A) It isn't that short.
  (B) What size is it?
  (C) Yes, we have.

04 We need to check your passport or your driver's license for identification.
  (A) Yes, I am.
  (B) Leave your car here.
  (C) Oh, I don't have either.

05 Which is the fastest way to get to the bank? Islington Road or the highway?
  (A) You can park your car in the garage.
  (B) They're both about the same.
  (C) To cash a check.

06 Do you need a lift to the convention?
  (A) I'd appreciate that.
  (B) I'm not sure I can lift this box alone.
  (C) I enjoy their conversation, too.

07 Where did you put my suitcase?
  (A) They'll discuss the case with me.
  (B) It is really suitable for you.
  (C) In the closet down the hall.

08 Which restaurant would you like to recommend?
  (A) Dinner is at 7 p.m.
  (B) How about the Korean one?
  (C) Yes, it's quite good.

09 Have you contacted the travel agency, or do you want me to call them?
  (A) Is that your phone number?
  (B) I don't have time. Do you?
  (C) No, I haven't had much yet.

10 Don't you want to take a taxi?
  (A) Thanks, I'll take some, please.
  (B) No, I'd like to walk.
  (C) No, I talked to him this morning.

11 How often do you check your email?
  (A) About twice a day.
  (B) We have about ten messages.
  (C) Email is a convenient invention.

12 Let's stop by the construction site next week.
  (A) I'll be out of town next week.
  (B) That's the resident's apartment.
  (C) To build a new convention hall.

01 How many chairs are there in the room?
(A) The room number is 808.
(B) There are twelve.
(C) Cheers! To our new living room.

02 Aren't you going to call the doctor this afternoon?
(A) At our last meeting.
(B) I go about twice a month.
(C) I gave him a call this morning.

03 The concert starts at 9 o'clock, doesn't it?
(A) That's the music store.
(B) I think the time should be on the ticket.
(C) I found the ending better.

04 Excuse me. Is this the train to Taipei?
(A) Yes, it goes northbound.
(B) You may leave now.
(C) Get off at the Taipei Main Station.

05 Are there any tickets available for today's play?
(A) It's probably the most valuable skill.
(B) I'm afraid they're all sold out.
(C) You must present your ticket.

06 Did you make it to the new exhibit at the science museum?
(A) No, but I plan to next week.
(B) That's good news.
(C) Yes, to build a new museum.

07 Didn't Ms. Johnson file the insurance paperwork last week?
(A) I'll ask her.
(B) The tiles arrived yesterday.
(C) The plastic ones look better.

08 Jacob will be able to reschedule the appointment, won't he?
(A) Yes, he's just been appointed.
(B) Yes, he will do it right away.
(C) Too many times.

09 Did you turn off the light?
(A) Yes, turn right at the corner.
(B) It is not light. It's very heavy.
(C) No, I always leave it on.

10 Do you have any plans for this weekend?
(A) We're going hiking on Saturday.
(B) No, it was a guided tour.
(C) I put the plants by the window.

11 Isn't that training session scheduled to last 2 hours?
(A) Yes, it will end on time.
(B) No, the train departs at 5:03.
(C) I believe it's yours.

12 This plant was constructed about two years ago, wasn't it?
(A) Yes, I think that's right.
(B) Was the result satisfactory?
(C) It looks like a good plan.

01 I think the picture in the booklet is too light.
(A) I thought we needed two lights.
(B) Could it be darkened?
(C) Several color photos.

02 I thought Ms. Wagner was going to lead the workshop.
(A) I haven't read it yet.
(B) No, she's on vacation.
(C) It comes in today.

03 Where is your boss sitting?
(A) We live in New York City.
(B) His seat is by the window.
(C) It is hanging from the ceiling.

04 I'd like to make reservations for dinner tonight.
(A) Can I have your name?
(B) Two nights only.
(C) Let's have a rest for a while.

05 What page is the phone number on?
(A) Did you check under the sofa?
(B) It is at the top of page four.
(C) It is 0933-909-876.

06 Can you please tell me where to find Mr. Tang's office?
(A) He works in the next door building.
(B) We haven't been booked yet.
(C) She found it this morning.

07 I've hired two software engineers.
(A) It's hard to use.
(B) Are they going to start within this week?
(C) We projected higher sales.

08 When did you buy your car?
(A) No, I rode a U-bike here.
(B) It cost me a lot of money.
(C) When I got married last year.

09 Do you know who's responsible for this project?
(A) Yes, the marketing manager is.
(B) Yes, it's next Monday.
(C) About new products.

10 The microphones in the auditorium aren't working.
(A) Sometime this morning.
(B) I'll get the technician.
(C) The desk is next to the computer.

11 Our sales fell by ten percent last quarter.
(A) Decreases in demand are the main reason.
(B) Our new sales goals.
(C) I'm getting used to this weather.

12 When will he return?
(A) He returned the book yesterday.
(B) He'll be back after spring break.
(C) Please make a right turn here.

Part 3

P. 387-390

Questions 1-3

W1: Hi, Maria. It's Joanna. Can you give me a ride to work this morning? My car broke down late last night, and it's being fixed in the repair shop.

W2: I'd be delighted to, but I have to go into work early to prepare for an important meeting. Do you mind leaving 30 minutes earlier than usual?

W1: Not at all! I will be ready to be picked up in 10 minutes.

W2: You can make that 20. I need some time to get dressed before going out.

Questions 4-6

M : Welcome to the exhibition. May I have your tickets, please?

W1: There you go. There are the two of us.

M : Sure. Please enter through the front door. There is a locker room at the very end of the first floor. Please check your coats, hats, and bags.

W2: Can we carry our cell phones?

M : Cell phones are allowed, but no food or drinks, please.

W1: You'd better finish drinking your juice now.

W2: All right. Give me a minute. Is there a tour guide for the exhibition?

M : Unfortunately not. But we do offer the audio tour service machines that include a multilingual system.

Questions 7-9

W : Can you please fix my red lamp for me? It doesn't work.

M : I am busy with my speech tomorrow. Can't you fix it by yourself? Or you can use the blue lamp in the garage. That one should work.

W : That one is too heavy. I am unable to move it alone without your help. I think this red lamp works better. Can you repair it for me, please? I can wait!

M : All right. Give me a minute. I'll take a look for you.

Questions 10-12

W : Thank you for calling Star Travel Service. How may I help you?

M : Hello, this is Antonio Chang from G&W corporation. I'm planning to go on a business trip this weekend. I'd like to leave for New York tomorrow night and return on Sunday morning.

W : Let me check. You can leave for 8 p.m. tomorrow, but all the economy class seats have been booked for Sunday morning. You may return Sunday afternoon, or you'll have to sit in a business class that morning.

M : Well, then book me on a business class. I have a meeting that afternoon. So, I have to come back before the meeting.

Questions 1-3

M : Good evening, Marie. How's everything going with your bread factory? I was in the area and thought I'd come by to see how the new baking system is working.

W : Oh, I find that the system you sold us is fantastic. It's a lot more convenient to have the bread dough shaped and baked automatically.

M : I am sure it is worth the money. It saves time and cuts back on flour use, and it should increase your production. Does it seem that you produced more bread this month?

W : Hopefully. We are expecting large orders next week, and I'm sure we can meet the deadline this time.

Questions 4-6

M : Hi, I need to make a reservation for tomorrow evening, seven PM.

W : Sure, may I have your name and number of guests, please?

M : It's Shaw. We need a table for eight. There will be six adults and two children.

W : I'm sorry, seven PM is all booked. But we'll have a table available at seven thirty. Would it be all right with you, Mr. Shaw?

M : Well, it's better than nothing.

Questions 7-9

M : Ms. Waldron? Did you hear the decorations you ordered for the company awards banquet just arrived?

W : Yes, I did. Could you pick up the supplies and deliver them to the main hall this Friday by 2:00? One truck should be enough. And please don't forget to hand the receipt over to the accounting department when you're finished.

M : Certainly. Don't you need a copy of it for your records?

W : Yes, I do. Please copy and give it to my assistant to file.

Questions 10-12

M : Good morning, Mary. You are early today.

W1: Yes, have you met Lucy? Lucy, this is John, our product engineer. John, this is Lucy, the new assistant in the sales department.

M : Nice to meet you, Lucy.

W2: Nice to meet you, John.

M : Hi, you look fairly young, Lucy. Are you still a student?

W2: Yes, I just graduated from High School last month. And will be admitted to night school of local university from September.

W1: All right, Lucy, why don't we start the orientation now? I'll show you around, and let's meet more colleagues from the company.

W2: Sure. Talk to you later, John.

P. 395-398

Questions 1-3

W : Good morning. Have you talked with Marsha about arranging for the sales meeting on Tuesday?

M : She just called. The quarterly sales report expected to arrive yesterday only came in this morning. She needs to analyze all the data, so she asked if we could reschedule the meeting for Wednesday.

W : Well, I'm leaving for a business trip on that day, but I can make myself available for an early morning meeting. Would you call her and reschedule the meeting?

M : Sure. I'll reach her as soon as possible.

Questions 4-6

W : Becker, how's the marketing manager search going? Did you find anyone who is a good fit?

M : No. The personnel department narrowed down the applications to two, but neither seems to be qualified. We're targeting young consumers in the clothing market. We need someone who has extensive experience in the related field.

W : I have a friend who is really qualified for the job. He's been with a clothing

company for decades. Why don't you contact him to see if he's interested?

Questions 7-9

W1: Excuse me, we'd like to know if you offer any training course for tour guides.

M : Let me see. Yes, we have a course for people who are interested in becoming professional tour guides or tour managers.

W1: Is it for Japanese division?

M : I'm sorry. We used to offer courses for the Japanese division, but now we only have English division left.

W2: Why is that? I thought the Japanese market ought to be quite big in our country.

M : Well, don't know why. But if not enough people register for the course, we will stop recruiting new students. Then gradually the class will be discontinued.

W2: Lorena, if we can't find a course we need here, maybe we have to check with other schools.

W1: That's the only thing to do now.

Questions 10-12

W : Excuse me, when will our table be ready? It's been a half an hour since we arrived here.

M : Well, I wish I could seat you right away. But you reserved a table for only 4 people, and now you have

8 people in your group. We have tables that can accommodate only 4 people at the moment.

W : I'm sorry that the others decided to join us just before leaving the office. We have to get back to work for a meeting at 2 o'clock. And it's already 1 o'clock now, so we don't mind sitting in two different tables.

M : Oh, that won't be necessary. The large group in the back room seems to be ready to leave soon. I'll go and check it out for you.

P. 399-402

Questions 1-3

W : David, I got a phone call from King Corporation. They want me to fax them a written confirmation for their reservations this weekend. Did you process that?

M : Well, let me check. Yes, I've given them all single rooms on the second floor for Friday and Saturday night and booked a conference room for Saturday afternoon. Is that right?

W : Actually, you missed one thing. They asked to reserve a banquet hall for dinner on Friday night, too.

M : Oh, I forgot about that. I'll book a banquet hall as well as prepare a written confirmation, so you can fax it to them right away.

Questions 4-6

W : Hi, my name is Sara Wilson, and I ordered some books from your store yesterday. However, I don't think I will be home next week to receive the delivery. Can you have the package delivered to my office, instead?

M : I'm afraid we've already sent your order, Ms. Wilson. If no one confirms the receipt of the delivery, the package will be returned to us. Then, we will call you to set up a new delivery date.

W : Then should I pay for an extra fee to get it?

M : In fact, yes, you should. There will be an additional charge.

Questions 7-9

M : Rachel, can you help Jeff with the work on how to market our new line of ice cream? Jeff asked me to find someone to work with him.

W : Why not? We used to collaborate before, and the results were always successful.

M : Yes, that's why Jeff suggested working with you. He is well aware that you're experienced in marketing ice cream, so he needs your advice.

W : Okay, let me call him to see if he can begin the project today. I want to get it started as soon as possible.

Questions 10-12

W : Hi, Mr. Jefferson. This is Miramar Travel Agency. We are sorry to notify you that your flight to Paris on Friday has suddenly been cancelled due to a local strike.

M : That's terrible. I have been expecting to spend the holiday there with my wife celebrating our anniversary.

W : We're very sorry. But it's really not something we can control. May I recommend another tourist attraction for you? Do you prefer European cities?

M : Forget it. We chose Paris because it was where we first met 30 years ago. It won't be the same celebrating it anywhere else.

P. 403-406

Questions 1-3

W1: Thank God it's Friday! I've been looking forward to today for 5 days!

M : Why? Do you have any plans?

W1: Yes, I'm going to see the movie "The Day After". Do you want to go with me? I have 2 free tickets.

M : I'd love to, but sorry I can't. I already have another pre-engagement. Maybe you can ask Clare.

W1: Are you free tonight, Clare? Do you want to go with me to the movie? It's an Oscar winning film.

W2: It seems like fun. A free movie, why not?

W1: Great! The movie is playing at the Sakura Theater starting 7:15. We can leave right after work.

W2: Sure. Since you are treating me a free movie, why don't I buy you a burger for dinner in return? We'll have a great time this evening.

Questions 4-6

W : Thank you for calling Ellen Jay Bookstore. What can I do for you?

M : Hello, I'd like to buy a newly released book, Back To Nature, reviewed in today's newspaper. But I don't remember how to get to your store. Is it on 14th Street or 16th Street? I'm going to stop by your store on my way home.

W : Neither. We're located near 17th Street, and you need to walk three blocks down. However, we're closing in five minutes. You'll have to come tomorrow, instead. We're open at 9 a.m.

Questions 7-9

M : Thank you for calling Dr. Johnson's office. How may I help you?

W : Hello, my name is David Wilson, one of Dr. Johnson's patients. I'm calling about the medicine he prescribed. I want to change it to another one.

M : I'm afraid Dr. Johnson is away from the office to attend a medical conference. Since it doesn't seem to be an emergency, let me put you through to Dr. Lee's office. She's been taking his job during his absence.

Questions 10-12

M : I am thinking about quitting my job and starting a business on my own. Being your own boss can give you more freedom, more dignity, and most of all, more money. What do you think?

W : Mmm…, all these benefits might come true if you succeed in this changeable market. And besides, you need a lot of money to get started. Do you have the capital?

M : Well, I can get a loan from the bank. Or have you heard of the Government Business Start-up Loan? Most of them are pretty good offers.

W : There is no harm giving it a try. But I suggest you not quit your job yet before you gather more information on it.

Part 4

P. 407-410

Questions 1-3

Hi, Erica. This is Madison Morton calling from Westwood Furniture store, and I'm a sales manager. I'm calling about the dress hanger you ordered from us last week. Unfortunately, the second type of model you selected is not in stock.

We can place a special order for it, but I don't think we can get it in less than two months. However, we have the third type model available now. So I'd like to know whether you want to order the third type model or would rather wait for the second type model. I will leave for the day around six, so please call me back as soon as you get this message. Thank you.

Questions 4-6

Thanks for calling THBC bank. Our lines are all busy at the moment. Please do not hang up and stay on the line, the next representative available will answer your call as soon as possible. If it is an emergency, please dial 0, our operator will take your call right away. Or if you know the extension number of the bank clerk you are looking for, please dial the extension number now. We can also be reached at our webpage www.thbc.com. Our office hours are 9 AM to 5 PM, Mondays to Fridays, and we are closed on Saturdays and Sundays. Thank you again for calling THBC bank. Your satisfaction is very important to us.

Questions 7-9

Hello, this message is for Mr. Jefferson. My name is John Franklin. I'm calling regarding the electronic engineering position posted in today's newspaper. I'm sure that I am an excellent candidate for the position. I have over 5 years of experience working for an electronics company. I designed circuit layouts for a variety of electronic products. Also, I was the leader of my team for the last 2 years. I will be visiting near your downtown office next week, so I was wondering if I could show you my previous work at that time. I will send you a copy of my resume this afternoon. I hope to hear from you soon. Thanks, and have a good day.

Questions 10-12
You've reached Countway Computers. We value your call. All of our lines are busy now. If you want to inquire about our computer products, hang up and dial 222-3456. If you would like to speak to a customer service representative, please stay on the line, and your call will be answered in turn. Right now there is a wait of approximately five minutes. Otherwise, please leave a brief voice mail message with your name and telephone number by pressing 2. Your call will be returned by our next available customer service representative. Thank you.

P. 411-414

Questions 1-3
Do you want to upgrade your occupational skills and earn more money? Hi-Q computer training school will help you attain your goal. We offer courses that are up to date and market oriented. All our teachers are academically trained and well certified. We guarantee you will learn what you need to know in a time of three months. Job hunting service is also provided for all trainees. Our courses are offered in the evenings and on weekends for someone who still holds a day job just like you. What are you waiting for? Call now and register!

Questions 4-6
As you all know, our network equipment sales have gone up. We expect that sales will continue to increase, so we're planning to start a new branch in Busan in early August. I've been appointed to head the sales department in Busan, so I will be leaving my position as sales manager in July. Several new employees will be hired to deal with the increased business. All of you are invited to consider the possibility of transferring to Busan. Please give us some feedback within next few weeks if you're interested in making this move.

Questions 7-9
Dear Ms. Jefferson, this is Melody Jones calling from Caves Art Gallery. My colleague left me a note saying that you called to inquire about the site rental matters. Our gallery has three different spaces available to the public. Two of them are on the upper floors of the

building. They are cheaper and has a longer lease period. There is also one on the first floor, which has a limited lease term of seven days. But the benefit is this showroom has French windows and pedestrians walking by can see your exhibition works from outside the building. The rental fee for this room is higher, but the ad performance is rather satisfactory. I will send you an email with a quote on these room types. If you have any questions, please give me a call back again. Thanks.

Questions 10-12

Attention, shoppers. Our store will be closing in twenty minutes. Please make your final selections and proceed to the checkout lane. Don't forget to stop by the produce department for today's specials. There are fresh vegetables and a variety of fruit, on sale, but only for a few more minutes. The customer service counter is now closed. Please direct all questions to the manager on duty. Shoppers purchasing fifteen or fewer items can use express checkout lanes. Just follow the red signs to the express lanes at the front of the store. Thank you for shopping with us, and we look forward to seeing you again.

P. 415-418

Questions 1-3

Welcome, everyone, to this year's Global Conference on Community Health. We're pleased to have more than 200 professionals who work in various fields of community health programs throughout the world give presentations. Our presenters will be sharing their experiences, survey results, and ideas for providing medical treatment to citizens of the world. Before I present our keynote speaker, I have an important announcement about the small group sessions on the program. Because of limited space, you need to register for the sessions in advance. Your tickets should be in your welcome kit for each session you sign up for. If not, check our website to confirm that you are really registered.

Questions 4-6

Welcome to our annual conference. Before we get started with this morning's program, I'd like to make an important announcement regarding the schedule. Our first group speaker will begin her presentation thirty minutes later than originally scheduled. She will now speak at 9:15, instead of at 8:45, in our main meeting room. At twelve o'clock, lunch will be served in the Red River Room instead of the Blue Mountain Room, which will be used for dinner. This evening, as listed in your pre-printed schedules, don't forget to attend our keynote speaker's presentation. Thank you.

Questions 7-9

Welcome, everyone, to today's lecture series. Our featured speaker today is Mr. John Park, once the chairman of the Stock Analyst Association. He is also an award-winning author of "Secrets of a Millionaire." Mr. Park will read excerpts from his book and answer questions from the audience. Following that, he will be available to sign copies of his book. You can purchase the book at the back of the auditorium for twenty-five dollars. To get more information on his other books, you may refer to the brochures available there. Now, let's give a warm welcome to Mr. John Park.

Questions 10-12

Hi, Jessie, this is Mary calling from the logistics department. The logistics officers are holding an on-the-job training at 3 o'clock tomorrow afternoon, and we need a conference room accommodating 15 people. The only room big enough is conference room A, yet, as I know that the sales department will have the routine monthly meeting in room A at the same time. Therefore, I am calling to see if it is possible for your meeting to be moved to conference room B, which is also fully equipped and can hold as many as 10 people. Would you please give me a call back as soon as possible to see if there can be a change in arrangement? Thanks.

P. 419-422

Questions 1-3

Good morning, everyone. I have an announcement to make. Our IT department will have a newcomer next Monday. Tina Gomez will work as our new system analyst. She has been in the industry for 12 years and is very skillful in dealing with different programming languages. She is also one of the participants in designing the famous Janova case. We are very happy to have her join our team. On Monday, Jessie Shun will give her an orientation showing her around the different departments of the company, the staff cafeteria, and most importantly, our computer systems and our processes for handling technical components.

Questions 4-6

The following is a public service announcement, brought to you by Radio ABC. Because of the drought, government officials are asking all city residents to conserve water. Residents are asked not to fill their swimming pools or water their gardens until further notice. Right now, the government is asking residents to do this on a voluntary basis, although if the situation becomes severe, it is possible that fines will be imposed. For more information, find energy conservation tips at our website at www.energytips.or.uk.

Questions 7-9

And now for this afternoon's lead news story. Residents of Melton city are still without power. The heavy rains and strong winds swept through the county last night and tore down power lines. As a result, 150,000 residents are without electricity until this afternoon. Work crews have been working hard to restore power, but the winds, which remain strong, are making their work difficult. The Power Company expects that the western part of the city will be able to turn on their lights this evening, but the rest of the city will be lucky to have electricity by tomorrow morning.

Questions 10-12

Good evening, this is Joe Butler, host of the Butler Live. Today I will be interviewing Mary Stein, one of the country's leading communication specialists. She will talk about useful tips from her new book, "10 Steps to Effective Communication" which has been on the bestseller's list of most major newspapers for more than 6 weeks. At the end of the interview, Ms. Stein has agreed to take calls from our audience. If you have any questions for Ms. Stein, give us a call at 555-4343, and we will try to get you on the show.

P. 423-426

Questions 1-3

Have you ever been late for an important meeting due to bad weather or heavy traffic? Looking for a comfortable way to get to your destination on time? Then check out Koreana Railways. Koreana Railways has trains to every major business destination throughout the country, and to better meet customers' business needs, we've just started providing wireless Internet service on board, so you can get on the Internet while moving to your destination. In addition, we are offering special discounts for new customers. This offer will be good until the end of the month. For more information, visit our website at www.koreanrailway.com. We look forward to seeing you soon at Koreana Railways.

Questions 4-6

Thank you. I hope you've all enjoyed the first half of our program this morning. I'd like to remind you that there will be another training session given in the afternoon. Our guest speaker, Dr. Harvey from The Harvard Consultation Center, is going to give a lecture right after the lunch break. There will be more trainees coming for the afternoon session, so the event will be held in the bigger auditorium next door. We are going to give out lunch boxes to trainees who signed up for the whole day session. Please get them from the staff members in yellow vests. Let's take a break for one hour, and please show your badge for re-entry. Thank you.

Questions 7-9

Hello, everyone, welcome to Big Mountain National Park. My name is George, and I'll be your guide for the day. I have a few reminders before we begin our tour. This morning, we will have a 90-minute drive to the Big Waterfalls. On the way, we'll see a lot of animals. We will stop a few times along the way so that you can take photos if you want. However, please don't attempt to feed the animals. Also, it's so warm today. It is recommended to drink water frequently. After spending an hour at the Big Waterfalls, we will have lunch for one hour at the Jinsan Restaurant where our bus will be standing by for us to move onto the next stop.

Questions 10-12

Dear passengers, may I have your attention, please. This is your train conductor speaking. We are approaching Karate Station and will be making a pause there due to damages to the track after a car accident. Passengers are required to get off the train there and transfer by shuttle buses to your destination. The train is being repaired now and hopefully will resume working

state tomorrow morning. For passengers who need to transfer to the shuttle bus, please get a free transfer ticket from the desk. Sorry about the inconvenience.

國家圖書館出版品預行編目（CIP）資料

全新制50次多益滿分的怪物講師TOEIC多益聽力攻
略+模擬試題+解析 / 鄭相虎、金映權 著. -- 初版. --
臺北市：不求人文化, 2018.1
　　面；　公分
ISBN 978-986-95195-3-3（平裝附光碟）
1.多益測驗
805.1895　　　　　　　　　　　　　　106018312

全新制
TOEIC Listening
50次多益滿分的怪物講師
多益聽力
攻略＋模擬試題＋解析

書名 / 全新制 50 次多益滿分的怪物講師 TOEIC 多益聽力攻略 + 模擬試題 + 解析
作者 / 鄭相虎、金映權
審訂者 / 怪物講師教學團隊（台灣）
譯者 / 高俊江、賈惠如
發行人 / 蔣敬祖
出版事業群副總經理 / 廖晏婕
副總編輯 / 劉俐伶
校對 / 林佳樺、紀珊、劉兆婷
視覺指導 / 姜孟傑、鍾維恩
排版 / 張靜怡
法律顧問 / 北辰著作權事務所蕭雄淋律師
印製 / 金濱印刷事業有限公司
初版 / 2018 年 1 月
初版六刷 / 2019 年 4 月
出版 / 我識出版教育集團──不求人文化
電話 / (02) 2345-7222
傳真 / (02) 2345-5758
地址 / 台北市忠孝東路五段 372 巷 27 弄 78 之 1 號 1 樓
郵政劃撥 / 19793190
戶名 / 我識出版社
網址 / www.17buy.com.tw
E-mail / iam.group@17buy.com.tw
facebook 網址 / www.facebook.com/ImPublishing
定價 / 新台幣 699 元 / 港幣 233 元
시나공 토익 Listening（전면 개정판）
Copyright©2011 by Jeong Sangho & Kim Youngkwon
Original Korea edition published by Gilbut Eztok, Seoul, Korea
Taiwan translation rights arranged with Gilbut EZtok
Through M.J Agency, in Taipei
Taiwan translation rights©2018 by I'm Publishing.Co., Ltd

總經銷 / 我識出版社有限公司業務部
地址 / 新北市汐止區新台五路一段 114 號 12 樓
電話 / (02) 2696-1357 傳真 / (02) 2696-1359

地區經銷 / 易可數位行銷股份有限公司
地址 / 新北市新店區寶橋路 235 巷 6 弄 3 號 5 樓

港澳總經銷 / 和平圖書有限公司
地址 / 香港柴灣嘉業街 12 號百樂門大廈 17 樓
電話 / (852) 2804-6687 傳真 / (852) 2804-6409

2011 不求人文化

2009 懶鬼子英日語

www.17buy.com.tw

2005 意識文化

2005 易富文化

2003 我識地球村

2001 我識出版社

2011 不求人文化

2009 懶鬼子英日語

I'm 我識出版集團
I'm Publishing Group
www.17buy.com.tw

2005 意識文化

2005 易富文化

2003 我識地球村

2001 我識出版社